OUR TIME

DARIUS RAHMAAN

ISBN: 979-8-9898170-0-9 (Paperback)

ISBN: 979-8-9898170-1-6 (Hardcover)

ISBN: 979-8-9898170-2-3 (E-book)

Library of Congress Control Number: 2024900337

This is a work of fiction. Names, characters, organizations, places, events, and incidents are either products of the author's imagination or are used fictitiously. Any references to historical events, real people, or real places are also used fictitiously.

Published by Darius Rahmaan in Memphis, TN.

First printing edition 2024.

www.dariusrahmaan.com

CONTENTS

DEDICATION

To my Auntie Tika, your spirit will live in my heart. Always.

PART ONE

DANNY

There are moments in life when one experiences a before and after. To make further sense of this peculiar phenomenon, let's look at my life starting from before the night of the infamous election that will forever go down in history, no matter what side you were on at the time. Life was relatively simple, I was a junior in college, making lifelong friends where we often discussed our dreams and goals. But politics became impossible to ignore. The mood and the vibe on the election day was hope, uncertainty, and fear. It was felt by everyone. I remember hosting an election party that night.

"Open the door, you hoe! Let's get this party started!" Libby hollered as Johannes beat on my door. I giggled as I walked to open it. The two were always a rambunctious bunch. As I let them in, the two did a conga line through the kitchen.

"Wait...where is everyone?" Johannes questioned.

"You guys are early...again!" I chuckled. "The two of you are *literally* the only people I know who shows up early to a party. Weren't you guys ever invited to parties in high school?"

"Oh, shut up!" Libby laughed as she threw her middle finger up. "Besides, we came bearing gifts!" She pulled out two bottles of wine from a couple of brown paper bags. "We're early because we thought we were running late picking this up."

"Well, I thank you for that!" I grabbed the bottles to put them in the refrigerator. When I tell you that I recall how they looked down to the very minute details, that should let you know how memorable this night was for me. Libby's rich, silky deep brown skin paired perfectly with her beautiful afro, accented with a blue flower. The floral piece accentuated her soft eyes and the colorful accessory matched her white shirt that said "Riperton, Tomorrow is Looking Great!" Johannes' style was particularly edgy, complete with dyed grey hair, a bandana wrapped around his head, aviator sunglasses, a leather jacket, and ripped, skinny black jeans. His clothing fit his tall and lean frame. Also, what I looked like that day stands out to me, as I looked so simplistic with curly black hair, skin the color of Café au lait, wearing a plain blue sweater on my medium built frame. I often looked back at those days as the best days of my life.

"I'm gonna go to the restroom. When I come back, I'll help with the snacks!" Johannes stated as he slowly backed away.

"Just make sure you wash your hands." I begged.

"I'll make no such promises," he chuckled. "Relax, I'm only kidding... or am I?" Johannes hurried away as Libby was left in the kitchen leaning her arm on the bar countertop. While I reached for the tortilla chips in the pantry, Libby asked me a pivotal question.

"What do you think will happen tonight?" She queried in her most serious expression.

"I don't know..." I said softly as the ruffle of the bag of chips overpowered my voice. I poured all of the chips in my red bowl and set the fresh salsa by it. "I mean, I hope Riperton wins, but I have some doubts."

"But Ace can't win, can he? You've seen all the stuff he's done!" Libby grunted in an exasperated manner.

"The polls have shown that most Republicans don't care. Plus, with the National Party backing Ace, he could win."

"How did the National Party even become involved in this election? I mean, they're just a fringe group." Libby said as she grabbed a chip and dipped it in the salsa.

"A fringe group with the same views as his own. Without them, I don't think Ace would've gotten this far. Yeah, he's a Republican, but he's more of a Nationalist. He's racist and homophobic unlike any of the other candidates that ran during the primaries." I stated matter-of-factly.

"Well, speaking of homo..." Libby giggled as I sat against the counter right next to her. "Did you invite Rafael?" She nudged me until I could do nothing but grin.

"Yes, I invited him." I smiled. "And before you ask, yes, I like him and I already made sure he was gay. You know my unfortunate history with straight guys."

"I was about to say..." She laughed. "You have the worst track record with trying to figure out if a man is straight or gay."

"I made sure to ask this time. Who would've thought I'd ever be attracted to a frat boy?"

"Yeah, I'm surprised by that too."

"Well, he's not the stereotypical frat boy. He's kind, funny, and extremely thoughtful. He has a lot to offer and I wanna date him, but right now, I'm just tryna talk to him."

"Talk to who?" Johannes interrupted and rushed to the chips. I looked at him, and somehow, he read my mind. "Look, I really was kidding, I washed my hands." He said as he continued to munch on the chips and salsa.

"I knew that, I just thought you were gonna help me with the snacks." I commented.

"I *am* helping with the snacks. I'm helping you eat them." He snickered. "But seriously, who did you say you were gonna talk to?"

"Rafael! He invited him to the party tonight!" Libby squealed.

"Finally, it's about time you worked up enough nerve to ask him out." Johannes said.

"I never said I asked him out yet." I replied.

"Then I take back my previous statement." He chortled as the doorbell rang. The election party was finally about to begin.

***

The main focal point of the party was the T.V. screen while the music softly played in the background with a nice crowd of people that I invited from the college. Since I was living in D.C., politics were all anybody could really talk about, besides a few mentions on how their lives were going. I remember Johannes tried to hit on a girl he just met and Libby drinking a tall glass of the wine she brought while remaining fixed on the T.V. I decided to take a break from playing host, poured me a small glass of wine, and sat beside her.

"See anything interesting?" I asked before I took a sip of my drink. She turned towards me and put her glass on the coffee-table.

"Right now, Riperton is winning! If she could just get Florida and Ohio, she could be the first female President of the United States!" She whispered, as if she was trying not to jinx the moment. "She has a chance! Aren't you excited!"

"I am, but..." I stopped myself.

"But what?" Libby questioned.

"I have this gut feeling, that no matter what... something bad is gonna happen tonight."

"Like what? Ace winning? Looking at the percentage and the recent scandal, now I doubt that he'll win." Libby took another sip of her wine "I can't imagine what could happen. A protest, at the most?"

"Maybe..." I sighed. "At least, this party is a success."

"You think Rafael will show up?" She asked in the most sensitive way that she could.

"I hope so, I was really looking forward to seeing him. He's probably busy tonight anyways." I muttered sadly. In the nick of time, before I got too into my feelings, Johannes hurried to casually sit beside me.

"Don't look now, but Rafael's here. Just play it cool."

I perked up. "When have I not ever played it cool?"

"Bud, that's gonna take too damn long to answer." Johannes responded. He slowly turned towards the door to see what Rafael was doing and then spun around and faced me. "Okay, what you're gonna do is take your wine glass, pretend like you're refilling it, and then act like you just noticed him Next, strike up a conversation."

"Okay," I whispered to myself. "Any other advice?"

"Yes," Libby responded. "Don't drool over him, now go!"

I grabbed my wine glass, took one last sip, and then I got up to get a "refill" when I heard Rafael call my name.

"Danny!"

I turned around and there was the most gorgeous man I'd ever seen. He had stark raven black hair, styled in a smooth undercut fashion. He was Latino and his brown skin seemed warm and invited me to melt into him. He was slightly shorter than me and was wearing his black and silver Sigma Phi Gamma fraternity jacket. And what could I say about his smile? His infectious smile was so magnetic that I could never say enough about it since it uplifted the mood of everyone in the room.

"Um, Danny? Are you okay?" Rafael asked curiously as he interrupted my daydream. I guess I did drool over him.

"Oh hey, Raf! Sorry, I didn't see you there! Just a little tipsy." I slightly lied while pointing at my wine glass. "Want a drink?"

"Yeah, I'm gonna need one for tonight. Do you have any beer?"

"Yeah, just follow me!" I said as I lead him to the kitchen and opened the fridge and reached for a cold bottle. I handed it to him, then I poured more wine for myself. "You appear to be nervous. Penny for your thoughts?"

He wistfully smiled as he opened his beer. "Am I that much of an open book?"

"I'm serious, though. If you ever need to talk to me, I'm here." I meant it fully.

He sighed. "I feel like I can trust you with anything, Danny. If I tell you why I'm afraid, you can never tell this to anyone." He got closer to me as he gulped and exposed his deepest secret. "The reason I'm nervous is because my parents are undocumented immigrants. Don't worry, I was born here, so that's not a problem."

"Raf..." I said in shock.

"Yes, I could worry about my parents being deported under any administration, but if Ace wins... You've heard how he talks about immigrants. I'm scared." He hushed into an even quieter whisper. "My parents are all I have, Danny. Dealing with racism is one thing, but the thought of ICE sending my parents back to Mexico. It's terrifying."

He set his beer down on the counter and turned back around.

"Danny, we've known each other for quite some time. And I know you like me."

My ears perked up, a lump gathered in my throat, and my heart started pumping so hard, it felt as if it would leave my chest.

"Now it's my turn to ask. Am I that much of an open book?" I blushed as I set my wine glass down. He smirked as I responded back with his original words.

"Touché. I've known you liked me for a while now. But I wanted to get to know you better." He slowly got closer to me and grabbed my hands, making my skin feel electric. I almost couldn't breathe when we looked eye to eye. "I waited because I'm very particular about men." He continued. "I wanted a man that was gentle, kind, and trustworthy. And you've shown that to me."

"I didn't know you were watching me like that." I said quietly.

"Oh, I watch everything. One endearing factor I've noticed about you, is your shyness. It's cute."

"You're trying to make me blush, huh?"

"No, I've just been waiting for you to ask me out." The room became silent as everyone except for us two became hyper-focused on the television.

"Well, in that case, would you like to get coffee with me?" I finally and boldly asked.

"Yes," Rafael smiled as he leaned in so close, I could feel the huff of his breath.

"Breaking news; the results are in." The newscaster stated. Before me and Rafael could kiss, we both turned around and leaned on the counter-top to watch the news.

"President Elect Ace has won the election and is preparing to give his acceptance speech."

The room rattled and shook with groans and shouts of disapproval. Someone stopped the music and the election results was all anyone could focus on. I turned to look at Rafael. His eyes began to water and swell with tears.

"I am thoroughly disappointed." Libby said as she commanded the attention in the room. "I am just disheartened and disgusted. What has happened to us?" She continued to no one in particular. "How did we let fear, hate, and anger overcome us to elect this man in office?! We as Americans are supposed to be great. We're supposed to promote equality, freedom, and diversity while we elect a man who goes against everything we stand for. Or maybe this is really what we are: divisive, ignorant, and hateful against anyone not like us."

Rafael had tears streaming down his face, not because of sadness, but because of anger. He squeezed my hands and I could only imagine his thoughts. It seemed as if he had a swirl of emotions building up inside of him, knowing how the country felt about him. But instead of bursting out in anger, he said only four words.

"I have to go." He untangled his hand from mine, and he left. While everyone still watched the T.V., I poured myself a full glass of wine. I was gonna need it to make it through the night. I looked at everyone in the room and even though we were all together, we kept our thoughts to ourselves the rest of the night. I remember my thought. There was a before. This was after.

LIBBY

I awoke to the smell of bacon.

"Finally, you're up. I bet you have a hell of a hangover." I heard Johannes say. As I began to gain my bearings, my head started to pound, and my stomach grumbled. I opened my eyes and saw my blue hydrangea on the floor. I sat up on the plushy leather couch. After picking it up and feeling the flowy texture of the white rug with my feet, I soon realized I was not in my apartment.

"Where the hell am I?" I thought aloud to myself quietly. Hearing the sizzling and frying in the kitchen, I quickly stood up and immediately regretted that decision. "Ah, crap! My head hurts..."

"That was the wine!" Johannes laughed. "To answer to your first question, we're still at Danny's apartment. I would've taken you home, but I couldn't since you were my ride." He flipped over some pieces of bacon, trying to avoid the hot grease to no avail. "Ah, dammit!" While Johannes made a lot of commotion in the kitchen, I looked at my shirt that I slept in: Riperton, Tomorrow is Looking Great!

"Oh God, please tell me last night was a dream." I panicked.

"Nope, it was real." Danny abruptly stated as he closed his bedroom door. "Tomorrow really ain't looking all that great. Morning, Johannes."

"Sup, Dan."

Oh no. I began to remember. Ace won. It felt impossible, but he did it. Complicated emotions swirled inside me. I felt concerned. I felt shock. I felt pain. I felt concerned for all of the people that the future administration would affect, namely immigrants from the other side of the border, as it was clear that the Ace Base misrepresented and misunderstood Hispanic people. I felt shocked because I never thought that Ace could be president, given his troubled history. I was never really prepared for anything other than a Riperton presidency. I was in pain because now I saw how some of the millions of voters actually felt about marginalized communities, how people truly felt about me. Even now, as I write this and look back, I still feel pangs of hurt whenever I think about how some people view blackness and femininity.

At that moment, I processed all the swirls of emotions within me, I slowly got up from the couch, and walked towards the window in the breakfast den. Drawing open the curtains, I saw the clouds covering up the sun, enveloping the world in a cold chill as if the moods and attitudes of citizens in this country affected the weather. I felt like there was gloom and misery everywhere, as raindrops began to pitter patter against the window. Gradually, my disposition started to lighten as the smell of warm biscuits wafted under my nose, leaving me to divert my attention from the world outside to the world within.

"I didn't know you could cook," Danny said to Johannes as he started to brew the coffee.

"Oh, I'm a man of many hidden talents." He smirked. Johannes started to make a plate for me and Danny, while I made myself some Rooibos tea. Inhaling the steam and feeling the heat of the cup cleared my head. We sat in silence as we ate, trying to avoid the elephant in the room. After a few moments, I needed to break the silence.

"Well, does anyone have class today?"

"Nope," Danny replied. "My classes were canceled because we needed 'a day of reflection.' Honestly, I feel like we deserve it."

"Johannes?" I asked.

"What makes you think I go to class?" Johannes chuckled as he sipped on his orange juice. "What about you, Libby?"

"I didn't have any classes today, anyways." I sighed. "Look, we can't avoid what happened last night."

"Oh, yes we can!" Johannes exclaimed. "We can avoid it by talking about Danny Boy over here." He said, making a huge gesture towards him. "I saw you and Rafael were awfully close last night, closer than ever So do tell, what happened?"

Danny blushed. "I asked him out."

"Finally!!" Johannes shouted. "Did he say yes?"

"Yes, it was super romantic, but before we could kiss or talk more, Ace ruined the moment."

"Damn, we're gonna have to talk about him, huh?" Johannes scowled.

"We can't just ignore this topic, as much as we all want to." I said. Before I could say anymore, my phone vibrated in my pocket. Surprised I still had battery life, I saw that it was my mother.

"Saved by the bell!" Johannes interjected. "Say hi to Mama Freeman for me."

I accepted the call and went into Danny's bedroom for privacy. "Hi Mama."

"Libby, where have you been? I've been trying to call you since last night." I could only imagine her worried facial expression.

"I'm sorry, Mama, I just spent the night at Danny's and my phone was on vibrate. I must have missed your call while I was asleep, that's all!" I replied.

"I assume you've heard the news by now. Now I pray you don't go to any of the protests happening."

"Afraid I'll ruin your political career?" I joked.

"No..." She said with a concerned infliction. "I just don't want you to get hurt out there."

I smiled. The only thing my mother has ever wanted was for me to be safe, especially considering her position.

"I'll be fine, Mama. And I wasn't planning on going to a protest anyways." I assured her. I gently sat upon the fuzzy and cozy blanket atop of Danny's bed. After a short beat, I said, "I guess that means you're going to be Minority Leader now that we've loss the majority?"

"Yes, actually, I was just about to go to the House today, start preparing for the next...administration." I could hear and feel her disgust at the thought.

"Well, I'll let you go. I'll be safe, I promise." I smiled. "Love you, Mama."

"Love you too, sweetie."

The phone hung up and I sighed. I opened up the bedroom to walk back out into the larger apartment area. For the first time, I really admired Danny's place. He had gorgeous and riveting art from the Harlem Renaissance on the walls, graciously spaced apart. It was a collection that his grandfather passed down. Danny was proud of his African American heritage. After my conversation with my mother, I felt better until I saw the frantic look upon Johannes as I got closer towards the kitchen.

"Don't worry, we'll be right there." Danny said on his phone with a panicked infliction. "Okay, I'll talk to you later. Bye."

The atmosphere of worry and anxiety was thick. I became nervous without understanding what was happening.

"Who was that?" I asked.

"We gotta go to the hospital, now." Johannes replied, quickly grabbing his jacket and his phone.

"What happened? What's going on?" I was still terribly confused, while also preparing to leave.

Danny looked solemn as he grabbed his keys. "I should've known something like this would happen once he won..."

"Danny, what the hell is going on?" I interjected while grabbing his arm to slow him down so he could explain.

"Rafael has been attacked."

APRIL

Hello readers. Around this point in history, one would have known me as April Freeman, Speaker of the House of Representatives. It has been an awfully long time since anyone has called me by my old title. But that is not important now as I do not want to drag along. What is important is that I tell you what happened after the infamous election. The next morning, I went to the House of Representatives, in order to prepare for the upcoming administration. It was quite dreary, I must add. I remember holding an umbrella, trying to cover myself and my nice green suit.

I walked into the empty House Chamber, as the House was not in session. Before I went to work, I just wanted to stand in the moment and imagine what I would go through the next four years.

"Enjoying the view, Mrs. Freeman?" I heard a voice say. I turned around. This was the first time I met Lynn Braun.

"I must say that congratulations are in order, Mrs. Braun. You are going to be the first female Vice President for Mr. Ace." I said cordially. She flipped her long brown hair away from her slightly tanned slim face. Her red dress showed off her slim figure. She grinned, taking the compliment to heart.

"Thank you. And congratulations, you're now the *Minority Leader*, I suppose?" She replied in a snarky manner.

"I suppose I am the Minority Leader now that your party has won."

"I imagine our sides will be fighting a lot soon. At least, if we have to fight, it'll be for the people." She smiled.

"It'll be for the people." I smiled back.

"It's been a pleasure seeing you, but I have to go." She sighed. She turned around to walk out and then came back to say one more thing. "It looks quite odd, but I think your green outfit is very becoming of you." She smirked. As she walked away, that was the day I truly met Lynn Braun and that was the day I began to despise her.

RAFAEL

The hospital room was cold and empty befitting to the way I felt. The walls were bare, and everything was dull. My emotional state reflected my actual reality. I knew stuff like this happened, but I never expected it to happen to me. While positioning my body to get comfortable, I groaned from the immense pain I felt radiate through my body. The jumbled memories of what happened the night before hurt just as much as my actual physical wounds.

"Raf!" I heard someone shout in the hall. Almost immediately, Danny swooped through the door with the face of distress and came rushing to sit beside me. "Raf, are you okay?" He said compassionately. Soon after he said that, Libby and Johannes came right in.

"Oh my God..." Johannes gasped in disbelief as he glanced at me. Libby covered her mouth in shock.

"Hey guys." I groaned out. "I'm probably a sight for sore eyes, huh?"

Libby slowly walked closer towards the edge of the bed, Danny put his hand in mine, and Johannes was still and solemn.

"Did the doctor come in?" Johannes asked.

"Yes." I said. "She said I had a broken arm and bruised ribs. And apparently, I also have a scar on the side of my face, but I haven't seen it yet. She said it'll most likely be there for life." I looked directly into Danny's eyes, full of worry just for me with him also caressing my hands. "I promise I'm okay, Dan."

"No, you're not, Raf. What happened? Who did this to you?"

My eyes began to swell with tears as the pain elevated not just from my bruised ribs, but also from my heart. Tears streamed down from my eyes and my words got caught in my throat.

"Take your time, we're all here." Libby whispered.

Once I gathered my voice, I began to recall what was, for a while, the worse experience I had ever lived through.

"It happened soon after I left the apartment to go back to my dorm room on campus." I began quietly. "After seeing Ace win, I just couldn't handle it. Seeing all the people celebrating his victory on TV. All of his supporters jumping up and down for a cause they so strongly believe in... I needed to leave the party to clear my head and go home to get some sleep." I started choking up as I reflected on that night. While walking back, I looked at the stars and the moon. The night sky twinkled as if the stars were gazing down upon the world, writhing at human actions and reactions. Over the distance beyond the hill, I saw the lights of D.C., shining brightly as if they were blatantly defying the stars with the pride of the faults and sins of humanity. Looking at the moon, it reminded me that throughout the ages, humankind have looked upon the moon and have wished and hoped and prayed for the same things: shelter, warmth, safety, and love. By being reminded of our basic human needs, I was assured that we are not all that different. I started crying, salty tears overflowed my tired eyes. My wishful thinking was wrong.

"I heard two guys behind me, uproarious and drunk with victory. Victory that what they believed in, their beliefs that they were better than and more deserving than the 'others.' They recognized I was Hispanic and one of them shouted 'Hey, Spic!'" I grunted through my teeth, grimacing at the hateful word. "I ignored them. What else was I supposed to do? What word could I ever call them that would hurt them? 'Racist?' 'Gringo?' They would just laugh that off. So, I kept walking, but at a faster pace. They were annoyed that I didn't respond so the other guy yelled out, 'Ace is finally gonna build a wall so people like you can't get in no more.' They laughed. They fucking laughed. I tried to keep walking, but they ran up to me and one of them grabbed me from behind."

There was not a dry eye from anyone at that point. Libby was crying with her hands covering her mouth again. Johannes, as wild, crazy, and fun as he could be, stood there, strong like a soldier, with tears falling from his eyes. And Danny, he kissed my hand as he sobbed. Me? By this point, I wept. "They grabbed me and just started beating me. I tried to fight back, but one punched me so hard in my chest, I could barely breathe. I was knocked down and one just stomped on my arm. I howled in pain. Then one took out a knife and said, 'Be quiet, you fucking piece of shit, you're gonna get what's coming to you.' He cut the side of my face, but before I got hurt any worse, someone heard what was happening and called campus security. They arrested the boys, thank God because I could've died."

"Do you know who did it?" Libby asked.

"No, I just know they had on red Alpha Tau Omega jackets. I told the police everything in case you were wondering."

"When I find who did this, I'm gonna make em pay..." Johannes muttered. "No one should go through something like this."

"This was a hate crime... I expected that to happen after Ace won, but not so soon and not to you." Danny whispered to me.

I replied by saying, "This is our world now... If this happened before Ace has even been inaugurated, then what's gonna happen in the next four years? May God help us all..."

JOHANNES

L.A. is the best place in the country, and you can fight me on that. There's nothing better than feeling the warmth of the sun pressed upon your skin like an affectionate hug, especially in May. School was finally over, and while I like D.C. and the east coast, nothing compares to the west. Something about the dry, arid winds and the feeling of dreams come true among the people in L.A. is something breathtaking. I especially felt it driving to the record store. I drove my dad's sleek classic red corvette with the top down. With an utterly alluring sky of azure, filled with puffy white clouds, I felt at home zipping through the streets lined with tall, green, and sturdy palm trees. My style in D.C. has always been edgy, but here, I felt normal. That day, I had on an American flag bandanna wrapped around my forehead with a white tank top and ripped jeans with a blue flannel shirt tied to my waist. It felt great driving with the radio on, it's something I should do more often. I was surprised at the gems they played with one song having a natural, euphoric California vibe with mellow synths dominated by an intense club beat. It was a song that was sure to be a summer hit because it had a catchy beat with a husky and deep, yet soft alto crooning voice of a woman.

After enjoying the ride, I finally arrived at the record store. This was one of my favorite places. I got out of the car, locked it, and started to walk towards the building. It was a very small building, and it was an aging structure. Walking inside, I smelled the dust in the place. In the background, one could hear the faint haunting melodies, the thud of a piano that could strike fear in your heart, and the wailing, powerful, guttural cry on the song. The blues could be felt even if you could barely hear it yourself. The flickering fluorescent lights somehow trapped the shop within a certain bygone time. Yep. This was my version of heaven.

"Glad to see you back home!" The shop owner said.

"Thanks Ed! It's good to be back for the summer! You have no idea how much I've missed this place." I replied. And it was the truth. I didn't realize how much I would miss home in general.

"You should make sure to visit more often. I am an old man, you know?" He laughed. I smiled as the man's eyes glistened with years of wisdom and pain. I don't know what he's been through, but I could tell he was a survivor.

"I know. It's just been a hectic year." I solemnly whispered, remembering what previously happened with Rafael and his attackers. I still hate that there wasn't much I could do. He's my friend. At least his attackers got arrested, but you know how it is with rich kids. I know I'm reading the hell outta myself, but its' true. I don't know if they stayed in jail or if they were able to go right back out into society. I reeled myself back in and focused on my conversation.

"I know, it has been for me too! I've had more customers than I've had in years! Did you know its suddenly cool to buy records again?" He joked.

"That's why I'm here, Ed! I desperately need some new records; I'm wearing my old ones out." I quipped with him.

"Go right ahead! Have fun! Let me know if you need any help."

I started walking around the rows layered with records. I looked through the Jazz and Blues section, which are among my favorites. I picked up a used Fats Waller record, feeling the roughed-up edges of the cardboard album cover and then took the vinyl out, touching the flat disk with smooth grooves throughout.

"Yes, this would do nicely." I thought to myself. Guarding it within my arms, I also spied a lucky find, an old Roberta Flack album, which pictured her in an afro that reminded me of Libby's. I walked over the soul section and picked it up, caressing the record. Humming the sweet yet intricate melodies of her music in my head as I walked over to the pop music aisle. Searching through the selections, I found one of my favorite artists of all time: Lumos. He's like the biggest superstar of all time. His music is a gorgeous and effective blend of R&B and pop, creating fans all over the world. His style of performance is impeccable as he dances with a crispness and sings with a velvety voice, while maintaining vocal stability and stamina. He just recently released an album and I picked it up because I had to have it. Being satisfied with my selection, I went ahead and bought the three albums. Walking out, I felt content.

***

I went back to my enormous house in Beverly Hills which was mostly empty except for my sister and me. It's not that our parents didn't love us, but they worked long hours and were frequently out of town to maintain our expensive lifestyle. Coming from the garage through the kitchen, it took a while for me to bump into my sister.

"Hey!" Anna casually said and signed since she is deaf.

"What's up?" I smiled as I embraced her in a hug, while tussling with her dirty blond hair, that was tied in a ponytail.

"Stop, you're gonna knock off my cochlear!" She laughed, pushed me away and grabbed her purse. "I'm on my way to a party, so I'll talk to you later."

"Wait, you're going out like that?" I pointed at her bohemian chic styled outfit. She was wearing a brown suede fringe vest with matching heels and a flowy cream shirt with daisy dukes. "It's a party! You should dress spicy!"

"I am spicy, thank you very much. If I became anymore fire than I already am, it would be literally impossible to keep the boys off me and that's already hard enough." She simcommed in both languages with a quickness.

"Alright!" I laughed. "Just be safe, okay? I love you, little sister." I signed 'I love you' with my right hand.

"Love you too, big brother." She walked out for her party, leaving me by myself. I smiled. I love my sister more than anything on this planet and I would do anything for her. But right now, I was alone. Again. I was hoping that my family would spend more time with each other, but it's fine. I went up to my room, which was spacious and filled with light. It was connected to a huge balcony. I set my stuff down on my desk and got myself comfortable and turned on the T.V. I wanted to catch up on the news because I hadn't had time to focus on the world because I was focused on coming back home for the summer. So, I tuned in to Broadcast News Service or BNS for short while I prepared my blunt.

Sitting at my desk with the T.V. on blast, I unrolled a white grape cigar, emptied out its tobacco content and laid the crinkly brown paper that was left. I looked up at the screen that was implanted in the center on the wall. All they ever do nowadays is talk about President Ace. Since his inauguration, he's been involved in nothing but controversy after controversy. Even the things that he manages to accomplish on his agenda are controversial. BNS was playing a newsreel of all the unpopular things he's said so far, the most recent being the new tax cuts that the Republicans were trying to push. Still reviewing his tenure as President, I pulled out my silver grinder and my bag of weed. I opened the bag and instantly smelled the earthy, woody, and pungent fragrant with the slight hint of citrus. I grabbed the green bud, pulled it apart and put it within the grinder to crush it.

While I did that, I glanced at the T.V., seeing all the protests against either the new administration or the causes that the administration support. Huge crowds seemed to march and fill the streets more times than I remember in recent history. Whether they were justifiably angry or not, I will never know. Then, the BNS coverage focused on the National Party. They explained how different they are to the actual Republican party, yet how frequently their beliefs overlap. The National Party was once a fringe section of the Republican party. Most of the Republicans believed that the Nationalists were nothing more than a cancerous tumor because of their hate, but nothing was done to wipe them out since they supported the conservative cause. Prior to the election, most liberals had no clue that they existed, but afterwards, no one could deny their existence. They were no longer just a sub-culture, but they became a part of mainstream America, especially since they were emboldened with Ace in office. They spewed hate everywhere, on the internet and in the streets. The men who attacked Rafael were found to be part of this hate group.

Feeling my anger slowly rise, I put down my grinder and decided to play the new Lumos record that I bought. After placing the album on the record player, I started to relax, letting the music play. Taking the weed out of the silver tool, I lined it within the creased paper, and I rolled it up, using my spit and a little bit of fire to make it stick. I opened the doors to the balcony, blasting the music even louder. I used my black lighter to set my blunt aflame. I inhaled the smoke, letting it fill my lungs to maximum capacity. I exhaled the smoke out into the world, creating a seemingly billowing cloud of smoke to float into the air. Watching the hue of the sky turning from bright crimson to violet and seeing the sun sinking down, slowly inviting an army of stars was one of the highlights of my life. I let the narcotized slow rhythms of a new Lumos song overtake me while the elation of the blunt uplifted me. Hearing the song gave me the best idea. Ever since Rafael's attack, I've wanted to do something for him considering he went through such a horrific experience. Since I couldn't do anything for revenge, I could do something not just for him, but for Danny, Libby, and even my sister. I could get tickets for the Lumos concert. It would be fun! And after the year we've all had, it would be a great release of tension. Yes, this is a great idea.

APRIL

I n May, I became better acquainted with President Ace and Vice-President Braun. During this time, I remember having a telephone conversation with my daughter Libby about the upcoming Lumos concert. She excitedly explained how Johannes bought her and her other friends' tickets to go to the event. I was happy for her, as any mother would be to hear that their daughter was happy. However, when I heard that the concert was taking place on the other side of the country, I must admit that I was slightly apprehensive. But then I realized she was a wise young woman and had demonstrated herself to be responsible. I told her that I trusted her and that she had my blessings.

Once I hung up the phone, I took a deep breath. That day was a day that I was not ready to commence through. At the time, there was great controversy in the House about the Tax Cut bill. In order to calm the roaring storm on the House floor, the President invited several key members of both the Republican and Democratic party. Since I was the Minority Leader in the House of Representatives, it was obvious why I was invited to talk about the new bill.

"Was that your daughter on the phone?" Charles Jackson, the Minority Whip, asked me.

"Why yes! She's going to a concert next month in L.A. She seems happy about it, and so am I. Quite honestly, both Libby and I have had a rough year. At least one of us has something to look forward to. Are you ready for this luncheon?"

"April, you know I'm not. If I'm frank with you, I do not want to go at all. Ace doesn't know the first thing about how to be a politician. To be honest, I trust Braun more. At least I feel as if I could reason with her." He said as we walked out of the Capitol building.

"I wouldn't trust her as far as I could throw her. As far as I'm concerned, she's worse than Ace."

"Nothing could be worse than him." Charles scoffed.

"She has the same beliefs he does; she just knows how to execute through her power in a way that he can't. She's something to be feared."

"Well, if you say so. My whole problem with this matter is, how is this lunch supposed to ease our conscience about the bill?"

"He already knows that he won't be able to convince us, but if he could convince more on the other side to support this bill, then he would've done his job." I said.

"Well, then Godspeed, woman. Let's hope we get through this unscathed. I swear if I'm insulted by that man just one more time..."

"One thing we can do, is do what we do best: debate. Hopefully, if our side could just discuss this, we could explain why this bill should not pass."

***

Charles and I pulled up to the restaurant. The concierge opened our car door for us. I got out and looked at the place. It was nice. When we went inside and we were greeted by our coworkers. We walked up a grand staircase that was lined with red velvet on the steps, which lead to a majestic dining room with only one table perfectly set for the twelve of us. There were place settings for five Democrats on one side, five Republicans on the other, the President at the head and the Vice-President at the foot of the table. The ambiance was dramatic, with low lighting to reflect the mood. All the representatives sat down while waiting for Ace and Braun to arrive. If my memory serves me correctly, - and it does- they arrived slightly late (if slightly meant 30 minutes). Once they finally arrived, they sat in their proper seat.

"Let us start with a toast." Ace began as he lifted his wine glass. "I hope that we are able to agree on a compromise, because what we should remember is that we serve the American people."

"I'll drink to that!" Braun interjected. We all drank the wine and almost immediately the first course was served.

"I brought everyone here today to talk about the tax cut." Ace followed up. "Now, I think it's a wonderful idea, you know? I feel like this is something that the people need. The economy has been absolutely terrible and our citizens have lost hope in us as a government. This is necessary!"

"I concur." Nick Patterson, a Republican Representative said. "It hasn't been a secret that I completely support the President on this. He has been wise to the plight of the American people, seeing how he's not an actual politician. He's a real person. A real person would recognize that passing this bill is the best thing for everybody."

"I agree." Said Ethan Nalls, another conservative Republican. "I think that passing this bill would be the best thing that the administration could do."

"I'm sorry." Tina Carter, a fellow Representative interrupted. "Are we praising the president and the bill? Or are we here to discuss the content of the tax bill?"

"I have to admit that she is right. Even though I support the plan, the whole purpose of this luncheon was to convince those who didn't." Nathanial Clements, another Republican replied. "Mr. President, would you like the honor of explaining why the bill would be good for the country?"

"Um..." Ace shuffled. "I think I'll give Braun the honor of explaining. You know, since she hasn't got a word in." There, I could tell that Ace did not even understand his own bill that he was proposing.

"It would be a pleasure." Braun smiled, as if she were the one who had the true power at the table. "This new tax cut bill provides for a reduction in tax rates for both businesses and citizens of this great nation. Also, by increasing the standard deduction, it creates for a personal tax simplification. Additionally-" I had to cut her off because I just couldn't take any more of the fake politicking aspect of this luncheon.

"I hate to butt in, but does anyone else besides the Democrats have a personal issue with the bill?" I had to ask. "Mr. President, Lynn, I have to say that this luncheon was about discussing the bill, not continuing with this farce. While the Republicans are seemingly trying to push this bill as something that will be beneficial, that is not the case. Only the businesses and members of the upper echelon in society will have something to gain, while the people suffer. And not to mention that voting this into law will add an additional Trillion dollars into the National Debt."

"With all due respect, April, I was in the middle of speaking and you ever so rudely interrupted me..." She grimaced.

"It was necessary."

"The bill is fine, April. If it weren't, then why would the conservatives endorse it?" Ace added.

"The conservatives are endorsing this because it only serves their purpose. If they continue to please the businessmen, they'll grant them money to fund their campaigns. You know. You used to do the same thing with your business in New York, Mr. President, am I wrong?"

"April, you know this bill is happening either way, so why don't you just accept that. We have the votes. Y'all don't." Nick responded.

"We may not have the votes. But the people deserve to know what their Republican representatives are willing to do to advance themselves, when you're supposed to be working for the citizens. I'll be damned if I let this bill pass without a fight." I stood up along with my fellow colleagues.

As we walked out, I heard Braun softly say, "Do your worst, April... I'll await the battle."

Danny

We rushed through the airport as soon as we passed the security section. Feeling the air whoosh past me and hearing the fast clickity-clack on the wheels of our luggage provided a mixture of adrenaline and anxiety. We made it to the right place just in time in that our plane was just about to board. After getting onto the cramped plane, we sat at our proper locations provided to us on our tickets. Me and Rafael sat together while Libby sat across the aisle.

"Thank God we made it in time!" Libby said as she buckled her seat belt. "We wouldn't have been late if it wasn't for the freaking traffic."

"We should place the blame on Mr. Pretty Boy over here!" I laughed, pointing towards Raf, when he smirked.

"Excuse me if I need my beauty rest! I didn't even get a full eight hours!"

"Well, now you can sleep if you want to. The plane is gonna take off soon." I sighed, making myself comfortable. The aircraft began to rumble as the it sped off the runway and we broke into the atmosphere as gravity forcefully pushed against us, causing us to sink into our seats.

Since I had the window seat, I leaned against the window watching the entire city of D.C. and the whole world become smaller, which really put things into perspective for me. I peered straight through the unbelievably puffy clouds and somehow it seemed as if we crossed the barrier into the heavens. The world was left behind, and the clouds covered the land below. All that was there was light and sky. Rafael propped himself on my shoulders and quickly dozed off. He was so cute that I didn't want to disturb him; I slowly pushed my earbuds in and just relaxed with music.

It was several hours into the flight. I looked over at Libby and saw she was deeply engrossed in her book. The drone of the engine had me slowly falling asleep, but then I was shocked when Rafael bolted upright. He was sweating, panting, and terrified.

"Rafael, what's wrong." I asked, grabbing his hands, attempting to reassure him. "Did you have the dream again?"

"Danny, it's nothing." Rafael said as he cleared his throat.

"Raf, I'm your boyfriend, you can talk to me. Was it about that night?"

"Danny, it's nothing! We're on our way to L.A. and let's focus on that!" He smiled behind troubled eyes. "Besides, the turbulence woke me up, that's all. Trust me, I'm fine."

I looked deep in his eyes, and while I knew he wasn't okay, I decided not to press the issue, since it was obvious he wasn't comfortable talking about it. We soon started our descent from the heavenly sky, back into the civilized world occupied by the sinful and broken people below. We left our plane, clueless and ignorant of the future because we had no idea that day would start a chain reaction that would be felt years later.

***

"I've been missing y'all's wack asses for too damn long!" Johannes exclaimed as he started driving towards his house. I partook in the view, since I had never been in L.A. before. The difference between D.C. and

L.A. was apparent. For one, the atmosphere was different because the air was much dryer, compared to the humid climate on the east coast. Also, the air was quite thick in a way I had never experienced, but I later found out that it was smog that made it quite difficult to breathe, seeing how Johannes' car had the top down. But I was happy and content. I was with all of my closest friends again along with my loving boyfriend. At that moment, I felt like nothing could touch us, that we would be young and carefree forever. I look upon that memory now with great nostalgia, seeing Rafael's smile, hearing Libby's giggle, and cackling at Johannes boisterous laugh. I wish that moment lasted forever. It was one of the few times I truly felt content. Eventually, we pulled up to the humongous house with the driveway plastered in gray stones. The architecture of the mansion was postmodern, and it definitely fit into Johannes' edgy style. When we walked in with our luggage, we entered a gigantic foyer with ceilings that never seemed to end. The floor plan was open with a sleek silver kitchen, updated with nothing but the best equipment. The sunken family room had a round, gray couch that created a semicircle facing the kitchen. The T.V. in the living room was implanted in the wall. The house was a marvel to take in.

"Ah, so you're my brother's friends!" Someone said as she walked in to hug her brother.

"You guys, this is my sister, Anna. Anna meet Libby, Rafael, and Danny! She's coming to the concert with us." Johannes introduced her to us, and we all shook hands.

"So how do you guys put up with my idiotic brother in college?" She laughed as she also signed in what seemed like American Sign Language.

"Awww, you know you love me!" Johannes kissed her forehead.

"Unfortunately." She giggled. "I can show you guys your rooms, so you can get ready for the Lumos concert." She showed Rafael and Libby to their rooms, while I stayed behind to talk to Johannes.

"Your sister is nice!" I said.

"Ehh, she aight." He turned to me and then we busted out laughing. "She's great. Although we joke around, we do love each other. Since our parents are often never around, we're all we got. I'll show you your room first, then I'll get the shots ready."

"Shots?"

"Yeah, you think I'm gonna be squeezing against people and being slightly uncomfortable standing up a good portion of the concert without *any* drinks? Think again!" He quipped. He led me up the stairs and showed me my room. I proceeded to get ready for the concert.

***

I walked out the bedroom in my stunning new outfit, a see-through shirt covered in crystals that sparkled like the night sky and simple black pants that hugged my waist along with a belt that had a silver buckle. I felt super attractive, I'm not gonna lie. I walked down the stairs and Libby was hanging out in the family room, girl chatting with Anna. They both looked absolutely stunning. Libby had on a sexy black strapless dress with a mermaid tail at the end. She wore dark red lipstick, where the pigment seemed to shine in the light. She had a red rose in her afro to match her lips. She looked flawless. Anna donned a short, bright red leather dress, with a matching red leather choker and a bold red lip. She looked gorgeous. Johannes came in and placed shots on the coffee table. He appeared to match with Anna as he had a red leather jacket with a white tee underneath. His accessories were a black bandana across his forehead and a gold necklace. We were waiting for Rafael when he came down the stairs in the simplest outfit out of everyone, but in my eyes, his was the sexiest of all. He had on a tight black tee with black leather trousers. We locked eyes and for a moment, it felt like the world stopped. But I was brought back to reality when Johannes gripped my shoulder.

"Let's have some shots now that we're all here!"

Rafael finally made it down the stairs, and I said, "You're the most handsome man I've ever seen."

"You don't look bad yourself, Danny…" he grinned just before he kissed me.

"Okay, after we take our shots, we must take a group photo, cause we all look damn good!" Libby stated. Anna was the first one to grab a shot and threw it back like she's done it a million times before. She looked up at us and noticed how shocked we were, seeing that she was only 17.

"Ooh, it burns…" She lied.

"Sis…" Johannes laughed.

"What, don't pretend you were pure and innocent in high school, big bro, I know all about your relationship with Ms. Mary Jane. I'm sure I'll see how wild you guys truly get once I join you at school."

My ears perked up. "You're joining us next semester?"

"Yep, I'll be a freshman, finally!"

"Well, we'll be your guide through life at our school." Rafael added in. We then took our photo, commemorating the night.

"Well, since I've already done my drinking for the night, I'm gonna get some music set up on T.V. to get us in the mood." Anna left for the living room, while the four of us stayed behind, with Johannes preparing a toast.

"Let us have a great night tonight! I thank you guys for being great friends and I thank you guys for being there, not just for me, but for each other. May life continue to bring us together with adventures far beyond our wildest dreams. Cheers!"

We knocked our drinks back and laughed, then we set our glasses down. All of a sudden, we heard a screeching cry from the living room. It was a scream that signified death. We rushed to the living room and saw Anna crying with her eyes stuck on the T.V. It was news that we never expected to happen. The blue and red flashing lights of sirens filled the screen as they replayed the scene coming from a cop cam. A black man was dead. Lumos was dead.

LIBBY

That was when everything changed. This was the event that changed our country and it created repercussions that will be felt for centuries from now. The night that Lumos died remains frozen in my mind's eye, forever stuck in ember. Upon closer inspection of the moment that will continue to be suspended in time, I remember all of us watching the breaking news. I remember the screen displaying images and videos of the shooting, with the newscasters explaining what happened. All Lumos was planning to do was visit his family that lived in L.A. The police officers were patrolling the area and they saw a black man that looked out of place because the rest of the neighborhood was white. He didn't even notice that the cop car was there. They got out of the car and attempted to arrest him. They claimed that he was resisting arrest, but the other neighbors accounted that they forcefully pushed him to the ground with his hands raised in the air. When he tried to reassure them that he was who he said he was and that he bought his family a house nearby, he slowly attempted to show his I.D., and the police reacted by shooting him 19 times. They claimed they were fearful for their lives.

That was a load of bullshit. I remember seeing the aftermath and I felt pain. But most of all, I felt anger. Lumos wasn't just a celebrity. He was a black man that was brutally murdered by the system that was supposed to protect us. It angered me because it showed that no matter how beloved you could be by millions across the globe, you are still black. In the United States, to be black meant you were to be feared; you were not to be trusted. No matter if you wore the finest clothes, you could still be seen as a thug. I was upset because if anyone could have avoided being targeted by the police, it was Lumos since he did everything that was "right." He made music that could be enjoyed by the masses, he wore clothes that were non-threatening, and he spoke in an articulate manner that wouldn't be deemed as "uneducated," but yet that was not enough. He had assimilated into a world where he would be accepted and that still wasn't enough.

Being black was both a blessing and a curse. There's a certain magic to being black no one can truly explain. We had all been through unspeakable trauma and we're all bonded through blood. We created a culture that was explicitly and uniquely our own since we lost our connection to our ancient past because it was washed away by the sea of Atlas. That was the twisted blessing we were able to receive. But the curse is far darker and sinister. Our people were enslaved for over 400 years. Our people went through horrific and shameful ordeals that no one should ever go through. Then we underwent segregation, otherwise known as Jim Crow, based on a spineless and pathetic minstrel character. Segregation was the result of slavery, with people believing that they were better than others, just because of their skin color. After slavery and segregation ended, many believed that racism was over, but how could it have been when no one had ever truly dealt with our country's shameful past. Our lives then were a culmination of both slavery and segregation. Because of those terrible times, we were the aftermath. We had to deal with racism still left over from the old eras. We had to deal with redlining, microaggressions, and school-to-prison pipelines. But the worse we had to deal with was police brutality. Police officers were put in place to protect us, but their sometimes-hidden bias against people of color can come out in a fatal way. I believed that police officers needed better training in order to accurately measure the danger in situations, but for Lumos, it was too late. Lumos was murdered.

I was angry, but everyone else was feeling different emotions. I looked at Danny. As black people, I knew we were thinking the same things. Rafael stared blankly at the screen, with one tear rolling down his face, bringing up a painful memory. Johannes was in disbelief. I later found out that he blamed the administration for emboldening racist police officers since Ace said things like "rough up the criminals" at gatherings with cops as the main attendees. He just didn't realize this happened all the time even before Ace and would continue to happen after Ace. Anna was perhaps the most shocked out of all of us. Yes, she knew of police brutality, but she never really thought about it. She realized that if it could happen to Lumos, it could happen to anyone.

The L.A.P.D. began an investigation into the shooting a couple of days afterwards. Major protests appeared across the country, as the nation was in uproar about the death of Lumos because he was a beloved icon. When asked about how he felt about the death of Lumos and the investigation, Ace stated that it was a "local matter," as if police brutality didn't affect everyone across America. That began to enrage even more people as small riots happened everywhere. That moment, that time, remains deeply emblazoned in my head. It's still almost impossible to fully describe, but those were the social issues of the time. Well, that was my tea. Sip it nice.

RAFAEL

I t felt good to be back in D.C., especially after a turbulent summer. No one could escape the aftermath of Lumos' untimely death. It weighed heavily on us. However, school was almost back in session and this was our senior year. Libby and I signed up to be guides for the new student orientation. We felt it was our duty to help out since we remembered how we felt when we were new students. The anxiety of becoming an adult combined with the thrill of freedom is an exhilarating mixture of emotions that we knew all too well. Aiding the next generation in any way to help them achieve success was a noble cause that we wanted to partake in. Libby and I guided a group of newcomers around the campus. Libby explained the history of this longstanding institution while I showed them the sights. Honestly, I should have appreciated how beautiful the campus was, with its stunning green grass and tall trees with wide canopies perfect for getting shade underneath the scorching heat of the sun. I should have smiled more when I saw people having picnics outside for no special reason other than to enjoy the company of their friends. To hear the sounds of grunting during football practice that showcased the hardworking spirit of our university. I wish I was present more at that time, but once we came upon a certain spot, I flashed back to the past.

Sensing that something was wrong, Libby said "Okay, everyone! It's time for dinner at the cafeteria! Please report back to Winston Hall by 8:00." She gulped in a panic when she looked at me.

"Raf, are you okay?" She asked, but she was unable to break through as the murmurs within my head became loud, reverberating echoes.

"Hey, Spic!"

"Ace is finally gonna build a wall...."

"You're gonna get what's coming to you."

"Rafael!" Libby shouted as she shook me out of my nightmarish daze. Shaking, tears started building up in my eyes.

"Libby..."

"Rafael, are you okay? You need me to take you to the nurse's office?"

"No... it's just that... every time I have to walk by here, at this spot, the only thing I can remember is that horrible night. Those boys didn't just attack me. They took my innocence. They took my hope and that's the worst thing to have taken from you. Before I used to have hope that everything would work out and be okay, but now? I have no faith in humanity anymore. Everyone is fighting each other now, standing up for their political beliefs as if they're the only one that could possibly be right. Everyone is fighting on how different a person is allowed to be. My faith is gone because I used to believe that no matter what, we humans would always support each other. Now you can get attacked just for your skin tone. You saw that with me. You saw that with Lumos." I said with fierce anger. "Every time I see that spot, I'm reminded that besides my friends, I can't trust anybody no more. Look at me! I've literally been scarred for life!"

"Rafael..."

"No! I'm tired of being pitied! I'm tired of being a fucking victim! This is something I'm gonna have to live with for the rest of my life and I..." I had to avoid breaking down. "I used to be so dreamy and idealistic. I used to believe that everyone had something wonderful to put out in the world. I thought that everyone was due respect and kindness, but dammit! I was attacked, and the boys bought their way outta jail and they're God knows where while they're doing stuff with God knows who. I hate them. I hate them for hating me enough to almost kill me." I grumbled out of frustration.

"I understand you're feeling awful right now. But you have to remember those are just a few people that believe in hate like that. And just because we're all fighting due to our ideology, that doesn't negate our love for each other as a people. Despite all of our flaws, we're Americans."

I wistfully smiled. "At least you still have some hope."

"I have to have some hope. That's how we as a people survive." She grabbed ahold of me. "Come on, let's go to dinner."

We started walking towards the cafeteria, enjoying the fresh air engulfing our lungs. We saw the sky begin the process of change and renewal into the night. We felt the humid air stick to our skin, but we didn't mind. It felt good to be home. While walking, we started to talk.

"I hear your mom is not letting the Republicans get away with this tax bill." I chuckled. "At least she's been letting people know what the full bill entails, even if the bill still passes. I know she's gained popularity all over the country, at least for standing up for the people."

"Yeah, she's fighting this as much as she can, even though she knows it's a losing battle. The response she's getting from some people is both uplifting and disheartening. But what can you do? That's the life of being a politician's daughter." Sensing it was a tough subject for her to talk about, I changed the topic.

"What do you hope will happen tonight? Do you think the police officers will be charged with Lumos' death?" I asked.

"I hope that they will, but with this country the way it is…"

"I thought you were hopeful?"

"I'm hopeful, but I'm also realistic. Like I'm hopeful that the cafeteria will have Jamaican jerk chicken wings, but I'm realistic in the fact that it'll probably be pizza again. You can be both. Don't let those boys take away your hope. That means they and all other Nationalists have won. And we certainly don't want that, do you?" She smiled assuredly.

We finally made it to the cafeteria, which we discovered was full of people, making joyful noises as the new students were talking to their new friends. This cafeteria was the busiest place on campus, wherein a majority of the tables were taken. For the first time, I came to appreciate the colorful murals that were painted by alumni from the past, as the murals were filled with swirling depictions of campus life through odd, yet life-like shapes. I grabbed a plate and immediately ran in line to the Jamaican jerk chicken wings. Hope did exist. After receiving my meal, I found Libby, Danny, and my parents sitting at a table near the television and joined them.

"Hi, mijo, did you have a long day? You look tired." Mama asked me.

"Yes, Rafael, your eyes are certainly puffy…" Papa added in.

"I'm fine, Mama! And Papa, it's just allergies, you know that D.C. is known for its terrible allergy seasons." I said as I sat down.

"Well, you missed a fun day with me and your parents!" Danny started to excitedly say. "We went to the Smithsonian and we went to the Union Market, we just had a blast! See, look at the pictures we took!" He paused to show me the pictures on his phone, with artistic filters used to spruce them up.

"Yes, we like your boyfriend. He listens to Selena! He's a keeper!" Mama nudged to me. Papa smiled and replied by saying "I'm happy we decided to accompany you back here." I was lucky and blessed to have parents that accepted me for who I was. I loved them, and they loved me, that was all that mattered.

"Has anyone seen Johannes and Anna? I thought they were supposed to come back together?" Libby questioned.

"They're still in L.A. I think they should be back sometime this week?" I responded.

"Well, I hate that we missed them." Mama said. "Maybe next time!"

We continued to eat merrily, laughing and having a good time until the term "Breaking News" streamed across all of the televisions in the cafeteria. Suddenly, the whole place went silent, paying attention to the nearest T.V.

"We have breaking news coming in from Los Angeles." one newscaster started. "The D.A. has declined to charge the former L.A.P.D officers involved in the shooting of the beloved celebrity icon, Lumos..."

The whole place seemed to rumble in a collective uproar. Hardly anyone supported this decision since he was a person who most everyone in our generation had genuine love for.

"Dammit!!" Libby cried, disappointed yet again.

"No Justice, No Peace! No Justice, No Peace!" People began to chant. Louder and louder, the students voiced their dissatisfaction at the results. The noisy chants came to a screeching halt, when officers from Immigration Customs and Enforcement barged through the door, frightening everyone and leaving them speechless. Terrified, I kept my eyes off of them, praying that they wouldn't notice me and my family. But my prayers were not answered that day.

"Get up!" One officer said forcefully, while pulling my mother up by the collar of her shirt. Papa tried to stand up for Mama, but another officer gripped his wrist. I was so scared, in a way that can never be explained.

"Officers, may you please grant us the common courtesy of explaining what is going on?!" I demanded, feeling everyone's eyes rest on me

"We've been watching your family for months. We know they're illegals." The leader said. I darted my eyes back to Danny, who got up to say something.

"Please, do we have to do this here? In front of everyone?" Danny begged on my behalf.

"Should've thought about that before coming to America!" one of the officers laughed. Their militant guards stood at the door, staring down any student who dared to look. My parents struggled at the mercy of the leader. I saw the fear in their eyes, an image I never wish to see again.

"Sir, they may not have been born here, but they're just as American as you and me. They've worked hard to make sure I had a better life! Isn't that the American Dream? They're an embodiment of that! Please don't take them away, they're all I have!" I begged with tears flowing down my face.

"I'm just doing my job." He responded coldly. They forced Mama and Papa to go with them, but they tried to fight it by holding on to me.

"Mama! Papa!" I hollered, trying to get to them before they could leave the door. One of the guards held me back, but I escaped, trying to run to the entrance before they left. I grabbed onto my Mama's hand, but the guard slapped me hard, knocking me on the ground.

"MAMA!!! PAPA!!!! NOOOOO!" I screamed in a blood curling cry as Libby and Danny rushed over to me. The cafeteria was hushed, not knowing how to act in this situation, as ICE took my parents in their truck to deport them back to Mexico. I did the only thing I could do. I wept.

ANNA

"Anna, I'm trying to teach you about college!" Johannes attempted to explain as he stuffed his mouth with sushi. We sat outside of the restaurant, enjoying the rays of the sun, taking in the atmosphere of L.A., and listened to the rhythm of the city as people hurried by.

Sipping on my Boba tea, I responded, "You're just trying to make sure I don't have fun, huh? I will have sex, Johannes, you won't stop me from that." The honey-flavored gummies coated my tongue in a sweet syrup. The wind softly blew across my face, leading me to adjust my strand of hair and place it on top of my ear.

"I want you to have fun, trust me! I've been screwing around since sophomore year! And I'm telling you, the football players at school are absolute trash! The cheerleaders, on the other hand..."

"You have first-hand experience in cheerleaders? Like any cheerleader would go out with you?" I joked.

"Cheerleaders are great because they're flexible..." He smirked.

"Ah, and here I was, thinking you were a feminist."

"I am a feminist! I believe that women should do whatever they want, and if they wanna have sex with me, I support it!" He quipped back.

"You're such a player, Johannes. Besides, I'm more interested in soccer players. They're sweeter."

"Wack! They're so boring! How about a dancer? They're full of passion!"

"You're speaking from experience again?"

".... Yes." He mumbled before he dipped his sushi in the wasabi and shoved it into his mouth. I chuckled as I chewed the Boba.

"I'll meet someone at school, so let's not worry about that, Big Bro. You wanna go shopping after we finish eating? I need to buy some stuff for my room." I asked him.

"You know I'm always up for more shopping, you don't even have to ask." He took his last bite and we went back inside the restaurant to hand back their plate. We walked back outside and just talked while we walked. It's so funny how a historic day could start off so ordinary. The smell of the food trucks tingled the senses with the delicious and homey whiff of chicken shawarma. The sights of the grandiose towers, stood over the city as a shining beacon of civilization. Cities are the grand achievement of mankind as we were able to settle in places to create great cultures and encourage migrants to travel with dreams and hopes to make their civilizations great. Even though L.A. was a part of America, it could pass as its own city-state, with its own exclusive culture. I watched people walk by in their flower crowns and their flowing hair. I watched women with their cornrows walk with confidence. L.A. was a different place, with a different ambiance compared to other cities; but on that day, I found this city was filled with its own problems and issues.

"I think I'll get a new T.V. for my room." I stated. In my mind, I had a vision for my dorm: a bohemian paradise with macramé tapestry hanging loosely in the corner of the walls, a bedspread set with simple patterns, fresh plants sitting by the window, and twinkle lights to make the room magical and whimsical. The T.V. was something that I needed because what would I watch while I pretended to study?

"Anna, why get a new one, you could just bring your old one?" Johannes questioned.

"Because we can get this one sent to the school directly and plus, look at the definition! It looks even more realistic than the ones we have in our house." As I admired the piece of technology, all of the T.V.s in this section of the store gathered the shoppers' attention when Breaking News streamed across the screens.

"We have breaking news coming in from Los Angeles." one newscaster started. "The D.A. has declined to charge the former L.A.P.D officers involved in the shooting of the beloved celebrity icon, Lumos..."

"Are you kidding me!!" I exclaimed. Johannes grabbed my shoulders and watched the news with me along with all of the other shoppers. "This is bullshit! How can this happen? The officers were obviously guilty, we all saw it! How could anyone deny that?!" I angrily signed.

"This happens far more than you think..." Johannes whispered. "Most of the time, when a black person is mistreated or killed by an officer, justice rarely ever gets served. Man, I was hoping for something different this time, seeing how Lumos was world-renowned."

Our eyes were stuck on the screen for what felt like hours. The chanting in the store became deafening and anger was felt by some as the pain in their hearts was excruciatingly unbearable. That was really the first time I understood how corrupt the system was and I was just disappointed. The crowd of people started to get restless, shouting and hollering out their frustrations. One person was so angry that they grabbed a T.V and threw it at the glass window at the front, causing the glass to shatter everywhere.

"I think we should head back home, like now." He said in a hushed tone as to not alarm me.

"I agree, let's go."

We ran out into the store and made it back outside where chaos had quickly already taken reign. The people in the streets began marching in protest of the court's decision. The massive crowd was an impromptu protest that came into effect. I don't know how it started but a huge confrontation began between some of the protesters and the police. A few of the people in the protest started breaking windshields on cars. Bricks began to be thrown into storefronts, causing glass to explode into the street.

"Anna, we gotta run! Hold onto me!" Johannes signed to me as he knew I wouldn't be able to hear anything over the thunderous noises. We ran across the sidewalk, attempting to dodge the rocks and bricks on the floor with the million pieces of glass. We were trying to find Johannes' car since we parked it near the entrance of the sushi place we ate at earlier. There was one problem: the car was missing.

"Where's my car!?" Johannes yelled. "Where the fuck is my car?! Someone stole my damn car!"

"How are we gonna get home now?" I wondered aloud.

"We're gonna somehow have to get there, the plan hasn't changed. We just have to improvise..." We kept running towards the heart of the city since we had to go through there to get back home. The scene had gotten worse. Cars were stuck on the road, with people looting and robbing stores. There were two cars on fire, creating a thick cloud of smoke and ash, with the heat blasting in our faces. We continued to run until we came upon the police.

"Stay back!" One officer said when he suddenly appeared. They finally responded to the reports of trouble.

"Please, sir!" I started. "We're just trying to-" he struck me with his baton. I assume he was scared I would do something harmful to him. I gasped in pain and fell to the ground where I earned additional scrapes and bruises. The world around me went quiet. "You knocked my cochlear off!"

I yelled, not hearing anyone's answer. I searched around for my cochlear, finding it near the boot of the officer. He lifted his foot up. I was afraid he was going to step on the most precious item I owned. Johannes was about to fight back for me, until the cop just left, presumably to chase after someone else. My brother lifted me up from the ground.

"Anna, are you okay?" He questioned.

"Yes, I'm fine, we gotta keep going!" We ran faster than we ever ran before. The sky became covered in clouds of pummel and ashes as buildings were lit aflame. The heat waves pounded against our skin. The hot air caused us to sweat profusely.

"We're gonna have to steal a car!" Johannes shouted. "We can't keep running home, it's too far!"

Johannes was right. I didn't want to do it, but I saw we had no other choice. We kept running until we saw another car with the top off. We hopped in and my brother hotwired the car, starting it up, just before the building with the blazing inferno started to collapse on itself.

"Johannes, we gotta go now! GO GO GO!!!" I bellowed. Johannes sped up while the tower fell, causing a wave of ashes to follow behind. While we drove, I looked in disbelief at the pandemonium that was happening across the city in such a rapid amount of time.

"How did this happen? Why are we destroying our city?" I cried as I continued to look on behind us.

"Centuries of pent-up emotions just came out into the open. It was bound to happen... I just wish it didn't have to happen like this." Johannes solemnly said.

Looking back now and then, the vision of the city in flames remains fixed in my mind. I had survived the Burning of L.A.

LIBBY

You know the feeling you get where you know something major is about to happen? The air felt thick with anticipation for a moment where everything changed as I left my dorm, walking in the heat of the summertime. My mind weighed heavily on the recent events that had happened with Rafael. The deportation of his parents, seeing his anguish depressed me, because the tears in his eyes told a story of deep despair. This walk across the Yard was something I desperately needed as I contemplated how the world was changing and yet, how much it remained the same.

The systemic issues within the country, how we viewed undocumented and even documented immigrants had never really changed. Consider the Irish and the Italians. They were treated as second-class citizens during the nineteenth and early part of the twentieth century. While groups that are thought of as inferior changes, the blaming and scapegoating of a group, along with the systems in place that keeps them viewed as inferior hasn't changed, they continue to remain the same. Also, my main thought was, had we lost our humanity? Had we lost the ability to put ourselves in someone else's shoes, to walk a mile in their footsteps? Could we no longer relate to one another? Had most people just assumed things about others and accepted it as fact now? Sure, Rafael's parents were undocumented, but did they have to be treated inhumanely with such force? Could the system be changed so that everyone could be happy? These were deep questions that I thought about as my walk was ending. I almost went back into my dorm building when a taxicab pulled up alongside me.

"Here, Sir. Keep the change." Johannes said as he and Anna got out of the mustard yellow car.

"Oh my God, y'all look a mess!" I exclaimed. Their clothes seemed to be covered in gray, ashen soot. Anna had bruises across her face and scratches along her arm. Johannes looked shaken and disturbed. I could tell they had been through something traumatic. "What happened? Y'all weren't supposed to come here till next week."

"We just came from the airport. After we left L.A., we just drove to the nearest airport, bought tickets for the next flight here immediately. There was no way we could pack a bag or anything, we just came here with nothing, but ourselves." Anna quietly stated. You could see her eyes twinkle in the slight remembrance of the event.

"What happened?" I inquired, still confused.

"Have you not checked your phone this morning?" Johannes cocked his head in a surprised fashion.

"No..." I answered.

"Don't bother, we'll tell you. Can we go inside? I just need to process this..." Anna said, visibly dazed.

"Of course. We can go in my room and talk. I have something to tell you as well." After walking up six flights of stairs since the elevators never seemed to work, I invited them into my room, decorated with posters of covers of classic literature, ranging from the iconic book *I Know why the Caged Bird Sings* to the illustrious cover of *The Great Gatsby* The morning light shone through, with the daily view of the Capital and the Washington monument directly ahead. I allowed Anna to lay down on my bed which was covered with a pink quilt and I gave Johannes permission to sit on my mini black couch while I sat on my desk chair.

"What happened? I can tell that something big went down."

"L.A. burned down. A city just went up in flames." Johannes said with a blank face.

"Wait, what?" I shuddered in shock.

"Yeah." Anna sighed. "It was in response to the announcement that the police weren't getting tried for their involvement in Lumos' death. Everyone got upset. Righteously so, but not enough to burn an entire city. Our home is gone. Least mom and dad are in Canada..."

"And then a cop struck Anna across the face. I wanted to go through him..." Johannes added.

"Oh my gosh, Anna!" I gasped.

Johannes continued. "But seriously, looking back at L.A., seeing it aflame, it killed a part of me. Yes, I'm sure the majority of the city is still there, but the spirit of it, what made Los Angeles bold and beautiful, is gone."

"You said that you had something else you wanted to tell us." Anna was attempting to deflect.

"Um, yes. Rafael's parents came to visit and while at dinner in the cafeteria, ICE came to take his parents for deportation in front of everyone." I replied wearily. Johannes was silent as was Anna since they did not know what to say. After a beat, he finally said something.

"Rafael has been through enough. How do we make him feel better?"

"I think the only thing we can do right now is be there and present for him." I said.

Anna was about to say something, but before she could say anything, my phone rang.

"I'm sorry," I interrupted. "Let me see who it is." It was my mother.

"Say hi to Mama Freeman for me." Johannes contemplatively smiled.

I answered. "Hi, Mama."

"I can tell by your tone you've heard about what has happened in California." She started off. "Or has something else happened? Your voice is worrying me."

"You can tell, huh, ma?"

"You have been my child for 21 years; I can tell your mood by the slight inflection in your tone."

"Yes." I confessed. "Johannes and Anna were in L.A. at the time."

"Are they safe now?" Mama said, concerned.

"Yes, actually they're here with me now, but there's something else that was bothering me."

"Are you okay, sweetie?"

"Rafael's mom and dad were deported right in front of him and everyone in the cafeteria. Mom, it was just awful how the officers handled the situation." I whispered. "I felt so bad for him."

"I'll see if there's anything I can do, but..."

"You're not sure, I know. Thank you for trying to fix it, but I don't think this can be fixed. I know you didn't call to just talk about what's happening in my life. What's going on?" I asked.

"Well, since my opposition to the tax bill has made headlines, BNS has invited me to a townhall in California to talk about the Burning of L.A. amongst many other things."

I soon became worried. "Mama, do you think it's necessary to go to the townhall? I mean, this just happened."

"I understand your apprehension, Libby. But I do believe it is necessary, because the people deserve leaders willing to talk to them about current events. I'm going." Well, that was certainly final.

"Well, I hope that you'll be safe, Mama. I love you." I meant that sincerely.

"I love you too, Libby. I'll talk to you later." She hung up and I was left standing, feeling the air thick with anticipation once again.

APRIL

Before the townhall began, I sat with Tina Carter, a fellow Democratic Senator and Nick Patterson, my Republican counterpart. I was able to be cordial with Nick, but I was better friends with Tina. I mentally prepared for the questions that the members in the audience would ask. People were upset. People wanted answers. The Burning of L.A. was something that all anyone could practically think about and people wanted someone to blame. They needed to know who to blame. Should they blame the two policemen who tragically killed Lumos? Should they blame the entire Los Angeles Police Department for its corruptness that bred men like the infamous two? Should they blame the system that was set in place for police brutality to occur? Or should they blame the leaders for allowing the system to continue?

As I made notes to myself, I noticed Braun walking though. I was perplexed. I did not know that she was meant to make an appearance for the townhall. I have to admit; she was graceful and appeared elegant. She greeted members of the staff as she made her way to the area where the rest of the politicians were, and she said hello to everyone, including me. While I never did like her, I always practiced hospitality.

"Lynn, I must say, you do look very nice today." I said. And it was the truth. She had on pearl earrings and a necklace and had on a soft red business suit that accentuated her thin figure.

"Thank you, April. You look nice today too. You look surprised to see me." She responded.

"I am, I cannot hide that. I was told to expect President Ace for this meeting with BNS." I replied.

"He was going to, but he was afraid they'd twist his words. He feels that BNS is fake news since they never give him credit."

"I can understand that, they do tend to twist our words." Nick interjected. "But the people expected to see Ace. He still should've come." Frankly, I was quite surprised to hear that from Nick. He usually was an avid and vocal supporter of Ace, but sometimes he could be rational and level-headed.

"Well, I'll be his voice today." Braun quipped. "I'll be representing this administration when they ask questions concerning it." The audience continued to grow while the staff equipped us with our mics. The auditorium was large and grand. It was one of the most politically charged townhalls in recent memory. It featured everyone on the political spectrum: members of the National Party, Republicans, Independents, and Democrats. The BNS anchors started the program.

"Hello, good evening everyone. I'm Woody Copper." The handsome silver-haired man welcomed.

"And I'm Tim Apples." Said the man with the small afro. "We are starting our special BNS program about the Burning of L.A. Thank you for joining us." They continued to explain the events that led up to the townhall and once they finished, they started handing microphones to the people in the audience.

One Korean woman stood and asked the question "Will L.A. be rebuilt?" A police officer responded by saying that one day, Los Angeles will rise again from the ashes, it just would take time.

Another man, Indian, asked "who will be paying to help build the city again?" No one could fully answer that question to complete satisfaction.

The next person to ask a question directed it towards Braun. The woman queried "Ma'am, who do you hold responsible for the Fire in L.A.?"

"Well, obviously the rioters who instigated a situation that could have been handled through peaceful protest." She said so matter-of-factly. "I don't hold any one group responsible. However, that shouldn't matter. Our focus should be on how to lift Los Angeles back to its former glory." Her statement gathered some applause. Although I didn't like her, her response better than I expected. The person who asked the question had something else to say.

"If it shouldn't matter, then why did Ace say this?" The woman pulled out her phone and pressed play on a video against the microphone. It was unmistakably Ace's voice.

Ace said: "I just quite frankly think it's disgusting how the blacks destroyed their own city, over the death of one man. I mean, the guy wasn't even a good singer... More respect should've been given to those policemen, they were just in fear for their lives. If you gotta shoot a black thug to feel safe, then I'm all for it... They're beasts."

That was all the people needed to hear. At that very moment, the audience began to check their social media and once they found out that what Ace said was true, the crowd cried in an uproar.

"Shit..." I saw Braun visibly mouth. Someone in the White House must have leaked the audio. Well, now the people had found someone to blame: Ace.

DANNY

The warmth of Rafael's body was pressed against mine as we laid relaxing in bed. My chin rested upon his shoulders with my left arm wrapped around his waist, feeling his stomach rise with every breath he partook. His hair made me sputter as a few strands landed on my lips. Rafael would have appeared to have been sleeping peacefully if the dried tears on his face didn't give away the fact that he was not okay. My heart sank at the thought that Raf was in a state of emotional distraught. I wanted to help him, for we shared the same heart, and if his heart was broken, so was mine.

I did not know how to help him. His parents were gone because ICE expedited their deportation. Since he was an only child, he depended on his parents as his guardians, his protectors, but nothing could have protected him from this. It was 6:00 AM that morning, and I was determined to get him out of the apartment since he hadn't left in a week. He had missed his first round of classes, but luckily, the teachers were understanding once I explained everything to them. He had always had outstanding grades, but at that time, he just couldn't manage to care. I carefully removed myself from being wrapped around his body and I went to the kitchen to start some coffee. The bitter yet comforting smell along with the dripping of the black liquid alerted me. As I poured myself a hot mug of straight black coffee, I was determined to help Raf out and get him up and going. If he loved me enough to bring me out of my comfort zone to ask him out, then I loved him enough to push him to continue living life, as difficult as it was.

I poured a cup of coffee, mixed it with cream and sugar (with more cream than actual coffee) as Rafael had more of a sweet tooth than I did. I carried it into the room and placed it on the nightstand next to him. I kneeled down on the coarse carpet and gently touched his cheeks and moved his one strand of hair away from his eyes. Rafael slowly, but surely began to awake from his slumber.

"Good morning, hon…" I whispered tenderly. He blinked and dolefully grinned.

"Morning, babe…" He groaned out. He looked over at the clock. "You wanna tell me why I'm up at 6 in the morning?"

"Drink your coffee and I'll explain why I'm waking you up this early." I said. He rose up, rubbed his eyes, and yawned a small roar. He scratched his head and looked at me as he grabbed his mug to sip upon.

"Mmm, sweet. Just the way I like it." He muttered numbly. I placed my hands on his knees.

"Raf, we have to get you out of the apartment. This is slowly killing you. Please, let's go somewhere, anywhere. I'll be with you."

"Danny…"

"I can't pretend to fully understand how you're feeling; I can't lie about that. What you're going through is truly awful, but sitting here, cooped up in this place, is definitely not making things better."

"Where would you have us go?" He questioned me. I actually didn't plan that far ahead. I pondered, and then I had a bright idea.

"Why don't we go to the March against Ace? Libby, Anna, and Johannes are going, we might as well join them." I responded.

"Again, Danny…"

"You have anger. You have hurt. You have despair hidden deep within your soul. If you take a stance and protest an issue that's bothering you, then you'll be accomplishing something despite what the world has put upon you."

He was silent for a moment. "What are we even marching for this time?" He asked me. That was good. I had him thinking about it.

"Really, ever since he made that comment about 'the blacks destroying the city,' a ton of people from multiple organizations have worked together to create more of an anti-Ace March. Personally, I don't think it'll do much of anything, but you need to express your emotions in some way. Protesting could help."

He set his cup down and got up from his bed. He contemplated the thought. I could see it from the way he crinkled his eyebrow when he's thinking.

"If you think that's what I need, then I'll go." He grinned. "You always have had my best interest at heart, even before we were dating. Besides, it'll probably be fun since the others are going."

My mission was accomplished. I kissed him on the forehead and he walked into the kitchen to start making breakfast as that was more of his specialty than it was mine. While he prepared our meal, I called Johannes.

"Sup, Johannes."

"Danny? Bitch, what the hell are you doing up so early?" He questioned. I could just imagine him starting to wake up as well.

"I was just letting you know that I convinced Raf to go with me to the march with you guys." I explained.

"At least he's finally gonna get out of that apartment." He yawned. "Do you want the three of us to meet with you and Rafael at your place?"

"Actually, yes, that would be nice. We could then get on a shuttle bus to get to the metro and go straight to Union Station where we could start marching. Does that sound like a plan?"

"Yes. But I was gonna ask you, how is he doing?" He inquired.

"Rafael... he's doing much better now that he has something to put his energy towards. I was really worried he would fall into a deeper spiral. He's already had a rough year and I hate it had to be even worse."

"You're a good boyfriend, Danny." He complimented me. "If I could be half the guy you are to my future girlfriend..."

"You'll be great, trust me. I'm gonna go take a shower and I'll see y'all later."

"Bye, bitch." He hung up and I had to chuckle. Even when half-asleep, he was still the life of the party. I walked in the bathroom and turned on the water for the shower, letting the steam fill the room. After undressing, I stepped into the blazing hot shower, intaking the warm vapors. After singing a few songs, I cleansed myself with a bar of lavender soap with its pale purple center and the outer shell was filled with sprigs of real lavender. The sweet floral smell arose once the creamy suds were lathered across my body. I put a towel on my waist, after rinsing myself off, then attempted to find something to wear. Provocative and protest-worthy was the look I was going for. I settled on the rainbow-colored shirt I got in June along with some black basketball shorts, to be comfy.

Walking out into the kitchen, the aroma of mushroom omelets topped with pepper sauce drew me.

"Bon Appetit." Rafael smirked. He knew he was and always will be better at cooking than I could hope to manage.

"Thank you." I managed to say after taking a bite of his scrumptious work of art. "Hey, Raf..." I caught his attention. "I'm really glad to see you doing better."

"I'm not totally there yet. But after this march, maybe I could get some counseling?"

"Whatever you need, I'll support you every step of the way." I meant it. He smiled. He went to change, and he put on his "Immigrants, we get the job done!" shirt. That was certainly a statement piece. For an hour, we waited until Johannes, Libby, and Anna showed up on our front door.

"Open the door, you hoes!" Libby laughed as Johannes rapped on the door.

Rafael opened the door and greeted them in by joking, "I think Johannes is the one that should be called a hoe."

"It's true." Anna agreed. "He's lost count on the number of cheerleaders he's slept with." She continued signing.

"It's not my fault these girls know I'm a bad, dirty boy." Johannes chuckled as he grabbed an apple from the fruit bowl on the breakfast table. They were all appropriately dressed for the situation. Libby had on a pink attire with a black power fist as a comment about the intersectionality of race and sex. Anna sported a shirt filled with the alphabet in American Sign Language. Johannes' shirt was relatively simple as it exclaimed in bold: Ally. He, of course, sported a bandana around his head. We were all ready to go and walk towards the campus shuttle bus, until Libby's phone rang. It was her mother, yet again. She put her on speakerphone.

"Libby, I know you know about the march today. This time I'm telling you, not to go." Mrs. Freeman started before Libby could even say anything.

"Mama, this is an historic event! They'll be talking about this march in the history books!" Libby rebutted.

"You are not going. That is the end of that."

Libby rolled her eyes at her mother's statement. "Why can't I go, Mom? I'm a grown adult, I make my own decisions." Libby's eyes became enflamed with passion.

"Because, have you seen what happens to protestors? Especially *Black* protestors? I do not want to hear from someone else that you died. You think I want that?!" Her voice rose not from anger, but from dread and anxiety. I think she understood Mrs. Freeman and felt conflicted – on one hand, she knew the potential danger existed for anyone attending a demonstration with opposing views in a massive crowd, on the other hand she felt compelled to follow her convictions and march.

Libby was silent.

"I love you, my darling girl." Mrs. Freeman continued. "You know I would not be a politician if I didn't believe in the causes for which the people are marching. I just have seen the atrocities brought from society against our black women. When I look at you, I see my baby. However, if there are protesters, Nationalists, or the police at the march against the movement, they might see you as just another 'angry black woman' and hurt you. I am not willing to live with that and I won't be able to do anything since I'm still in California. I love you, but my answer is you cannot go to this march."

Libby hung up the phone and left us all hanging in suspense.

"I'm gonna do something that goes against my upbringing." She said. "I'm gonna do something that is rare for me to do. I am going to disobey my own mother." She placed her phone in her pocket. "Let's go." She commanded. We followed.

***

We made it in time for the shuttle bus to take us to the nearest station. Mr. Kaleka was the nicest man you would have the honor of being your bus driver. The conversations that he carried were often thought provoking and full of ancient wisdom and knowledge. Once he dropped us off, we went underground, which exposed a whole new side to the city. The underworld was crowded, even more so than usual. People from all walks of life filled the station. Once our metro came, we made sure to hold onto each other, so we didn't get separated and we squeezed in, pressed against people, feeling the beads of sweat develop on our foreheads. The train bumped along the track, causing the people to get slightly jumbled. When we finally made it to Union Station, me and the rest of the gang finally got out of the tightly packed metro and walked up to the grand entrance, with huge overarching golden columns and clean marble floors, signifying opulence.

Once we walked outside of the crowded and congested halls of Union Station, my friends and I became aware of what a historical moment we were witnessing. Standing on the steps of the station, we saw the multitudinous sea incarnadine. My eyes fixated on the variations of bright crimson red hats to signify the lost blood of Lumos, stretched across the city as far as my eyes could see swaying harmoniously together like the waves of the ocean. We saw every race, sex, and creed out in the city to protest the Ace administration and to support equality for all. Walking down towards the crowd, I felt so proud. I was proud that I had become a part of America's legacy: fighting for what is right. Chants and yells filled the city, as we all recognized that we were becoming a part of history. Multiple signs surrounded us, with statements mentioning women's rights, gun control, and respect for immigrants. Later on, we marched with a ferocity like soldiers marching towards their enemy ready for battle, following the people towards our destination. Throughout, we heard iconic chants like "we don't want your tiny hands anywhere near our underpants" and "Hey hey, ho ho, women's rights will never go" along with "Hands Up, Don't Shoot" and "Enough is Enough."

"Do you know where we're going?" Rafael basically had to shout.

Libby responded in kind. "We're going towards the National Mall where several people will be giving speeches."

"Who?" Anna signed.

"I don't know, but my feet hurt." Johannes complained.

The crowd that day was simply massive. I came to learn that 1,000,000 people marched, ferociously fighting the emboldenment of people who believed in absolutely the wrong things. Even some Republicans marched alongside with us, since they couldn't believe what their party had come to. They used to be the party of the great Abraham Lincoln and they wanted to capture that essence back since they felt that Ace and other Nationalists were never true Republicans at all, but imposters. They were imposters in the sense that the Nationalists and others who believed in their cause used the Republican party as a mask. The ones who believed in true conservative values were no longer the face of the party, the Nationalists were. And they too were standing up.

Different groups bonded through shared experiences, especially over the death of Lumos and the president's outrageous comments on the matter. With this march, there was unity. My friends and I finally arrived at our destination, amid a vast horde of people, standing shoulder to shoulder. Celebrities and protesters appeared on stage to sing freedom songs and give speeches about the values of decency and humanity. They preached about how President Ace would no longer divide us as people and that it was clear the American people had had enough. Suddenly, the crowd erupted into an enraged roar.

"Can you see what's going on?" Libby questioned, jumping up and down.

"Is...that who I think it is?" Johannes furrowed his brows, causing his bandana to slightly sink.

"This doesn't make any sense...why would he be here, of all places?" I wondered aloud.

"Who is it?" Anna asked. It was Ace and Braun, walking across the stage of a rally that was against them. It was unfathomable. It didn't make any sense.

"People, you should give me a chance to explain for once! The Fake News Media has what I was saying all wrong!" He addressed to the protesters while the audience booed him loudly. "What I was trying to say is that the police have a right to shoot criminals! It's the criminals that are animals!" People booed him even louder than before as he still couldn't understand why people disliked his comments. "We should be protesting against the thugs that destroyed the beautiful Los Angeles." That was a bad thing to say to an already agitated people.

Braun had to step in. "What he is trying to say is that what he says gets misconstrued. We should be willing to listen to -"

Amid the roars, an ear-piercing shot rang across the National Mall.

"OH MY GOD!! SOMEONE GET HELP!! THE PRESIDENT HAS BEEN SHOT!" Braun wailed at the top of her lungs. Pandemonium and mayhem commenced. People began shoving and pushing to run in the opposite direction from the shooter, wherever the shooter came from. My feelings went from confusion to panic as we began to try to run. Things were happening so fast that my head was unable to wrap around what was happening. Me, Rafael, Libby, Johannes, and Anna tried holding hands together, so we wouldn't get separated. However, the security at the march tried to rush towards the area of the shooting, splitting the crowd up while people were still running.

"Rafael, hold on to me!" I shouted. The pressure of people running towards us caused us to separate into two groups as I lost my grip on Rafael and Anna lost her grip on Johannes.

"Anna!" Johannes yelled out, colliding against others alongside Rafael. "Stay with them!! We'll find our way back to you!" He raised Rafael's arms up to signify that they were still linked together while me, Libby, and Anna were forced to go another direction. Eventually, we lost sight of them as we had to run far from the area we were originally located. The police started to try to bring law and order back into the crowd, but it was futile since everyone felt like they were running for their lives.

"Where do we go now?!" Libby panicked.

"Anywhere but here! Johannes and Rafael will find us when they can!" I hollered. We kept running until we were out breath, away from the larger crowd, closer to the college.

"We gotta stop..." Anna said. "I need to breathe." We sucked in air and fully realized the situation.

"Is...is the president dead?" Libby spoke. It was a thought that I hadn't had time to process amid the chaos.

"I...I don't even understand! How did he get shot, why was he on that stage?!" I pondered frantically, attempting to find reason among madness.

"What about Rafael and Johannes..." Anna started crying, fearing for her brother. "Where could they be, oh God, where are they?!" Libby took ahold of Anna to hold her as if to shield her from the thought that her brother could be in danger. I silently started to shed tears. I suggested this event in order to take Rafael's mind off of his parent's deportation and now? I had no clue where he was. Illogically, I blamed myself. In walking the long way back to the campus, the only thing I could say to ease the situation was "May God help us all."

JOHANNES

When I say the night the president got shot was hell, I sincerely mean that shit. It was absolute hell. Rafael and I got separated from the rest of group while trying to escape from the area where the shooting happened but here's the kicker: we got lost. I mean, you can't blame us, D.C. is freaking huge! But anyways, we wandered around for miles attempting to go in the direction of our campus, looking for familiar landmarks. The sun was about to set, and we stopped in an alleyway to rest for a moment. The alleyway was filled with tires, broken glass, and I think there was a wild black cat, but I couldn't pay much attention. Rafael leaned his head against the red brick wall and I squatted down by the tin garbage cans, then I got back up because I couldn't stomach the offensive smell.

"We gotta... keep going..." Rafael gasped. I could tell he was exhausted trying to find our way home. "We need to get back to campus. Danny, Libby, and Anna should be back there."

"Rafael, we need to rest!" I said, exasperated. "Look around! We're lost! We need to get our bearings straight, which I realize may be hard for you."

"Ha ha, very funny. Nice gay joke, but this is serious!" He exclaimed. "But the police are everywhere and there's bound to be a curfew soon! God, I still can't believe Ace got shot... Is he dead?"

"I don't know, but you're right, there will be a curfew soon, so the police can look and examine the streets." I replied. Mentioning the police gave me an idea. "If we ask the police to take us home, do you think they will?"

Rafael's ears perked up. "I don't know about that. I mean, that literally sounds like the worst idea I've ever heard in my short and miserable life!" He looked absolutely incredulous.

"We don't know our way home! We need to ask for help." I argued back

Rafael stood straight and wiped the beaded sweat from his forehead onto his arm. "Do you really think we can trust them? The same people who you said knocked your sister to the ground? The same people who are 'just doing their job?' Johannes, get a grip! We are the only people out in the city after the president of the fucking United States got shot and you wanna run up to Mr. Dunkin Donuts with our suspicious-looking asses?"

I was shocked at the outburst from Rafael and the assuredness of his statement. I hadn't heard that level of frustration from him before. But I also never heard anything so funny.
"Mr. Dunkin Donuts? That's a new one!" I laughed aloud. It was a brief moment of lightheartedness.

I understood where Rafael was coming from, however I managed to convince him that this was our best option. Reluctantly, we appeared back on the street and searched for the nearest officer. It was twilight and I swear I felt the emotions of people within the city. They wanted change, but not like this. We wanted it done the right way, through law and order, not by chaos. With the Burning of L.A. still in recent memory, I was cautious, always ready to run just in case. A police car came from behind us and the sirens whirred. The car caught up to us. We found an officer within. He had slightly pink skin, with a thick, bushy mustache.

"Sir? Can you please help us?" I asked him as he got out of the car. He smiled and was patient with us. I mainly talked to him to cast any suspicion off our backs.

"How can I help you boys?" He asked in a helpful manner.

"We got separated from our group after all hell broke loose." Rafael warily said. "We're trying to get back to our campus, but we're lost. May you please take us home?"

"Of course, as long as you tell me the address."

We provided it to him and he allowed us to enter his car. He started on his way towards the school, and I started noticing the familiar landmarks, to my relief. On the way, we noticed that the police and military blocked off certain parts of the city, in an attempt to find the suspect who shot Ace. We heard blaring alarms and loud booming voices placing a curfew in the city. The streetlights began to flicker on while the cars on the roads were sparse. We struck up a conversation with the officer.

"Do you know what's been happening since Ace was shot?"

"Ace has been officially pronounced dead." The officer stated.

"Se lo mercia..." Rafael muttered under his breath.

"We have been scouting the area for the suspect since he was able to blend in with the rest of the protestors."

"Are you worried about any pushback? I can't imagine the Ace supporters as anything but upset about his death. They'll blame it on anybody that's not a Nationalists." I noted.

"Actually, we've been preparing for a riot and we've set up for a -"

All of a sudden, we heard a gunshot. We felt the tire lose pressure and the officer lost control of the car as we spiraled on the road, feeling panic and fear overtake us. The car skidded to the right, hitting a pole. My head banged against the car as the glass around us exploded into a million pieces. Pain suddenly overtook me. I blacked out. Minutes later, I was awakened by Rafael who was shaking me harder than a baby shakes a rattle.

"Johannes, wake up!" He scrambled to undo his seatbelt as I groaned aloud. I regained my vision, although hazy at first. I noticed how awful my head felt so I gently touched the area that was impacted, and I drew blood. Luckily, Rafael and I weren't hurt too badly. I just had a concussion and several cuts from the glass. I wanted to help the police officer but I could tell through the bars of the back seat that it was too late for him. He was dead.

"I smell gas..." Rafael warned me. I did too. I could hear it leaking steadily.

"Go! Kick open the door on your side, Raf!"

He used all of his strength and energy to kick the door that was ajar a little from the accident and we rushed out. The car exploded behind us and we fell forward onto the pavement from the heated impact. The inferno blazed with a fiery passion with the smoke seemingly brushing the heavens.

"What the hell happened?" Rafael screamed.

Over the distance, we heard shouting noises coming from the other side of the neighborhood we were in.

"Justice for Ace! Blood and Soil!"

"Oh God no, the Nationalists are rioting..." I whispered. "Do you know where we are, Raf?"

"We're just a couple of minutes away from the campus, if we run, we can make it." Rafael panted. Another gunshot, bang! We ducked and started running towards the school. We heard even more rounds of fire.

"Who's shooting at us?!" I yelled. I really wasn't in the mood to be shot at considering I had just survived a car crash and a gas explosion.

"Justice for Ace! Blood and soil!" said a man who instantly came from behind. He was angry and vengeful, upset that the man he regarded as the savior of conservatism (twisted as it may be) was gone. While that was understandable, that still didn't give him the right to shoot at me! I turned back and saw him aim his gun towards Rafael. Before he had a chance to pull the trigger, I grabbed Rafael and pulled him into the bushes.

With high adrenaline pumping within me, I had to think quickly. "Rafael, can you get over the gate?" I said, holding the metal bar.

"It's too tall for me!" He whispered.

"Not if I push you up quickly. Once you're on the campus, I need you go to Winston Hall and get help. I'll dodge this crazy son of a bitch. We don't have time to debate this shit, let's do it." I opened up the palm of my hands where Rafael pushed himself up over the gate quickly. Before the gunman could start shooting yet again, I popped up from the shrubs to get his attention.

"Hey asshole, suck on this dick!" I yelled, grabbing my crotch once he turned around. What? I had to get him to pay attention.

"You're gonna regret that..." He continued shooting. I dodged him by zigzagging him. I eventually made a sharp turn into the main entrance of the school. In hindsight, I shouldn't have put the others at risk, but what was I supposed to do, I was flying by the seat of my pants, okay! I heard him losing his breath. Since it was finally nightfall, it was easier to try to hide. I tried hiding behind a tree. Guess how long that worked out? He spotted me almost immediately and grazed my shoulder with a bullet. I was not having a good night. I gasped when the blood started dripping down my arm. I still had to keep going.

Ducking from the gunshots, I entered the library, trying to hide in the bookcase beside the door. I saw the gunman come inside searching for me. "What the absolute fuck was going on?!" I contemplated. Luckily, I was the only other person in the library besides this crazed madman in a fruitless effort of revenge.

"Come out, come out wherever you are!" He teased. "I just wanna talk about where you were today."

"Bullshit!" I thought to myself.

"I just wanna know that you snowflakes weren't involved in killing Ace today, man!" Yep, this guy was absolutely insane. I saw him go past the area I was hiding in, as he searched for me. I saw a chance to escape from my hiding place to a better one, so I ran for it.

"Was that you, little man?" He whispered, so he could hear me I was running faster so he couldn't catch me. "I see you, punk."

I looked behind me and saw that he was catching up to me.

"Don't get away from me, little man," he screamed. I was running so fast, that my heart was pounding, and I was out of breath. "Tell me where you were, or I'll kill you!" giving a bloodcurdling scream.

I ran harder than I ever ran in my life. So basically, I ran like a racehorse. I turned left in an attempt to go up to the second floor. I glanced behind me one last time and I saw that the crazed man had fired two warning shots into the ceiling. I saw the plaster falling to the ground and then he fired three more shots at me. I dodged the bullets and ran upstairs as fast as I could. He fired some more shots and a bullet would have hit me, had I not made a sharp right turn to hide out in the elevator. I was fast, but he was keeping up. I then went into the elevator and pressed close rapidly many times. The door started to close, but the man forcefully pushed the elevator door open and got inside and he held the gun up to my head. I have never been so terrified before in my life. He pulled the trigger. He was out of bullets.

With us both stranded in the elevator, he pulled a knife that was hidden underneath his shirt. "I don't wanna hurt you, much less kill you._" In a quick life-and-death decision, I grabbed the knife before he could process what happened.

"Well," I said preparing the knife, "Neither do I." I struck him in the heart. He tried to fight back, but I was too quick in killing him. After he lost all consciousness, I removed the knife from his heart and slit his throat, making sure he was dead. I stood up and dropped the knife and stared at the dead corpse. How could I do this? How could I kill someone, even though he might have killed me? I could be anything, but not a killer. I just stared at the cadaver for the longest time and when I just couldn't take it anymore, I went to the corner of the elevator and cuddled myself and sobbed. I thought about the past hour. I thought about the death of Ace, being separated from my friends, almost dying in a car accident, getting shot at, and how I killed the man. I cried on just about everything. After I calmed myself down, I looked down at myself and noticed how bloody I was. I got up and hard-pressed the down button. Once I got off the elevator, I looked at the dead body one last time before the door closed.

ANNA

I couldn't stop glancing at my phone, hoping to get a call or get a text from Johannes. My footsteps left slight dirt marks as I paced across the gray carpet floor. Waiting in the lobby of Winston Hall filled me with nervousness and anxiety. Libby sat on the single chair with blue fabric that was in front of the window, looking in the distance to find them. It was nightfall by then, and the streetlights within the city steadily began to shine.

"Anna, they'll be back..." Danny tried to resolve my uneasiness. He was as worried as I was, yet he had a calm demeanor. While he was thinking, he expressed a stoic facial expression that I had never seen. His stillness was scary.

"How can you remain calm like this?" I frustratedly grunted. "Johannes and Rafael are out there in the city and we have no idea where they are!"

"I'm remaining calm because what else can I do? You've seen the curfew alert on your phone, so we can't go out looking for them. I've tried calling them and they are not answering so their phones are most likely dead. All we can do is wait." He said.

He was right, and I hated it. I hated not being able to do anything, but pace with a frown upon my face. My head remained hanging with my shoulders slouching as I bit my fingernails to sooth me (a bad habit that I've still carried through childhood.) The only thing that I could even concentrate on was Rafael and my dear brother. They should have been back by now, I remember thinking. All I could think about was the danger the two were in. The president was dead, and the city was bound to have Nationalists start appearing. Tonight was too dangerous of a night for them to be out, because they could be mistaken to be the shooter who killed Ace, whoever that might've been. Then I looked up and gazed at both Libby and Danny and realized that pain is not a monopoly.

Libby looked worried sick, peering through the window with some sign of them. She steadfastly paid attention as if she was a solder assigned to post. I turned to Danny. I should have realized his heart was utterly broken behind his composed mask. Rafael was the love of his life and he felt as if he was supposed to protect him. In his mind, he failed to look after him. I later found out that indeed, he felt guilty and responsible, even though he was not.

I must say, I learned something profound on the human condition of worry. Worry impacted the three of us in three strikingly different ways. Danny was worried but hid himself in an invisible black veil of composure in order to conceal his pain. He did it to show outward strength, to assure everyone that there isn't much to worry about when it was clearly a lie. Libby was more vigilant, keeping an eye out and actually putting her worry into use. However, I was useless in my worriment. My anxious tension did not put anyone at ease and my frantic nerves allowed me to be of disservice.

I heard the chime of the elevator located behind us on the left side. Shifting my focus, I turned around to see a group of students exit the lifting machine. The leader was a man I had not yet met before. He had sweeping, almost majestic blonde hair that reached down to just above his shoulders.

His attire was very preppy, he had on a pink polo shirt with a baby blue sweater wrapped around his collarbones. He noticed that the three of us were apparently waiting for something and he had a sneaking suspicion of what it was.

"Hey, y'all. What's going on?" The boy questioned as he made his way down the three steps to get into our level.

"Hey Josh, uhm…" Danny found himself saying. "I don't know if you met Johannes' sister, Anna." He was obviously trying to avoid the subject

"Nice to meet you, Anna." He shook my hand with a firm, yet gentle grip. His eyes seemed to pierce into my soul and could further sense that something was wrong.

"You never answered my question, Danny. Are Johannes and Rafael lost in the city?"

"Yes." Libby interjected, never taking her eyes off the window.

"Me and the rest of the Young Republicans are gonna go downtown to find some other lost students. I'll search for those two personally." Josh said.

"Republicans? Yet, you don't seem to be bereaved over the president's death." I mentioned.

"No man should be gunned down the way he was. However, and I am speaking for myself, I did not feel that he represented the true values of the Republicans. But then again, I am much more of a fiscal conservative." He responded. "We must start heading into the city. About 15 of our own have not made it back, including Rafael and Johannes."

"You talk as if we're in the middle of a war." Danny whispered somewhat in a quiet state of fear.

"I'd consider killing the president the first casualty. You don't realize I have been hearing words from the Nationalists. To say they are upset is an understatement."

"How are you hearing words from them if you are not one yourself?" I questioned.

"Unfortunately, some of my family are part of the National Party. I was always considered to be more empathic to people. My sensitivity to issues has allowed me to see through the propaganda and conspiracies of the Nationalists, to the chagrin of my family." Josh smiled. "Besides, you don't have to be related to a Nationalist to know how they're feeling. Just check social media. The Nationalists... they want revenge. And they just might get it. We should look for the others now before something happens.

"I'm afraid that's not gonna happen." Libby said without moving an inch. "There's a curfew that's been put in place. No one can leave campus right now."

There was a collective concern. The curfew has been in effect and the 15 others were out to fend for themselves. I hated the silence that followed. No one knew what to do and everyone was powerless.

"Well..." I felt compelled to speak against the silence. "You guys can join us and just pull up chairs." They did just that, dragging chairs from the other side of the room. It was, at that time, quite an odd scene. Both self-proclaimed conservatives and liberals sat together in quiet. There was no bickering or arguing about the other's point of view. We were just scared. Our friends, partners, and family were out in D.C. where chaos was sure to happen. We all just waited for what seemed like 10 minutes.

Quickly, Libby rushed to her feet as she saw a figure running towards Winston Hall.

"Y'all, there's someone coming!" We all got up and rushed towards the window to see who was approaching the building.

"It's Rafael!" Danny shouted, relieved. Danny pushed past everyone and ran out to help him. Watching from the window, we saw Danny embrace Rafael tightly, and Danny helped Rafael inside the building as Raf limped the rest of the way. When they arrived back into the building, we gave them space, yet we were curious. I was too, especially on the whereabout of my brother. I gazed my eyes onto Rafael. He was physically and emotionally shaken. He was bleeding, covered in scratches and other marks of pain.

"Rafael, what happened? Where's Johannes?" I asked frantically, kneeling beside him as Danny sat next to him on the couch. The others surrounded, eager to learn of what had occurred.

"I don't know where he is." Rafael panted. "He told me to run here to distract off the Nationalist that were shooting at us."

"What?!" Libby said in shock. "Explain everything that has happened since the two of you separated from us."

"We have been through utter hell." Rafael shuddered. "When we got lost after everyone dispersed, me and Johannes were trying to find our way back home. An officer was so gracious to offer us a ride home, but some ASSHOLE shot us." With anger burning deep within his heart, he continued. "The Nationalist must have thought that since we were in the police car, we had something to do with the murder of Ace. He shot the tire, causing us to get in a car accident, hitting a pole. The officer was killed on impact."

The murmurs of the small crowd began to rise to a crescendo. Rafael had to take a moment to breathe before he started yet again. "Johannes and I had to get out of the car because we smelled gas. We rushed out before the car exploded. We tried running back to campus but the same guy that shot at the car, followed us and kept shooting at us. Johannes told me to come back here to get help while he'd make the guy go away but I have no idea where he is now. I should have stayed with him. Fuck the Nationalists! I'm so sick and tired of my life being ruined by them!" He was clearly frustrated beyond belief.

"Is he on campus? Johannes?" Josh asked. "If he is, we can look for him. There may be a curfew in D.C., but there ain't one here. Let's go, y'all.

We're gonna find him." Josh gathered the rest of the Young Republicans and hurried out of the building to find him. I looked at Rafael. Danny and Libby can take of him, I thought. I was gonna help find my brother. So, I followed the rest of the group.

"Hey guys, wait for me!" I yelled, catching up to them. I ran up to Josh and walked besides him.

"Anna, what are you doing? It's not safe out here for you, there may be a killer at large here on campus." Josh questioned.

"I'm going to find my brother. Besides, I'm surprised you would care whether a Nationalist would kill a liberal."

"See, that's what the Nationalists have done. They've poisoned our minds to return us into our ancient tribalistic ways. Them versus us. They have divided us. Literally, the Republican party is divided in half because of them." He whispered.

"But it's the Republican party that spawned them. If it wasn't for the deep-rooted phobias against anything that goes against the social norms, the Nationalists would never exist, now would they?" I challenged. "The Republicans conservative values are filled with hypocrisy. You call for family values, but yet split families apart. You praise religious freedom yet want to ban those who practice something different than the norm."

"That's not us."

"But it is. The Nationalists claim themselves to be Republicans. Has the party renounced them outright? I haven't seen that. What has happened has been the results of your party's making, like it or not. If my brother is dead, I will know who to blame." I gritted through my teeth.

"If anything, blame Thomas Jefferson and Alexander Hamilton. They started this two-party system." He chuckled, trying to uplift the mood as we walked across the campus. With the moonlight bathing us in a blue hue, we searched through every blade of damp grass. Suddenly, a figure walked out from the distance. We were on guard, but I recognized the limping man. It was Johannes. It was my brother.

I ran up to him. "Johannes!" I hugged him immediately upon impact, feeling the soft strength of my brother but he wasn't hugging back. In fact, he was more in a daze. I broke the hug and stared down at my shirt. It was covered in blood. In shock, I looked at my brother again. He had a trickle of blood coming down from his forehead, his arms and neck covered in gashes, and an open wound that was gushing blood. Looking further down, he carried a knife. Once I let go of him, he continued walking, ignoring the people. He just walked towards Winston Hall by himself, taking the lonely way home.

***

He stumbled into the building, squeezing the knife as if he still didn't believe that he was safe. Rafael, Libby, and Danny all caught his eye, astonished at Johannes. Johannes sunk his head down in shame. Rafael seemed to have been the only one that remotely understood what happened as he got up and lifted my brother's head. "You did nothing wrong. You saved my life and you saved yourself." He said. "Don't be ashamed." He returned to his seat next to Danny and Johannes continued on to the elevator. I was the only one that followed. Even the R.A. knew not to bother him as he seemed to exist in a state that was neither living nor dead, lost in the darkness trying to reach his way back into the light. He did something that was unspeakable. Walking into his room, he threw the knife on the floor.

"Johannes. Please talk to me." I said assuredly. He replied with silence. He slowly took his bandana off.

"Anna, can you wrap this around my shoulder where I got shot?" His voice quivered. "I'll go to the hospital in the morning, I just don't wanna go back out there." I did what he asked after I cleaned the wound. He was shaking and slightly winced in pain.

"Talk to me, Johannes. I'm your sister, whatever happened out there, I'll understand."

"No, you won't... Instead, what I will do is go to bed. I'm tired and I want to go to sleep. Please..." His eyes were watering, ready to burst at any moment.

"Johannes..."

"I killed a man, Anna!" He cried out, falling to his knees. I took a knee to be right beside him in his suffering. As he was being held, he sobbed with his tears flowing behind my neck.

"I know you, brother. You would only do it in self-defense."

"It doesn't matter! He was a person, a human being with consciousness and I took his life. What kind of a person am I?!"

"One who defended himself and saved everyone else on this campus. Despite what you're thinking, you're not a murderer."

"I am. There has to have been something else I could have done. He's a man, a man that has family and friends. His mother could be waiting for him to come home. Do you realize the scope of this? I didn't just kill him; I ruined the lives of everyone that surrounded him. Oh God, what I have done?"

"He came after you. He was responsible for his own death. Better yet, what has happened to you was entirely out of your control. You didn't know that Ace's death would snowball into your experience tonight." I reasoned.

"Do you know what it's like to watch the life drain out of someone's eyes? To see their pupils, turn to glass as you're the last thing they'll ever see? I hate myself, Anna. What is done cannot be undone."

He melted in my arms, attempting to cry his emotional and physical pain away. I was there as only a sister could for her brother.

RAFAEL

"You've seen the doctor, right?" Libby asked me as she arrived to the table with a plate of sausage, scrambled eggs, and hash browns. I could feel the hot steam coming off of the plate when she sat it underneath my nose, undertaking the savory, yet greasy smell of the university's cafeteria food.

"No, but I went to the nurse's office, considering my injuries weren't as bad as Johannes. I just got bandages as you can see." I explained. She took a seat next to me and sprinkled sugar onto her grapefruit; for the life of me, I could still never understand how one enjoyed the bitter pulp. "And before you ask, Anna took Johannes to the hospital earlier this morning. They should return back later this afternoon. I've gotta email my professor, tell her I can't make it to class this morning." I said, while salt and peppering the potatoes.

"I'm sure she'll understand once you tell her the situation." Libby agreed, biting into the pinkish citrus. "And what about the others? Have they been found?"

"I don't know, you, Anna, and Danny are the only people I've talked to this morning." I said with a full mouth. I looked around the cafeteria, feeling the eyes of the people on me, leaning in and whispering about me.

"You know, he was down there! In the city!" I heard someone whisper.

"It's amazing that he survived at all! The poor thing, he's been through so much lately…" I heard another say.

"I saw his parents get deported. Oh yes, it was heartbreaking."

I abruptly stood up, interrupting my own and everyone else's meal. "If you guys want to talk about me, I'd appreciate it if your gossip about me was spoken out of my sight cause all y'all loud AS HELL." I shouted, shutting up everyone in the room. I sat back down, as they just tried to continue their meals while feeling guilty. I cleared my throat and grabbed my fork to stab at my sausage. "I'm sorry for that, Libby. I'm just tired of people talking about me."

"You want to go? The food is not that great anyways. As you see, the only thing I can stomach here is a grapefruit and that's saying something."

"No, I don't wanna give these people the satisfaction. Besides, their food is not that bad, sis." I chuckled. I looked at the T.V. that was hanging on the wall near our table, which was on the BNS channel. The scene I have to admit, was quite frightening. Woody Copper was on screen, giving the news for the day alongside Tim Apples. The images that flashed across the screen turned my stomach.

"Today, a nation is still reeling after the death of President Ace." Copper started off. "The reaction throughout the United States have been highly emotional, no matter which party one falls in. The Republicans have been lamenting, the Democrats have been in a state of confusion and apathy. It is important to mention that this was an appalling and egregious crime to commit in front of a million people and the killer will be brought to justice once they have been found."

"And it must be said," Apples picked up, "that we must mourn not only for the president and his family, but for the country. We should remember that no man should die based on political beliefs alone. We must mourn that the country has felt the need to come to that, to assassinate a president. Also, we have to warn the citizens of the nation tonight. Since the leader of the Republican, or more specifically the Nationalist, party has died, there have been some posts on social media mentioning 'revenge' on members not of the National Party."

Copper continued. "All over, there are reports of violence in major cities, especially in Washington D.C. There are descriptions of mass rallies planned tonight by the Nationalists. It is our recommendation that citizens everywhere across the country stay indoors tonight. Please stay safe and may God bless America."

"That concludes our segment on 'Hot Takes,' coming up next, we will discuss the funeral plans for President Ace." Apples finished.

"I suppose I should call and tell my mother to not leave California." Libby said, still spooning at the bitter fruit. "I don't want her to be caught up in an experience like the Burning of L.A. There's less Nationalists there. She should be safer."

"I pray nothing else happens anytime soon, my poor heart can't take it after yesterday." I halfway joked, while being halfway serious. I couldn't imagine anything with more calamity than what existed the previous night before. The memory of the events will forever remain clear in my mind, with the sharp image of running away from an attempted killer.

"Speaking of yesterday, they found the body of the man that Johannes... killed." That word was a hard one for her to swallow. "I don't know if there'll be charges, but it's clearly evident from the security footage that was in the library and the elevator that the man was chasing Johannes, meaning to kill him."

"News travels fast around here, huh?"

"I'm just always the first to find out the tea. It's a small campus, remember that."

"Thank God he's still alive. I should have helped." I said out of remorse.

"You did the right thing by listening to him to come to the dorm. If you hadn't, you might be dead. Imagine Danny, his heart would've been utterly broken. Speaking of Danny, where is he? He usually comes to eat with us by this time."

"He's helping to set up this campus wide meeting. He didn't explain what it was about though."

"Oh yeah, I had a text alert about a meeting later this afternoon. Honestly, that's the last thing I wanna do after my math class, but I'll go. It must be important since this seemed to have just appeared out of the blue."

"You want me join you later?" I asked. "I could wait for you outside of the Cleary building, where the meeting is taking place."

"Sounds like a plan. Well, I have to get to class." Libby got up and put her cutlery in her plate. "I'll talk to you soon." She kissed my cheek and left to put her plate in the proper place. When she finally left, I ate my final bites of egg, then I left as well to avoid peering eyes.

***

I placed a blanket underneath the canopy of one of the largest trees on campus. I intended to sit underneath the shade and study. The fall weather was just starting to appear with a gust of cool wind shaking the leaves. I covered myself in my fraternity jacket, which was warm and comforting. I hadn't spoken to my frat brothers in a while since the ICE incident. I had become reclusive, with good reasons. So much stuff had happened in such a short amount of time. I decided that studying would be the best thing to get back into school life. I leaned against the tree and read my history textbook on the chapter regarding the Mexican-American war. While the dull words made me half-drowsy, I felt accomplished. I had pushed through something I normally couldn't care less about. I moved onto my lessons on intersectionality with a paper written by Kimberle Crenshaw. I was actually interested in that paper as it focused less on academic jargon and more on real-life experiences. In fact, I became so enthralled in my reading, I didn't hear anyone walking towards me.

"Doing some light reading?" I looked up to see Johannes with a slight smirk.

"Mind if we join you?" Anna said and signed, standing alongside him.

"Of course, I don't mind!" I smiled, scooting over so they both could have a seat in the shade and be one with nature. "How do you feel, Johannes?"

"Like my old self again." Johannes attempted to put on a brave face when I knew it wasn't true. He looked different. He changed in one night. But I could tell he didn't want to go into that at the moment. "But in all seriousness, I'm okay. My concussion was very minor, and all my wounds have been sewed in and bandaged. It sucks, but it could have been worse, right?" He pensively smiled. Yes, it could have been worse.

"The most curious thing happened in the hospital. The cops just questioned Johannes and left." Anna was clearly puzzled by this.

"Well, I'm sure they know what happened since they're investigating. I'd say not to worry about that right now." I said as a bird whistled, sitting on a branch near us.

"What else is there to worry about?" Johannes wondered aloud. "I murdered a man."

"You didn't murder anyone. You acted in self-defense!" I added.

"A person is still dead because of me, Raf. That's not gonna change. I did kill someone. I say that gives me plenty to worry about!"

"The meeting this afternoon!" I jumped up, almost hitting my head on the branch, scaring the bird away. "That's something to worry about right there! I was so into my studying, I totally forgot about it! Libby's probably walking there right now. You guys should join me."

"What meeting are you talking?" Anna asked, getting up to help her brother up as well.

"Danny helped set this impromptu campus-wide meeting. I have no idea what's happening, but what I do know is that we're almost late! Come on!" I led them to Cleary, where I saw Libby waiting.

"I'm sorry, Libby!" I apologized.

"No worries, I just arrived. Are you okay, Johannes?" Libby said.

"I'm okay, I'm more curious about this meeting..." Johannes responded

"Yeah, what are we doing here?" Anna signed.

"Let's find out, shall we..." I opened the door to guide them in and immediately, there was a noisy commotion throughout the building.

"Looks like we're in for something special..." Libby says while we walked to the gym where hordes of people were in the bleachers and a massive crowd was on the court.

"Quiet down, people!!" Josh's voice carried above the racket as he yelled into his bullhorn. "We're trying to come to a solution here!"

"You know Kyle, I've heard many stupid things from you, but that is the dumbest shit I have ever heard in my short-ass life!" Danny exclaimed, not noticing that we were closing in on him. I had never really seen him that infuriated. "Kyle, do you hear how you sound? Like do you hear yourself? Do you hear yourself? How can you say that we're not in any danger? Tell me, Kyle!" I intervened before Danny really went off on him.

"What's going on?" I probed.

"You wanna know what this idiot said?" Danny started off. "He believes that we're not in any real danger."

"Look, all I'm saying is, if they're gonna march, let them march! The liberals got to march in protest of Ace!" Kyle protested.

"Are we really gonna go down this road?" Danny continued.

"I'm just saying, you saw what happened at the march! The Republicans weren't the bad guys." Kyle clapped back.

Danny pointed at Kyle with emphasis on every syllable. "You're proving my point! You're right! We saw what happened at the march! Ace is dead! I want us to survive. You're saying the Nationalists that are coming here won't be looking for revenge?" The crowd got riled up again, seemingly picking sides to agree with: Danny versus Kyle. "You say you doubt that they will do anything to harm us, but I know something you don't. Check your social feeds, there's pictures and videos of Nationalists packing up to march to D.C. with guns and blunt force weapons. They mean to harm us, Kyle, despite what you believe. Imagine if a liberal wanted to shoot conservatives at like, a baseball game or something, everyone would be upset and rightfully so. Look around, Kyle. We live in the freaking District of Columbia, where there are more liberals in the city and this school has educated half of the damn democratic senators in the country. We are a target."

"Then we should do something about it." Anna interjected. "I was there when Los Angeles burned to the ground around me. I will not stand and do nothing if they're coming."

"They're not gonna do anything! All of this is simply fake news! Nothing will happen, let the Republicans have a march for once! You claim you're about equality, then be about it."

"This is not a matter of equality, this is a matter of survival, you jackass!" Danny screamed. "How is it that you're making it about parties, when this is not about politics. All we are proposing is to figure out a way to protect ourselves, not to choose sides in a petty squabble. I'm tired of this bullshit and I'm tired of you, Kyle!" Anna had to adjust her cochlear because the gymnasium was full of commotion, which was slightly more than she could handle. Seeing the campus in such a state of unrest rattled within Johannes' soul. Amidst the clamor, Johannes grabbed Josh's bullhorn.

"Everyone SHUT THE FUCK UP!" Johannes bellowed with his echo reverbing in the room. "I was out in the city, surely everyone knows by now!" He was sarcastic in that sentence. "I was chased around by a Nationalist and almost killed by one! And you sons of bitches wanna argue about fake news!! How wonderful to see how everyone cares about politics, but nobody cares about people anymore! Why don't we focus on helping each other, instead of tearing each other apart for no damn reason? Kyle, when I sincerely say 'go to hell,' I mean 'go to hell.' I'll greet you there myself." He dropped the bullhorn and exited the gym, leading his sister to follow behind him.

"Johannes! Johannes wait!" Anna shouted with her voice trailing off when she left.

"He is right. This is above party matter; this is about us." Josh said. "It does not matter. This argument is over."

"But... but..." Kyle stammered.

"Respectfully, Kyle, I'm asking you to get the hell out. Your argument is invalid and therefore if you can't help, then you betta step! Byeeee." Danny condescendingly smiled. I couldn't help but slyly chuckle. It was pretty funny seeing Kyle's astonished face while he exited the premise.

"Well, at least that's over." Libby said as the crowd began to murmur. "What do we do? The Nationalists have organized quickly, perhaps too quickly if you asked me."

"I agree. And I have an idea, but I don't know if y'all will like it." Josh's face was serious.

"What is it? If we need to do something, we should do it now." I added.

"Guns." Josh blankly voiced.

A hushed silence fell over us while the crowd tried to listen in on our echoed conversation.

"Guns?" Libby whispered. "We shouldn't have guns on campus! Someone could commit a mass shooting if we gave students here guns."

"Normally, I would agree with you." Josh said. "But what other options do we have?"

"We could try leaving the campus." Danny suggested.

"And go where?" Josh responded. "I have intel that the Nationalists will plan to march from all across the city, there will be nowhere to go. Besides, there's still the curfew. There's no way all of us could find somewhere else to stay before curfew."

"Where would you even find so many guns in such a short amount of time?" I asked. It baffled me that this was even a possibility.

"I have my ways of getting things done, don't question it. Just announce to the people to stand outside their respective dorms by 7:00. After all the weapons are dispersed, we will protect the gates of our school." Josh said. "I will be back." While he was leaving, Danny grabbed the megaphone and publicized to everyone to wait outside of their dorm by 7:00, just as Josh had instructed. People were whispering amongst themselves as they departed from the gym. Danny, Libby, and I gazed into each other's eyes with intense fear and worry.

After the gym cleared, the three of us walked out into the halls to see Johannes sitting crisscrossed, leaning against the brick wall that was next to the trophy stand encased in glass. Anna was changing the batteries of her cochlear when we walked in, almost startling her.

"Sorry." I signed to her as I picked up some sign language by hanging out with her.

"It's okay." She said, flipping her hair back in order to let the magnetic device connect to her head. "What decisions have been made? Everyone seemed confused."

"Is Johannes okay?" Libby asked to evade the question, making it clear that she was uncomfortable with the agreed-upon decision.

"I'm fine." Johannes said loudly so we could hear him. We moved closer to him, so he wouldn't feel left out. "I'm sorry I lashed out earlier. I just couldn't handle hearing Kyle and his rhetoric."

"At least people heard you." Danny replied. "What you said needed to be said and we have come across a decision. Josh is gonna help us protect this campus, the best way he knows how."

"What do you mean?" Johannes turned his head from Danny to Libby.

"How about Danny and I get some takeout from the cafeteria and we can have dinner outside on top of the hill and Libby, you can explain to them." I jumped in, attempting to run away from an already tense situation. I grabbed Danny by the arm and pushed opened the door, hearing Libby stammer to explain what was planned for tonight.

"What was that about?" Danny asked as I guided him to the cafeteria, making shuffling noises across the sidewalk.

"I didn't want to have to hear and see Johannes' and Anna's reaction about Josh's plan."

"Do you think it's the right thing to do?"

"All I know is after last night, I'm gonna be protected. I don't think guns should ever be handled on a school campus but if Nationalists are on their way here, I'd rather hurt them than to have them hurt me." A strong gust of wind blew our way, displacing the strand of hair that was in front of me.

"Rafi, I won't let anyone hurt you. I promise." Danny stopped me. His hand was intertwined with mine. "I will help protect you from all harm or danger. That is my vow to you." He kissed me with a warmth and passion that I hadn't experienced before. It was a covenant of love. It was a promise of safety within his arms. I melted into his arms and I felt he was sincere in his statement. The wind surrounded us as if Mother Earth approved of the intimacy of her two creatures. "Come on. Let's get dinner for us and our friends. Let's enjoy tonight before...before whatever happens." Danny put his arms around me and we went into the cafeteria.

We both paid for five meals to takeout and the cashier gave us five Styrofoam containers. God seemed to shine on us because that day was a rare day where their food was actually good. There was Jamaican Jerk Chicken. There was Lo Mein. There were quesadillas. We packed each container with different food items so we could all share it. It seemed like even the food staff knew that the student body needed sufficient nourishment for the night that was divinely planned. We placed our food and water in paper bags and walked towards the hill, trying to enjoy our time together. The trouble was, the way towards the hill was where I was assaulted.

"Hey, Spic!"

"Ace is finally gonna build a wall so people like you can't get in no more."

"Be quiet, you fucking piece of shit, you're gonna get what's coming to you."

I kept smiling at Danny so he wouldn't think that anything was wrong. I kept smiling to hide the pain that was hidden within the setting.

"Y'all are finally back with the food!" Libby awkwardly chuckled as she grabbed the bags. Johannes and Anna were sitting beside the pavement on the grass overlooking the city. The District of Columbia, the political capital of the world, was brimming with energy and life. The structures of the city told the history of this significant town, with the Washington monument standing tall with the pride of being a symbol of liberty and democracy to the glorious dome of the capital building to the left from our view, embodying equality. Washington D.C., in my opinion, was a crown jewel in regard to cities across the world. The beating heart of the city was the Capital. The metros and roads became its vein. The blood within the veins are the citizens, people from all walks of life from all over the world. The memories within the artificial organism were the museums, recalling joyous moments and horrific terrors in the subconscious mind of

America; and the mind of America was the White House, but uncertainty lied there, like a brain in a coma. The lights in some areas were starting to be turned on, seeing as how dusk was steadfastly approaching with storm clouds gathering. The wind was picking up, but since we felt no rain, I gently sat upon a grassy patch next to Johannes, who just grabbed a water bottle and was probably silently reflecting upon what Libby had to tell them.

"We shouldn't do this, you know." Johannes softly said to me while the others began sharing the food amongst themselves. "The guns will only bring more problems and you know it."

"No, it will not."

"Yes, it will!" He hissed. "Look at me! Now, I'm a mess after stabbing a man, how do you think others will react to the possibility of killing someone. They'll be weak, just like I am now."

"You are not weak." I assured. "You are the one that came up with the plan for me to escape. You managed to dodge him while he was firing bullets at you. You took a gun shot and kept pushing yourself. And when you were cornered, with nowhere to go, you did what you had to do. You're not weak. You're strong because only a strong man would be able to do what you did. You saved my life. And you saved your own, without hesitation or malice. That is the mark of a strong man, my friend.'

Johannes took a breath and gulped down some of his water. "Thank you, but I still don't agree with the decision that you guys came up with and I'm positive many others won't either."

"I know. But I will be at the front of the gate guarding our campus so no one else will feel the fear that we went through yesterday." I said, grabbing a piece of chicken from our 'pot-luck.' "Knowing the kind of man and friend that you are, I know that you'll be right by my side."

He sat in silence and just stared at the city. He made a curious face as if something piqued his interest.

"Hey guys!" He gathered everyone else's attention while Danny, Libby, and Anna were in middle of slurping noodles. "Do you guys see that?"

"See what?" Anna signed while chewing her food.

"There! In the distance!" Johannes pointed.

"Are those protestors with torches?" Libby questioned. I peered towards the marchers. They were coming by the hundreds, perhaps thousands, flowing through the streets like a river of fire. The stormy backdrop made the scene more dramatic. Faint, but clear, the orange blaze was illuminated not just by the gasoline on the torches, but from their burning and passionate anger over the death of President Ace. They weren't marching from just one direction. They seemed to surround the city, fueled with the fury of Pele. The Nationalists were coming.

"We should try to find Josh," Danny began to say before we felt the ground shake a little.

"Oh, my God!" Libby exclaimed. She saw the Washington monument fall to the ground, collapsing onto the people below. The monument was bombed. Clouds of smoke and ash blended in with the dark clouds. I gasped because I was not expecting such an American symbol to fall right before our eyes. Next, the Lincoln Memorial suddenly burst into flames, with parts of the structure forcefully exploded, killing the people that were nearby. Someone was attacking our nation and it was from within.

"We need to find Josh now!" Danny shouted but as he did more memorials began to be destroyed. Explosions were seen all around the city, with our national museums demolished and our history destroyed, including the Rotunda of the National Archive building. The Declaration of Independence, the Bill of Rights, and the Constitution of the United States of America were all up in smoke, intermingling with the clouds of ash in the air. The sky became dim gray. Anna began to sob as she had seen this familiar image before. The heart of the city, the capital of the world blew up with a loud and deafening boom, killing the unsuspecting people within and surrounding the building. What I saw must have been what Dante saw as he entered into the inferno. The loss of hope and the feeling of absolute despair overwhelmed me as the world crashed before my very eyes. Then the unthinkable happened. The White House was on fire. The pillar of the free world, the brain of western civilization was destroyed. The greatness that was the District of Columbia was no more. The veins were stopped. The blood was stilled. The memories were forgotten. The heart stopped beating. And the coma became death. Meanwhile, the Nationalists still approached.

The sirens sounded.

"Rafael, we need to go now!" Danny shouted. I stood in disbelief, watching all of the bombings happen within seconds and minutes. "Rafael!" Danny shook me and grabbed me to start running towards Winston Hall, trailing behind Libby, Anna, and Johannes. A multitude of people came out of their respective buildings, confused as to what was happening. A white truck quickly pulled up in front of Winston and Josh got out of the car.

"Looks like things are gonna have to happen sooner than I thought. The guns are in the back, I've got other people distributing them to people in the other dorms." Josh panted. He seemed to have narrowly escaped the chaos that was happening in the city below.

"What about the R.A.s, won't they question us?" Anna spoke up. "We're breaking the law."

"Just like your brother broke the law last night, right?" Josh argued. "We don't have time to debate. Help me give the weapons to the people here, then we will walk to the edge of campus. I don't intend to die tonight by the supposed members of my own party." Josh grabbed a handgun and gave it to Anna. "All you do is pull the trigger. Just make sure to shoot the right target."

Anna gulped and placed it in her purse. I helped passed out weapons to the students over at Winston. While they were scared and confused, they knew that defending our school was of the upmost priority. They knew their duty, even if they didn't agree with the method, seeing how it was a liberal college. Josh handed me my gun. It felt heavy, both physically and metaphorically, knowing that this weapon could kill someone. We were finally doing what the conservatives wanted and part of me hated it, but another part of me was certain that the Nationalists would get a taste of their own medicine. I didn't know how they pulled it off, but they murdered probably half a million and that's just an underestimation. I was pissed that they could even have the audacity to commit such an atrocious crime.

Josh gave Johannes a gun. He hesitated, but he grabbed it and held it before putting it behind his belt. He looked at me and nodded in understanding. Danny grabbed my hands and said, "I'll be by you the whole time."

Libby seemed to have heard what he said. "As will I. I'll join you wherever you guys are."

"And so will we." Johannes responded, speaking for both him and his sister.

The chanting from the Nationalists grew louder with mentions of blood and soil, draining the swamp, and with death to the opposition. I remember their chants sending chills to my bones as they voiced racists and perverse thoughts.

"We should head to our borders!" Josh shouted. "May God be with us tonight as we fight for what is right! No more Democrats versus Republicans. We all have a new enemy, a common one. It is the Nationalists. Let's remember who to point our weapons towards. Understand?"

There was a cacophony of agreements.

"Then let's go. If we die, we'll die an honorable death." Josh and his other accomplices lead us to all the edges of our campus. We were stationed with Josh, the five of us. We were at the front gates, which for some reason was never actually closed. I wished it was that night. The noise from the marchers became louder and the heat from their tiki torches could be felt. I noticed there were less protestors. Instead of thousands, most had dispersed across the rest of the city, gracing us the presence of several hundreds. They made it to the front. They had weapons themselves, just as Josh predicted. There was silence. We were scared.

Josh was the first to approach. "Declare yourselves!" He forcefully commanded. "What business do you have here?"

Someone from the crowd stepped out, appearing in a red hat with camouflage clothing. "We have come to claim justice for Ace!" He hollered. He cocked his rifle.

"'Vengeance is mine, saith the Lord'" Josh quoted. "I'm sure you proclaim to be a Christian, just like I am. If you believe in His words like a true God-fearing Republican, then you know this is wrong."

"President Ace's death was wrong!" The man grunted. "D.C. and this school are a cesspool, full of those who want nothing more than to destroy us. It deserves to burn."

"So, this is how another civil war begins..." Josh said. "A battle with brothers against brothers, citizens against citizens, just because one side doesn't agree with the other."

"It's deeper than that now."

A single gunshot rung out, placing both sides on guard. To this day, no one knows who fired the first shot, but mass mania resumed. Josh ducked and rolled to the nearest tree before the man in the red hat blasted his weapon towards him. Screams and yelps were the sounds that will forever be ingrained within my mind. Thunder rumbled as I dodged bullets. I jumped onto the ground and shot towards no one in particular and I heard a groan. Someone threw a torch, setting a patch of area on fire. Others followed suit, blazing the tree that Josh was positioned behind.

"Get away from the gate! Get positioned in the Yard. We'll fight them from there!" Josh barked the order as he was running backwards while shooting. Anna kneeled behind a bush and continued shooting until Johannes came by. Anna rose up and they both shot people together, circling while having each other's back, making their way towards the center of campus. Johannes yelled in anger, possibly at the Nationalists for shooting at his sister, or for the Nationalists forcing him to kill yet again. I ran towards Danny once the Nationalists came in past the gate. He was forced to elbow someone in the face when she came behind him, then shot someone clear in the guts.

"Come on Danny!" I shouted before having to duck from a torch aimed towards me. He followed me and we came across Libby, who was beating a man with a heavy flagpole, with the flag having a symbol of the Nationalist: a black canvas with a large red circle in the middle and in the center, a white saltire. Libby's gun was in the back of her belt and once she finished beating the man, she ripped the flag off, tossed it in one of the fires, and kept the pole as a weapon. She came behind me and Danny and we ran towards the center of campus. The thunder rolled, and raindrops began to pour onto our heads. We were facing a storm. The wind howled in our ears as if the sound of war wasn't loud enough. At least the fires were put out by the outpour of water.

As I ran, the rain impaired my vision and my shoes got muddied but I pushed onwards, until we made it to the center of campus. We had killed the majority of them, but they also killed so many of our own students. The images of their corpses stuck in mud was all I could think about at the moment. The people I went to class with were dead. The people I partied with were dead. My fraternity brothers, dead. The city I loved, dead. I felt dead inside, but I still had so much to fight for as Danny, Libby, Anna, Johannes, Josh, and so many others were right by my side.

There were still some Nationalists that were foolish enough to want to continue the battle. We were proactive. Instead of waiting for them to come and slaughter the rest of us, Johannes turned to Josh.

"Josh, hand me your rifle, I've got an idea. Don't worry, I can handle it. I'm tired of these bastards fucking up my life!" Johannes firmly told him. Josh took a look at him and realized that Johannes was up to the job. He nodded and gave Johannes his rifle while Johannes gave Josh his handgun. I saw Johannes quickly climb up the tree where I was studying earlier that day and steadied himself on a sturdy branch. He started silently picking off Nationalists. Unknowingly, at the time, there were other students from the rooftops of our dorms, including Winston, that were shooting at the Nationalists militia. The few that were left were shot by us, the rest of the front line. I learned that others ran away from the scene, not prepared at the fact that us students would be strapped. The fighting seemed to have ended almost as quickly as it started. The first battle of this civil war was won by a group of kids that have now turned into adults who have witnessed the blood of battle. We won the Battle of D.C.

We were cold, wet, and sore. Many of us had wounds. Johannes climbed down from the tree and dropped the rifle to join us as we all walked back to our respective dorms. Even those that had bad injuries knew it was better to get help another day. Libby limped back to Winston, using the flagpole as a staff. Anna and Johannes walked as Johannes eyes swelled with tears, but he didn't make a sound. Josh looked back at the massacre and took a knee to pray for all of the souls that were lost in battle. Danny intertwined his fingers in mine as we made our way towards Winston, trying not to think about all of the lives we took to save ours. Lightning flashed, and the earth shook as God expressed His anger at this wicked world. It almost seemed that He would break the promise that was granted to us through the rainbow. But He didn't. We were still there to live another day.

We made it back to the dorm and crashed in the main area. No one spoke a word. Some were crying. Others were withdrawn. We were in silence until a beep went across my phone. Then another notification popped up on Anna's phone. Beeps were starting to appear on our phone as if our phones were meant to be instruments orchestrating a melody. I took out my phone as did a multitude of others as we began watching a live update. It was Vice President Braun.

"I've come to speak to you, the people, on this horrendous day." She said on screen. "Our nation has come under attack by violent criminals. It was not terrorists from other countries that have attacked us, but our own brothers and sisters. Our ideals as Americans were first attacked when President Ace was murdered in cold blood. Now, our capital lies in ruin. Most of our politicians are dead. The constituents are dead because of a band of vicious people who label themselves as liberal and progressives. The president is dead because of them and D.C. burned because of them! Our constitution, all our laws have been destroyed. It is clear that the great American experiment has failed. I have taken it upon myself to lead with force so that these rebels may be wiped out. They won't win. They may have killed America, but they will never hurt us again. They will be exterminated under the might of our new country." She gave a chilling grin which struck fear into my mind, body, and soul. "All hail Freedonia."

PART TWO

LIBBY

I t had been 13 months since Braun took over the government. Times were hard, and things were changing. Shopping for groceries was a clear example of just how difficult things had become. The florescent lighting was harsh in the small store and it was especially bright since it was night and two hours before curfew. The store was no bigger than a mom 'n' pop shop of old. The shelves were not as a stocked because there were not as many options like before the new government was established. Now, there were only a few brands that were left to choose from. I had just finished grabbing all of the essential items that I needed: eggs, bread, milk, and cheese. I also got some potatoes, tomatoes, carrots, along with beef. I personally debated on buying beef since I knew it would be more expensive. However, we needed protein and it was okay to indulge every once in a while. After perusing the aisles for other products, I decided what I had was enough. I went up to the counter and pushed the cart near the woman that was working her late shift. It seemed that I was her last customer of the day.

"Hey, how are you today." I smiled attempting to make small talk as she scanned each item.

"I'm okay, I'm just ready for the day to be over." She smiled back.

"I hear you. At least it's Friday!"

"You got that right!"

We both stayed in silence as she continued to swipe the food and put them into a paper bag.

"Okay, that will be $100."

My mouth gaped open. I couldn't believe how expensive simple groceries had become. I looked at the receipt. The bread was $20, when bread used to be $3.

"You have to be kidding, $100 for just this?!" I gasped in shock.

"The inflation has gotten bad, ma'am. You know no one can really afford even the simple things anymore." She tried to explain.

"But $20 for bread? Keep it, I'll make my own." I said as she took the bread away from the bag.

"Cash or social credit?" She asked. Social credit was a new thing that came about as the Freedonian government became more established. It was based off our social standing and relevance to society. If you were a rich person and was the head of a tech company, your social credit would be high, but if you were struggling, it would be low. It was also a way of punishment. If you misbehaved in any way that was deemed unacceptable, the police could lower your social credit. Additionally, it could be used as a form of payment where it would only drop your score moderately. I looked down at the barcode tattoo on my wrist that allowed us to access our social credit which we were required to get during the transition. I was wondering if I should use some of my social credit.

"I'll use cash, I've used enough of my credit." I pulled my money out, paid and grabbed my bag.

"Hail Çaé Braun." She quickly said uncomfortably.

"Hail Çaé Braun." I whispered in return before heading out of the store. Luckily, I didn't have too far to walk from there to the apartment. But it was tragic remembering how lively D.C. used to be rather than how it was at that moment. It was war-torn. Our majestic society crumpled. Because so many institutions and neighborhoods got bombed and destroyed by the Freedonian government and Nationalists, homelessness was rampant. By our block, there was a tent city, occupied by families that surrounded barrels of fire just to be warm. I was blessed that I wasn't a part of that unfortunate crowd as no one deserved to be homeless. I was blessed that my friends weren't a part of that crowd. Danny wouldn't have been able to afford the apartment he used to own, but because Johannes' parents were wealthier, Johannes has it in his name while still allowing Danny, Anna, Rafael, and me to live there. Danny was grateful that he got to keep his home, even if it technically wasn't his anymore. At least the art of Harlem still stayed on the walls. While walking, I saw the moon shining its blue beam onto the new national flag of Freedonia, the same exact flag as the Nationalist's flag. Every time I set eyes on it, it stung me that although we won the battle and defended ourselves, they ultimately won. Every morning, they blared the National Anthem through the loudspeakers and they did the same thing every evening just before curfew. It was entrenched in the minds of the population.

Freedonia,
Freedonia,
God bless our shores,
Forevermore.
Freedonia,
Freedonia,
Our Çaé's our lord,
Forevermore.

The tune was quite haunting and so damn insidious, you'd find yourself humming it unconsciously. It worked well to make sure that people never forget where they are living and who was ruling over them: Braun, our Çaé our leader. She drilled it into our heads that we were no longer America, we were Freedonia. The anthem started playing right on cue as I entered the apartment building. After walking up the stairs, I pulled out the key from my pocket. I pushed the door open and set the bags on the counter, before greeting my friends.

"Hey guys! Finally made it back from shopping." I said while pulling out the food from the bags.

"Finally, we were starting to get worried about you." Danny smiled as he approached to start putting some of the food in our bareboned refrigerator. "You know you shouldn't stay out too late."

"I know, but I made it before curfew. I'm not trying to get caught by the police." I replied with a potato in my hand.

"We were also getting bored without you!" Johannes yelled out from the couch, while holding a book. "There's nothing fun to do anymore. Most sites on the internet are expensive, porn is illegal, and I can't buy weed. I can't do anything!"

"Ignore Johannes." Rafael laughed when he walked in from the restroom, finally sitting on the armchair next to the couch. "He's just grumpy because there's nothing on T.V."

"Damn right!" Johannes jumped out from his position on the couch and put his book down on the coffee table to face me from his seat. "The only thing that's actually somewhat entertaining is the news, and even that's fake. Listen to this bullshit!"

Johannes grabbed the remote to turn the volume of the television up. The newscaster was a white, blonde woman with straight hair. She was the standard of beauty in Freedonia, which used to be the standard for beauty in America, so that part didn't change much. She had on a bright red business suit and was standing in front of a digitalized Freedonian flag waving while the anthem played quietly in the background.

"Hail Çaé Braun, our glorious leader!" She exclaimed cheerfully I couldn't tell if it was a forced expression or legitimate happiness. "Today was a great day for our country and for the Çaé. Today, our government police were able to capture several of the disruptive rebels that were plotting to overthrow our government. Also, the Çaé visited Philadelphia to see how the new Capital House was coming along. It will be finished soon and will be furnished with the finest furniture and newest technology so our Çaé can continue to lead our glorious country in peace and style. She will be able to keep enforcing moral policies that strengthens the foundations of our nation. Furthermore, we have news about our economy. The new Freedonian economy is doing much better than the traditional methods. The introduction of social credit to the economy has benefited people from coast to coast. It has allowed for a booming system and will lead to a new golden age of economic prosperity. We will now take it over to Chris for the weather when we come back from our commercial break. Hail Çaé Braun and All Hail Freedonia!"

It was disconcerting having to watch the broadcast. I grimaced at the thought that a new generation of kids will never have heard of America and will view what I had watched as a valid news source.

"You see this crap!" Johannes said. "The only reason why it's entertaining is because it's so damn laughable. Who would actually believe our economy is great when it's hard to even buy guacamole!"

I laughed. "Next time, you're doing the shopping. You have more social credit to use than I do. Then, you can buy guacamole. Hopefully, it's not as expensive as bread."

"What are you even making?" Johannes asked as he stood, allowing the other boys curiosity to be stroked as well.

"I'm making Layrow stew. It's an old recipe from my great-grandmother down from Alabama. She made it as a way to use all of what she had. It's absolutely delicious and it'll last for several days. I could use some help preparing the dish. That is, if you're not too busy with your book." I joked to Johannes.

"No, it's just a stupid story about how a murderer pities himself and hates the situation he's placed into. You know, same old, same old." His jokes had gotten a lot darker than they used to be, but at least he was joking again.

"I'll help, just let me know what I'm supposed to do." Rafael offered.

"Same here." Danny replied. "It's supposed to be my turn doing the cooking."

"I'll still help. Just clean the vegetables and chop them up, I'll take care of the rest." I was truly grateful for their help. I couldn't imagine living through that time without them.

"If it's your great-grandma's recipe, I'm sure it's absolutely delicious. Grandmothers have a way of making a dollar out of 15 cents." Danny commented.

"Try making a hundred out of dollar." I grunted. "This inflation is just ridiculous! A year ago, a meal like this wouldn't have costed more than $30, maybe even less. But we have to do anything to survive." I noticed someone was missing from the conversation. Danny was there. Rafael was there. Johannes was there.

"Where's Anna?" I questioned.

"She's in the bedroom." Rafael answered. "She's working on some kind of board. Actually, you should check on her, she's been in there for hours."

I placed all of the necessary vegetables on the cutting board for the boys to wash and cut. Curious as to what Rafael was talking about, I left the kitchen and entered the bedroom to see Anna intensely focused on the board she had placed on the wall that was covered with pictures and documents.

"Anna?"

She got startled once I closed the door.

"Next time, please knock! I didn't hear you come in." She said, still staring at the board.

"Did you make this?" I asked, wondering how all of the pieces were connected as she had red string tied to certain pins.

"Yes, I made it, but you didn't ask why or how. Most people forget to ask those questions."

"What is this about?"

"Don't you ever wonder how Freedonia came into existence? I know this is gonna sound crack't, but I can't help but think that Braun has had all this planned. Look." She said, pointing at a picture from the anti-Ace march. "It never made sense for Ace to be at a rally that was against him. Why would he be there unless Braun knew he would get shot? And think about how quick the Nationalists were there to march, how quickly D.C. was destroyed. This was all some elaborate plot for Braun to create an authoritarian regime! It's no secret that she felt that Ace was a weak president and that she could do better. See this article where someone reported her saying that in private. Of course, she denied it, but Libby, this has to be more than a coincidence. She had to have this planned for a long time. Don't you care about how a solid institution like the United States fell and collapsed into a dictatorship like Freedonia?"

"I do care, but what can I do? All I can focus on is trying to survive, day by day. Maybe the rebels will be successful and this whole thing could end tomorrow, but I'm just trying to make it through the next meal. Speaking of which, I could use your help with dinner. We're having stew tonight."

She took one last look at the board. "Okay, I'll join you. I think I'm driving myself crazy." She signed. She went ahead of me and I almost walked out of the room until a phone rang. Anna looked at me. It was my burner phone. The only person that called on there was my mom.

"I'll leave you in the bedroom. Say hi to Mama Freeman for me." She smiled before closing the door. I answered the phone.

"Mama?"

"Libby! Oh, thank God, you have no idea how much I've been wanting to talk to you."

"It's why I kept this burner phone. It's slowly draining some of my social credit, but it's worth it to talk to you." I whispered. I truly missed her. "Are you okay? Braun has been jailing former politicians that used to oppose her."

"I'm fine. Following your advice to stay in California was the best thing I ever did. Truth be told, her influence isn't as strong here, but it's still powerful to say the least."

"Is that why it took so long for you to call me?"

"I've been trying to find the right time and moment, but it's hard in this society." I heard noise in the background.

"What was that, mama?" I asked her.

She ignored my question. "Just stay safe. I'm still trying to find a way to get you and your friends out here with me. Everything is....:." She didn't finish her sentence, leaving me forever curious   "I'll call you next time I can. I love you Libby."

"I love you, mama." The phone hung up. It was a quick conversation, which worried me because she could usually ramble on and on in a way that only politicians could do. That let me know that she was in a dire situation, but there wasn't much I could do. All I could do was pray that God would continue to look out for her safety. For once, instead of her worrying about me, I worried about her. I put the phone away on the dresser. I headed back out into the kitchen where everyone was chatting and carrying on. I worked on preparing the beef, while everyone else cleaned, chopped, and seasoned the carrots, onions, tomatoes, and potatoes. As the pot became filled with food, I started on the tomato broth. The smell was divine, and everyone was feeling at home. Throughout this difficult transition, we all had become a family of sorts, leaning on each other through hard times.

Oddly enough, even with the anxiety of the outside world, I felt content. We had prepared a simple meal that represented us as friends. A pot filled with different kinds of tastes and textures yet mixed to bond well together.

We finally finished making our stew and got our bowls ready. I was just about to pour stew into a bowl with a ladle until we heard three knocks on the door. We quickly hushed. Hardly anyone went walking around after curfew. Anna cautiously walked towards the door. She peeped through the door. She gasped. It was someone that was unexpected.

"Who is it?" I asked, setting the ladle back into the pot.

She opened the door. It was someone we hadn't seen in months It was a man dressed in all black. It was a man with a buzzcut. It was Josh.

JOSH

The door opened, and it was clear that no one was expecting me. Anna's face was one of pure shock. "Hi." I said, clearing my throat. "May I please come in?"

"Josh..." Anna was aghast. "You're alive!" She threw herself at me and greeted me with me with a hug. I slowly reciprocated the warm welcome by wrapping my arms around her. It had been a long time since I embraced someone like that. Anna backed away and continued to grin.

"Oh my, you're back!" Danny dropped his spoon on the counter and came to give me a pound shake. Johannes gave a head nod, Rafael waved in surprise, and Libby offered the best gift: a meal. She poured me the first bowl of stew, something which she called Layrow. The smell was intoxicating and comforting, giving me a feeling of home, even though I never had that particular dish before. Setting it upon the dinner table in front of the windows, everyone else had gathered their meal and sat with me. I could tell they were curious as to why I just suddenly appeared on their doorstep, as I know I would be. Amongst the commotion, I prayed silently to myself. Once I opened my eyes, all of their eyes were on me. I took a sip of the simmering broth and smacked my tongue as the flavors burst in my mouth.

"Mmm... this is the best meal I've had in months." I groaned as I savored the stew.

"Speaking of which, where the hell have you been for months?" Johannes asked. "When you left after our school shut down, we had no idea where you were. Some of us thought you had died."

I laughed. "You thought I was dead!"

"Is that really so hard to believe? These are not exactly idyllic times. Prices are rising every day to the point that there's no middle class anymore, people are dying on the streets with no shelter, we're all expected to act certain ways..." Anna started.

"So not much has changed! The only difference now is that everyone knows the government sucks!" Johannes joked. He really did change from the last time I saw him. He was much bleaker.

"You shouldn't say that out loud!" Anna elbowed his stomach.

"Cause what, big brother is listening? Like they weren't doing that before." Johannes sardonically replied.

"She's right, Johannes." Danny said after biting into a carrot. "We can't be too careful these days. The other day, Rafael and I were out walking. We wanted to see the ruins and remember old times. I imagined how people in the Dark Ages would look at the ruins of Rome, knowing that your home was once majestic and glorious, but now had fallen to barbarians. I imagined the Athenians looking upon their ruins, knowing that their experiment in democracy ultimately failed. I imagined how the Aztecs must've felt when they saw their entire civilization was destroyed by conquistadors and there was absolutely nothing they could do. Looking at the few pillars standing from the old Abraham Lincoln memorial and Lincoln's head on the ground with parts of his face crumpled into dust steered up emotions for me. Naturally, Rafael held my hands. Unfortunately, a policeman that was walking by told us that engaging in homosexual behavior in public was grounds to arrest us. Luckily, all he did was lower our social credits. Now we can't exceed past 2,000 credits since we're now known gay men and were considered as likely to defect from the laws of Freedonia. That's 2,000 out of 5,000 credits. That was just a spank on the wrist, Johannes. If you get in trouble, there's nothing we can do."

Johannes grunted in agreement. "Fine, but Josh, you never answered my question. Where the hell were you all this time?"

"I suppose it is better that I tell you before I ask for a favor." I said, chewing on the beef that was well-seasoned. "My recent behavior will let you decide on whether or not you guys would grant me that favor."

"What have you been up to?" Rafael questioned.

"I've been a part of the rebellion, the 8Crow..." I whispered.

"Well, that explains your new style." Libby said under her breath.

"After our school had to close down, I just needed to do something. The fact that our republic just swiftly fell because we couldn't come together. It was almost like we allowed this to happen to us and I was just so angry. We had freedom and we allowed it to be snatched from under our feet. I left to go to do something. I sought out 8Crow because I had heard rumors that they were trying to sabotage the government. They recruited me and I graciously accepted. What I didn't realize was that they weren't just doing sly sabotage jobs. This has actually turned into a civil war. I've been involved in so many battles now between us and the military of Freedonia. It's amazing I've survived. It's amazing that I haven't been captured either."

"Can you give us any clue as to what's going on? The news says that the government had wiped out most of the rebels." Libby leaned in, interested.

"You can't believe anything they say, they're required to say and do anything the Çaé tells them. The truth is, we're getting stronger every day. We're mostly set in the west, where Freedonia has less power."

"Wait, the Çaé can't control the west?" Anna questioned.

"She proclaims that she controls all of the land, from coast to coast, but she really only controls the east side of the country. The Freedonian government can't afford to really send any military assistance to the west, especially with them attempting to build a new capital over in Philadelphia. Throughout this civil war, 8Crow has managed to gather some territories in the west."

"But what about the Nationalists who support her?" Libby further wondered.

"Ha!" I chuckled. "They're making things worse with their vehement worship of the Çaé. I'll explain later. But 8Crow, we're gonna make a big move here in D.C. We're gonna attempt to take back control of this city."

"Won't that be extremely dangerous?" Anna inquired.

"Yes. I almost ruined the plan because I tried to do a supply run which ended up actually with me running away from a policeman. Speaking of which, could you imagine my father hearing that I ran away from a cop? Anyways, I managed to dodge him, and I headed to the only other place I knew in the area, here. I want to ask if I can spend the night. I would completely understand if you guys denied me because harboring a rebel is against the law."

There was momentary silence as I could see the cogs in their heads almost working together in sync, as if they were all thinking the same thing. Finally, Danny spoke up. "Josh, it's not even a question. You've saved our lives before. We'll save yours. You can stay as long as you need to."

My heart swelled. I arose from the dinner table at the same time as them and I hugged everyone. I was truly grateful because I was in a desperate situation and they came through for me, even though the consequences could have been death. While being a part of the rebellion gave me a new family, I was reminded of my original family, the ones that fought with me in the Battle of D.C., the ones that were there when it all started. It was quickly approaching bedtime for them and while at this time I would have been keeping watch at our camp, I helped with the dishes to express my gratitude while they pulled out a camping bed (since that was the best they had to offer). Once I finished cleaning up, I laid on the bed and it was the best rest I had in months. I could finally let my guard down once again.

APRIL

In those days under Braun, I woke up early to fix myself a cup of tea to start my morning. I got dressed quickly, reusing the same clothes that I packed when I came to California about a year ago. I wore my favorite green business suit. At that time, I lived in a humble trailer that was close to the large, formerly abandoned warehouse that was the headquarters of 8Crow. We were in the desert, far from ordinary citizens so they wouldn't know where we were stationed. I prepared my papers and put them within my briefcase along with my laptop. Even though it felt like the end of the world, I still wanted to maintain my professionalism. I walked out of the trailer and to the warehouse in the early dawn. I heard the 8Crow militias training and going over plans in the background once I walked in the incredibly spacious building.

I never got used to seeing all of the weapons hanging on the walls which included guns of all kinds, clubs, and knifes. Armor was on the walls as well. It was like 8Crow was a military base. I climbed up the metallic stairs that had open gaps. Once I got up the stairs, I looked down below on the whole headquarter, seeing the soldiers grab whatever tools they needed before their next mission. I still couldn't believe all the changes in my life.

I went into the boardroom with the open window. I was the second one in as Angelique had already arrived. To explain her position, she was one of the most well-known actresses in what used to be called Hollywood. She was rich enough to help fund our cause as was I. She was attractive, but also extremely intelligent. She was an incredible asset to the movement and the fight to bring back our freedom.

"Ah, would you look at that? For the first time, I'm earlier than April Freeman. I wish I had another witness to this rare occurrence." Angelique chuckled.

"Don't think that it'll happen again!" I joked back with her.

"How was your sleep last night?" She asked while sipping on her coffee.

"I didn't get much rest. You'll see why once Charles come in." I replied.

"I still don't believe it. Former Minority Whip turned into an 8Crow military leader. These are indeed strange times." She laughed.

"Says the actress actually backing the 8Crow organization financially. In all seriousness, I thank you for all your help. Without you, we wouldn't have been able to fight this dictatorship."

"It's not just me, it's so many other people in Hollywood that have supported us and gave us millions. I suppose making movies about totalitarian governments have given people the knowledge that doing nothing is just as bad as personally helping the Çaé." She said. "The real question is, who would have thought that you were be the one to start a rebellion."

"I needed to! When I saw what Lynn had done to the country, I knew we needed to fight back. I hated that woman from day one. And let it be known that I knew she was a conniving son-of-a-bitch before anyone else did. But let's not go down a beaten path. We have good news to share. I'm just waiting for Charles and the others to come."

"You won't have to wait any longer!" Charles laughed out loud as he walked into the room along with Gianna Martinez (a former Democratic mayor), Liam McPherson (a former Republican senator), Jerome Presley (a former Hollywood director), and Barbara Riperton (the former candidate for the presidency of the United States), among others. It's amazing that Riperton was able to escape Braun's brutal political genocide.

"Good morning!" I said arising to my seat, shaking hands with everyone. "Thank you again for backing this cause, not just financially, but with all of your heart and mind. Thank you for putting aside our differences so that we can all focus on a common goal: gaining our freedom back. General Charles Grant and I have called you all in for a very important development." I sat back down, taking out my briefcase to pull out my computer and papers that were meant to be passed around. I plugged in my computer and showed my content on the projected screen.

"Last night, General Charles and I stayed up late watching this." I pressed play on the computer. It was a video that was shot by a hidden camera by the leader of that certain division. You could feel the tension of the battle within the video, hearing the gunshots ring as if they were right outside our doors. You could see the opposition fighting against the 8Crow, both the Nationalists and the Freedonian military fought us. "Luckily, we won the battle. That's not the only battle we won last night. We won three. We overtook the three most strategic cities in Nevada: Reno, Carson City, and Las Vegas."

Charles picked up from there. "We started with invading Las Vegas first, because that was the area with the most armed forces sent in from Freedonia. By ambushing them first, they had no time to think about our militias entering into Reno and Carson City. Since there were no official Freedonian military there, we were able to put down the cities' Nationalist militias as they weren't as well-trained as our forces. By controlling these three key regions, it should make it easier for us to control Nevada. The 8Crow that died in these three battles did not die in vain. Getting those cities insured that Nevada is now part of 8Crow territory, along with all of California, parts of Oregon, and all of Washington state. The 8Crow rebellion now has enough land and power.”

“What about the rebels on the eastern side of the country?” Jerome asked.

“The rebels are having a harder time establishing territories on the eastern side since there’s more Freedonian armed forces. Plus, because it’s harder for our supplies to reach them. However, the land they do manage to take are in areas that are less occupied by government officials. But the eastern 8Crow have a plan to take back D.C. While it is not the capital anymore, taking it back will give people hope that Braun’s tyrannical rule will be over someday. It would boost some sort of morale to start to get people fighting for our side.” I continued.

“Now there is only one thing left to do.” Liam said.

“And what is that?” Gianna questioned.

“Create a new country.” Liam stated. “We can’t leave the people thinking that they’re occupied by another harmful force. We have enough land and people to form our own nation. Not to mention, it will send a powerful message to the Çaé that we are a formidable force and that we have enough support to build our own nation.”

“What about our economic circumstances? We can’t give false promises to the people.” Riperton added.

“We can worry about that later. Besides, we Hollywood elites can help ease the pressure on that side.” Angelique started. “What we need to start doing is drafting a constitution. We need to lay out what freedoms the people would be granted.”

“Why don’t we start right now? There’re no more military ambushes scheduled for today. We could get started on an Article of Freedom to depart from Freedonia and start building on a constitution.” I exclaimed. “We don’t have to finish today, but we need to start. Building a new nation that will grant the rights that everyone deserves and will boost hope in these dark times."

"I couldn't agree more." Charles said. "We should band together to come up with something and spread it to our people and beyond. Let's open up the computer and get started on it."

I began typing while they spoke on how we should break away from Freedonia. Here is the beginning of the now famous Article of Freedom: "When it is necessary, throughout the history of mankind, the people must disengage from the political powers that unfairly bound them to laws that are unjust. However, a decent respect to the opinions of mankind requires that they should declare the causes which impel them to the separation. We, the people, find that it is true that we are all equal and that we are all ordained with rights granted by the Creator of our beliefs. The rights that should be granted are those concerning one's freedom and one's happiness. To secure these rights, governments are established among men and women, deriving their just powers from the consent of the governed. Whenever any type of government becomes damaging to these ends, it is the right of the people to amend or to abolish it, and to organize a new government, laying its foundation on such principles of liberty and equality. Also, it is the right of the people to organize its powers in such form, to affect their safety and happiness. Let it be known that governments should not be changed for trivial matters; but when constant usurpations of equality are caused under laws of absolute despotism, it is their right and their duty, to overthrow such a government, and to provide new guards for their future safety..."

Somehow, we were so passionate about our work that we finished by noon. We printed it, scanned it with all of our signatures, and sent it to the 8Crow IT department so we could break through the firewalls of Freedonia so that every citizen with a phone could go out and share the news. Of course, we hired the best person from Silicon Valley to do it.

We also printed copies, so the soldiers could share it to the world. We became proud that we were able to accomplish the Article of Freedom in one morning. We decided that we would write the constitution another day because we had accomplished so much work already. With the Article of Freedom, the world was about to change again and this time for the better.

ANNA

The sunlight beamed through the window, awaking me with the warmth from the sun since I was sleeping on the couch. I groaned and looked at my phone to see the time and discovered it almost noon. Part of me wanted to leave my cochlear on the coffee table so I could just relax and browse through the free websites that were allowed or read a book online that was permitted by the Freedonian government. But I remembered that we had a guest and one thing I was taught by my mother, who was a socialite, was that I should always be ready to entertain. I put on my cochlear, and I winced when I heard loud laughter, since I just entered from the world of silence to the world of noise.

"No, I'm telling you, my fraternity, Sigma Phi Gamma was better!" I noticed the camping bed was put away and I could hear Rafael joke when I sat up to listen in on the conversation. He and Josh were in a deep conversation, while Libby and Danny were in the den eating some of the potatoes that Johannes fried earlier from the shopping trip that Libby went on the day before. Johannes was sitting on the armchair, writing in his journal. He looked up to see me.

"Ah, you're awake! I made fried potatoes, with onions too!"

"What are Rafael and Josh talking about?"

"Whose fraternity was better." Johannes replied while still writing in his book.

"Frat boys are something else." Libby laughed when I got up to prepare myself a plate.

"I will have to disagree with you on that." Josh said after taking a sip of water. "Zeta Delta Beta was the best, I would know, I was in it."

"Oh, really? Tell me, did you guys have step teams like we did? Can y'all stroll in style? Did y'all have dance chants like this?" Rafael proceeded to do a step and song routine.

A, B, C, D, E, F, G
Sigma Phi is the one for me.
We're the men boys want to be,
We treat our lovers so heavenly.
You wish you could be just like us,
But we'll just stomp you into dust.

He continued to dance until the end of his number. It was actually quite impressive. Once he finished, he sat back down at the bar and said "Josh, don't tell me you can beat that."

"Um," Josh stammered while Libby laughed in the background. "At least we were um...great at beer pong." There was dead silence and then everyone just burst out laughing.

"I hate I got to miss out on the college experience that you all seemed to have had." I said while pouring a glass a water for myself. "I feel slightly cheated. You guys had so much fun while the only fun I had was surviving a damn battle."

Johannes chuckled. "I'm sorry, sis. You did miss out on the fun part. Hey Danny, what was that big party we went to during our first semester?"

Danny cackled. "I'll never forget! It was the Heaven and Hell house party! I remember the whole campus being so excited for this party, especially me, Johannes, and Libby. I was in all-white cause I felt like I was a perfect angel. Libby followed suit, although she had on red pumps. Johannes, however, was in all red, looking as sly as the devil himself. We all walked to the party together, which was right across the street from campus. It seemed like it was a small house on the outside, but when we got inside, the house was huge! Everyone was dancing, and the music was bumping, let me tell you! The DJ was on point. We were in the upper level or 'heaven' where the beer was flowing literally for free. Libby and I were dancing to some song, I can't remember what it was, but it was like a banging Trap song. I accidently bumped into a frat person and he spilled beer all over me. Guess who it was? Rafael, in his Sigma Phi Gamma jacket, and he was super buzzed. When that first happened, I thought he was gonna be a stereotypical, frat boy and just be a jerk; but he immediately apologized, and we started talking. That was when he and I first met and became friends. Johannes was getting stone cold drunk and then said that he was going down to 'hell.' That meant that he was going down to the basement that was filled with smoke because the basement was for the stoners. Hours passed, and Libby decided that we should find Johannes and leave. Rafael said he'd join us. When we got down to the basement, Johannes was sprawled on a couch, just completely high and drunk. We heard police sirens, so we quickly got Johannes' arms wrapped around us and left through the back door of the basement. Imagine us walking back to campus and through our dorm with this man who could barely walk and move by himself. God, that was a time. At least I got to meet Rafael."

"It took you a long time to ask him out!" Libby chuckled. "Gosh, if I could go back..."

"I'd never thought I'd say this, but I wish Ace was our president again." Rafael smirked. "Things were so much simpler back then, even in those complicated times. Now we live under this godforsaken Çaé. But at least we have the memories. I agree with your brother, Anna. I wish you could have been there with us earlier. You shouldn't have to go through what you went through, but we're here. What else can we do?"

A knock on the door.

"F.I.I, open the door!" A gruff voice exploded from the other side. Tension and anxiety gathered in our throats

"Josh, go hide in the closet, now." I whispered in his ears. He quickly and quietly went in the bedroom and closed the door.

"You're required by law of the Çaé to open the door immediately." The officer continued.

Johannes rose up to open the door. He gulped when he saw the buff and bulky man enter the apartment.

"Hail Çaé Braun." He said.

"Hail Çaé Braun." We all said in return, complying with the custom.

"I'm here on official business for the Freedonian Internal Investigation."

"What business do you have here for the F.I.I., sir?" Libby shakily asked.

"A rebel has escaped, and he is a danger to the Freedonian government and the Çaé. We believe he came through this apartment complex and we are searching every part of the building. By the law of the Çaé, I am required to search your premise with or without your permission."

"Then I suppose we should make it easy on all of us and allow you to do your job." Danny said with the slight twang of panic in his vocal cords.

"Spoken like a true, cooperative subject. The Çaé will be pleased to hear how well people are following the law." He nodded and began his search. He looked at the counter and saw two glasses of water side by side. One was mine and one was Josh's.

"I count 5 of you here, yet I see six cups that have been used?" The investigator asked.

"Um... I forgot that I had already poured a glass. You know how it is in the morning, you just don't think about things." I lied.

"Hmm..." He glared at me. Once he turned away, Johannes looked at me and I just shrugged and shook my head. It was the only lie I could think of on the spot.

"Why is this door closed?" The investigator questioned.

"You mean the bedroom door? I don't see why it shouldn't be. It's a bedroom door. If it's crucial for you to check..." Libby stated, clearly sweating and biting her lips.

The investigator went into the bedroom, seeing the messy bed. He stared at the closet, leading my breath to linger in my throat. He forcefully opened the closet and there was nothing but a spare amount of clothes. Josh seemingly vanished. The investigator looked in the bathroom and just saw a messy counter with different toothbrushes. He walked back into the main room and looked around. He still wasn't convinced that there was nothing wrong.

"Who owns this apartment?" He asked.

"I own it now." Johannes replied.

"I need to see your social credit." The investigator said mindlessly as if he's said that a million times. Johannes showed his barcode tattoo on his wrist and the man pulled out the scanning machine to read his social credit.

"4,075 credits, huh? You must be very wealthy, yet you're living with other people when you could easily afford a place of your own."

"They're my friends, sir." Johannes responded clearly.

"And your name... Johannes Jansen, there's not a lot of people here with that name."

"My grandfather immigrated from Amsterdam. I'm named after him." He smiled, trying to be polite.

"You're also named after the man that killed a patriotic Nationalist in the middle of a library." He stared dead in his eyes while Johannes' face dropped.

"Those charges were dropped because it was self-defense. If you watch the tapes that were captured on video, you'd know I was running for my life." Johannes whispered.

"Those charges were dropped in America. We're in a whole new country with new laws enacted by the Çaé. You killed a Nationalist. If I can't catch myself a rebel, then the next best thing is a murderer. Now, give me your wrist." The investigator took some of his social credit scores and lowered it by about 1,000 credits. He then made Johannes lift him arms behind his back and linked his elbows with new black Freedonian cuffs. "Now let's go." He pushed Johannes out of the apartment. "Hail Çaé Braun and All Hail Freedonia!" He then slammed the door, leaving the five of us in shock.

"Oh my God, what are we gonna do?!" I panicked. "My brother has just been arrested by a Freedonian Investigator. Oh God. We have to do something! We must do something!"

"Anna, you have to calm down!" Danny grabbed ahold of me, even though there was anxiety hidden in his eyes.

"How can I keep calm, when a Freedonian who wants to protect Nationalist scum has arrested my brother!" I yelped. "This man just barges in here, looking for something and when he didn't get what he wanted, he walks away with my brother. How the hell am I supposed to keep calm!"

"We'll do something!" Josh barged in from the bedroom.

"Where did you go, we thought he was gonna find you!" Rafael exclaimed.

"I hid in the bathtub behind the shower curtains. I prayed he didn't look there. But I heard everything. We don't have much time. Grab everything essential that you need and put them in a backpack, there'll be more F.I.I.s here soon. I'm gonna take y'all to my 8Crow camp, I'm positive they'll be able to help Johannes. Let's go!" Josh commanded.

I had to pull myself together. I grabbed my old high school backpack and packed both my rechargeable and renewable batteries for my cochlear along with a couple of shirts and pants. I also grabbed Johannes' journal as I knew he would want it. After the speedy packing, Josh made sure that we were all ready.

"Once we do this, you'll all be considered rebels. Are you prepared for this?"

"No." I said. "But I'm tired of letting these Freedonian bastards keep walking all over us. Let's go get my brother back." Josh led us out of the apartment complex and I looked back, knowing that life would never be the same. I became an outlaw.

DANNY

The weight of my bag against my back strained me as we crouched behind a dumpster. We tried to hide from the rest of the population, fearing that people might be compelled to obey the laws of the Çaé and call-in suspicious behavior. We rushed to the other side of the street. Josh was leading us to his 8Crow regiment in order to report back after his failed supply run and to also receive help in retrieving Johannes from the F.I.I. We had been walking for a considerable amount of time to the camp when we came upon a tent city.

"All right, we're here." Josh said, taking a breath and smiling while he looked around at the olive-green canvas sprouted around, with people walking about seemingly finding shelter on the grounds and people being huddled together near cans of fire.

"This is it? This is the 8Crow camp?" I asked in a confused manner, dragging my footsteps among the dirt, allowing dust to rise up as the chill of the wind made me shiver. "I was expecting something...better."

"I agree, where the hell are we?" Libby questioned, with Rafael and Anna slightly lagging behind. "I thought it would look more sophisticated than this."

"That's why this place is perfect. People expect us to look like an obvious rebel base, but if you surround the base with a poor tent city, hopefully government officials would never think to enter. Look further." Josh responded. Walking closer, the scenery slowly changed. There were a few oddly placed weapons here and there and a few men and women in all black armor, standing out from the inhabitants in the front of the tent city. As we began approaching closer into the interior, it became more like a military base, with more soldiers walking with guns. It was quite a shock to see the area go from poor and desolate to full of energy and fervor within a few minutes of walking inwards. There were people packing stuff as they were preparing for something. In the middle, there seemed to be this large pavilion in the dead center, with the very back of the tent highlighting the symbol of the 8Crow (which was the number eight next to a rudimentary image of a crow.) There was action from all over and we stuck out like sore thumbs, dressed out of place.

All of a sudden after Rafael accidently dropped his bag, guns cocked from everywhere. 8Crow were alert. We froze. Only Josh was confident about this new mission of ours, while we were scared. We were finally face-to-face with the rebels that were "destructive to the progress of western civilization," as was said by Çaé Braun.

"Don't shoot unless I say so!" A voice said from behind. "Turn around, slowly. Any sudden moves, and you will be shot." We moved 180 degrees and saw an Indian man, dressed in all black and covered in a bulletproof vest. "Josh! You survived!" He said in shock.

"That seems to be the running theme, huh?" Josh joked.

"Are they with you?" The man motioned his head at us.

"Yes, and I trust them with my life, Hasan. They're with me." Josh said.

"Everyone put your guns down." Hasan ordered. "Come here!" He pulled Josh in for a hug and patted him on his back. "I'm sorry, guys." He apologized. "I can't be too precautious. The Freedonian government has been making our lives a living hell for the past few weeks, but I assume you came because you heard about the good news."

We were puzzled.

"There's, um, good news around here?" Rafael stammered.

"You haven't heard yet, have you? Headquarters have penetrated through most of the internet, but the Freedonian government have been working hard against the citizens seeing this fantastic new development." Hasan responded. "Come with me, we'll go to my personal office in that tent over there, we'll discuss what has happened and then we'll discuss what to do with the rest of you."

Hasan summoned us into his tent which had a cheap poker table as a desk, which was covered with differing papers and maps, including a color-coded map of D.C. He motioned for the guards to remain outside. It was clear that Hasan led this regiment.

"You can put your bags down here." He motioned near his table.

The temperature of the room was odd, where part of the tent was warm and other parts were cooler. There was a rolling, metallic container in the corner, which I was sure contained weapons. He pulled out his phone and smiled (speaking of which, I still have no idea how he managed to receive electricity to charge his phone without paying Freedonian Light, Gas, and Water. I assume that will forever remain an 8Crow secret).

"The good news is contained on this phone. I assume that you all would have received the document but I'm sure that Josh told you to get rid of your phones as to not reveal our location. I will get you all some burner phones."

"You taught me well, Hasan." Josh smirked.

"That's the job of being a leader. But anyways, the 8Crow organization has made incredible gains in that we have won territories in all of California, all of Washington, part of Oregon, and we just won territories guaranteeing the entire state of Nevada. Because of that, our leaders from the top of the organizations have released an important document: The Article of Freedom. You can read it for yourself." Hasan said, handing us the phone. We all huddled together to read the tiny text. It gave us hope knowing there was a potential light at the end of the tunnel. However, there was a shock when we finished reading the document once we got to the signatures. Libby gasped when she saw that April Freeman, her mother, signed it.

"How did my mom get involved in this?" Libby whispered.

"Is your mom April Freeman?" Hasan curiously asked. He took his phone back after we were done.

"Yes... I'm happy she's a part of something that will give people hope and I'm proud that she's a part of something that could provide change but how did she..." Libby was baffled.

"What's your name?" Hasan asked.

"Oh, how rude of me!" Josh exclaimed. "This is Libby, that's Rafael, she's Anna, and he's Danny."

"Well, I guess it's important to know." Hasan turned to address Libby. "Your mom, she's a real hero. She actually created the 8Crow organization."

Libby's eyebrow went up. "Well, that does explain a lot of things, how she could barely call me."

"Well, I'm honored to be in the presence of her daughter. Speaking of which, why are you all here?" Hasan questioned.

Josh was about to answer, but Anna took the lead. "We've come to ask for a favor."

"Any friends of Josh are friends of mine. He's saved my life more than once, believe me. What is it?"

"We need your help to save my brother. An F.I.I. arrested Johannes on a charge that was dropped before the Çaé became the ruler. We need your help in breaking him out." Anna bluntly stated.

"Um...excuse me?" Hasan paused.

"I know it's a lot to ask, but Johannes was apprehended trying to hide me from them." Josh explained.

"I'm sorry, but I can't. We can't! There's too much on our plate, especially our plan... *the* plan." Hasan responded.

"They already know about the plan, Hasan. I had to tell them why it was necessary for me to stay at their place. Now it's even more important that we save Johannes because he might blurt out the plan once they start torturing him." Josh said.

"Josh... tell me you didn't do that..." Hasan pleaded.

Josh shrugged.

"Now, it's even more important that we carry out our plan to gain control of D.C. now." Hasan said.

"How will you do that, if you don't have the support of the people?" Libby suddenly interjected, shocking even me.

"What do you mean, of course we'd have their support." Hasan faltered. "The people want back their country."

"What the people want is security." Libby rebutted. "I don't know if you realize, but most people here don't have phones because it's too expensive. We're the lucky few that have them. They haven't seen the Article of Freedom yet."

"So?" Hasan replied.

"They're gonna think that you're just another occupying force because they don't know what you stand for. I know my mother. She'll have physical copies of the Article sent in, but that will take weeks to arrive. Once you overtake D.C., who is to say that there won't be a rebellion against you. They won't really know nor understand your mission. You have to get it, just taking D.C. won't work. You have to make them want to fight for you. You can take back D.C. and help us get Johannes. I am my mother's daughter. I know a way we can have our cake and eat it too."

Libby was a force to be reckoned with. I saw the gears turning in Hasan's head. Finally, he gave in.

"What's the plan?" He asked.

Libby smiled. "We'll call it Operation Eagle."

LIBBY

"Do you have everything prepared?" I said aloud, shoving all of our bags into the large, black van and putting the jugs of gasoline in their proper place.

"I had some of my people copy down the preamble to the Article of Freedom since we didn't have time to write down the whole thing." Hasan grunted as he carried a case of handwritten papers that were to be passed out and placed it inside the van.

Danny walked back from the outside of the base. "Josh, Rafael, and Anna are leaving to get into their position along with some of the people in your regiment, Hasan. They understand the plan. They're gonna wait for our signal and they will accomplish their mission."

"Good." Hasan stated. "Libby, I hope this plan works."

"It will. I am my mother's daughter after all, aren't I?" I smiled. I got in the passenger seat and Danny was in the far back while Hasan drove outside of the camp towards the location of our mission. He drove down what used to be Ohio Drive. The roads were almost practically empty since hardly anyone could afford gas or their cars anymore. Only people with the highest social credits had the road available to them. While in the van, we were quiet, going over the plan within our minds. Each word that I thought of was absolutely crucial. I needed to motivate people to join our cause and move the Freedonian government out of our city. My brain worked overtime as Hasan was driving. My anxiety was through the roof. I already had influenced history before with the Battle of D.C., but here, I would be directly involved in the interference of time. The blood was rushing through my veins and I gritted my teeth.

"I believe we're here." Hasan said as he drove the van into the grass to park. "I'm surprised this memorial still exists."

"The Jefferson Memorial? I was too, but apparently, that was the only place where the bombs didn't go off." I explained. "They tore down the Jefferson statue, though."

"But why here?" Hasan questioned. "It's just a tent city."

"The biggest tent city in D.C., I should remind you. It's close to the water so people can boil it for drinking water, wash themselves and their clothes. I think we would have ended up here if Johanne hadn't rented out the apartment. Plus, the dome provides good shelter during the rain. If you get the people here committed to your cause, then we can get them to fight against the Freedonian government officials and the F.I.I. which is right across the bridge of the tidal basin. Also, we can give Josh the signal from here. He'll be able to see it and follow through with his portion of the mission." I continued.

"Okay," Danny grunted, carrying the papers. "I have the flare gun in my pocket to signal Josh. Hopefully, it'll also charge people to go towards the Freedonian Government House."

"My troops are in position both over here and on the other side of the basin." Hasan confirmed. "I believe we're ready. Libby, you can lead us in."

I cleared my throat. It was go-time. I walked ahead of Hasan and Danny with my bullhorn, walking into the tent city. It was a pitiful sight. The people within were clearly hungry and tired in more ways than one. They were hungry for nutrients and nourishment for food, yet they were also hungry for the old days of when they had plenty and wanted for nothing. They were physically tired, but they were also tired of just trying to survive hour to hour, day by day. The people had dirt on their skin and their clothes were tattered. It was emotional seeing children walk barefooted, knowing that Freedonian government officials slept comfortably every night on plush pillows. It was emotional knowing how one could allow people to live in these squalor conditions.

It was getting close to sunset, yet time seemed to slow down as I saw dozens shiver once the chill started to settle in. I saw others huddle close together near the inactive cherry blossom trees. The sound of the fire cackling in the distance caught my attention. I got to the steps of the memorial, where people were laying, trying to rest their weary eyes and weary souls. As I made it to the top of the memorial steps, I saw people gathering water from the basin to drink, the same water people were bathing in. I couldn't handle seeing the injustice that was done in this city and the country of Freedonia. That gave me conviction to do what was right. Danny got into his position, prepared to pass out the preamble to the Article of Freedom on my mark. Hasan was behind me, protecting my back. His job was also to let me know if the F.I.I. from across the bridge would start to arrive. My next job was to gather the attention of the dwellers surrounding the memorial.

"Hear me and hear me well!!" My voice boomed into the bullhorn. The commotion throughout the area stopped. "Once upon a time, we lived under a system of freedom, liberty, and equality. Once upon a time, we used to live in a nation that was a shining city on the hill. Once upon a time, we were Americans, whose ideals meant that every man and woman were given rights that allowed us to live freely. But now in Freedonia, a country that has no legitimate claim as a nation, our rights have been tarnished.

No longer are we promised freedom. No longer are we promised liberty. No longer are we promised equality. We are living in a system where we're not valued as human beings." The crowd started to pay attention. "We're valued by our social standing, as if those who exist on a different caste from the wealthy are worth nothing to society. You are worthy! You matter!" Some of the crowd roared in agreement, while others stood watching, curious to decide if my speech had anything to offer. "We should be judged by the content of our characters. Our lives shouldn't be dictated by a government that cares nothing about us. We shouldn't be starving. We shouldn't have to decide between feeding our children or feeding ourselves. We deserve rights that the Freedonian government aren't willing to give. We deserve help!" By now, seemingly all of the tent city cheered and clapped in agreement to my speech, people were listening.

"There is one group that will help: 8Crow." I shouted. "You may have heard of them as murderous rebels, but those are lies perpetuated by the Çaé, a brutal tyrant that does not and will not identify with our struggle. 8Crow is fighting to gain back our freedom, liberty, and equality. And they're winning. Out west, in the former states of California, Nevada, Oregon, and Washington, they're giving back God-given rights to people. You can see it in the Article of Freedom, which was signed by the leaders of the 8Crow militia and its territories." Danny heard his cue and started handing out copies of parts of the article for the people to read. People joined him in the handing out of the papers.

"The Article of Freedom states this: When it is necessary, throughout the history of mankind, the people must disengage from the political powers that unfairly bound them to laws that are unjust. However, a decent respect to the opinions of mankind requires that they should declare the causes which impel them to the separation. We, the people, find that it is true that we are all equal and that we are all ordained with rights granted by the Creator of our beliefs. The rights that should be granted are those concerning one's freedom and one's happiness. To secure these rights, governments are established among men and women, deriving their just powers from the consent of the governed. Whenever any type of government becomes damaging to these ends, it is the right of the people to amend or to abolish it, and to organize a new government, laying its foundation on such principles of liberty and equality. Also, it is the right of the people to organize its powers in such form, to affect their safety and happiness. Let it be known that governments should not be changed for trivial matters; but when constant usurpations of equality are caused under laws of absolute despotism, it is their right and their duty, to overthrow such a government, and to provide new guards for their future safety."

There was uproarious applause. The people began chanting as they were provided hope which had long since been denied. I continued. "8Crow knows that you are worthy. They know that you matter! You can help 8Crow and start again out west where your rights will be guaranteed. If you want to further help the cause, then you can help us by overthrowing the Freedonian Government House, where we can get back control of the District of Columbia. Join us in the fight for freedom! Help us maintain equality! In the yet-again relevant words, give me liberty or give me death! Let the Revolution begin!!"

The people were riled up, with their anger and frustration of their situation finally beginning to rise. My speech had worked. About ¾ of the people in the tent city started to march out towards the bridge across the Tidal Basin, determined to no longer remain in the conditions they were living. At the time, I was surprised how many people went to join the fight. But now that I'm older, I realize that they had nothing else, but their lives to lose. Many had already felt that life was not worth living, but the speech ignited passion and fury and they aimed that emotion towards the Freedonian Government House. On their way to go across the bridge, they were singing an old bar song of freedom which kept spirits up while holding hand-held weapons.

Hark, the sound of war is heard,
And we must all attend:
Take up our arms and go with speed,
Our ideals to defend.

I looked at Danny and Danny looked at me. He nodded and knew what to do. He pulled out the flare gun and shot it upwards towards the sky. It's bright trail of light inspired the crowd and let the rest of our crew know to carry out their part of the mission. Hasan was on his phone and had received words from the troops. Once he got off his cell phone, he breathed outward in relief and held his breath in apprehension.

"The troops are in position." Hasan said. "Operation Eagle is now in full effect."

JOHANNES

Shackled in chains, I was alone at the table, unable to escape. I had been in there for hours after that prick locked me into that hellhole. I was hungry and tired, as I had not been seen in hours. The florescent light in the room flickered and the air was cold, with the temperature matching the appearance of the sterile environment. I stared directly at the mirror that was in front, grimacing and frowning. I was pissed. The Investigator had just arrested me with no grounds for it, other than he couldn't get the person he wanted.

"Hey!!" I screamed at the mirror. I shot up, kicking the silver chair away from me. It hurt my wrists because I was still chained to the table, but I was furious. "I know you're listening in there! I have been in here for hours and no one has seen me! I demand respect, dammit! I have rights!" I yelled seemingly at myself. I looked at myself in the mirror and I laughed. It started from a chuckle that reached to an absolute cackle. I looked crazy for yelling at myself towards the mirror, even though I knew there were people behind it, watching me. "This is what you wanted to see, isn't it?" I hollered. "You want to see me lose my fucking mind? Well, here I am!

I'm breaking down right before your very eyes! I hope you're enjoying the show, motherfuckers!" Yeah, I admit, that wasn't my proudest moment.

The door suddenly busted opened and in walked the officer that arrested me.

"I assume I finally got your attention, Mr. Investigator." I said, staring him down.

"Please, call me Joe." He smirked, setting up his computer, while sitting at the table.

"Joe." I grinned. "I knew a Joe back in the day. In fact, you remind me of him. You guys are both utter assholes."

Joe got up and punched me in the face, hard enough for a back tooth to fall out. I started bleeding from the impact, due to the rings he had on that helped tear some skin. I gathered my breath when he chuckled.

"You're a typical rebel scum." He spat in my face and I tried to go at him, but I couldn't with my arm movements limited.

"I am not a rebel! Where's my attorney? I want an attorney! You're supposed to comply with the law!" I argued back.

"You keep forgetting what country you're living in now. By the laws of the Çaé, there are no attorneys, only Observers."

"Where's my Observer, then?" I snarled.

"They only come once trial begins, only to make sure that you're in compliance with the law during court. You should be lucky that you're even allowed a trial. If it were up to me, you'd already be in front of the squad in the line of fire, you little punk." He said as he got in my face, where his breath was close to my nose.

"You know what I think?" I started to say. "I think you could use a mint." I laughed. Joe then knee-ed me in the guts.

"You know what I think? I think you're a brat." He snipped. He got the silver chair and set it under me to force me to sit. He sat on the other side and just stared at me. He stared at me for what seemed like an uncomfortable amount of time. The silence was somehow more piercing than the voice of an opera singer. Finally, he spoke. "We know that you're hiding the rebel."

"I don't know what you're talking about." I lied.

"Stop lying!" He slapped me across the face.

"If you hit me one more goddamn time, I swear you will regret it." I fumed in pain and anger.

"Ah, there it is! The anger that I was expecting from a rebel." Joe smiled.

"How many times do I have to tell you, I am not a rebel!" I scoffed.

"Aiding and abetting one makes you a rebel!"

"Listen, buddy boy." I seethed through my teeth. "I haven't done anything."

"But you did! Killing a Nationalist brings your allegiance to the state into suspicion. That leads me to think you are harboring a criminal, since you're a killer."

"I am not a killer! Period." I was getting really upset with this guy.

"Oh, then what about this video?" He turned his laptop around and I recognized the grainy footage. It was me, stabbing the man in the heart and then taking the knife out to slice his throat. I looked down in shame and gulped.

"That was taken out context and you know it." I said, looking at the table. "You didn't show how I ran in the elevator. You didn't see his gun aimed for my head." I stood up and faced the Investigator. "You didn't see the look of sheer terror on my face! He came after me! He was the one that was trying to kill me. I defended myself. You took the tape and edited it to fit your agenda."

"Edited it?" He huffed. "Why, I see what you really are, a cold-blooded murderer. All I see is someone brutally stabbing an innocent man and then immediately after killing him, you cut open his throat as if your bloodthirst wasn't satisfied. In fact, it looks like you took pleasure out of it. My God!

You're so cold that you went after someone who was mourning the death of their president. How are we to know you wouldn't conspire against the state and against the Çaé?"

"I WAS TRYING TO SURVIVE!" I bellowed in his face. "I had no other choice and you're making it out to be like I'm a sociopath, when the real sociopath is you. You are the sociopath. You are taking pleasure out of the task of trying to mentally break me. You are taking pleasure out of beating the fuck out of me. You're the sick one, you son of a bitch!" Joe immediately shot upwards to grab my throat and began to choke me.

"No one calls me a son of a bitch." He murmured. He let go and then sat back down. As I was panting for air and sat back down as well, he started laughing. "You know what? You're good, you're entertaining. The Audience will love watching you be sentenced to death by the Ruler in court."

"Then I'll be as boring as you, so they don't get the pleasure of watching me die." I smirked.

"You'll die nonetheless when the court finds you guilty because this video is mighty incriminating. But what if I told you that you didn't have to die. If you give us the rebel that you're harboring, then we can make this whole thing go away."

I paused. I turned my head ever so cockily. "You know what? I've given it some thought. All I have to say is... Suck. On. My. Balls." He grabbed a fistful of my hair and was about to pound my head into the table when there was a loud explosion in the building. The alarms started blaring. He looked at me. I could tell he was thinking hard, which I'm sure for him was no easy feat. After what seemed like minutes, he made up his mind to check out whatever happened outside.

"What the hell?" The Investigator said. He let go of me and went rushing out the door to see what the problem was. I was left alone, staring at my bruised and battered face in the glass mirror. I laughed at myself again.

"I hope you bastards had a good show. Let the Audience be entertained by this." I spat out blood. From that day forth, I became a different man.

Rafael

J osh, Anna, and I, along with several other 8Crow soldiers waited on the side of the building located next to the Bureau of the F.I.I. The building we hid in was partially scorched, abandoned and uninhabited. Panels were missing on the ceiling and the infrastructure seemed to be crumbling to dust. The burns on the walls created a sort of apocalyptic atmosphere. It was astonishing that the building was still standing. Anna, Josh, me, and several other soldiers all stood around in one area next to a window, so we could look out for Danny's signal. I stared across the distance of the sparkling body of water, seeing the ancient dome which resembled the great works of antiquity. I saw the memorial in a brand-new light. Before the pillars of America collapsed, I barely paid it any mind, but it had become a symbol at that moment of how things maybe *could* change.

Anna tapped my shoulder. "Do you see anything yet?" Anna both said and signed while leaning against the wall.

"No." I replied. "But give them a chance. Knowing Libby, I'm sure her speech is inspiring and...long. It'll take them a second."

Josh chimed in from the other side of the window. "Rafael's right, we just have to wait this out. In the meantime, we should go over the plan again."

"We know the plan well enough, Josh!" Anna sniped. Clearly, her patience was running low.

"It doesn't hurt to go over it again. It's especially important when people don't know how to follow through." Josh was being shady to a soldier. I laughed and then covered my mouth as to not be rude. Josh was never one that I expected to dabble in the art of shade.

"I swear, you make one mistake…" The soldier hissed.

"Brune, we almost died in Richmond because of your ass, okay?! We're doing this again!" Josh corrected him. "Now first, soon after Danny shoots the flare gun, most of the lineups in the F.I.I. will go towards the bridge to see what all of the hullabaloo is about."

"Hullabaloo?" I laughed. "What the hell kinda talk is that!"

"Anyways…" Josh rolled his eyes and continued. "Once the majority of the Investigators leave, Rafael and Anna, you will shoot the two security guards with the special tranquilizer dart guns."

"Where *do* you guys get these things?" Anna questioned as she felt her dart gun in her weapons utility belt that was given to her.

"That's not the point!" Josh focused her in.

"Seems like a plot hole to me…" I mumbled.

"ANYWAYS… we want to have the least number of casualties as possible, to legitimatize our cause. Brune, you will sneak through the front door and place smoke bombs to confuse people while I hack and dismantle all of the technological locks which includes the cells. The rest of the soldiers, y'all will be in the back of the Bureau so you can successfully help get all of the political prisoners and journalists out. Brune, you'll also help lead them out towards the back as well. Rafael, Anna, and I will find and get

Johannes out personally. Then Brune and the other soldiers will be taken to safety back to our camp by our vans."

"Speaking of, how are you guys getting this much money?" I asked.

"NOT THE POINT!" Josh frustratingly yelled in a hushed tone. "I am going to continue and there will be no more interruptions! Got that? Good. *Anyways...* Rafael, Anna, Johannes, and I will meet with Hasan, Libby, and Danny at the Jefferson Memorial while the tent people and our battalion infiltrate the Government House. Now does that plan make sense?"

"Yes, Josh. We know our part. Both Libby and Hasan drilled it into our heads before we left." I said. "We got this. The hard part is just waiting."

"You don't have to wait much longer." Anna replied. "Look, there's so many people marching across the bridge." She was right. It was a multitude of people running in what seemed to be excitement. Because there were so many, their faces mixed into a vague color of beige. But I saw enough to know the faces had expressions that embodied the confusion of these times, the bizarre emotional combination of anger and inspiration, exhaustion and empowerment. Libby's speech did the job. With the forces of the citizens and 8Crow, it was hard to see a possibility of losing. Then, from the memorial, an illuminizing blaze of light was ejected, which lead a trail of white smoke. Danny gave us our sign. Our part of the mission began.

We went outside and stealthily made our way over to the Bureau of the F.I.I. We hid behind bushes and trees when we saw the Investigators come out of the building. Some were rushing through with cars that blared across the city while other rans on foot. It was like an army was sent to interfere with the uprising. However, it was hard for many to completely succeed to making it all the way to the bridge as we had sharp shooters located in inconspicuous areas. We heard rapid gunfire near the bridge. Knowing that we were safe and couldn't be spotted, we hid on the side of the large building. Hasan was right. How he knew F.I.I. protocols still baffles me to this day. Hasan knew that when a significant number of Investigators was called into action, there would be two security officers on the steps in front of the entrance. It was meant to broadcast a look of calmness as to not arouse the feeling of worry (or perhaps rebellion) if something was happening, which was a really stupid rule if you think about it. Once we saw the two security officers standing alone, we knew it was our moment.

"Anna, you ready?" I signed as I wanted to be as quiet as possible.

"Yes. I'm ready." She signed back. We both grabbed our dart guns and discreetly aimed towards the guards. For them, the darts came out of nowhere. They were barely able to register the fact that they had been hit with something because they immediately fell to the floor. They were knocked out, unable to do anything. No one noticed because too many people were gone. I nodded to Brune and he nodded back. He knew it was his turn when he made his way up the steps. The rest of us waited as he did his task. He rushed out in a hurry and had a grimace on his face upon his return.

"I um...messed up..." Brune chuckled, trying to ease tension.

"Brune, what did you do?" Josh violently stared into his soul. If looks could kill, Brune would have crumbled into ash and dust.

"It wasn't my fault; I swear they looked the same." Brune stammered.

"Brune... so help me, if you ruined this mission, I will make your life so miserable that you will wish that you were a personal shooting target for the Çaé herself. What did you do?" Josh fumed. Suddenly, there was a thunderous explosion that was in the center of the Bureau, allowing pieces of materials to fly in every direction. We had to put our hands on our heads and dropped down to protect ourselves from the impact of the detonation. An alarm blared. I got up and saw a giant hole was exposed in front of the partially mutilated edifice.

"I mistakenly used a regular bomb, thinking it was the smoke bomb." Brune whispered.

"Brune, you utter idict." Josh said when he rose from the ground. "The Investigators from the bridge might come back, further complicating our mission. Brune, you will be reprimanded for this later, but right now we have to do what we 8Crow do best: improvise. Brune, you will go to the back and help the rest of the soldiers get the other prisoners out. I'm sure the locks are broken now since it looks like your explosion hit the computers. The three of us will get Johannes out as the layout suggests that he's in the interrogation room. We don't have much time, go." He ran. Anna and I followed. It was hard to avoid the rubble on the steps. There were several pieces of the stairs that had been destroyed and I almost tripped as I got to the top. I didn't even take a look at the building since I was focused on the mission. The alarm was blaring, as Josh led me and Anna deep into the complex. The walls and interior changed when we turned a corner and broke through an entry door. The silver and metallic ornamentation transformed the ambience quickly. It felt like we were breaking into a high-tech dungeon. The hallway we ran in felt like a maze, striking fear and confusion. I was slightly worried we could get lost, so like Theseus, I made note of where we were going and noticed slight differences as the halls started to look the same. Before we made a right turn, Josh stopped us by holding his arms sideway to block us.

"Shh..." Josh whispered.

"What the hell?" Someone yelled. It was the voice of the Investigator that arrested Johannes. All three of us peeked our heads out of the side of the wall one by one and saw the officer leave an interrogation room. He didn't turn and go straight because he would have run into us. He went the other direction, to his left. We slowly made our way towards the door but froze when we heard laughter. We realized it was Johannes' laughter and continued making our way down.

"I hope you bastards had a good show. Let the Audience be entertained by this." We heard him cackle.

"The Investigator must have broken him." I remember thinking. I heard it in his voice, which was strained and tired. Josh slightly jogged ahead and gently pushed opened the door from which the Investigator left. When we tip-toed into the room, we all simultaneously gasped at the sight of Johannes. He was beaten black and blue, with several scars on his face. Parts of his face were swollen. It was clear that he was tortured for information as Freedonian Investigators were known to do. His hair was a mess, ruffled every which way. His eyes offered a glimpse into his soul, which burst forth the feelings of anger, but his soul was also shattered just in the span of a few hours.

He was slightly startled but calmed down when he saw it was us. He attempted to grin but whimpered in pain. "Right now would be a great time for a joke, but I need you guys to get these chains off of me."

"Of course, give me a second." Josh said, suddenly pulling a machete from behind his shirt. He forcefully slammed against the chain with his weapon, effectively breaking it in half.

"Does he have every weapon available in the book?" I wondered to myself.

The chains fell on the ground and Johannes groaned when he slowly arose from his chair.

"Johannes..." Anna tried to hug him, but he winced in discomfort. "I'm sorry, I should've realized you'd be hurting too much."

"We should probably get going now. The F.I.I.s and other officers will be on their way here soon." I said.

"You're right. I don't want you guys to get the grand treatment that I got once they get back here." Johannes replied. "Someone give me a gun. If you think I'm walking out of here defenseless, you've got another thought coming." Johannes held his hand out, waiting for someone to give him a weapon. Anna budged and reached behind her shirt, in the back section of her belt, to pull out a handgun. She gave it to him and he prepared the firearm. "Now we can go." While he was hurting still, he sucked in air to cope. He wiped the blood from his face with his shirt. Josh led us once again, but it became clear that the twists and turns of the labyrinth started to confuse him as we were in a hall that split into two.

"Dammit, I can't remember which way we came from." Josh stated in frustration.

"I do." I said. "You see that slight dent in the metal panel right there on the left. We turn around there, then we make another left, then a right, and then another right, and continue all the way, until we turn another corner to make it to the entrance of this damned corridor. I can lead the way. I memorized it."

"Then what are we waiting for?" Anna gestured. I took the lead and we walked through the halls with our hearts in our throats and beads of sweat drenched the collars of our shirts. I gulped in fear, knowing that anything could happen. And something did happen. We heard the shuffle of movement that were not ours. Johannes reacted faster than the rest of us and fired the first shot with his gun. I turned around to see the Investigator that previously held our friend, fall on the floor before he could reach for his own weapon. The bullet hit him on the side and he spewed a red river of the iron-filled liquid. He laid gasping for air. Johannes limped towards the man and chuckled while waving his gun without care.

"Well, well, well... Mr. Investigator, I didn't think we'd see each other again so soon." Johannes smirked. He was gagging, he must have been hit close to the lungs. "Aw, Joe. You're speechless. I thought you'd be happier to see me. I thought we were friends. Friends just love to rough each other up, right?"

"Johannes, we need to go, we don't have time for this!" I hissed. He ignored me.

"I just wanted to tell you, Joe, that you might be right. I may be a sociopath. I am sick because I want to make you suffer and watch you bleed until you're nothing but a pale, rotting carcass. I want to rip out your intestines and wrap them around your neck as you gasp for your last breath. But most of all, I want to kill you just like you tried to kill my sanity."

"Johannes!" Anna yelled, while Joe struggled, and his eyes stared at us, pleading for help.

"I guess I'm a murderer, but if I'm going to hell, I'm gonna drag you down to that fiery abyss with me." His eyes were raging with fury, the likes of which I had never seen. "Say hi to the devil for me, you son of a bitch." Johannes started firing off a multitude of rounds aimed at the Investigator's head with blood being sprayed across Johannes' face and pieces of flesh stuck and stained the walls, along with the sounds of pieces of skull clattering on the floor. When he was done, Johannes spat at the corpse.

"Rafael, lead the way." He said in a deadpan voice. I listened. I guided us out of the building. We saw chaos in the streets of D.C. once again. We hid when we heard gunshots all around from the sharp shooters aiming at officers while other police officers and protestors from the tent city were clashing.

"Shit!" Anna groaned. "How are we gonna get across the bridge. There are too many people fighting."

The officers started to hit people with their batons and the citizens were throwing rocks and bricks.

"We're lucky their forces are too stretched out to focus on us." I replied. "But I agree with Anna. The road is filled to the brim, it would be hard to get past them, even if we got past the violence."

"Oh, we will." Johannes gritted his teeth. "We'll get to where we have to go by sheer luck."

"And by the grace of God." Josh added.

"Are you two actually insane? Are you crazy because this is actually dumb? Are you dumb?" Anna was baffled.

"I guess when you've been through hell, you can go through anything." Josh sighed, looking at Johannes. "Brune and the others should be gone by now, taking the other prisoners back to camp. Our only backups, besides the sharpshooters, are located on the other side of that basin. We are going to get there. We are going to make a run for it."

"That's it?!" I said. "That's the grand plan?!"

"Yeah." Josh stood up. "Just don't get hurt. I'll meet you guys at the front of the memorial. We are gonna do what 8Crow does best: improvise." He ran into the crowd.

"Fuck..." I muttered. I followed Josh. Anna and Johannes were behind me.

I dodged smoke bombs and tear gas from the officers and Investigators. I bumped into a multitude of people. I almost got shot, but I ran harder than I ever did in my life. As I got closer to the main road, I pushed my way across the crowd, shoving people to get to my destination. My heart was pounding, banging against the rib cage of my chest. My lungs burned as I struggled to breathe in enough oxygen. My muscles were getting sore and tense. I pushed through and ran miles, outrunning a champion at a marathon. I made it to the van in front of the memorial, with Johannes and Anna appearing minutes later.

"Raf, thank God you made it!" Danny said as he appeared out of the van. He hugged me while I panted for air.

"That was the dumbest idea you ever came up with, Josh!" I exclaimed to him while he was leaning against the van.

"You guys survived. That's all that matters." Hasan said as he helped Johannes into the van. Afterwards, Hasan gave Libby a map and a set of instructions. "We've arranged a safehouse for you guys to go to. I can't guarantee your safety here as we may get some resistance from the Freedonian government, but I can if you head out west."

"But the Government House..." Libby stammered.

"We'll handle that." Josh stated.

"You're not coming with us?" Anna questioned with a sad infliction in her tone.

"My place will always be with 8Crow." Josh responded. "But I will see you again soon." He held Anna's cheek with the palm of his hand.

"Thank you for your help." Hasan shook our hands. "Now please, be safe." He made sure we all got into the van. Libby was at the driver's seat, getting the car into motion where we were sent to the next part of our adventure.

APRIL

I t was late at night, or early in the morning depending on one's view. I sat in the same conference room, in the same compound. I remember being tired and exhausted while doing my work. I poured over papers involving the takeover of D.C., the western front against the Nationalists in Idaho, and the distribution of the Article of Freedom. Anxiety overwhelmed me, but I could not let it hinder me from my responsibilities. The lives of people rested upon my shoulders and I did not have time to get the proper amount of sleep that one should receive.

"I brought some coffee." Barbara Riperton suddenly announced, bringing in a pot and some cream and sugar on a tray.

"I'm just drinking tea. I can't have too much caffeine in my system, you know." Angelique barged in as well, holding a large teacup.

"What are you two still doing here?" I asked them. "Shouldn't y'all be asleep in your cabins?"

"How can we sleep knowing how stressed you are?" Angelique replied.

"We thought it would be best to join you. We think you could use a break." Barbara said.

"There's no way I could take a break, I have too much on my mind." I responded.

"Then share your thoughts with us." Angelique said while pouring a cup of black coffee for me. "Us women should support each other. We know you have the weight of the world on you right now. Take a break, you've been going nonstop." She served me and placed the cup in front of me. The bitterness and robustness of the smell did entice me and they raised some good arguments for me to take a break.

"There's just so much going on right now that I can't sleep until I get some answers." I sighed before taking a sip of the coffee. "For example, the Nationalists are giving us hell in Idaho, because they know that if Idaho falls, so could Montana and Wyoming. They are putting in such a good fight that even Charles himself had to go to fight alongside the rest of 8Crow near Boise where the fighting is bloody. We had to send some of the troops that were stationed in Nevada and Oregon to join the fight."

"Silver lining, we quickly got control of all of Oregon!" Riperton interjected.

"That is good." I mentioned. "But it's hard to appreciate it when your troops are dying. I sent in armed forces from the boarder of Washington state to infiltrate the northern part of Idaho. Hopefully, that plan will work. And hopefully, Charles is safe. I haven't heard from him in a while. And then the Article of Freedom. In areas where it has been read, my covert men within key cities have seen positive results, but the damn Nationalists seem to burn down cities and hunt down people with copies of the document."

"I still don't understand why they do that. They don't try to convert anyone, but they just decide to kill anyone that doesn't agree with them. What that is doing is driving refugees towards us. Do they not realize they're helping the 8Crow cause by being so combative and more militant than even the Freedonian government is able to be?" Angelique said.

"It's a double-edged sword. They're forcing people to leave their homes, but that ultimately means more numbers for us. I just feel bad for the people who have been chased out. And the worry at the top of my head is D.C." I responded, taking in another sip of the hot liquid. "It has been days since we heard from the troops in the former capital. I don't even know if the mission failed or not. I do not know if we can win this fight."

"Don't you dare doubt yourself. Whatever April Freeman wants, she will get, don't forget that." Riperton tried to cheer me up. "You know, when I was running for the presidency, I looked up towards you. I thought to myself, 'how would she handle this or that situation.' April, you're an inspiration to me. Even though I lost the race, I never doubted myself. When I lost, I thought about you and that led me to realize that I'd have to keep fighting. Look at us now, we're fighting for an even bigger cause: absolute freedom. Times are hard now, but things will get better and maybe sooner than you think."

I smiled, looking at the women and felt glad that they supported me, and they supported the cause. We continued to talk, and it was a riveting conversation all about the past, especially on the old Hollywood gossip story of Angelique and Monica and how the paparazzi tried to paint them as bitter enemies, even though they were friends. We all dished on our hatred for Braun and were able to tell personal stories of why we did not like her. I gave the story of how she insulted me wearing one of my favorite outfits. We laughed about that. It was nice to feel like a normal human again and not a military figure. It was nice to be surrounded by powerful women who completely supported each other, and it makes me sad to remember how society once pitted powerful women against one another when they didn't do the same towards men.

Suddenly, the computer lit up and started to ring a video call. I was surprised to see someone calling this late/early. The other girls were curious too. I answered and saw it was Hasan from the District of Columbia. He was calling from a different location because the walls in the building did not have 8Crow emblems, but rather Freedonian emblems.

"I'm sorry to call so late, Mrs. Freeman." He started off. "I hope I am not interrupting anything important." He said, seeing Angelique and Riperton next to me.

"Not at all, in fact, we have been waiting for your call." I said.

"Well, I am happy to report that after fighting hard, we have regained complete control of D.C." Hasan smiled.

I sighed a breath of relief. "What took so long, was the plan hard to implement?"

"Actually, we had to change the plan. In all honesty, I don't think we could have won D.C. without the help of your daughter and her friends."

If you could only imagine my face of shock. "Libby?"

"I will give a more detailed report soon, but your daughter is a hero and you should be proud to have raised such an intelligent person. And I would also like to commend Josh as he has been my second-in-command. He has helped me tremendously, especially in the past hours. He got information from officials working within the Government House and found plenty of classified documents of which I will also share with you later."

"You have no idea how much I needed some good news." I said.

"And there's even better news. Libby and her friends are traveling west towards California. It will be a long journey, but you will get your daughter back."

When he said that, tears welled up in my eyes. "That's the best news I've heard all day. And I will make sure to ensure Josh gets the promotion he deserves. In fact, if you read me some of the classified details, I may already have a job for him in place." We stayed up the rest of the night talking about how Libby led a revolution and managed to save both her friends and the city she loved best. We also talked about what would be Josh and his new second-in-command, Brune's new assignment. It was good to hear that the citizens of D.C. responded well to the Article of Freedom and to the message of 8Crow. But I still knew that while a battle was won, the war was still going strong and that I could not back down until I won the war.

JOSH

The pride I felt after 8Crow and the citizens fought valiantly for independence was immense. It was a tough battle after Anna and the rest of the gang went their way down the interstate highway. We had major pushback from the Freedonian Internal Investigation, along with official Freedonian military that was called in. However, even though it took hours of brutal violence, we finally won. Without the help from the inhabitants of the tent city near the Jefferson memorial and help from the other people in the surrounding areas who had had enough of the government, 8Crow might have been overpowered by the military with our original plan.

While many were dead and injured, there was a form of celebration the day after the violence ended, with people burning the national flag in the streets all across the city. While some parts of the city were cleaning the blood of the fallen, other parts were parading around with effigies of the Çaé, which were hung up and/or burned. It was a victory. The officials within the Government House surrendered and we were able to obtain valuable intelligence as well as classified documents. Hasan, after we formally occupied the city, video called the heads of 8Crow from across the country on a secure network. He then began to file a report and requested that I personally meet him regarding something within the classified information.

I mentioned before that I was requested to see Hasan in his new office. I cannot express the happiness I felt seeing Hasan sitting at the desk of the former Representative of the Çaé or the R.O.C. It felt right. It felt proper to have someone else be in temporary control instead of a puppet for the fascist state under Braun. The Government House was finally under control of people who truly wanted the freedoms that Freedonia would never offer. Hasan was looking over documents before he motioned me to sit down.

"Josh," he started off, putting his pen down. "Let me begin by saying how proud I am that you have served beside me as my second-in-command. You saved my life and the lives of countless others. You've helped us bring back liberty in this city."

"It's for the Cause." I said. "I don't do it for the glory, I do it for the people, despite putting my own life in danger."

"That's what makes a hero. And the leaders of 8Crow agree."

"Sir?" I questioned.

"I'm promoting you. But before I go into any further details, we're waiting for one more person."

Almost as soon as he said that, Brune came rushing into the room panting.

"Sorry I'm late, I just fell down some stairs, but it's all good! I may have almost broken a finger, but I'm okay!" He smiled.

Hasan laughed while I groaned.

"You're right on cue, Brune." Hasan said.

"Thank you, sir!" Brune beamed.

"I'm sorry sir, but what is Brune doing here?" I asked.

"Brune will be your second-in-command from now on." Hasan stated plainly.

"Um, excuse me?" Brune and I both stammered.

"Sir, Brune is about as clumsy as a three-legged horse!" I exclaimed. "He confused a smoke bomb with an actual explosive!"

"Jeez, some people will never forget anything!" Brune defended.

"We almost died in Richmond because of you!" I said, exasperated

"That was an accident! How was I supposed to know that-?"

"Enough!" Hasan commanded. We followed our orders and stopped arguing.

"The reason why I am also promoting Brune is because he helped free the other prisoners, people that 8Crow could use to spread our message. Brune helped free journalists like Woody Copper and Tim Apples. Both of you have done a great service, but I'm assigning you two on a new mission." He gave us papers that detailed our new operation. "One of the officials that we have captured, Ryan Oakland, was guaranteed to be promoted as a Representative of the Çaé or the R.O.C. Strangely, he looks identical to you, Josh. In fact, the only difference is that he has longer hair."

"How ironic." I thought to myself.

He continued. "The mission is for Josh to take his place and Brune, you will act as his assistant."

"When do we go?" I asked.

"Effective immediately. We made one of our covert operatives located in Baltimore make the R.O.C. of the city believe that Mr. Oakland escaped the takeover of D.C. We've already prepared the necessary I.D.s. Then from there, you guys will go to Philadelphia, the new capital, where you will act as the new R.O.C. of the city. You will feed us valuable information as you will, for the time being, work closely with the Çaé herself. You two only have a few hours to prepare and read up. I'm gonna miss you boys, but you're doing 8Crow the greatest service by spying in the capital of Freedonia."

Brune and I left the office dumbfounded as this was a position we never expected to find ourselves.

***

I put on a tie like one that Mr. Oakland would wear and looked myself in the mirror of the bathroom of the Government House. I also looked at the picture of Oakland. The similarities were uncanny. The only real difference was that the other guy was slightly older, but I felt I could hide that fact considering I carried myself more maturely. I prepared myself by breathing in and out slowly. Brune suddenly walked in with a black suit-and-tie.

"Oh sorry, I didn't know you were in here." He apologized.

"No worries. I'm just about done." I said.

"Well, the car is ready to take us to Baltimore, but first, we need to clear the air."

"Okay."

"I know you think I'm nothing but a bumbling clown, but I take being in 8Crow as the greatest honor of my life. I will fulfill this mission. You have to understand how much is at stake for me. Under the laws of Freedonia, being a transgendered man is illegal. Had I not joined 8Crow, I would have to had to deny being who I truly am. 8Crow and its promises are the only things I can depend on in these times. So yes, I make mistakes and I will continue to make them, but don't ever for a second doubt that I wouldn't do anything to bring back the America that we once knew, flawed as it may have been."

"Do you really think you can handle this mission?"

"Yes, just as I can handle being your second-in-command." He responded as the florescent lights in the bathroom flickered.

"That's all I need to hear. Now let's go put on the greatest performance of our lives and win an Oscar." I said.

"We'll do that once I finish using the restroom." Brune slightly bounced.

"I thought you were trying to find me."

"No, I actually really have to piss badly, so I'll see you later." He said, entering a stall. I chuckled and left the restroom. I made it downstairs and waited for Brune. Once he got in the car, we began our short trip. Soon we were in Baltimore and we were dropped off in front of their Government House. I sighed to myself and walked first with Brune following behind me, showing the order of succession in Freedonian customs. I walked into the building and was immediately greeted by Kylesworth, the R.O.C. of Baltimore.

"Oakland, it's good to see you escaped the savagery of the rebels in D.C. Who's he?" He asked, motioning at Brune.

"That's Wesley, my assistant. I must say he is not as competent as I would like, but it's hard to find better help these days. However, let's focus on the matter at hand." I said, acting like I had a large ego like Oakland.

"Of course. Follow me to my office and we'll wait there for the limo to Philadelphia." He led us upstairs and showed us his main headquarters.

"Oakland, you wouldn't mind if we talked privately for a moment."

I cleared my throat. "Wesley, stay out here. I will let you know when we're ready." I walked into his office.

"Okay, I'll wa-" Brune was rudely interrupted as Kylesworth slammed the door in his face.

"What the hell are you doing here?" Kylesworth fumed.

"Watch who you're talking to!" I exclaimed.

"You left D.C. to the rebels. You took an oath that vowed to fight for the Çaé."

"And I did! I maintained my position until I realized it was a losing battle!" I lied.

"You should have stayed there and continued fighting for the honor of the Çaé."

"You clearly have forgotten who I am. I am an Oakland. I am a part of a proud legacy that upholds the values that Freedonia should stand for. We support the Çaé and all of her ventures. Whereas you are nothing, Kylesworth. If you want to bring up an oath for the Çaé, why don't we talk about how you're breaking that oath by taking money from the government and putting it into your own pockets. If we're to talk about honor, it seems you have none. What kind of man cheats on his wife with *three* other women? Don't try to fuck me over." I hissed, fully getting into character.

"How did you know..." Kylesworth stuttered.

"I'm an Oakland. I know everything." I said. "Are we done? Because, unlike you, I have somewhere important to be."

He scoffed, and I grinned. "The limo is ready now." He said after putting in a call.

"Good. I hope to see you again, that way, you'll never forget who I am."

"Trust me, I won't." He grunted.

"Ahh, now you know how to treat someone right. I hope you'll carry that lesson along in your marriage. But I'll keep your secrets if you do this one thing: don't ever try to play me again." I walked out of his office and snapped for Brune to follow me. "Wesley, our limo awaits!" I walked away with confidence. Damn, I was a good liar.

DANNY

By following the instructions that Hasan handed us, we spent days traveling throughout both the states of Virginia and West Virginia. The latter state was where our safe house was located. Hasan's instruction had us zigzagging between the two states to avoid military checkpoints. All five of us took turns driving, however when all of us were too tired to continue, we'd pull over and parked behind gas stations in small towns that had no security cameras. This worked because no one noticed us and we were able to steal tanks of gas for the van while also breaking in to steal food. The times called for desperate measures.

We were getting close to our destination at this point. What could have been a seven-hour trip from D.C. felt like a week's worth of travel. We were finally in West Virginia, near the southeastern boarder close to Kentucky. Rafael was in the front, since it was his turn to drive. I sat next to him in the shotgun seat. Libby, Anna, and Johannes were talking amongst themselves. The only view they had were the windows of the back exit of the van, as they watched the world fall behind while we pushed forward. The stale freon air enveloped the vehicle just as the feeling of anxiety for what was to come enveloped us.

To avoid thinking about what was next, Libby, Anna, and Johannes tried to keep busy by talking about old Broadway songs. Libby was reminded of a song that pertained to our depressing situation, from the musical *The Wild Party*. She cleared her throat to sing *When it Ends*. She had a beautiful bluesy voice. If things were normal, she could have obtained a record deal. The atmosphere was bitterly cold when the song ended. It took us back to innocent times, back to college; but it reminded us that the party was over and now reality must set in.

"Damn, Libby, way to bring the house down." Johannes joked in masked pain.

"We could sing a happier song. What about 'This little light of mine?' That would be happier and that should uplift our spirits, right?" Anna suggested. They agreed.

This little light of mine, I'm gonna let it shine
This little light of mine, I'm gonna let it shine
This little light of mine, I'm gonna let it shine
Let it shine, let it shine
Let it shine!

While they sang to pass the time, I started noticing the environment. The road was a two-lane expressway, with only one lane for one direction. I looked out of the window to my right to appreciate the rural beauty of West Virginia. Occasionally, there would be a singular, quaint house, surrounded by nothing but land. There were still some houses that illegally waved the former United States flag.

In the background, the rounded Appalachian Mountains loomed as its ancient magnificence awed me. Since it was Autumn, the trees surrounding the mountains blazed with colors. The leaves were a cacophony of gold, red, and orange. The Fall was and still is my favorite season. At any other time, I would have been completely in love with the setting, but that day I was focused on us arriving to our destination. To distract myself, I looked at Rafael. His face encompassed more beauty than any art created by Michelangelo or Leonardo da Vinci. In fact, Rafael was art itself. He was molded and sculpted by God to portray and signify infinite love and unending commitment.

"Danny, stop drooling over me and pay attention to the map." Rafael laughed.

"I'm sorry I just got distracted. But let's be real, do you really think I know how to read a map?"

"You've used maps before, right?" Raf questioned.

"I've used a GPS, but I've never used an actual, physical map before. It's... odd." I said.

"God. I'd give anything to go back to the days where my biggest problem was trying to use a GPS while traveling under a bridge."

"The old days... it's not so long ago."

"But yet it feels that way." Rafael pondered while driving. The song that Libby sung still left us feeling nostalgic. "Who would have thought as a nation, we'd undergo the transformation of a republic to a dystopian nightmare? Who would have thought we'd be in a civil war against this dictatorial government? Who would've thought we'd be responsible for so many deaths...?"

"Let's not focus on the negatives. Let's think about something more positive. It may sound unromantic to talk about in a van, but we should discuss it." I smiled. "Here, in Freedonia, it's illegal to have a relationship like ours. But when we settle down out west, we should get married."

Rafael diverted his attention off the road briefly and then smiled when he turned his head back to pay attention again. "I would love nothing more than to call you my husband. What kind of wedding do you have in mind?"

"Well, it would be a blend of both traditional and non-traditional. It would be in a Baptist church."

"No, it should be a Catholic church." He quipped.

"Baptist."

"Catholic."

"Baptist."

"Catholic."

"Jesus, are you two trying to start another holy war?" Johannes shouted from the back, making us blush when we realized he heard us.

"Anyways, I'd be in all-black with a white tie. You'd have a white tuxedo and a black bowtie. We'd both have red roses pinned to our suits. Johannes, Anna, Libby, Josh, and maybe some of your sorority friends and frat buddies could be part of our wedding party. Of course, my family doesn't approve, so they won't be there. But we will find your parents, Raf, and they'll be there as well. It will be the most romantic spectacle of the century. Our first dance at the reception should be to *Let it be me* by Roberta Flack."

"Or *Dreaming of you* by Selena." Rafael mused.

"It can be anything, as long it's a nice, slow song where we can just enjoy the moment and enjoy each other." I said.

"And the honeymoon?" Rafael grinned and raised his eyebrows.

"You and me on a beach... alone." I smirked.

He giggled. "Shut up and let me drive." He continued to steer the wheel. I guided him with the map. I'm still amazed how I was able to read it. Soon, the road turned into gravel, causing us to go through a bumpy ride. Then once Rafael made a turn, the gravel transformed into a red dirt road. The dirt somehow reminded me of clay. We had to drive through the forest with golden leaves gently falling everywhere. Suddenly, the road stopped at this vast property. There was a small house. Slightly further from the house, there was a decently sized recreational vehicle, otherwise known as an R.V. It was an odd and interesting sight. We had seemingly reached our destination. We all slowly and carefully got out of the van. We stretched as we all had been in the car for hours. Libby then walked up to the porch, which had two rocking chairs. Libby knocked on the door three times, as instructed. An older white woman opened the door.

"The birds may enter my nest." She said, knowing who we were. That saying was to let us know that for now, we were safe.

LIBBY

Mrs. Ewing granted us permission to enter. Her house resembled a small cabin. The entryway led directly into her living room where the walls were covered with wood. The wooden planks also hung a multitude of photos. There were portraits that were significantly aged, but there were also pictures that were relatively new. In all of the pictures, however, there was a constant theme of love for family and friends. To tie in the country aesthetic, she had a brick fireplace stuffed with thick hunks of logs. The ashes suggested that it was recently used. The furniture was noticeably older, but it was kept in nice condition.

"Thank you for allowing us to stay in your home again, Mrs. Ewing." I said.

"It's no issue, it's our Christian duty to help weary travelers. And besides if y'all can help us regain freedom, then staying here for a couple of days is the least I can do, for my son, for 8Crow, and our home." She replied in such a sweet, charming voice. Her gray hair was styled in an upwards fashion. Speaking of fashion, her white shirt consisted of blue flowers, which matched her blue pants. It was clear she dressed up in the expectation of company. "Now, why don't y'all get your bags and set them in the rooms I've prepared for y'all. The rooms are down the hall. The first room is for the boys and the second room is for the girls. Y'all can use the bathrooms that are co-joined to the rooms to wash up while I cook supper for y'all. My husband and my son should arrive beforehand." She led me and Anna to our rooms while the boys gathered all of our things. The room was cozy with two twin beds that were covered in handmade quilts. I took in the alluring energy of the place.

"I've heard of southern hospitality," Anna started off while charging her rechargeable batteries that her brother gave to her with her bag. "But wow, Mrs. Ewing seems so nice and..."

"The hospitality is throwing you off, huh?" I chuckled as I sat upon one of the beds.

"No...yeah." She laughed. "I guess I'm not used to people being this nice, especially after the past few years. Wait, is West Virginia even southern?"

"That's a complicated issue. But I personally don't care. At least we have a bed to sleep in for the next few nights. Then we can keep going to California."

"It would be nice to be home again." Anna got lost in her memories of her city before the Burning of L.A.

"It would be nice to see my mother again." I said. "I still can't believe that my mama is behind 8Crow."

"I can. You see her as your mother. I see her as the no-nonsense politician that dared to challenge Ace and the rest of the Republican party. She's fearless. She had to be to survive the political sphere. But she's also empathetic to people's pain. That's why she had to create this rebellion."

"And now we're rebels." I groaned.

"So, what? At least we know we're on the right side of history."

"But will history see it that way? As Danny and I have learned as history majors, history is written by the victors."

"Then we'll just have to claim victory. But we'll do that after we get cleaned up. I feel absolutely disgusting."

"You can go ahead and shower first, I'll go after you since it'll take a while to clean my hair. The boys can wait!" I laughed.

"Thanks, Libby. And in case I forgot, which I'm sure I have, given recent events, I want to thank you for helping to save my brother."

"He's one of my best friends just like you are. We're in this together, Anna."

"Till the end." Anna smiled. She took a shower first, much to the chagrin of the guys. Soon, it was my turn to take a shower. To this day, I can't recall a better shower as the water was boiling hot. I inhaled the steam, clearing my sinuses. I used the clean bar of soap that Mrs. Ewing offered. I covered my entire body with suds and cleansed the filth that had accumulated. The two-in-one shampoo and conditioner (while it wasn't particularly black girl friendly) fared pretty well. Once I finished drying off, I got into some fresh clothes. I was completely clean. While the rest of the boys washed up, Anna and I relaxed and talked as we barely had time to hang out together alone.

"So... you and Josh, huh?" I nudged.

"What about him?" She asked.

"I saw that moment where you had to say goodbye. I saw how he caressed you. Admit it. You like him."

She blushed. "How can I not? He's so well-mannered and he knows how to command attention."

"You're forgetting his jawline." I giggled.

"Oh my gosh, it's so sharp, it could cut diamonds! And his eyes... but we could never work out right now. He has an important job to do and we're going home. Maybe once this civil war is over, it could happen."

"I get it." I said. "The timing is awful." As soon as I mentioned timing, Mrs. Ewing announced that dinner was ready. I will admit the smell was heavenly. I had to walk through the kitchen to enter the dining room which had a certain antiquated visual aspect to it. I could tell that this room and the dining table was present at every important event in the past 100 years. At the head of the table was Mr. Ewing. He had a blue-plaid shirt tucked into his belted blue jeans. He had completely white hair and a trimmed beard and glasses. His son, which Hasan told us was named Lionel, was sitting next to him in a t-shirt and cargo shorts. He appeared to be close to 30 years of age.

"Y'all are gonna have to excuse me and Lionel." Mr. Ewing said with a gruff voice. "We had to get the Vacation Permit, so Lionel can transport y'all without detection."

"We understand." I said, sitting myself next to Mrs. Ewing's chair. I noticed how the table was set beautifully, with champagne-colored table-cloths and maroon placemats.

"It's quite an ingenious plan that Hasan told us to follow, for us to be hidden under the guise that we're on a family vacation in an R.V." Johannes said as he sat next to his sister.

"It's the only way to completely avoid the military checkpoints." Lionel replied. "If an officer stopped me for a routine check and I show them my permit, then we're good."

"Okay now!" Mrs. Ewing walked in holding plates of foods, serving us individually at the table. "I made chicken-fried steak with mashed potatoes and gravy along with biscuits and sweet tea."

I gasped in astonishment since we had not had a hearty meal like that in over a year. The divine smell entered my nostrils and tingled the senses, making me salivate in anticipation. "Mrs. Ewing... this meal... we can't possibly accept this... this must have wreaked havoc on your social credit!" I stammered.

"Puedo aceptarlo!" Rafael smiled and stared at the food.

"It's okay!" Mr. Ewing responded. "We don't hardly have company over anymore for dinner, especially since the Change."

"The Change?" Danny said, already cutting into the meat on his plate.

"That's what we call it around here." Lionel said. "The Change was when we transitioned from the United States to Freedonia."

"That makes sense." Danny shrugged, already cutting into the meat on his plate.

"Hold on now, we haven't said grace!" Mrs. Ewing exclaimed after serving her husband last. She sat down and bowed her head, holding her hands out for us to grab. We followed suit.

"Our Father, who art in Heaven, hollowed be thy name, thy kingdom come, thy will be done, on earth as it is in Heaven. Give us this day, our daily bread and forgive our debts as we forgive our debtors. Lead us not into temptation but deliver us from all that is evil. For Yours is the Kingdom, the Power and the Glory, forever Amen!" Mr. Ewing prayed aloud.

"Amen." We all replied.

I wish I could say we were more mindful of our manners, however the Ewings seemed to have understood that we were hungry. All we had had to eat that entire week beforehand was stolen food from gas stations. All senses of my taste buds were delighted. The chicken-fried steak had intense umami flavor. The creaminess of the mashed potatoes was extremely satisfying. The biscuits were nice and buttery; the gravy was a perfect companion to all of the dishes.

"Mrs. Ewing, this dinner is exquisite." I said after washing my food down by sipping on a glass of the sinfully delicious iced sweet tea.

"I'm glad you enjoyed it!" She beamed.

"Yeah, Ma always makes the best food." Lionel commented. "It's the best meal we've had in months. Our social credit ain't the best, so a good meal is far and in-between."

In trying to make conversation, Danny asked Lionel a question. "I'm curious, how did all of y'all get involved in 8Crow? I don't mean to pry, but it is interesting to see a whole family be a part of a rebel organization. The five of us got pulled in, but I just wanna know your stories."

"Well, I have a personal reason. Ya see, I am an addict, an opioid addict. Don't feel sorry, it's sorta common around these parts here." Lionel responded. "It's still my hardest battle to fight. Even now, after being sober for several months, I still have to fight against the cravings. I needed to join something that could take my mind off of the pills that I so desperately wanted but could no longer afford. It seems extreme that I joined a rebel organization as a distraction, but that's what I did."

"If you mind me asking, how did the addiction start?" Anna questioned.

"I was prescribed pain pills after a coal mining accident. Then I became dependent on them."

"I'm sorry for such an insensitive question." Anna apologized.

"No, it's okay! I need to learn not to be ashamed of the circumstances I was given. The real question is why did my parents join? That's something I wanna know too." Lionel stared at his dad. "I'm happy for the support, but you ain't never explained why."

After a beat of silence, Mrs. Ewing finally spoke up, stammering. "We joined because we felt...guilty."

"I've explained to y'all, it's not your fault I have an addiction." Lionel said.

"That's not why we feel guilty." Mr. Ewing responded. "Lionel, you already should know the answer, why we feel responsible for this government."

It seemed to click in Lionel's head. But the rest of us still felt left in the dark.

"What do you mean?" I asked.

"We voted for Ace and Braun." Mrs. Ewing explained. When she broke the news, there was a slight shock from the five of us. Here was a family who seemed so kind and so gracious, yet they voted for someone that represented the antithesis of what we believed in. Memories of the toxic political environment of the previous government surfaced. The racist, sexist, homophobic, transphobic, and xenophobic ideas that permeated the Ace Base and the Nationalists struck fear into our hearts again. Not to mention, if Ace was never voted into office, Braun would have never wielded power after his death.

"Were you... Nationalists before?" Johannes gritted his teeth.

"Oh Heavens, no! We were just pure, red-blooded Republicans." Mrs. Ewing defended herself.

"Well, that somewhat makes it better." Rafael muttered.

"It's just surprising." I said. "You don't seem...bigoted."

"Las apariencias engañan..." Rafael whispered.

Danny and I locked eyes and peered into each other's soul to see that we were both screaming internally.

"I didn't like the things he said about women, of course. But as an Evangelical, I could not comfortably allow progressive laws on things like abortion and same-sex marriage to pass." When she said that, Rafael and Danny shifted in their seats. She continued. "Yes, I had my doubt on Ace's commitment to God, but I thought he could push religion back to the lives of American families. See, I feared that religion was becoming unimportant."

"You were wrong on that. There are still Christians out there, but they felt they had been abandoned by the organization within the church." Danny started off. "If you want to pull more people to Christ, give them the message of love because that's something everyone can relate to. Love is love, just like God is love. I'm gay, Mrs. Ewing. I plan to marry Rafael one day and I still have my faith in Jesus. Yes, homosexual relations might be interpreted as a sin by some people, but so is your outfit. Leviticus 19:19 mentions that you should not wear clothing woven with two kinds of materials. No sin is greater than another in the eyes of God."

"Except murder maybe..." Johannes chuckled, sipping on his tea.

"But that doesn't matter because if you actively believe in Jesus, you will be saved, you and your whole household. Acts 16:31." Danny finished.

"Well, the reason I voted for Ace was because he promised to bring back the coal industry by rolling back regulations." Mr. Ewing said. "Ya see, my family has been mining coal for generations and then we all lost our jobs under the president before him? It didn't feel right to not vote for someone that could have helped the coal mining industry. Ace made us, the silent majority, feel heard. But if we're being honest, our biggest reason was that it felt like the country was changing too fast."

"Like the changes in demographics?" Rafael rebutted. "Say, like an increase of immigrants?"

"Yes." Mr. Ewing responded.

"We had no clue that Braun would turn around and infringe on our rights." Mrs. Ewing said.

"Just like some Evangelicals and some Republicans tried to infringe on ours?" Danny raised his eyebrow. "It was okay if that happened to others. But once you realized it could happen to you too, that was the bridge too far?"

"Listen. I am ashamed that I helped bring the Freedonian government along, but by joining 8Crow, I remembered our motto: Mountaineers are always free. I realized that everyone should be free to make whatever choices. That's why me and the misses joined the cause. Plus, those Nationalists gave us Republicans a bad name." Mr. Ewing articulated. "All that matters now is that we're in this fight together."

There was a silent agreement.

"So...anybody want moonshine?" Mr. Ewing asked.

Johannes immediately jumped up. "I sure as hell could use a drink after the recent bullshit I went through. Lead the way, sir!"

Once they both left the table, the rest continued eating. After the meal was over, I stayed to help Mrs. Ewing clean up. I had one final statement to say to her.

"I understand that change is scary, but nothing remains the same. Learn to embrace the new, no matter how foreign it may seem."

She understood. Once I finished helping her with cleaning the dishes, I laid in the bed they provided me and I rested without fear.

JOHANNES

Mr. Ewing had some strong ass alcohol; I'll tell you that much. I only did two shots as my tolerance was low and the shit burned like hell. But Mr. Ewing was a fun drinking buddy. He told old stories about deer hunting. It wasn't my scene, but I appreciated the conversation. However, dark thoughts swirled around in my mind while drunk, so I wrote down a poem after I asked for paper and pen. It went like this:

Man or Monster.

Am I a demon or am I civilized?

I don't know,

But I wouldn't be surprised

If everybody had both inside.

Man or Monster.

How can I continue

When the sin of my blood is on the menu,

On the menu of righteousness.

Am I righteous?

If I do what I have to do?

Am I a devil if I enjoy seeing blood pierce through?

Man or Monster.

Josh

Riding in the limo was quite an experience, at least for me during that time. The luxury was unprecedented. As Brune and I traveled towards the capital, I noticed the lifestyle of the people who were in charge. While in the limo, Brune and I were offered champagne. We both refused, or rather I made Brune refuse the offer. I did not want either of us to be inebriated. The flooring of the car was velvet, an enormously expensive material for the times. The details of the limo were entrenched in the finer things, befitting for a royal. I must say, it was quite astonishing to see government officials living way outside the economic norms of the average citizen. The partition was up since it was customary for the plebeians to lower their interaction with the upper-class. The reflective surface of the partition showed me in my new style, masquerading as Ryan Oakland and I was disgusted with myself. I had, before the Fall of America, lived a privileged life. Quite frankly, I was rich, white, from Charleston and I never knew the struggles of the so-called everyday man. But when things changed, and I had to struggle to survive with my fellow soldiers, I realized that all of the things I owned were superfluous. Other people deserved more than I did.

I guess that's another reason I joined 8Crow. I felt that I didn't deserve to live comfortably with a high social credit while I saw others making it day by day, with hunger pangs and thirst disrupting their lives. Looking at the grandness of the interior of the limo just made me feel slightly guilty that even though I was undercover, I would still enjoy the luxury items that were there. I made a promise to myself to never get too drunk with power. I did not want to become like Ace, or even worse, become like Braun. She was calculating and cold, much like brutal leaders are known to be. Shivering at the thought, I turned to the monitor screen to watch one of the movies that were personally rated and certified by the Çaé to take my mind off my swirling thoughts and emotions. *The Wise One* was a movie about how a younger Braun saw the injustices in the United States and sought to correct it. It was a deep fabrication of what happened, and it made it seem like her rise to power was necessary to improve the lives of the common people. It was propaganda, plain and simple. If I were not a part of 8Crow and I didn't know anyone connected to the rebels, I might have believed the movie.

It showed me how good Braun was at selling lies. She was clever, slick, and cunning. She was no ordinary villain. She was everything that Ace was not. Ace played checkers, while she played chess and she had used the former president as a pawn. She had us all fooled before and I became determined to never be fooled by her again. Watching the movie diverted my attention even though I rolled my eyes a lot. Brune just fell asleep during the ride. His snore would sometimes be loud enough that I laughed at how funny it sounded. He sounded like a cartoon duck blubbering in a quacking noise.

I looked off out of the window and I noticed that we were finally in Philadelphia. It was about 7 o'clock in the evening and the nightlife was just beginning. Already, I could see key differences in the Capital versus any of the other cities that I visited as an 8Crow officer. In Philadelphia, the people were more affluent and they were able to afford wearing the latest fashion trends. They wore office attire and they were often in the colors of the flag. Some of the women wore black sheath dresses, while others wore white business suits with large shoulder pads and red heels. The majority of the men wore white button-up shirts with black ties and red suits. It was odd if you considered the dressing styles before, but those were the fashions of the time. I nudged Brune to wake up. He was startled, but he quickly arose and cleaned the drool off of his face with his sleeve.

"Woah, we're here, huh?" He said in amazement as he looked out the window while we were stopped at a traffic light. He observed the down-town area as people rushed past. The lights of the advertisements covering the cityscape made up for the sun's disappearance. It was another world. Outside the city, people were starving, and people were homeless. Within the city, however, the people were working for the Çaé, either directly or indirectly. Because of that fact, many had the right amount of social credit not just to survive but thrive. It made me angry. Nay, it made me furious. I thought about the people in D.C. who had to figure how they could stretch food to last for several days. I thought about the people in Richmond who had their homes repossessed by the government if they couldn't afford it. But in the Capital, people were fine. There was such a large disparity of wealth that it could have given anyone emotional whiplash if they saw what I saw.

Finally, we drove up towards the gates of the Capital Building, formally known as the Aurea Palace. The gates of the palace were made in gold, blocking the commoners out in style. The limo drove into the front of the palace, making Brune and I gawk at the greatest example of hedonism in architecture. Even though the Capital Building used to be the Philadelphia Museum of Art, the home of the Çaé became the epitome of opulence. The Aurea Palace was bathed in warm golden lights.

If I could describe the place, it was a lesson in perfect symmetry. The main pantheon had branches that extended into an opposing L-shape that housed the other two pantheons which faced each other at the end of each branch. The stairs leading up towards the Capital were larger-than-life, making you literally lose your breath by the time you reached the enormous courtyard. In the center of the courtyard, there was a gigantic fountain with a bronze statue of Çaé Braun placed atop. The exterior design of the building seemed to have taken inspiration from both the Ancient Greeks and Romans, resulting in a Neo-Classical design. The large and imposing columns of each entrance were of the Ionic Order and the Entablature were meticulously carved to command awe and respect.

While Brune and I were equally astonished, we quickly remembered our mission and we assumed our roles with Brune as my assistant Wesley Morehouse; I became Ryan Oakland once more. A servant of the Capital Building opened our limo door and a female employee was sent to show us around Aurea Palace. The grand entrance set the tone for the interior of the building. Some of the finest works of art greeted visitors. But instead of people standing around to gaze at the art, people moved about in a fast pace, busy with the work of upholding the state. The woman guided us through a large portion of the palace. The Capital was both a home and a workplace. The higher-ranking officials lived and breathed inside the palace. Even though the place no longer had an open floor plan because of recent renovations, it displayed more workspaces with rooms to sleep. However, it was still spacious enough.

The employee showed me and my partner our adjoining rooms. The rooms obviously used to be to be a gallery, with a new wall put up to create the separation. They were beautifully decorated and furnished. The beds looked extremely comfortable and there were gorgeous paintings on the wall with colors that were so vibrant they appeared to leap off. The woman implored us to continue our tour of the palace. We walked past people rushing through the halls, hurrying to complete their work. We were finally escorted to the East Wing, where my office was supposed to be. I was nervous since not only would I have to act like Ryan Oakland, I would have to work like him too. In the hall, we walked up to a door and inside there was a mini suite. Immediately, to the right of the room, Brune was supposed to work there and impersonate Wesley at his own desk. The curtains were open to let light into this part of the room. The wallpaper was adorned with golden decorations. To the left of the desk was another door which led to my office. It was expansive and contained two couches and a large desk. The windows ahead were draped in golden curtains and the sights of the water showed the rippling waves glistening under the lights of the city and the moon.

"The Çaé will arrive soon specifically to meet you before she goes to New York City to attend to business." The employee said standing next to Brune in front of the door.

It became clear that it was time to fully personify Ryan Oakland. "Excellent. You can leave me be, Miss. Whatever-your-name-is." Ashamed, she bowed and walked away. While it was harsh, I had to sound like the man I was impersonating and quite frankly, the real Ryan was an arrogant son-of-a-bitch. "Wesley, I'll let you know when you're needed. And don't forget to close the door on your way out." Brune nodded and shut the door. I sighed, wrecked with anxiety about the difficulty of the assignment. I adjusted my tie and looked over to my desk to see a pile of papers stacked on top. I decided to get a head start at my "work" while also taking mental notes of things that would be helpful to the resistance. While I read the files, my eyebrows furrowed. I can't get into what was within all of the papers as some are still classified today, but what I saw was shocking. I got so caught in the reading, I was almost startled when someone barged through the door. I looked to see who it was: it was Braun.

I stood up in a commanding stance and saluted, even though it pained me to do so. "Hail Çaé Braun and All Hail Freedonia!"

"At ease." She replied in a surprisingly calm demeanor. Her posture was not at all how I expected. I remember thinking that she would be way more forceful, but that was her power. She commanded respect by giving an air of strength and docility. "I just came to see how you were adjusting to your new position, but I see you are already hard at work."

"Well, I always like to get a head start on your agenda. Can I just say, I am honored that you choose me to help make your vision for the great nation of Freedonia?" I lied.

"I knew you would be a good addition in the government." She said. "After I heard about that horrendous fight in D.C. and how you tried to hold on, I just knew you would be a loyal R.O.C."

"The rebels were out of control. If it were up to me, I would have tortured and killed every last one." Saying that churned my stomach, but I had to stick to the assignment.

She smirked. "Personally, I would have done worse, but I like your attitude. The rebels are gaining too much power because people still believe that absolute freedom is the best way to live life. They don't realize that someone needs to be in control of their mundane lives. I've always said that too much freedom can be a bad thing. Which gives me a good lead-in into what I really want to talk about. The fight in D.C. had me thinking about what could further limit people's thinking about independence. I made a list of books I want you to burn and censor all around the country. I do not have the time to engage myself in trivial matters, so I will leave you to command that order." She gave me a list and I hid my anger.

"Of course, Çaé Braun. I will do whatever is necessary, so nobody will get the bright idea of hopefulness. It is too dangerous, as it will lead them to fight with the rebel group."

"Good. People need to know that I am in control forevermore. Free-donia will be the greatest nation on earth and the opposition needs to be crushed." Her face contorted into the stern look of power, but she quickly became "nice" again. "Anyways, I must be going to New York City. Get this done."

"Of course, my Leader." I saluted once more. "Hail Çaé Braun and All Hail Freedonia."

She immediately left, and I shuddered at my actions, even though it was an act. But even though I was just acting, the laws I had to implement were real. I looked over the list she gave, and I was stunned. I hit a buzzer on my desk to get Brune in the office. He came in and waited for me to say something.

"Wesley, do you want coffee?" I said, making him remember our secret code that we prepared. It was a code to check the office for hidden bugs or security cameras. We did that thoroughly and briefly. Once we found no signs of any listening devices, we huddled together and whispered quietly.

"How was the meeting with the Çaé?" Brune asked.

"She scares me, Brune. I mean, she is worse than I imagined. She said that too much freedom is a bad thing and that she would do worse than just kill and torture rebels."

"What's that paper?" He responded, acquiring to the list I was holding in my hands.

"She wants me to order the burning and censoring of these books across the country." I handed it to him, so he could read it.

His face expressed emotions of confoundment. "She... wants to get rid of some of the greatest literature. She intends to destroy books like 'The Jungle' and '1984.' She even wants to burn 'Fahrenheit 451!'"

"I know! The irony is not lost on me..."

"She wants to burn the Quran and other religious texts not pertaining to Christianity. She even wants the Bible changed into a Çaé Braun Version by taking stuff out. Josh, we can't do this."

"I know, this is something I don't want to do, but we have to follow our orders from Hasan. We have to do our job, no matter what. As Ryan Oakland, the R.O.C. of Philadelphia, I have to order you to send the message across the country. Remember who we are really doing this for."

He gulped and nodded. He took the paper and before he opened the door to leave, he said "I hope you know what you're doing."

"I hope so too." I somberly replied.

He shut the door and I returned to my desk. I swiveled my chair around and I stared out into the city. A million thoughts ran through my mind that night, but one voice was clear: Josh, what the hell have you gotten yourself into?

RAFAEL

"Danny, we've known each other for quite some time. And I know you like me."

"You're trying to make me blush, huh?"

"No, I've just been waiting for you to ask me out."

"This is just in; we now have the results."

"Hey, Spic!"

"Candidate Ace has won the election and is now preparing to give his speech to the audience."

"Every time I see that spot, I'm reminded that besides my friends, I can't trust anybody no more. Look at me! I've literally been scarred for life!"

"The D.A. has declined to charge the former L.A.P.D officers involved in the shooting of the beloved celebrity icon, Lumos..."

"Should've thought about that before coming to America!"

"Ace is finally gonna build a wall so people like you can't get in no more."

"MAMA!!! PAPA!!!! NOOOOO!"

"You have anger. You have hurt. You have despair hidden deep within your soul."

"People, you should give me a chance to explain for once! The Fake News Media has what I was saying all wrong!"

"OH MY GOD!! SOMEONE GET HELP!! THE PRESIDENT HAS BEEN SHOT!"

"Be quiet, you fucking piece of shit, you're gonna get what's coming to you."

"Look around! We're lost!"

"Ace has been officially pronounced dead."

"Ace is finally gonna build a wall so people like you can't get in no more."

"Justice for Ace! Blood and Soil!"

"I just know they had on red Alpha Tau Omega jackets."

"Johannes wake up!"

"Rafi, I won't let anyone hurt you. I promise."

"Hey, Spic!"

"MAMA!!! PAPA!!!! NOOOOO!"

"Be quiet, you fucking piece of shit, you're gonna get what's coming to you."

"I will help protect you from all harm or danger. That is my vow to you."

"Are those protestors with tiki torches?"

"May God be with us tonight as we fight for what is right! No more Democrats versus Republicans. We all have a new enemy, a common one. It is the Nationalists. Let's remember who to point our weapons towards. Understand?"

"So, this is how another civil war begins..."

"I've come to speak to you, the people, on this horrendous day."

"Hey, Spic!"

"Our nation has come under attack by violent criminals."

"Ace is finally gonna build a wall so people like you can't get in no more."

"It was not terrorists from other countries that have attacked us, but our own brothers and sisters."

"Be quiet, you fucking piece of shit, you're gonna get what's coming to you."

"It is clear that the great American experiment has failed."

"Hey, Spic!"

"Ace is finally gonna build a wall so people like you can't get in no more."

"Be quiet, you fucking piece of shit, you're gonna get what's coming to you."

"HEY SPIC!"

"ACE IS FINALLY GONNA BUILD A WALL SO PEOPLE LIKE YOU CAN'T GET IN NO MORE."

"BE QUIET, YOU FUCKING PIECE OF SHIT, YOU'RE GONNA GET WHAT'S COMING TO YOU."

"HEYSPICACEISFINALLYGONNABUILDAWALLSOPEOPLE-LIKEYOUCAN'TGETINNOMOREBEQUIETYOUFUCKINGPIECE-OFSHITYOU'REGONNAGETWHAT'SCOMINGTOYOU."

"All hail Freedonia."

I gasped aloud as I jolted upwards, escaping my never-ending nightmare. I accidently awoke Danny as I began sobbing.

"Raf, did you have that nightmare again?" Danny asked in his most calming voice, despite the fact that his sleep was interrupted in the middle of the night. He removed the covers and sat upright to place his arms around me. My tears streamed down my cheeks as I looked out of a moonlit window.

"All I see is them, violating me every night... and no matter what I do, I can't escape it. All I can think about are those boys who tried to kill me." I touched my scar that was still visible on my cheeks. "Even though I've been in worse danger since then... I don't think I felt more scared than I did that night. I've been in battle and I had to face death many times. Mi madre y padre... watching them being taken away hurt me to my core. Yet still, all I see, even now, is the hatred in their eyes. Eyes as dark and cold as a demon. And they laughed. The indelible laughter is seared in my memory. I can't get any fucking peace. When I look in the mirror and see my scar, they're there. When I'm alone, they're there. When I close my eyes, every night, they're always there. I'm tired, Danny! I'm tired of always being reminded of that horrible night. I wish I could forget, but I can't! They are there. And they won't ever leave. And that's the worst fate of all...knowing that they will never leave."

"Raf, I don't know how to help, but I promise that I'll be here to listen to you. Whenever you need to talk about it, I'm here. I can't tell you not to think about them, but what I can say is that you are better than them. They're lowlife scum. And wherever they are, I hope they go through hell, because you are a slice of heaven and they messed with the wrong angel." He continued to stroke my hair to calm me down. "When we get to California, we'll both get some mental health specialists. I think we need it."

I softly smiled. "You always know how to calm me. I'm sorry for waking you up."

"It's okay. Let's go back to sleep, we have a long trip in the morning. You can lay in my arms if you want."

I laid back down and felt the warmth of his body and the warmth of his love as he wrapped his arms around my chest. It took a while, but I finally closed my eyes again.

"Danny, we've known each other for quite some time. And I know you like me..."

ANNA

The few days that I spent at the Ewings were relaxing. I remember saying to myself, "finally, a break from the madness." It was a necessary mental pause, considering everything that happened earlier. I was able to be without my cochlear for at least a day and meditate. Unfortunately, those days couldn't last forever. We had to move on.

I got up bright and early on the last day in order to pack up my belongings. I passed by Rafael, who seemed exhausted. Libby helped Mrs. Ewing make breakfast and Danny was in the shower singing some of Broadway's greatest hits. After I finished shoving my clothes into my bag, I accidently bumped into Mr. Ewing in their living room.

"Oh, I'm sorry, Mr. Ewing. I was just on my way to the R.V. to store my bag." I apologized.

"No, problem, thank you for attempting to be on time, unlike our dear R.V." He grunted in his gruff voice.

"Is there anything wrong?" I asked.

"Nothing that me and Lionel can't fix. Y'all will be on schedule."

"Again, thank you for allowing us to stay here and for letting your son take us on this journey."

"We're just trying to do the right thing this time around. I'll take your bag to the vehicle." He timidly smiled.

"Thanks." I handed off my bag and leaned against the door. I watched Mr. Ewing through the screen door, and I happened to see Johannes' shoe as he crossed his legs. Curious as to what he was up to, I walked out onto the porch. Johannes was sitting on a tan wooden rocking chair, drinking orange juice from a glass. He set it on the small table next to the chair once he noticed me.

"Hey, Anna." He said dryly.

"Are you ready to go?" I asked as I leaned on the column that supported the roof of the porch.

"Yeah, my stuff is already in the R.V. I'm just biding my time right now." He replied, intertwining his fingers as he laid his elbow on the arm of the rocking chair. He looked...different, that I can definitely remember. He was less fashionable than usual, only wearing a gray sweatshirt and black sweatpants. He had a 5 o'clock shadow, his hair was ragged, and his gray hair dye was starting to fade away. Also, his bandana, his statement fashion piece, was nowhere to be found. He had changed tremendously, and I could tell.

"Are you okay, Johannes?" I emotively questioned.

"Yeah." He sighed. "I'm trying to nurse my hangover. I drank too much last night, but Mr. Ewing is actually a cool guy, surprisingly. You know, he once hunted down a- "

"Johannes. You know that's not what I mean. Answer me: are you okay?"

His piercing eyes started to water. "Anna..."

"I'm your sister, I can tell when something is wrong with you. You've been distant, strange, and you've been drinking every night since we've been here. You're not okay, are you?"

There was a long pause of silence and a single tear came out of Johannes' eye. He took a breath and looked in the distance, trying to focus on something other the pain that resided inside of him. "No, I'm not okay."

I sat in the rocking chair that was on the opposite side so I could pay attention to what he had to say. "Talk to me."

"Anna, you wouldn't get it." He scoffed.

"Maybe not, but it helps for you to get your feelings off of your chest."

"I don't even understand my own emotions. I feel…"

"Feel, what?"

"Conflicted. I feel emotionally conflicted right now and so many other thoughts have been swirling in my head. Remember when Rafael and I got separated from the rest of the gang, after the anti-Ace March?"

"How could I forget? I was so worried about you two, and when you came back…" I shifted.

"After killing a man. That's what you were gonna say." He took a sip from his glass and continued onwards. "After that night, all I could think about was how terrified I was. It's the only way I could justify the murder."

"It wasn't murder, Johannes, it was self-defense."

"Try convincing the F.I.I. of that. Or better yet, try convincing me." He made his elbows go upright on the arms of the rocking chair and placed his chin on his knuckles.

"You've told me yourself. He was shooting at you, and then when he ran out of bullets, he pulled out a knife while on that elevator. You had to act quickly. You took his knife and killed him before he killed you."

"But why did I have to slit his throat?" Johannes winced at the memory.

"You wanted to make sure he was dead. It's simple."

"No, it's not that simple. I killed that man along with God knows how many at the Battle of D.C. back then. When I think about how many lives I've ruined… It's not just about killing people; it's knowing that you have effectively destroyed the lives that they were connected to. I've not only harmed the ones I've killed, but I've harmed dozens of others. Countless dozens... God, what kind of man am I?" He closed his eyes to catch his breath, seemingly to prevent from breaking down.

"The person that you killed in the elevator and the people you killed in the Battle of D.C., they wanted to hurt you first." I assured him.

"But that's the thing, I had no intention of hurting them. Never did I want to hurt them."

I noticed something was off. He didn't mention his most recent killing: The Investigator that arrested and tortured him. "You've talked about killing the others, but not about the F.I.I. officer. Why?"

When I brought him up, his demeanor changed ever so slightly. It was a blink-or-you miss it moment. His voice changed a tad. "He made things more...complicated." He said.

"Complicated?"

"Yes...complicated." He had an odd glimmer in his eyes, one that I had never seen at that point before in my entire life as his sister. "As guilty as I feel for killing the others, I have no remorse for *Joe*." He said his name was such distain as if it was the most vulgar word in the world. But honestly, I remember being surprised by his different reaction towards the killing of Joe and the killing of the others.

"You have *zero* remorse?" I questioned. "That doesn't make sense. You clearly feel remorse for killing people."

"Not only did I not have any remorse killing Joe, but I enjoyed it." He had a sinister grin.

"What?"

"I feel guilty for killing the others because I never wanted to harm them. But after he tortured me, I wanted him to feel what I felt, Anna. I can't explain it, truly I can't. But when I shot him, watching him bleed and then shooting his brains out was somehow a pleasure. I wanted him to die brutally. My issue is that I didn't have time to slowly kill him and enjoy it even more. That's sick, isn't it? I've become a monster. But yet, I feel guilty about not feeling guilty." He reverted back to his old behavior, slinking back in the rocking chair, gulping in his remembrance. "God, who've I become? Look at me, throughout all of this mess. The person I'm fighting with the most is myself."

"Johannes..."

Suddenly, the doors swung open. There was Danny, oblivious to our conversation.

"Y'all ready to go?" He asked with a bright smile, carrying his backpack. I could tell he was anxious to go to California and hopefully gain a fresh start away from the rule of the Çaé.

"Yeah, I'm ready." Johannes said, getting up. He headed to the R.V. without looking back. Danny followed. Libby and Rafael were next as they came out together, talking about how nice the Ewings were. And speaking of the Ewings, the parents kissed their boy, Lionel, on the cheek. They hugged him hard and the father shed a tear as they had no idea how long it would be until they saw their son again. I just sat in that rocking chair until it was time to go as I realized that my brother, once so carefree, had now changed beyond recognition.

APRIL

It had been a long day and Charles had returned from leading several battles. In the conference room, several of the other leaders and I gathered together to greet him back. We celebrated his safe arrival. We were scattered across the room, but Charles Grant, Liam McPherson (the Republican senator), and I were talking in our own group.

"We're glad you made it back." Liam said. "I know Idaho was a hell of risk to take."

"It was an important one. If Idaho fell, our chances of taking Montana would be moot." Charles replied.

"Montana is also a big risk." I stated. "It's a state with wide terrain and their Nationalist militia is a force to be reckoned with, are we sure we should take 8Crow out there?"

"Ma'am, Montana is sparsely populated." Charles assured me. 'While their militia and the Freedonian army are good, they're not a match for us."

"Well, that is good to hear. I will advise that once we take Montana and the northern part of Wyoming, we start securing the territories we have amassed." I responded.

"That sounds good to me." Charles said. "The next thing to do is to gain some international allies. I'm sure the rest of the world views Freedonia as we viewed North Korea."

Liam came up with an idea. "Why not do a backchannel with the Prime Minister of Canada and the President of Mexico? If we can convince them to back us, we might be able to win this civil war!"

"I don't see Braun backing down that easily." I articulated. "The most she'll give is us having our own country, but I will never underestimate her, no matter whether her methods make sense or not."

"Well, since we're on the subject of the war, I wanted to thank you, General." Liam heartfully expressed to Charles. "I didn't get a chance to tell you, but my son was with you under your leadership in Idaho. I'm grateful that you were able to keep him safe."

"My soldiers mean the world to me, so I try my hardest to make sure my soldiers can come home." His voice choked up. "I'm sorry, I'm not usually this emotional."

"Charles, I must thank you too." I said as I gripped his hands for a handshake. "Without your military expertise, I don't know how this rebellion would have ever survived."

"The resistance would have gone on without me, April. It is you who gave the movement its fire." He wistfully smiled.

"Ahh, Angelique!" Liam expressively raised his voice in excitement. Angelique walked in holding some papers. I noticed she had a face of concern.

"Hello, Liam! I'm sorry to cut your party short but I need to borrow April and Charles, if that's okay with you." She politely uttered.

"Of course, I'll just tend to my work, I actually have quite a lot to finish. We'll catch up more later, alright?" He grinned. Liam left Charles and me behind.

"Are there any new developments, Angelique?" I asked.

"Yes, actually. Hasan would like to videoconference as soon as possible with the both of you. Apparently, he has some new information he needs to share immediately."

Curious as to what the news was, I asked Angelique to take us to a private room so that we could communicate with Hasan. The computer was already set for the conference, in fact it was he that waited for us. When he saw me sit down, he looked relieved.

"I'm glad to see you, ma'am." He gulped.

"Hasan, is everything alright?" I questioned.

"I actually don't know, ma'am." He said quietly, leaving me, Angelique, and Charles concerned. "I should explain further. As you know, Josh is acting as Oakland which means he's privy to certain information as the R.O.C. of Philadelphia. He came across intelligence that Braun is forcing or rather, enticing Nationalists to move from the West towards the South."

"What?" Angelique was confused.

"What is she getting out of this?" Charles quizzed.

"She's realizing that she can't win the west and she has to consolidate her power. She realized that it is impossible to rule a country this big. But also, she realized that it is impossible to control the Nationalists because they're still terrorizing people, forcing them to migrate to the West. She feels if she makes all of the Nationalist come back east, she can control them." Hasan explained.

"I still don't see why that's bad." Angelique said, unaware of the consequences.

"I do." I replied. "Did she promise what I think she did?"

"She promised the Nationalist could have the South as their own nation. It appeases them and allows her to only have direct control of the North and she can control the South as a puppet state. A state with whom she could trade goods."

"Does she not realize the implication this could have for the people of color in the South?" I grunted in frustration.

Hasan shook his head. "I don't think she cares. All she cares about is keeping her regime. I have notified and alerted all 8Crow people throughout the South to start moving people towards your position."

"With the Nationalists moving towards the East and the South, and people of color moving to the West... It'll be a Mass Exodus!" Charles exclaimed.

"And there's 33 million black people in the South alone." I added.

"We won't be able to save everyone." Hasan lamented. "It'll be a crisis, but we will try to save as many people as we can."

I sighed. "Thank you for keeping us posted."

"Of course. I will keep you updated." Hasan said before he signed off.

"Well," Angelique piped up as she made her way to the front of the room, "what can we do now?"

With a deep breath, I thought aloud, "We can start making provisions for the migrants who won't have places to stay, but other than that? There's nothing more we can do than wait."

DANNY

We traveled from West Virginia to Kentucky without much trouble. I enjoyed looking out of the window, watching the landscape transform and appreciated the vastness of the country. However, on this particular day, I spent most of it sleeping, trying to get some rest while bracing for the impact of potholes or sudden swerves. When I was awoken by Rafael, I briefly kissed him, and he smiled.

"Are you awake now, my sleeping ugly?" Rafael laughed as he threw a shirt for me to put on. The road was clearly bumpy as I almost fell out of bed.

"You're just jealous that I'm prettier than you!" I joked, hopping out of the top bunk.

"Vain much?" He retorted back.

"Me? Vain? Never!" I grinned. "I'm just telling the truth!"

"Oh really?" Rafael said, tongue-in-cheek.

"I am, however, a big enough man to admit that you are a very, very close second." I responded.

"A 'big enough' man? Wow, you are conceited." He smirked. We leaned in to kiss, but were stopped as the R.V. jolted when it halted.

"Hey guys, we're at a gas station now." Libby said as she walked from the front. "We can empty out our mess and get some gas."

"And also get some more food!" Johannes shouted. "I'm hungry. All we have left are corn chips."

"I swear, once we get to California, I'm going to become a vegetarian. All of this kind of food is making me bloat..." Anna muttered.

"Remember to pay with cash!" Lionel said when he left the driver's seat. "Paying with social credit can lead the government to track us down."

"Affirmative." Rafael answered. "You guys go ahead and buy the food and pay for the gas. I'll fill the tank and clean the mess. It's my turn anyways."

"Remember, we're on 'vacation.'" Lionel reminded us as we began stepping out of the vehicle.

"Hey Danny, if you can just buy some nachos, I'll be forever grateful." Rafael begged.

"Your wish is my command." I smiled.

"Love you."

"Love you too."

Walking out of the R.V., I noticed the gas station was dingy. It hadn't been upkept in a while because customers rarely came by at that point. The convenience store was small, and it was an off-white color that had grime and dirt of years past built upon each other. Once we went inside, the fluorescent lights flickered and gave the place a cool and dull undertone. The faint smell of urine lingered in the air. There was only one cashier there and it was clear that he did not want to be there. He was working with the greasy hot dogs on the rollers under the hot lights. Lionel paid for the gas and I tended to getting the slimy hot dogs, the oily fried chicken, and bright-orange nachos while Johannes and the girls stole food from the aisles. In hindsight, I think the cashier noticed, but he could not care any less. In the right corner, next to the cigarettes was a small T.V. The quality of the screen was glitchy and the colors were subdued. The T.V. grabbed my attention when "Breaking News" went across the screen.

"Hey, dude!" I said to the cashier. "Can you turn that up?"

"Whatever..." He moved to turn it up. Across the screen appeared the woman with the blond hair. The anthem of the country played in the background.

"Hail Çaé Braun, our Glorious Leader!" She exclaimed. "Out of West Virginia, we have breaking news!" Hearing that made Lionel curious and he got closer to listen. "Members of the local Nationalist militia decided to take justice into their own hands. They discovered that a family was working against the state by helping the criminal organization that seeks to destroy our government and way of life. The Ewings were found to be guilty by the militia of helping 8Crow, the rebel group. As their punishment, the man and his wife were burned alive in their home." The screen shifted its focus from her to the Ewings' home in a blazing inferno. "We are showing these images to let our citizens know that going against the Çaé and her rule will result in consequences." The focus went back to her. "Remember to obey the law and order of this land! Hail Çaé Braun and All Hail Freedonia!" The screen went back to the home in flames as the music continued to play.

Freedonia,
Freedonia,
God bless our shores,
Forevermore.
Freedonia,
Freedonia,
Our Çaé's our lord,
Forevermore.

Lionel was in a state of shock and started breathing heavily.

"No…God, no." He whispered. His knees buckled. The cashier, not knowing or understanding what was going on, went to the back after he thought he was done serving us. Lionel fell to the floor in despair. He bit his lips to keep from wailing. "Why? Why, God, why?" He was gutted as his face turned red. Johannes, Libby, and Anna didn't have to ask what happened because they heard it on the television. We attempted to calm Lionel, but he was almost inconsolable. He had lost his home and more importantly, his family. His deluge of tears only stopped when his 8Crow burner phone started ringing. Calming down, he cautiously picked it up.

"Hello." He timidly said. "I just heard about my family, yes. Yes, we're still driving west. New location? St. Louis? Why? A Mass Exodus? So, the roads will be completely full by then? Okay, what do we do once we're in St. Louis? You'll provide us a small plane and a pilot to fly to Los Angeles? Weird strategy, but okay. Will do, sir."

"Lionel. Are you okay?" I had to ask him as his parents just died.

"No," Lionel sniffled. "But I already made a promise and a commitment. I need my family's death to mean something. We have a new plan. We're gonna quickly go to St. Louis before there's a Mass Exodus of sorts. St. Louis is an 8Crow stronghold, so they'll grant us a plane to fly to California. You'll be home."

"Are you sure you can do this?" Libby sincerely said.

"I have to. I will not allow Ma and Pa's death to be in vain." He got up off the floor and drug his sleeves across his eyes to get rid of his tears. He pushed forward. We grabbed the materials we gathered and walked outside. We discovered another problem: the R.V. was stolen.

"No, no, no, no…" I started to panic as not only was our mode of transportation gone, Rafael was missing. "Where's Rafael?" The others started to get fearful for Rafael's safety.

"Rafael! Rafael!" I shouted, hoping to find him. "Where are you?!"

"Danny, stop shouting! We can't draw attention!" Lionel tried to put some sense into me.

"Lionel is right, Danny. But Lionel, we have to find Rafael." Anna said.

"How? We don't have time!" Lionel yelled back.

"Dammit, we can't just leave Rafael! He could be God knows where, with God knows who!" Johannes defended. I was too shocked to speak.

"He could have gone in any direction. Look around! There's no way we can find him right now. Plus, we need to go before the masses arrive!" Lionel responded.

Anna spotted the cashier's truck. "Johannes, remember the Burning of L.A.?"

He noticed. "Yeah, I'll get the car started."

"Y'all, we can't just leave Rafael!" I cried out.

"We can find him once we're safe." Lionel said. "I'm not letting my parent's death be for nothing."

"This isn't right! We have to find him! Rafael! Rafael!" I yelled out as Lionel drug me kicking and screaming.   My face grimaced in agony, and I tried to escape from Lionel's arm to run. I just wanted to run. I wanted to run and find Rafael. I wanted to run away with my lover and escape this hellhole. Running was not an option. I got angry at Lionel for holding me back, so I scratched and clawed against his arms and chest. The traumatizing realization swallowed me whole: Rafael was gone and so was my life.

We got in the truck and Johannes was able to jumpstart the car. While we made our way to St. Louis, the mood was morbid. The R.V. had been stolen, Lionel's home and family were burned to ashes, and Rafael was missing and possibly kidnapped. Our lives as fugitives went from worse to just plain disastrous. There are no words to describe the pain we all endured as each one of us felt helpless.

JOSH

I walked out of my meeting with other government officials from the West Wing of the Aurea Palace feeling sick to my stomach. The distance from the west to the east side was still surprisingly long. Time seemed to slow as I went through the halls, watching everyone rush past me in a fury of chaos, attempting to do their jobs. All I could do was think about the meeting. We had to come up with a plan to coerce or force people from the west side of the country to move towards the east and the south. Regarding the south, we had to discuss plans on how the south would be used as a puppet state to trade with other international organizations who wouldn't trade with us. It was for the economic benefit of the state, but there was just a feeling that everything I was doing was wrong.

I was a part of the inner workings of the government I had come to despise as a spy. It was a whirlwind of a day, listening to the people who truly believed in the Çaé. They felt that they had secured a great nation for the citizens when the country was only truly working for the top 1% and barely even that. I felt like I had the backbone of a chocolate éclair when I realized all of the legislation and laws I had passed on behalf of the Çaé. Laws such as the Erasure of Falsehoods which served to censure books that were critical against the kind of government we were living in and the Media Protection Act which worked to perfect our image toward the outside world were enacted under my role as the R.O.C. of Philadelphia. While logically, I knew that my main job was to gather intel for 8Crow, I continued to feel bad for the role I played acting as Oakland.

I was in my own head when I entered into my side of the building. I almost didn't notice Brune running up to me.

"Josh, I need to talk to you right away!" He whispered as he started to catch his breath. When he referred to me by my real name, I knew it was really serious.

"Wesley, let's step into my office for coffee and bring the important papers." I said, still trying to remain undercover. Before we went into my office, he hurriedly grabbed some papers and shut the door."

"Is the coffee pot boiling?" I asked, another code to check for bugs. There were none.

"Josh, we have a serious problem." Brune panicked.

"Can you explain?"

"When I was going through the emails that are addressed to you for you to then forward to the Çaé, I saw this." He handed me the papers. "We can't stop this from happening. Hundreds of thousands of people will die." When I read the email, my eyes widen in shock and fear.

"We need to get a message to Hasan pronto! We have to let the operations of 8Crow know immediately. Now!" I exclaimed. Brune went out of the room and did his job. I sat down, winded from the news that was delivered, knowing I could never stop it in time. "God help us all." I remember praying. "God help us all."

LIBBY

We finally made it to St. Louis, Missouri, but we were all emotionally battered and mentally bruised. Johannes did all of the driving since he knew how to jumpstart the truck. Also, Lionel's hands were shaking throughout the trip, so there was no way he could have driven even if he wanted to. We followed the instructions given to us and went to what used to be the St. Louis airport. That airport had become a center for 8Crow, and their headquarters were there. After getting out of the truck, we got out onto the concrete floor of the parking garage. I stretched because I had been spoiled with the R.V. and had been forced to be in a cramped space riding from Kentucky to St. Louis.

I noticed that everyone was in a terrible mood. Lionel's family was gone, and all his property destroyed. He kept gripping his hands, and his eyes were streaming tears even though he remained silent. Johannes attempted to hold his sister's left hand as Anna kept biting her nails. Danny was a nervous wreck and rightfully so. We all were in a bad predicament. We were all scarred both mentally and physically. One of the leaders of the center came to greet us and guide us to the small plane we were to fly on.

"I'm glad you guys made it safely." She said. "Please follow me, I'll show you the plane and we'll take off." Seeing how exhausted we all were, she never said much else. We hurriedly walked through the airport, seeing a mini city as there were people who were soldiers, regular citizens, doctors, and more. We were walking and Johannes observed the whole complex. Suddenly, he stopped.

"Guys." He plainly said. That made us all turn around and listen to what he had to say. "I've thought long and hard about this. I've made a decision to stay here and help 8Crow."

Anna furrowed her brows and I was surprised. "What?" We both said in confusion.

"Look at me. I'm not the same person I once was when I used to live in California and I never will be again. I've changed too much. And I know I can be of some use to the troops on the ground." Johannes sighed. "This is where I belong."

"Then I'm staying here with you." Anna abruptly said.

"Anna- "Johannes tried to interject.

"You're my brother and I'm not leaving you here by yourself. My place in this world is wherever you are. You can't get rid of me that easily." She went forward to him and grabbed his hand. He faintly smiled, something I haven't seen in a long time.

"I'll join you." Lionel responded, moving forward to them as well. "Those bastards have destroyed everything I ever loved. My family is dead, and I need to make sure they receive justice."

"I guess I should stay too." Danny tried to say.

"No, you will not." Johannes replied. "Rafael would want you to stay safe. We'll look for him. I promise."

"Y'all..." I stammered. But I had no words. I ran to hug Johannes, Anna, and Lionel. Danny did the same too. Our parting was sad, but it had to be quick. Danny and I went on to the plane, but I turned around to look back. Lionel waved and both Johannes and Anna did the I Love You sign as a form of goodbye. I shed a silent tear.

Danny and I left the main airport and went onto the airstrip. We boarded the small plane and felt heaviness in our hearts. I gulped as the plane took off, knowing that I left my friends who had become like family in order to start a new life. I could only imagine the pain Danny was feeling, as I could see the emotional drainage on his face. I thought we were well into our journey to the west, but then something unexpected happened. We heard loud explosions.

Both Danny and I looked out of the windows and we saw missiles and projectiles fall down towards the city of St. Louis and caused the blazing inferno that we saw in the air. It was abhorrent. I screamed as I witnessed the Blitz of St. Louis, knowing that so many were dead. It was an unspeakable tragedy. Danny and I knew that the war had escalated to a level that was never thought possible. After that day, our world changed forever, once again.

PART THREE

DANNY

Even after some 20 years, the Blitz of St. Louis, the Freedonian Civil War, and all that happened beforehand still laid heavily on my mind. It would always remain in my conscious. Through it all, I managed to become a professor of history at a prestigious university in Seattle. I taught about the history of the war; I was an expert in that field. On this particular day in the spring, I wore an old-fashioned neck shawl, navy blue sweater with jeans as I waited for my class to start. When the students started to come in, I somehow noticed my age looking at the younger people. At that time, I had grown a beard that had speckles of gray.

The students were in the latest fashion. Some of the women had loose, flowy outfits that resembled the Greco-Roman style. It was also similar to the fashion of the neoclassical period or the counterculture era. Pastel colors seemed to be popular although there were certainly extravagant patterns. The makeup style was minimalistic at the time because the time period after the war placed a concept of scarcity in people's mind. However, eyelid colors were the main focus, alongside kohl liners and glossy lips. A few of the men also wore eyelid colors and kohl as the stigma of men wearing makeup faded within a generation, although it was more muted. For the males, loose fitting kurtas were all the rage with different designs; the kurta became popular as more Indian immigrants came into the country because of worsening climate conditions in their homeland. But everyone was still individualistic with their own sense of style. I, however, dressed like a vintage hipster from decades ago.

"All right everyone!" I exclaimed, attempting to get the class started. "Please take your seat." The classroom was set up for accessibility, with the desks arranged in a semi-circle so everyone could understand what was being said. "Did everyone remember to bring their holo-lens?"

"Um..." One of my students sheepishly blushed.

Smirking, I handed him one of my extras. "You're lucky I had an additional lens. I keep telling y'all to remember! Put it on and we'll start with today's lesson." They put on the holo-lenses. This relatively new classroom technology was a form of augmented reality or AR for short and was recently made affordable. The student would see charts, maps, and pictures as if it was right in front of them in real life. This was also great for accessibility as they could still see and hear me. I had their holo-lenses connected to that day's lecture through my AR PowerPoint on my thin computer.

"Last time, we left off right before the Blitz of St. Louis." I showed my students the holographic pictures of the ruins that were there 20 years ago. "The leader of Freedonia knew that St. Louis was an 8Crow stronghold. Don't forget that 8Crow was the insurgent army that led the rebellion against Çaé Braun. Anyways, she used the missiles as an attempt to try to crush the rebellion, but it backfired on her. It caused the war to escalate to a whole new level. Without April Freeman's permission, a small group of members in 8Crow decided to Blitz New York City and Philadelphia as well with their own projectiles from the west coast." On the PowerPoint, I displayed a rocket missile hitting the former great cities into rubbles. "That led to retaliation by the Çaé, who survived the Blitz of Philadelphia and moved her capital to Lynn in Illinois. She intended to send missiles to Los Angeles. However, the launch failed and hit a small town in Utah, completely obliterating it." I showed them a video of crushed buildings and dead bodies lying around the city, clearly burned. The students were sensitive to the material, but I felt it was necessary to show the horror of the war.

"More fighting took place on the ground." I continued. "The Battle of Memphis and the Battle of San Antonio were especially brutal. Not to mention, the Mass Exodus was occurring." I pulled up a map of North America for them to see along with charts and infographics. "Since the Çaé demanded that the Nationalist move either to the east or southeastern part of the continent, it was imperative that the people who were from disenfranchised communities move towards the west. The majority of the black population had to leave the South alongside with people whose cities had been destroyed. The New Yorkers that wanted to leave Freedonia illegally migrated to Canada." With the tap of my finger, I showed them pictures of travelers from both sides, looking weak and weary. "Here is a picture of me and my friend, who you know as Senator Libby Freeman, after we arrived from St. Louis just before the Blitz. There, we didn't know whether the friends we left behind were dead or alive. We still don't know."

The picture of us showed how worn out we were 20 years ago. "We were an early part of the Mass Exodus. The five years after the Blitz of St. Louis were among the worst years of the war. Countless millions of people died. We suffered more casualties than during the American Civil War. It got to the point where other countries needed to intervene. Canada, the then-new country of Quebec (since the locals won their referendum), and Mexico made both the heads of government in Freedonia and the leaders of 8Crow come together in Toronto, Canada." I showed a picture of the powers, including April Freedman signing a piece of paper. "This was them signing the Treaty of Toronto. It ended the Freedonian Civil War or the Elysian Revolutionary War, depending on your point of view. It also established the different territories."

I pulled up a map of a divided continent with color schemes to represent each of the different countries. "Freedonia inhabits the northwestern part below Quebec. Their territories extended from the top of Maine and their borders ended at Minnesota, Iowa, part of Missouri, Kentucky, and Virginia. The Confederate States of Dixie encompasses East Texas (extending through Dallas and Houston), part of Arkansas, Louisiana, Mississippi, Alabama, Tennessee, North Carolina, South Carolina, Georgia, and Florida. The Republic of Elysia comprise of the states of Washington, Oregon, Jefferson (which used to be the northern most area of California), North California, Silicon Valley, Central California, West California, Los Angeles (which inhabits federal land as our capital), South California, Nevada, Arizona, Colorado, Utah, Santa Fe (part of which used to be most of New Mexico under a new name), Wyoming, Idaho, Montana, Alaska, Hawaii, Puerto Rico (which took some tough negotiating), the Virgin Islands, Guam, the Elysian Samoa, and the Northern Mariana Islands. To be a barrier between the two hostile nations, Mexico gained most of Texas, the rest of New Mexico, Kansas, Oklahoma, the rest of Missouri and part of Arkansas. Finally, there's the Demilitarized Zone that inhabits the former states of the Dakotas and Nebraska. Freedonia has border patrol on the eastern side of the zone, we patrol the west. Canada patrols the north side and Mexico patrols the south side."

"We had won the war and it was time to build a new nation and President Freeman knew how to do that." I showed one last picture of her standing in the front of her desk. "Without her, we wouldn't have gotten through that difficult time after the war, but with the help of the Founders, the Heroes, and the Citizens, we made it through." I ended the AR PowerPoint by showcasing the Elysian flag which was green and had

24 gold stars in a circle to represent our states. I also had the call of the Crow, our national bird, placed just for special effect.

"Okay, you may take your holo-lenses off. That concludes our lesson for today. Enjoy the rest of the day and do your readings! Be prepared for what is on the syllabus next week. See you later." The students left the classroom and I left too, towards to my apartment.

***

I entered my apartment at the Addison Complex. The Addison Complex was a cohousing neighborhood, which is an intentional community of private homes clustered around a shared space. Each of the separate apartments have traditional amenities, including a private kitchen; shared areas typically feature a common house, which included a large kitchen and dining area, and recreational spaces. The outdoor spaces that we share include walkways, open space, and gardens. Community activities that we do together as neighbors are regularly scheduled shared meals and meetings. We all gathered for parties, games, movies, or other events. Cohousing made it easy to form clubs, and to establish child and elder care.

Cohousing enabled interaction among the neighbors and thereby provided social, practical, economic, and environmental benefits.

My apartment was pretty simple. My furniture was sparse and in-between as I was the only person living there. In the main living room, the couch faced towards the thin, yet huge television that was encased within the tanned-colored walls. Throughout the apartment, I had large frames that contained digital pictures that changed within minutes. One frame was more like a screensaver, showing exquisite pictures of nature ranging from The Trails of Ritidian Beach in Guam to the Mojave Desert in Nevada. It was larger than the other frames as I always found myself staring in the awe of nature. The second digital frame that I had focused on historical paintings and pictures that changed every day. On that day in particular, there was a painting from the Harlem Renaissance. The last frame I owned was more personal and focused on family and friends and it changed every hour. This frame had a specific picture of Rafael, Libby, Johannes, Anna, and I on the night of Lumos' untimely death when we were prepared to go to his concert. I stared at it for several seconds, remembering the times before everything changed. But before I went down a rabbit hole, I remembered to add some things to my grocery list.

"Digita?" I said aloud to my voice-controlled, intelligent personal assistance device.

"Yes." The computer replied.

"Please remind me to pick up some avocados, limes, onions, and tomatoes along with tortillas and some beef."

"Of course. The aforementioned items have been added to the list. Would you like to check the list?" Digita made the refrigerator screen light up with the grocery list. I went over to the kitchen and looked over the smart screen. I touched the screen to access the list and sent it to my cell phone. My cell phone made a blinking sound to let me know that I had received it. I took my phone out to examine it. The phones at this time period were extremely thin and sleek but had more power than it ever did before. By examining my phone, I noticed the date.

"Digita, what do I have on the calendar for tonight?" I asked while searching for recipes on the refrigerator.

"You have a community dinner scheduled for tonight. It is your turn to help with the dinner as you're signed on to make the salad." The computer reminded me.

"Thanks." I said as I left the apartment, not realizing that I had just been courteous to a machine. I left my apartment and made it to the common kitchen. After greeting my neighbors, I smiled as we enjoyed each other's company and participated in the dining experience. The savory aroma of the roasted chicken with rosemary and thyme filled the air along with the salivating smell of mashed potatoes with garlic. We all shared a moment together and broke bread as neighbors should do. The comradery was and still is important to me as it allowed us to be truly human; we're social creatures not meant to be secluded all of the time. The laughter of the children made my heart soar and the adults drank wine while sharing old stories that made us smile.

After the dinner, I returned to my apartment. The lights slowly dimmed back on, and I put my leftovers in the refrigerator. Suddenly, Digita talked to me to let me know something.

"Miriam wants to do a holo-call." Digita stated plainly.

"Send her a message, that I'm getting in position."

"Affirmative."

I went into my office and turned on the holographic projectors. I stood on the opposite side of the room where one of the projectors could record me. Miriam, my friend who lived in the state of Los Angles, appeared on the other side of the room in holographic form. The device was pretty brand new. The form of the person was rudimentary and appeared in black and white. Plus, you had to stand in one spot. But it was a cool device that I knew would improve over time.

"Miriam! How are you?" I asked.

"I'm doing well! I was just wondering if you were still coming to Los Angles for the party." She responded.

"Wait?" I was confused. "You're having a party?"

"You didn't get the invitation? I emailed it to you!" She replied.

I pulled out my phone and searched for it. "I can't believe I missed it, but it was under all of my students' paper submissions."

"No wonder you didn't RSVP back. Well, I'm having a party next week celebrating the ten-year anniversary of my journalistic news organization. I was hoping you'd come! I'll let you crash at my place when you get here."

"Miriam..."

"Please! It's only about an hour and a half trip on the hypertrain from Seattle to L.A. Plus, we haven't seen each other in two months since Libby and Andrew Li's wedding! Did I also mention they'll be there?!" She was clearly trying to entice me into going.

"I'll go! Just have those banana balls that I like there! And don't forget!"

"To make the pepper sauce extra spicy! I knew you'd come."

"How could I ever refuse you, Miriam? Have a good night and please get some sleep! You're always working late at night."

"Only because I want to. Besides, I want to try to cover as much news as I can. The world never sleeps, so neither shall I."

"Sleep tight!" I chuckled as the holoprojectors turned off. I went into my bedroom and got comfortable and went back into the living room to sit on the couch. I contemplated watching my favorite soap opera, but I was too far behind. I finally made a decision on what I would do for the rest of the night entering into the weekend. I decided to take out my pack of marijuana joints from a company named Mary Jane (a very befitting name). It was an Indica strain and I rarely ever smoked, but that night, I just needed a good night sleep. I lit the joint and smoked it.

"Digita, play some Minimalé music please." I was in the mood to hear this relatively new subgenre of Hip-Hop and R&B music (two of the most timeless genres). The best way to describe the sound is a blend of traditional Hip-Hop beats and Jazz elements mixed with powerful and soulful vocals along with lyrical rapping. The intricate and detailed, yet sparse instrumental created an atmospheric and hazy landscape. Minimalé is categorized by the utilization of elements such as introspection and seeks to engage with elements of human emotion. It best reflected my state of mind. Looking over, I saw the digital frame that contained my personal pictures not move. It was stuck on the group picture that we took on the night of the concert that we planned to go to.

"Huh, must have broken..."

There I was in the picture, so young and shameless in that see-through shirt covered in crystals. Libby, with her dark red lipstick and her black strapless dress, looked so beautiful. It was hard to look at the others without feeling emotional. Anna and Johannes looked youthful and carefree compared to the last time I saw them. I didn't know if they were still alive or if they were dead, a thought that often occurred to me. And Rafael, looking at him made me realize how lonely I was without him. I started crying because I was never able to find Rafael and have him by my side again. The pain of the past 20 years bubbled up, reminding me that time can never heal all wounds.

MIRIAM

I'm Miriam Tabbara and before the war, I was a first generation Lebanese American. In fact, I was a senior in high school when Braun took over the country and became the Çaé which changed my life forever. The public school that I went to was altered, as I no longer could say the Pledge of Allegiance, but the Loyalty to the Çaé. I still remember it:

Loyal to the Çaé
Forever, I must be.
Her guidance, we pray,
Will always be best for me.
Freedonia, a country divine,
Will always shine bright.
The Çaé, ruler of mine,
Will always be right.

In the schools, they also made everyone wear only the colors of the flag; my uniforms only consisted of black, white, and red. Also, the books were censored. Stories that I had read previously were no longer allowed. Even my place of worship as a Catholic was never the same, since I only could read the CBV version of the Bible. Life became harder as my family became poorer. We were never rich before, but we at least were financially stable. Under the rules of Freedonia, we could barely afford our home, much less enough food. There were days my mother and father didn't eat just so my sister and I didn't go to bed hungry.

It got so bad that once I finished high school, I couldn't afford to go to a university. College was a dream I had stolen from me during that time. Desperate to make more money, I became a maid, for some of the wealthy elites in Manhattan. I was not treated like a human being. But the work I did was still not enough. My family lost our home and we lived in a tent city for a while. In the tent city, we heard that people were packing up to move to the west after they read the Article of Freedom. My time in New York City was fraught and perilous because many of my friends died trying to resist. Once the Blitz of St. Louis occurred, I knew it was time to leave. It got to the point where, just like my parents did before during the Lebanese Civil War, we immigrated to a new country. However, we did not go west. It was too far, and we could not afford to travel that long of a distance. While the rest of the country participated in the Mass Exodus, a small percentage (mainly people from New York and other New England states) moved further north. I thank God we left before New York City was attacked.

Through a hazardous journey, we arrived in the new-founded country of Quebec. Just briefly before, since there was a rise of right-wing politics around the world, the Bloc Quebecois found the perfect opportunity for a referendum in Canada. They won and were able to create their own country. Even though being a refugee in a new country was rough, I just tried to put myself in my parent's shoes. Instead of learning English as an additional language like my parents did, I had to learn French. While I dealt with some discrimination, I found I could handle it better than I did with the discrimination in Freedonia.

My family settled in an historical Syro-Lebanese community and we started getting our life back. Both my sister and I worked as waiters at a typical Middle Eastern restaurant. My parents found jobs that were suited to their service. Eventually, I made enough money to start going to college in Quebec. In fact, I got my degree in Journalism when the Treaty of Toronto was signed. After I graduated, my family and I were finally comfortable again. We were one of the lucky ones. However, I had a restless spirit and I wanted to start my own life with my degree. I moved to Elysia. The Republic was in a state of creation and I decided to document the change that took place as Elysia tried to build a new system under the old foundation that crumbled.

In the 16 years that President Freeman held office, I met other journalist who documented the events of the war and the Mass Exodus. In fact, an interview between me, Libby, and Danny was the start of our friendship. But I wanted to do more than just do freelance reporting. I wanted to help create my own journalistic organization. Some of my fellow journalists created a news cooperative in the sixth year of Freeman's presidency. The reason why we created a cooperative was because the time was right. Elysia was a more liberal country as a backlash against the Freedonian Civil War.

The Standard was created as a cooperative so that everyone involved would have the objective of creating and maintaining sustainable jobs and generating wealth, to improve the quality of life of the members, dignify human work, allow for the workers to have democratic self-management and promote community and local development. It was perfect for us with the flatter management structure. The multiple roles for everyone created a sense of shared responsibility, shared reward, and a common purpose. Also, it allowed us to be thorough gatekeepers, only allowing important news stories and reports to be heard, instead of the partisan hackery that existed in the previous systems. Our system changed businesses through-out the Republic of Elysia as more businesses created cooperatives to maximize net and real worth of all owners as well as having policy set by directors elected by the workers, or by assembly of members.

This news organization was the most important job for me as I would think about how much I enjoyed my work in the night and in the morning. It was on my mind when I awoke from the night after I talked to Danny. I remember arising thinking about what was the most important news of the day. Even though it was the weekend, I wanted to stay current and up to date for both our online and televised content. I started thinking about the heightened tension between Mexico and the Confederacy and I made a note to myself to write a story on that for Monday's broadcast.

While thinking about this, I went into my restroom and attempted to start my morning routine.

"Digita, may you please change the light color to a pale pink?" I asked aloud, talking about the LED lights around my mirror.

"Affirmative." The light and the atmosphere of the room changed. To further get myself into a good mood, I asked Digita to play some Dream-mood music, a regional subgenre of pop and rock from Seattle that was mellow, synthesizer heavy and reverb-rich. The style frequently contained elements of psychedelia such droning resonances and dreamy cadence. While I listened to the music, I brushed my teeth with my bamboo toothbrush with compostable plant-based bristles and my glass jar of toothpaste. Later, I flossed with the silk dental floss and placed the waste in the small compost bin I had next to the toilet. I then washed my face and got dressed.

I wore a light mint-green flowing shirt, with the sides draping to the knees. Parts of my caramel arms and shoulders were exposed and was tied together with stylistic silver pins. I wore a lot of kohl eyeliner and wore my thick and curly hair down. I chose to wear white pants although I debated whether to wear a skirt. I was ready to complete my errands for that day once I asked Digita to stop the music and dim the lights.

I went into the living room, finding my partner, Chamorra, on the couch typing on a vintage laptop. I smiled at her.

"Good morning babe." I said, kissing her cheeks.

"Good morning! I put the water on for your tea." She replied as she continued on her assignment. I went into the kitchen and got my tea ready while I ate some breakfast pastries.

"I noticed you're hard at work. What are you writing about?" I asked her.

"I'm working on a report for *The Standard* about the former territories and their transition into states for the Republic of Elysia. For the past 16 years, the island of Guam, for example, has benefited from the new government. Before, the American military occupied 29% of the land, and now the Elysian military only occupies 15% of the land. Plus, the government has been in the process of returning land back to the citizens. Most of the population are happy with the new change but some argue that it doesn't go far enough. Some want independence. There are similar stories on the other island states and its quite a fascinating subject." She explained, going through her notes. I enjoyed seeing how expressive she got when she went into a topic she felt passionate about.

"Speaking of Guam, how's your family?" I asked as I sat next to her with my cup of tea. I pushed aside my couch pillows and snuggled closely. Her slightly wavy hair, which was in an updo and decorated with flowers, tickled my nose. I also noticed her pink floral dress and admired her great sense of style.

"My family is doing good. My younger brother just signed up for the army and apparently, my cousin is moving to Silicon Valley, in San Francisco." She grinned.

"He'll only be about forty-five minutes away by hypertrain! That's great news!" I exclaimed, sitting back upright.

"I'm happy he'll be on the mainland with me." She said. "I'll be able to hang out with him more. Also, he'll be here for the 10th year Anniversary party for *The Standard*, so you'll get to meet him."

"Oh, I'm so excited for the party. I've already got the catering service. We're gonna have a myriad of cuisine! There'll be Lebanese, Native American, and traditional Americana food."

"It'll be great!" Chamorra chimed in. "You'll be the perfect host." She kissed me and I blushed.

"Let me finish with my tea and I'll do the grocery shopping for the day." I smiled, sipping the last bit of the warm liquid.

"Love you! Be safe!" She said.

"I will!" I replied as I went to the refrigerator screen and sent my list to my phone. I also gathered all of my mason jars, reusable bags, metal containers, and several other items.

"Bye!" I exclaimed.

***

Los Angeles had significantly changed since the infamous Burning of L.A. After the war, the city had to rise from the ashes like a phoenix. The high-rise towers throughout the city were reimagined as vertical forests. Buildings sprouted greenery with rooftop gardens and whole façades were draped with plants and terraces teeming with vegetation. It led architects to embrace the benefits of using extensive foliage on buildings, extending from energy-saving insulation to mitigating air pollution, increasing urban biodiversity, and increasing the quality of life.

I was appreciating the sights as I rode my tricycle, with my carriage in the back holding my grocery materials. I also appreciated how different city life had changed since I was younger. When I was in my adolescence, cities were full of traffic and noise and chaos (at least in New York City). That all transformed as Elysia invested in hypertrains and their stations. Hypertrains were a part of the city skyline just as subway trains were part of NYC's skyline. It allowed people to take quick trips from different cities that would have taken hours or days before. For example, a trip from Los Angeles to Las Vegas took 30 minutes by hypertrain, when it took 3 hours by plane. Also, there were electric cars but people in highly urban areas used them less. To replace that need were bikes, scooters, hoverboards, walking, an efficient underground metro system, and faster streetcars that were operated outside of the superblocks of Los Angeles.

A superblock was synonymous with the new way of life in Elysia. A superblock consists of a three-by-three-block square made from nine existing blocks. The traffic of the streetcars and the electric cars were limited to the streets on the perimeter of the superblock. Intersections within maintained the steady flow of the traffic of electric cars, which were limited to the speed of 6 miles per hour and were restricted to one-way lanes. Because the speed limit was so slow, traffic barely existed aside from a myriad of people using bikes, scooters, and hoverboards within the superblock. The streets transformed into walkable, mixed-use public spaces where pedestrians, cyclists, and citizens traveled around in safety. The purpose for this new style of urban design was for all citizens to enjoy the benefits of rural living (as it allowed for green spaces) plus the benefits of city life (which included the mass distribution of goods and living amongst a diverse group of people). Different superblocks in different neighborhoods used their public spaces in different ways. For example, there were outdoor concerts, sporting events, block parties, green and garden spaces, playgrounds or places for gathering like areas with picnic tables and benches.

In fact, while I was biking to my supermarket, there were people hanging around in the garden areas, sitting on the benches enjoying the sunshine and the fresh air. I was also enjoying life as I had my Mini-Mic wireless music earplugs that fit perfectly within my ears. I was listening to Toshi Pop, a new genre that had emerged that was uniquely Elysian. Toshi Pop comprised of different styles such as Jazz, R&B, Hip-Hop, Disco, Soft Rock, Caribbean, Latin, Polynesian, Korean-Pop, Japanese Pop, and Bollywood music. The fusion and mix of all of these different types of sounds shouldn't have worked, but it created an amazing original genre. Some songs were breezy and lush, while others were thumping club bangers. It was a truly modern sound as it exemplified the journey of life in Elysia, both romantic and hopeful, along with melancholy and loneliness; these are feelings that many Elysians related to after the war as we were living a better life than we had before, but we still harbored pain from the past. The smooth beats and gleaming grooves along with heartfelt lyrics made it my favorite music.

I finally arrived at the front of the supermarket and I parked my bike. After locking my bike, I grabbed my shopping materials and went inside. It was a sizable store, but I had a plan of attack. I grabbed a cart and went to pick some fruits and vegetables and placed them in my reusable bag in the cart. Afterwards, I moved on to the rest of the store. The local store looked more like a wholesaler than a grocery store of the past. Items were stored in clear self-service bins or dispensers, to be poured into the containers I brought from home. I bought all sorts of goods by weight, from chocolate chips to sugar to oats to spices, taking only as much as I needed. Next, I stopped by the bakery to pick up some fresh bread to place in another one of my cotton bags. Also, I grabbed some glasses of juice as my partner loved juice in the mornings. Next, I went to the butcher area and purchased some chicken which the butcher placed in my metal containers. Lastly, I made sure to shop for any additional items like shampoo bars, toothpaste in glass jars, and tissues packaged in recyclable paper. After my shopping list was complete and paid for, I went back to my bike and placed everything in my carriage and biked home.

When I returned back to my place, Chamorra had gone to South California to interview someone in San Diego. I put up the groceries by myself and told Digita to remind me to cook dinner in a few hours. I then watered my houseplants and made sure to listen in on my favorite podcast. While listening in, I did my household chores. Unexpectedly, I received a call from my burner phone, a sign that it was one of my sources for a story I was working on.

"Hello." I answered.

"Hey, it's me." My source responded. "I wasn't sure I'd be able to call you; it's been risky."

"How so?" I wondered aloud. "Are you okay?"

"When is one ever okay in Freedonia?" He huffed. "There are spies everywhere here and the Çaé doesn't make it easy to communicate with the outside world. The fact that I'm even talking to you is baffling to me."

"What is going on there?" I asked while taking notes of the conversation.

"Here in Freedonia? Life is always the same, struggling to survive under an oppressive regime. We're barely eating while the government officials are pigging out. We can't even buy fresh produce; we're stuck with straight canned products. And we can't travel far. There are few countries willing to trade us cars and even if we had working cars, gas is so fucking expensive..." He went on a rant.

"Wait, slow down! You're going on a tangent!" I exclaimed.

"I'm sorry... It's just been a hard couple of weeks. We've been traveling but anyways, that's not what you wanted to hear. I have some news to tell you. Really, not news, more like rumors."

I was intrigued. "Rumors? What do you mean?"

"There are rumors spreading around about something happening down south, in the Confederacy of Dixie. We got some information that Dixie might be operating slave labor camps."

Shocked, I gasped. "How is that possible? Surely, we would have seen it by satellite!"

"They're supposed to be hiding the labor camps as prisons. That way, no one would catch on that there are human rights violations occurring in Dixie. But some have escaped to tell the story."

"My God... Is there any way you can confirm this?"

"We're trying as we speak. This is personal to my heart as well."

"Well, thank you for calling me. Your information has been very helpful."

"No problem. Wait for my next call." He hung up quickly. I stood there and the shock and horror overtook me as I realized the implication that this had not just in Dixie, Elysia, or the whole continent. This had implications that shook the very foundation of humanity. Slavery was, quite possibly, alive and well in the South.

APRIL

Hello readers. Around this point in history, one would have known me as April Freeman, the first President of the Republic of Elysia. It is important to understand the aftermath of the Elysian Revolutionary War. After the Treaty of Toronto, we used the foundations of the Article of Freedom and the Constitution of the Republic of Elysia to establish our independence. Within the constitution, we created our state to be both a representative democracy and a constitutional republic, similar to how the previous government of the United States of America was founded. The similarities did not end there. We had an Executive, Legislative, and a Judicial branch, where we had stronger checks and balances, so no one like Ace or Braun could rise again. Our lower house is known as the House of Constituents with 235 seats and our upper house is known as the Senate. The House of Constituents is based on population while the Senate gives the 24 states equal representation by giving each state four senators, leading to 96 senators nationwide; 331 people occupied congress.

As previously stated, the government system was similar to the older United States system. We had a Supreme Court as well, except we had 15 Justices instead of the original 9. We realized that it was foolish to pretend that the Supreme Court is not political, but we wanted to make it as fair as possible. There were 15 Justices, 5 liberal judges and 5 conservative judges along with 5 other judges that both the liberal and conservative judges agreed upon, as well as other conditions to make the Supreme Court as impartial as possible.

We also changed the system of voting to make it fairer to every citizen in Elysia. In the United States, we used to vote on a "winner take all" system. It was not a great system because it created elections that were not competitive. It also forced people to pick for candidates as the lesser of two evils, instead of the one they most agreed with, as they were afraid of the third-party spoiler effect. Continuing on that point, in the old system, there were only two parties to choose from that had a better chance of winning. Furthermore, gerrymandering by both of the old parties was a huge problem.

Under this administration, we got rid of the electoral college voting system and we set up a Single Transferable Vote system, which worked so much better. The Equal Representation Act requires that primary and general elections for Congress and the Presidency be held with ranked choice voting. The goal with this system is to maximize the number of voters who help elect a candidate. The ballot gives voters the freedom to rank candidates in order of choice: 1st, 2nd, 3rd, etc. It gives voters a stronger voice by not limiting their vote to one candidate. If a voter's first choice loses, their vote immediately goes to their next choice. It creates fair results, where it upholds principles that not only the majority earns the right to decide, but all voters. Also, under the Equal Representation Act, we established multi-winner districts. Instead of gerrymandered districts that only elects one representative, larger districts were created to elect more than one member. This way, more voices were heard with fair representation and real competition in every district. A majority of voters can always elect a majority of seats, but at least voters that are not in the majority still elect their fair share. The candidates and parties elected in a district represented a proportional representation of the population.

This led to a natural formation of multiple parties as voters had more choices. The most prominent parties during the early period of Elysia, on a scale from the furthest left to the furthest right were The Rose Society Party (RSP), the Green Party (GP), The People's Party (TPP), the Libertarian Party (LP), the Unity Party (UP), the Christian Democratic Party (CDP), and The Conservative Party (TCP).

The Rose Society Party held 35 of the 235 seats, which was 15% of the House. They are a democratic socialist party, although they also contained legislators that were even more left leaning. They increased the power of the working people. The Green Party held 47 of 235 seats, which was 20% of the House. They are a progressive party of environmental protection and the party that sought to defeat climate change. The People's Party held 70 seats of 235, which was 30% of the House. As the liberal and social democratic party, they had the majority, seeking to provide government intervention and regulation in the economy.

The Libertarian Party held 12 seats out of 235, which was 5% of the House. They are a centrist party due to the fact they were somewhat socially liberal and economically conservative. The Unity Party held 12 seats out of 235, which was 5% of the House. They were also a moderate party that was more socially conservative and economically liberal.

The Christian Democratic Party held 24 seats out of 235, which was 10% of the House. It is a party that was formed out of Christian values from different denominations ranging from Mormonism to Catholicism. They were right-of-center on social issues and moderate with economic and labor issues. The Conservative Party held the last 35 seats in the house, which was 15% of the House. The Conservative party supports lower taxes, the free market, a strong national defense, deregulation and restrictions on labor unions.

I was especially proud of the 16 years I spent as president, since I was able to guide the newfound country from war into an economic miracle. The 16th year was the year I decided to retire, as it was time for the country to prepare to move on with a new leader. The administration was able to accomplish transforming the nation (I believe it partially because I had no affiliation with any party and because right-wing politics left a bad taste in most people's mouth after the war). We were able to make Election Day a national holiday as well as automatic-voters registration as a law. The government also accomplished guaranteeing federal jobs with a family-sustaining wage, adequate family and medical leave, and retirement security to all people. We also established high quality healthcare for all, tuition-free public colleges along with quality public education, and access to clean water, clean air, healthy and affordable food, and nature.

During my terms, we met 100 percent of the power demands in the Republic of Elysia through clean, renewable, and zero-emission energy sources. We repaired and upgraded the infrastructure as well as all existing buildings in the nation. The administration built new buildings after the war to achieve maximal energy efficiency, water efficiency, safety, affordability, comfort, and durability. We also eliminated as much pollution and greenhouse gas emissions as we could as we became more technologically advanced. We did that by overhauling transportation systems to eliminate pollution and greenhouse gas emissions from the transportation sector through investment in zero-emission vehicle infrastructure, manufacturing clean, affordable, and accessible public transportation, and high-speed hypertrains. There was massive growth in clean manufacturing in Elysia and we removed pollution and greenhouse gas emissions from manufacturing and industry alongside working collaboratively with farmers and ranchers to eliminate pollution and greenhouse gas emissions from the agricultural sector.

I believe it is important to give a background on the formation of the new nation to fit with the context of the narrative. Elysia represented hope and a new beginning for us as citizens. I am honored to have had a positive impact for a country and the world.

LIBBY

To say a lot had changed in those past 20 years would be an understatement. One way to show the magnitude of the change would be to describe the night of *The Standard's* 10-year anniversary party. I prepared for the gathering, rummaging through my closet. I attempted to find the right dress, but I got frustrated because I was trying to look fashionable, but also portray a certain image.

"Andrew, what about this one?" I asked, pulling out my green dress with an angular edge on the ends.

"Hmm," He winced while sitting on the bedroom couch. "Representative Giovani already wore that last week to an event." He pulled up a picture from his phone.

"Why does it matter if she wore it first?" I groaned.

"It doesn't, but people will make it a thing." He sighed in his undergarments. He arose from his seat and went into the closet. He pulled out a blue dress that had a black belt with a silver buckle. "How about this dress? You look amazing in this."

I smiled. "I do, but I wore that to my first debate."

"I know." He grinned, placing the dress next to me. "I remember the day I first met you. You caught my eye because you were simply gorgeous beyond compare." His hands caressed my face. "That's when I knew you had to be Mrs. Li."

"It's ironic, isn't it? The first time we met, we had to argue." I chuckled. "You had it so bad for me, you fumbled during the debate."

"I did not!" He dropped his jaw jokingly.

"Yes, you did! You looked at me, then you tripped on your opening statements." I laughed.

"Well, I remember it differently." He chortled while putting the dress back. "I remember after the debate, I had to ask you out. Your intelligence and passion for the issues won me over. Even if we are from different parties, what with you being in TPP and I being in the RSP, I knew that it was the people you truly cared about."

"Our solutions were not that different from each other although our endgames may be slightly different. Besides, we both became senators and were able to represent our state." I said, while picking out another outfit. "Remember this dress?" I showed him my gorgeous gray dress with a sparkling silver cape that draped across the floor.

"Yes. You wore that stunning little number to our first date." He whispered as if it was a secret only for me to hear.

"You don't think I overdressed? You just asked me out for drinks." I laughed.

"It is a glamorous dress that started a glamorous relationship." He said, taking me into his arms. "That date was amazing, sharing drinks and sharing our life stories. We stayed and talked for hours, about everything underneath the stars and beyond the heavens. Your titillating conversations stimulated the deepest depth of my subconscious. Your beauty, your smile, your eyes, your intellect, your fervor for change, your charisma, your charm, the way you disarm and take away a person's walls with just a smile. Man, I'm totally into you."

"You have a way with words." I swooned by his romantic remarks.

"And you have a way with time. The party is gonna start in 20 minutes." He chuckled.

"Oh!" I said, startled. "What am I am going to wear!"

"Here." Andrew pulled out a black, long-fitted sheath dress with long sleeves with puffy shoulders. The dress was made of velvet, patterned with a red design that resembled the art nouveau fashion that stretched down to the calves.

"Oh, that's perfect!" I marveled. "That's what I'll wear!" I grabbed the dress and went into the bathroom to change into the clothes. After I got into my outfit, I put on the rest of my makeup, added the final touches of kohl liner and the perfect nude lipstick with gloss. I styled my hair into four cornrows that ended in two low buns, with the braids accessorized with gold hair cuffs. I came out into the bedroom, ready to show off my completed look for the night, when I didn't see him. He came out from the closet and was almost ready. He wore an ensemble that matched mine, a red velvet suit decorated with a pattern of black roses. Attempting to put on his tie, he looked at me with a smirk.

"Wow, look at you!" I exclaimed. "You look sharp, hon!"

"I knew that would be the dress you'd go for, so I was already prepared."

"You know me too well." I smiled. "I also know that you probably need my help with your tie, huh?"

"You know me too well." He laughed. When I was helping him, I looked up into his face, I couldn't help but notice his handsomeness. His brown eyes were warm and loving. The fact that his jet-black hair was at shoulder's length and his soft smile made me blush reminded me of our wedding day. I remember him looking at me the way he did at that moment, with the smile and twinkle in his eyes. I can remember my red wedding dress and his matching piece. I can remember the difficulty of merging Chinese and Black traditions, but we did it in a glorious way, as I wore my qipao and we jumped the broom in a Baptist church. I still remember the feeling of the ring slipping onto my finger and I felt that same happiness then, helping him with his tie. I felt I found the love of my life.

"What are you thinking about?" Andrew said, noticing I was getting lost in my flashback.

"I was thinking about our wedding. It was such a beautiful day." I replied. "That day was a moment I'll treasure forever. All of my friends and family watching us make our lifelong promise to love each other."

"Let's not forget, that reception was pretty lit." He laughed, taking ahold of me.

"Lit? My God, you sound old." I chuckled in return. "But yeah, it was amazing. Everyone was dancing and having a good time, except..."

"Except who?" Andrew questioned puzzledly.

"Danny. He sat at a table by himself. He's never been the same since Rafael..."

"He's coming tonight, you know. Miriam was able to convince him to come." He said.

"I hope I get to talk to him. We didn't get a chance to speak much at the wedding."

"I know you care about him a lot."

"How can I not? We've been through so much that there's a lifelong bond. But ever since we arrived in what was then California, he never got through the tremendous suffering we went through. I'm worried about him."

"He seems to be doing okay. He's a professor at a prestigious university and from what I heard from him, he loves his job."

"It's been almost 20 years since we left Missouri before the Blitz, and he still carries the weight of the past. It's like he feels guilty for leaving

Johannes, Anna, and Lionel there, even though it was their decision. He feels guilty as if he condemned them to death himself. And he never felt whole after we lost Rafael. He's felt incomplete. I'm worried for him." I whispered sincerely.

"I know you are. Maybe you can address your concerns for him when you see him. Don't stress yourself out." He hugged me. "It's time to go, or we won't just be fashionably late. We'll just be late. Periodt." He said.

"God, you're an old man with your dated lingo!" I laughed while grabbing my handbag.

"You love me, I'm your bae!" He replied without missing a beat.

"You're insufferable!"

"Ahh," he said after chuckling, "I know."

***

We arrived at the large rooftop park, and I can't express how magnificent the arena appeared. The space was filled with wonderful vegetation, rivaling the hanging gardens of Babylon. The plants were bright with their bioluminescence, shining like LED lights. Soft hues of blue, yellow, and green colored the atmosphere. The structure above made the garden feel like it was in a glass dome. The stars above were alive and gleaming. As I looked on the sides, I looked at the rest of Los Angeles. The state that acted as the capital of Elysia looked marvelous in the nighttime, with the city never sleeping. The plants that hung around the buildings were also glowing with their bioluminescence, matching the digital lights as well. Flowers surrounded my path as my husband, and I walked through. Roses, Daisies, Lilacs, and many others made for a wonderful sight.

Another wonderful sight were the people. Everyone wore delightful and memorable outfits. One woman I saw had the most elegant outfit which glowed and changed colors and patterns. She was able to switch back and forth from animal print to a metallic shade of bronze. Her hair was styled in the contemporary nighttime fashion of the Freeman era; it was piled on high and was incredibly voluminous with the outer layer containing crimped hair. Her makeup look was neutral, as to not clash with the changing outfit. There was also a man dressed in a pink asymmetrical kurta with a purple waistcoat that contained silver embroidery, while wearing white pants. He had hair that was quite decently long (shoulder-length) and he had on kohl liner along with a royal blue smoky eye. His wife had a darling royal blue toga gown with a thigh-high slit and a cape that draped magnificently. There were older people who wore the traditional black suit and ties and still looked amazing.

There was also a makeshift dancefloor of sorts with a deejay set up, playing his multiple different playlists through the Mini-Mics of the people dancing. It was a silent party with people dancing at different speeds. One group listened to the same mixtape, while one group danced to another. They had the choice of whatever playlist they wanted to hear. I also appreciated the buffet of food. It had a variety of cuisine to accommodate the diversity of people that were there at the rooftop park. There were buffalo ribs with blueberry barbecue sauce, fry bread, sfeeha, banana balls with a spicy pepper sauce, and hamburgers and French fries to represent old Americana cuisine.

After Andrew and I ate some food at the surrounding tables, we enjoyed each other's company underneath the stars and mingled around with the other guest. I had an enjoyable conversation with Representative Carmichael from the Green Party. We discussed politics, of course, but we discussed the things we enjoyed about Los Angeles. I also talked to Senator Garrison from the Conservative Party and conversed about *The Standard*. She cracked a joke about how *The Standard* has definitely set the standard. We had deep admiration for the journalistic organization because it always strove to tell the truth from a non-biased view. I meandered around the party until I finally ran into Miriam.

"Miriam, you look absolutely incredible!" I squealed as I hugged her. She looked beautiful that night. Her dark hair was curly, and she wore a shimmery golden eyeshadow to match the art deco embroidery in her pale pink one-shoulder gown with a chiffon cape sleeve.

"Thank you! And you look divine, yourself!" She gushed. "Where did you get this dress, I love it!"

"Oh, I bought it from a local store here in Los Angeles actually!"

"Really! You have to tell me where!"

"I can't remember, but I have the receipt for it back at home."

"You still keep paper receipts?"

"Girl, I always keep the receipts! How do you think I can go toe-to-toe with these senators?" I laughed. She giggled along with me. "Look at us talking about receipts. You know I was just talking to Andrew today about our old slang."

"We are not old!" She lightheartedly gasped.

"Andrew used the phrase 'lit,' which hasn't been used by anyone cool in the past 20 years."

"Now don't you give him any grief; you use dated slang yourself!"

"Like what!" I questioned.

"You use the word 'tea' like a twitter stan."

"...tea." I muttered out before we both busted out into cackles. "You just said 'stan' so you're just as bad as me." I said.

"You're right, but we are not old!" She laughed. "We're only...40-something..." She muttered which turned into a giggle.

"Excuse you, I look younger than 35 myself."

"You don't look a day over 30. The only time I've seen you look even younger than that was your wedding day. You were positively glowing with the dew of youth."

"I hope you got to enjoy the wedding!"

"Oh, it was amazing! The vows you two exchanged were breathtaking."

"I just had to ask because I didn't get much of a chance to spend quality time with everyone at the wedding."

"Believe me, I understand, I'm sort of experiencing that right now. Being a good hostess is hard."

"Y'all managed to throw a spectacular party! The food, the ambience, everything is great! Congratulation on the success of *The Standard*."

"Thank you!" Her phone started to ring in her handbag. "I'm so sorry, I have to take this!" She pulled out a vintage looking burner phone. "What do you mean, what do you mean you're working with the Mexican military on this?" I managed to eavesdrop on her before she left. After wondering around, I started to look for my husband, but then I managed to see Danny. He was sipping on champagne, setting it down on a table once he saw me.

"Libby!" He smiled as he came in for a hug.

"Danny!" I said excitedly. "It's so good to see you! You look great!" He wore a black, raw silk suit that had a golden embroidered pattern with black pants and shoes.

"Thank you! It's the best thing I own, so I thought it would be fitting for the occasion. I bought it from my neighbor's shop."

"It really 'suits' you." I quipped.

"Ahh, I just got it." He chuckled after taking a few seconds.

"How are you? We didn't get a chance to talk much at the wedding."

"I'm good. I'm enjoying my job as a professor. My students give me joy and sometimes they also make me laugh at how stupid some people can be."

"Really?" I said, surprised at his bluntness. "Can you give me an example?"

"While on the way here from Seattle, I graded some papers. Do you know a guy just straight plagiarized from my own actual words about the war?"

"Did he not realize?"

"No! At least when I worked on my papers in college, I changed it around a little bit. Kids these days, huh?"

"Wasn't so long ago when we were kids like them." I whispered.

"Yeah..." He managed to mumble out. "They don't know how easy they have it nowadays."

After a pause, I said, "I wanna know how you are really doing."

"I'm fine." He fidgeted.

"Danny. It's me. I've noticed some things and I'm worried about you."

"What do you have to be worried about? You've moved on with your life." He snapped back. "You have a job that actually affects the world. You're with the man you love, whereas I'm not. You're happy, so don't try to pretend like you're worried."

"Do you think I've actually moved on?" I grimaced. "There is not a day that goes by where I don't think about all that's happened. You wanna know what I thought about just today? When I played my music on my way to work, I remember us getting the news of Lumos death. When I'm in this city, I'm always reminded about the Burning of L.A. Whenever I see a gun on T.V., I can recollect the trauma of the Battle of D.C. And when my fireplace is aflame, I can see the millions upon millions getting scorched in St. Louis. I remember Johannes, Anna, Lionel, Josh, and Rafael. I've never forgotten and how dare you assume that because I've been able to get through the pain, that it meant I forgot about them. I could never do that." I calmed myself down and his eyes began to water.

"I'm sorry I didn't mean to snap on you." He apologized.

"I just want you to get some help, that's all." I brushed his arms

"Rafael and I promised each other that we'd seek mental health treatments together..." He murmured. "I should go." He walked away, but he turned around as he remembered to say something. "It was a really lovely wedding, by the way. It was in a Baptist church, the way I would have done it." He voiced sadly.

"Danny." I said, but it was too late. I was left standing, wondering how our conversation went so wrong.

"Oops! Sorry, that was loud!" Miriam said as her microphone created a feedback loop. She tried to get everyone's attention in the rooftop park as she stood on a platform. "I just want to thank you all for coming to support this ambitious endeavor in journalism. I feel so grateful that we made it to 10 years and I'm happy that you are here to celebrate with me. That's basically all I have to say, so continue to enjoy yourself!" She stepped off of the platform and people clapped before they continued what they were doing.

"There you are!" Andrew beamed, swooping in by my side. "I tried looking for you when I started talking to Jamie Thompson. You know she wrote that successful book series that you love? I had an enlightening conversation with her, but I wish you were there."

"I was talking to Danny, probably."

"It didn't go well; I can tell by your face." He stated.

"Yeah. God, I probably should've been more sensitive or something? I don't know. I just wish the conversation didn't go south the way it did." I groaned.

"Well, I've got something that might cheer you up." He took out some Mini-Mics from the deejay. "I got the deejay to use an old-school playlist, some music from our high school and college years that we can listen to together. I'm throwing it back."

"Hmm, you know my music taste so well."

"So, madam, will you allow me the honors of dancing with you?" He said before kissing my hand.

"You're so cheesy! And romantic. Of course, I'll dance with you." We put our Mini-Mics in and slow danced together to an old Alternative R&B song. The song took me back to my high school memories and I laid my head against Andrew's head while we enjoyed the warmth of each other. I briefly closed my eye and then opened them to see Danny sitting by himself at a table, downing scotch with a tear running down his eye. It was the same thing then, just like at the wedding. Danny was alone.

Rafael

I awoke gasping from my nightmare only to look at my surroundings to realize that I was living one. I got up from my cot and looked around my cell. My cell had a small and thin opaque window which only allowed me to see whether it was day or night. It was early morning. The white dingy walls had peeling wallpaper and the water leak thankfully fell into the sink that was next to the toilet. I was the lucky one because I had one of the best cells with a private wall and door. In terms of how the others were sleeping, I was in a better position. I looked in my mirror (a luxury item in my circumstance) and noticed how much I changed. My hair had gray and silver streaks from stress and my face was gaunt from malnutrition, which made my scar even more pronounced. I saw my orange outfit that I had to wear to stand out from the other slaves since I was a foreman. The other slaves wore different colored jumpsuits that denoted status. White and black stripes for the newcomers, blue for the workers, orange for the foremen, brown for the overseers and the guards (who were usually always white males) were the standard uniforms.

I sighed as I put it on, knowing I was in for another day of pain and humiliation. I was teary-eyed that morning.

"What hell had my life become?" I whispered to myself. As I was the foreman, I was up early to count the slave numbers. I knocked on my door for the guard to let me out. They wouldn't let me out. They liked toying with me, making me almost late so I could get in trouble with the overseer. They taunted me. I was forced to rap on the door rapaciously for them to let me out. That day, it took them maybe 3 minutes to open the door. I say maybe because there was no clock. The only way to tell time was to keep it yourself. Light was day. Dark was night.

When I finally left my cell, I walked around the prison. I saw the sadness and the anger in the slave's eyes as I passed by the open-walled cells. Some were upset that I went along with this. And why shouldn't they have been? But I knew the truth. I had become complicit in this inhumane travesty to survive. I marched down to the underground tunnels. There were different tunnels leading to different places. My assignment was at the steel mill factory. They placed the tunnel underground so it would be harder to escape the complex. Also, it was to hide the fact that the government of the Confederate States of Dixie was using slave labor.

I arrived at my first post of the day through a long trek in the tunnels. My job was to read the slave numbers as they march through the tunnels and check them off to make sure no one escaped. It was designed to make the idea of escaping worthless as someone would always notice you were missing. It always pained me as I looked into their eyes. These men of color were my brothers and I was forced to condemn them to a hard day's work for no money, only to return to their terrible conditions in their cells and then start anew to look me in the eyes again. I became numb as I read out their numbers in the glass booth along with the other foremen.

"Number 12573...Number 40475...Number 42648...Number 71298." I repeated aloud in the cacophony of noise between all of the foremen reciting the numbers. We had no name. We were dehumanized. My number was 33127. After all the slaves for the steel mill factory were found to be in place, I went to my position to supervise the steelmakers. This was the hardest part of my day, I believe. We'd be forced to work in the hot heat all afternoon until lunch break, only to work until dinner, where we returned to our cells. The men toiled and sweated under harsh condition, producing steel that would be used for the everyday Confederate or Dix as we liked to call them as a derogatory term.

That day started off ordinary. I was watching the slaves work as they were told to do while the overseers watched from high above through a window that shielded them from the heat. The sight of the hot, red molten steel being poured into a mold was common. My men worked with dangerous materials and equipment with the bare minimum for protection. They handled sharp objects that were blistering to the touch. It was my job to see the men through and make sure that they kept working. However, that day, Number 61891 was injured. He was limping because he dropped something on his toe. I didn't report it in, as his lunch break would be revoked if he wasn't working. Lunch and dinner were all we had to eat. Plenty died because they couldn't survive such malnutrition.

Number 61891 was struggling, and I tried to pick up his slack. I was doing so to divert his injury from the overseers watching from above.

"Hey, are you doing okay?" I whispered, darting glances between Number 61891 and the guards.

"I'm trying my best. I'm in so much pain." He winced.

"I'm gonna try to help you. You're gonna have lunch if I have anything to do with it."

"Hey!" One of the overseers yelled aloud, striking fear in everyone. In our section, we all froze. "What is going on around here?"

"Nothing Mister Richards. I am doing my job, as instructed." I replied in as a calm manner as I could without him seeing the fury in my eyes and soul. I was trying to help a man, but in the overseer's mind, I was not following orders.

"Oh really? Is your job to help an injured worker?" He scolded. "You know your duty."

"Yes. I am the foreman. My job is to make sure they get their work done."

He slapped me across the face and I just had to take it. Otherwise, I could have been killed. It wasn't the first hit I've received from an overseer or guard.

"Number 61891 is obviously injured. You're supposed to report it though the chain of command, so we can assign a new worker."

"He can work. He just needs a little help." I stood my ground. "He's a good and valuable worker. Let him stay."

"He can work, huh?" Mister Richards smirked. "Guards! Handcuff his ass up to this rail." The guards came and responded to his order All of us slaves could only watch and gulp in fear. He forced Number 61891 to bend over in a humiliating fashion and tore off his uniform. The overseer briefly left and returned with a tong carrying some molten hot steel With a devilish grin, he then pressed the hot metal and seared the man's back. He screamed so loud; the whole facility took notice.

"Please stop!! ARGH." That was all the words he could muster as we heard his skin sizzle. I wanted so badly to help him, but I was all too aware of the consequences by then. I still feel guilty. I was worried about my own survival. The sudden smell of burning flesh overwhelmed my senses. This description doesn't even give a glimpse into this horrific sight. The guards laughed cruelly, mocking the man as he passed out once his bones became exposed. I panted hard through my nose as I wanted to curse all of the guards and overseers out, but I bit my tongue.

"Now, he definitely can't work." The overseer said to me, holding the tong of metal dangerously close. Internally, I was panicking. He whispered into my ear in a chilling tone, "Handle your workers, before I do." He placed the steel back in the proper place when he got out of my face. "Take him to be transported to the Camps of the Undesirables. He's disabled now, so he won't be worth anything." When he caught all of us just staring, he hollered "Get back to work!"

The guards removed Number 61891, and I couldn't contain my pain in as I started crying. The tears kept rolling down while I did my job. Life was a hellish landscape in this slave complex. That one experience of the man (whose name I never learned) having his back seared with red-hot metal was not even the pinnacle of torture people had experienced. People got beat, raped, and killed by the overseers and guards. Some of the women gave birth to some of the guards' children. There have been children that grew up and toiled their blood, sweat, and tears in the same place as their parents. There were teenagers and young adults that never knew a life outside of the prisons and factories. We all helped raise them ourselves because the state never gave them legal status and protection because to do so would recognize that they were slaves. However, slavery wasn't enforced on all people of color in the Confederacy of Dixie. Slaves only became slaves if they were born inside the prison or if someone "broke" the law. You'll notice I use the term "broke" loosely as law enforcement could take anyone if they needed more workers. Blacks and Latinos with a few East Asians were living under an apartheid system of second-class citizenship and segregation.

As you'll notice, I only said Blacks, Latinos, and East Asians. Secretly, other marginalized groups were sent to the Camps of the Undesirables. Groups such as people of Arabic and Semitic descent, Muslims, Disabled people, and people within the LGBT+ community were sent to these camps to be hidden from society. Those camps were death sentences. Most of those who were sent there didn't make it out alive. That's why for almost two decades I never revealed my sexual orientation. I always hid my true self in fear, and I had not been with a man romantically since I was with Danny. That is why I was horrified when Mister Richards decided to send Number

61891 to the camps. It's partially why I helped to take care of Zero. At that time, Zero was a five-year-old born in the camps. He was born from a rape between Mister Richards and Aniyah (or Number 59384 in the official records). We called him Zero for short because he had no real name; his identity was Number 02849. Mister Richards never acknowledged the child or the mother after his brutal contact with her. That fact is the reason he had no issues sending Aniyah, the only stability the child had known, to the Camps of the Undesirables was simply because she was found kissing a woman. She was a lesbian. That was all the reason needed to be banished and condemned to eventual death.

I was often reminded how cruel life was in the containment prisons, but that day really shook me to the core. When we left for lunch, all of the men from the steel factory integrated with the women at the prison who worked at a clothing factory. The children, ranging from newborn to 16, were there waiting for us because they always stayed behind since they were the maintenance crew for the prison. While the adults worked, the older children took care of the little ones. I felt so horrible that the kids were robbed of their childhood. But at the time, there was nothing I could do, but help care for them. Zero was the one I looked after during the day before he's forced to sleep with the other children in the "crib," a cell block of young ones.

"Thirty-Three!" He called me as I ran up to him and hugged him. He was often the only joy I could find in that godforsaken hellhole.

"How are you, buddy!" I said, balancing on my tippy toes to talk to him at his level.

"I'm good! You wanna know what I did today?" He asked with an infectious bubbly tone.

"What'd you do today, Zero?" I replied with a smile, hiding the pain of life as a slave from the child. That was something he didn't need to know about at that moment.

"I helped the older kids clean the windows!" He excitedly said as if that wasn't something forced upon him. "I tried peering through it as hard as I could, and I saw something that was big, and the color looked like the nasty pea soup we have to eat."

"The color green." I smiled at his happiness, but I was disappointed that he didn't get to know what a tree was. I didn't tell him as not to raise his hopes unnecessarily.

"Yeah! And I tried to look for my mommy outside, but I couldn't find her. People keep saying she's outside, but I never see her."

I didn't know what to say to that. I knew he missed his mother terribly and it hurt me so that he would likely never see her again as I could relate to that feeling. A mother was taken from her child. That was why I bonded with Zero because I understood somewhat the loss he was going through, even if he wasn't fed all of the information. "Come on! Let's go to the cafeteria and get something to eat." I grabbed his hands and led him to the eatery. We got in line, where we were served bread, pea soup, and water. The green color of the soup looked slimy, the bread was stale, and the water had a strange aftertaste to it. But I ate it because I was actually starving. I had to coax Zero into eating his soup.

"Zero, it's important that you eat to be a growing boy." I nudged while he stirred his spoon in the soup.

"But I don't like it! It doesn't taste good." He complained. He was right. It didn't taste good at all.

"I know. But you should still eat because you need the energy. Come on. Watch me." I showed him me eating the soup and tried to smile, even though I absolutely despised the taste. "Do you think you could eat it for me? Please?"

He looked at the atrocious meal and sighed. "Okay, Thirty-Three." He leaned over and took a sip, only to cartoonishly frown. He looked back at me and sighed, knowing I wasn't going to ease up on him unless he ate the whole thing. I made sure he ate everything while also being as picky as he was, making sure the water didn't look contaminated.

"Don't forget to eat the bread." I said.

"But it's hard." He whined.

"I know. Just chew and sip some water to make it go down. Do it with me. See?" I said after intensive chewing and gulps of water.

He followed my lead and chewed for what seemed like ages. But I managed to get him to eat his entire meal, which I took as a huge accomplishment. Some of the other children were too finnicky and not eating stunted their growth. I finished my meal and played with Zero for the remainder of my time even though I was tired because I cared for his happiness or whatever counted as happiness inside those walls. He was sad when I had to leave, but I promised to eat dinner with him. I grew to love and care for Zero like he was my own child.

I walked back to the factory, getting into the same routine by calling out the numbers in the booth. Then I watched over my men, still scared with the recent memory of a man's skin essentially being burned. It was shaping up to be a standard and normal day for the most part. I did my job for hours until I heard, "All foremen, report to the transportation room immediately." I complied. I walked through the underground tunnels to enter a giant garage, basically. I was so close to the outside world but I couldn't reach it without being shot dead. Mister Richards approached me, chewing tobacco in his mouth.

"We got a new shipment arriving." He said callously. The other overseers talked to their respective foremen. I was the unfortunate soul that had to have Mister Richards as my supervisor. "I expect you to take the time this weekend to show your workers around and tell them how things are run round here. Course, it wouldn't be my fault if they didn't pay attention and I shot em for breaking the rules."

I didn't say anything, I just nodded.

"You not gonna say anything? You not gonna show me any respect, you dirty shitskin?" He grunted in a rage.

"I'm sorry, sir." I said, grinding my teeth.

He then proceeded to spit his tobacco right in my face. I wiped off the gross black tar and saliva. I felt utterly humiliated and emasculated since I was not able to fight back. He proceeded to laugh and say "You're damn right you're sorry. You wanna say something else, boy?"

"No, sir."

"Now there's that proper respect I'm fucking talking about. Now shut up. When the truck brings in the new workers, I'll pick the ones that I'll assign to you."

The large garage door began to open and brought in a bus of new arrivals. I watched them as the guards took the new slaves out of the vehicle. They were shackled and chained while wearing blindfolds.

"Line one will be for you." My overseer said after talking with his peers.

I looked at Line one. They seemed rattled and scared. The myriad of black and brown faces standing before me.

"Take Line one to the prison. Number 33127, you will meet the new workers alongside me. Is that clear?"

"Yes, sir." I replied.

He led the line towards the prison, and I followed behind him, alongside the blindfolded slaves. The guards forced them to move since they were shuffling around, most likely afraid of where their final destination might be. We arrived in the prison and the line stood in place.

"Okay, boys, take off their blindfolds." The overseer said to the guards. They did just that. I stood behind Mister Richards and I saw the shock on their faces as they saw the bright florescent light and the coldness of the prison. I looked around at their faces. Some were young, too young. The law enforcement may have justified their reasoning for bringing them here. But I knew the truth, that they either committed crimes of survival in order to live or they hadn't committed any crimes at all. There were older faces, in their elderly stages, who I knew would die inside those walls. I perused all of their faces until I saw one face I recognized.

"Hasan?" I accidently whispered. Lucky, the overseer didn't hear me. But yes, it was Hasan, the same man who was the leader of the D.C. branch of 8Crow decades ago by that point. He looked weary and tired, yet determined; for what, I did not yet know. He almost looked the same, just older.

"You've arrived in the Cook Containment Prison, one of many across the country." Mister Richards started off. "Y'all some unlucky sons of bitches, I'll tell you that! Don't y'all ever forget. You sure won't escape cause the only way out of here is death. And I don't care about niggers and shitskins dying." He coldly laughed.

One woman tried to escape, but she was still in chains. The overseer pulled out his gun and shot her straight between the eyes. The sudden thud shocked everyone, and people stood still.

"Too bad she couldn't just follow the rules. She was beautiful. Could've had her in my bed tonight. Oh well. Number 33127 will tell you all of the rules as he is a foreman. I expect you to follow him, or you'll end up like that unlucky whore. Number 33127, do your job."

"Yes, sir." I replied in compliance. I told them what they're meant to do. I assigned their numbers and I let the guards lead them to their new cells. But before they all exited, while still dragging the body of the dead woman, I whispered in Hasan's ears, "Meet me in the cafeteria during dinner, Hasan." He did a slight acknowledgement to let me know that he understood, like back in the 8Crow days. They left and I was left standing alone. I walked back to the factory, contemplating what my next step should be. If Hasan was here, what did that mean for me?

***

I entered into the dining area, exhausted, but still remembering that Hasan was here. I saw him in the corner, dressed in the white and black striped uniform. He mostly kept his head down while I was in line getting dinner. I walked up to him with my tray and sat on the table, sitting next to him.

"Rafael!" He whispered. "Man, you have no idea how happy I am to see you."

"I'm glad to see you too." I said in a hushed tone, leaning towards him. "But you can't call me Rafael. Call me Number 33127. I'll call you by your designated term, Number 172080"

"Why can't anyone call you by your name?"

"They make us call each other numbers to dehumanize us. And if we say our real names, we're punished through various means. But it feels so good to hear someone say my name again. But how are you here? You'd be at a Camp of the Undesirables. You're a Muslim."

"Good thing I changed my identity. We had heard rumors, but we weren't sure if the information about the camps were true. When I arrived in Tennessee, I changed my name from Hasan Rahman to Ricky Ricardo. They think I'm Latino."

I erupted into an unexpected giggle. I hadn't laughed like that in a while. "Ricky Ricardo? From *I Love Lucy*?"

"These young'uns don't know nothing bout the classics. Especially around here, since that would be promoting interracial marriage. But I am glad to see you, truly I am." He smiled.

"What are you doing here?" I asked.

"I'm working with the remaining 8Crow left." He quietly said.

"What do you mean remaining? Tell me everything, I don't get much information outside the country."

"What do you know?"

"I know we're somewhere in Mississippi, I suppose? I know that the war is over, but aside from that, I know almost next to nothing."

"Nothing?"

"Not a lot of people talk to me much. I'm a foreman and people here barely talk to us. Hell, it makes sense because I don't talk to the other foremen hardly. I don't trust them either."

"How did you end up as a foreman? Matter of fact, how did you end up here?" He asked while taking a sip of water, frowning at the aftertaste.

"Well, I was in the R.V., on our way to California, and we needed to stop for gas. The others went into the station and I got the gas. I went back inside, and I went into the bathroom area. All of a sudden, the car jolted, and all of the waste landed on the floor. I went out to complain to Josh, who I thought was driving, but it was two people who I'd never seen before. They had stolen the R.V., not knowing I was inside. We all panicked. I grabbed the nearest weapon I could, but someone behind me pistol whipped me. I blacked out. Next thing I knew, I woke up in the back of a van along with other people. We were all tied up and had duct tape around our mouths."

"My God..." He was astonished.

"It turns out...well, I won't get into all the details. Thankfully, I was able to escape. I had no idea where I was, but I stumbled into a small town. I stole food. I stole a loaf of bread and that was enough to send me to what these stupid Dixs call a prison... Estas malditas personas son tan crueles!" A little bit of anger jumped out of my vocal cords. "I'm one of the original occupants of this slave labor camp. I tried to escape, but the guards caught me." I showed Hasan my left hand. "They cut off my ring finger to deter me from ever escaping again. It worked. I've worked long enough to make it to the position of foreman, which granted me to my own private room. Lucky me...Suerte la mía."

"At least you're alive." Hasan tried to assure me. "The underground 8Crow have been looking for all our fallen comrades, including you."

"You keep saying underground or remaining 8Crow. What happened to us?"

"We were able to create a new country, the Republic of Elysia, out west. But the Treaty of Toronto required that the remaining 8Crow cells in Mexico, Freedonia, and the Confederation could not have any more support from the head of 8Crow, April Freeman, who became the first elected president of Elysia. But don't worry. Right now, we have support with the Mexican government because we are working with them to help free Mexican private and public citizens captured at the boarder of East Texas and taken into these slave labor camps."

"Why not just take the army into the Confederacy?"

"That risks breaking with the Treaty. But that might happen anyways. There is word that Mexico and the Confederacy will end up going to war. But we have a plan. I have a plan. I need to get word back to my 8Crow cell that you're alive."

"How are you gonna do that?"

"Don't worry about that." He said as Zero walked up to sit in front of me with his plate of food.

"Hi, who are you?" Zero questioned to Hasan.

"Hey, I'm... I'm Number 172080. I'm new here."

"That's too long. I'm gonna call you Seventeen." Zero stated.

"This is Zero." I introduced Hasan to him, both of us smiling. "I promised him I'd have dinner with him."

"Nice to meet you, Zero." Hasan said. "How long have you been here?"

"What do you mean? I've lived here my whole life." Zero said in confusion. He couldn't really imagine much of a world outside of these walls.

"He was born here." I clarified for Hasan. He felt bad for Zero, I could tell.

"Hey, you're from the outside!" Zero exclaimed. "Have you seen my mother working?"

"Um, I'm sorry, but I just arrived here." Hasan didn't want to go into the fact that he was blindfolded on the way in, so he would have no idea either way.

"Listen up, newbies! Time for your labor lessons. Dinner is over for y'all. The rest can stay and eat whatever the hell kinda slop you eat." Mister Richards yelled, walking into the dining hall.

"I have to go." Hasan said. "Trust me, you all will get out of here." He whispered to me.

"I will talk to you later." I voiced.

Zero kept eating when Hasan left and said, "Nice to see you made a new friend!"

"Yeah, I'm glad to see I made a new friend too...Hey, eat the hoecakes." I instructed. I was left siting there, happy that there was some hope now, but I admit I was scared because I still was nervous, wondering if freedom was even possible at all.

LAURALEE

I will admit that while it may feel that my story won't align with the rest, I assure you, it is important with the overarching narrative. I was a 16-year-old girl in this timeframe in the Confederate States of Dixie, living in a small town in Mississippi. I didn't know much. Rather, I knew what I was taught. I grew up as a Clayton, one of the wealthiest families in the entire South. I was taught that my father was a prominent businessman. I knew my mother was a Southern Belle, raised in the state of Georgia. She was a housewife, but she was heavily involved in charity programs and organizations such as the Daughters of the Confederacy. I had twin siblings, Thomas and Jolene, who were in their mid-20s and were born before the war. I was the youngest and I was among the first generation to grow up in Dixie.

Growing up, I had a great life. My mother was loving and attentive. My father worked hard to provide for us. I wanted for nothing. My house was simply beautiful; it was a gigantic mansion built in the typical Southern fashion. On the outside, the house was a pure white color with a secondary color of green on the shutters and was supported by large pillars that stood on all sides of the house. There was also a wrap-around porch and a wrap-around balcony that had railings with ornate design. That was a feature of the house that was great for shade during the hot days and for entertainment. Huge windows and a central entrance made for an even and symmetrical look. The inside of my house contained an aura of extravagance and class. We had a massive foyer with two sweeping stairways that ran parallel to each other. It was a home that I absolutely adored.

My adoration for my home was especially clear on this special spring weekend. The image of the sunset remains unforgettable. The golden hour made the property feel like I was living through a snapshot of a memory. The light cast a beautiful shine on our expansive garden. I admired the view while I stood on the porch, leaning on one of the pillars. The Spanish Moss trees extended from our house to the entrance of our land, creating a fantastical canopy. While enjoying the elements, I breathed in the fresh air and closed my eyes to appreciate the cool breeze. The wind slightly ruffled my flared, white shirtwaist dress with a special red belt. Thankfully, the wind didn't dishevel my chestnut bouffant flip.

After letting my mind drift and daydream, I came back to reality when I saw one of our cars come through the property from the distance amidst the dangling moss flowing gently in the wind. Happy that my mother and father were arriving, I jogged down the steps from the porch to greet them. Our valet, Juan, got out and opened the car door to let Mama and Daddy out.

"Oh Daddy! Mama! I'm so glad you're home. Y'all must tell me about your day! Come on, let's go inside before the night chill starts to set in."

"Hold on, baby girl, we have a surprise for you!" My father said as my mother smiled. There were other figures in the vehicle, but I couldn't see them as the windows were tinted. Juan opened the door and let my brother, my sister, and her fiancé Samuel out onto the driveway.

"Ahh! Thomas, Jolene, what on God's green Earth are you doing here!" I shrieked as Thomas lifted me up and Jolene squeezed me with affection.

271

"I wanted to surprise you!" Mama said with enthusiasm.

"Yes, I couldn't possibly imagine missing your debutante ball!" Jolene gleefully squealed.

"You're finally making your debut into high society and I couldn't be prouder." Daddy added in.

"Plus, I will be a part of this family soon and I see you like a little sister. Jolene didn't even have to convince me to come." Samuel said.

"That's because you're a true gentleman." My mother replied. "Let's go on in and eat supper. I'm sure our fabulous cook, Auntie Yolanda, has made a great dinner as per my instructions."

The rest of us went inside and prepared for dinner. My father stayed outside briefly to monitor Juan as he took our guest's suitcases into our home. He also demanded that the car needed waxing, to which Juan said he would do. The driver drove off to the garage away from the house. As my father came inside the house, I looked out of the window to admire the land known as Dixie, a romantic and genteel country that I was blessed to live in, a country that was a legendary land of moonlight and magnolia, an idyllic territory that felt like living in a dream. I felt peaceful and content. I was happy.

***

Our dining room was elegant. We had a china cabinet that was the envy of our town. On the main wall, we had a simple, yet striking painting. The painting was of fruits such as grapes, peaches, plums, cherries as well as figs and barley along with what appears to be a glass of sparkling cider. All of the objects were placed upon a marble slab in the painting. Furthermore, there were two columns behind the fruit. Above the fruit and covering the majority of one column was a red velvet curtain raised at a certain angle.

It was my favorite work of art in the entire house, as I studied the details time and time again. We had a cherry wood table that was covered with a champagne-colored tablecloth. On top of that were maroon placemats. It was an extremely classy setting.

My father, dressed in his suit-and-tie, looked clean-cut and professional. He commanded the room by sitting at the head of the table. My mother sat on the other side of the table and Mama looked regal. She had perfectly curled and coiffed brown hair along with her tasteful red swing dress with white stripes on her skirt. Sitting beside her and across from me was Jolene. My sister was often very stylish and up to date on fashion as she wore a navy-blue shapeless shift dress and a similar hairstyle to mine. Next to me and Daddy was my brother. Since he was in the Army of the Confederacy, he possessed a buzzcut and he wore a gray uniform. Across from Thomas and next to Jolene was Samuel. He was the same as Jolene in the fact that he was trendy and dressed his age. His hair was greased on top and slicked down on the sides. He also matched Jolene by wearing a navy suit jacket and khaki pants. He looked young and professional.

Our butler, Uncle Terrell, served us the food that Auntie Yolanda prepared. There was buttermilk fried chicken, crispy and golden brown, along with some warm and buttery biscuits. Also, there was a side of some smoky, slow-cooked black-eyed peas, made with onions, garlic, bell peppers, tomatoes, and Cajun spices stewing in its own broth. Another side that was available was collard greens cooked with ham hocks. To drink, cool and refreshing lemonade was on the menu. Dessert was also present in the form of peach cobbler. After we said grace, we began to eat and passed around the dishes.

"Oh, darling, may you please be a dear, and pass Mama the biscuits?" My mother said to Jolene.

"Yes, Mama." Jolene complied. "Oh, I didn't get a chance to ask about your day in the car. What'd you do?"

"It was a nice day. I was working with the Daughters of the Confederacy." She said while placing a biscuit onto her plate. "We're commissioning several statues around Mississippi of Ace, who died a martyr for our rights, and Çaé Braun, who helped us establish this country. We also helped set up sites dedicated to Jefferson Davis, Fielding Wright, James Eastland, and Zack Claiborne who was a veteran from the Freedonian Civil War."

"Sounds like you had a full day, Mama." Thomas replied.

"It was, but it was fulfilling. Helen told me to say hello to the family, as well." She smiled.

"Give her our blessing, will you?" Daddy responded. "Jolene, how's life in Jackson?"

"Oh, it's wonderful! Jackson is the perfect city to be a socialite in; I'm starting to get to know everyone."

"Look at you, trying to be a city girl!" I joked with her.

"I'm still a country girl at heart." Jolene smiled.

"But she does fit in perfectly." Samuel complimented her. "You should see her, how well she gets along with all of the state congressmen and their wives."

"I keep forgetting that you're the youngest representative in the state." I mentioned before taking a bite of the greens.

He chuckled. "It's something I'm reminded of quite often. It's a very humbling experience, getting to learn from the older members."

"Well, ol boy, what's been going on in the state congress?" My Daddy asked.

"Oh Hunter! You should know better not to discuss politics at the dinner table." Mama reprimanded him.

"Margret, it's fine! I'd rather hear what's happening from him than to hear B.S. from the guys at the country club."

"Daddy!" I was shocked to hear the vulgarity. Thomas laughed at me because obviously, he'd heard worse.

"Well, to answer your question sir, there is a bit of a squabble within the state congress right now."

"Why would there be?" My mother asked, perhaps from a place of ignorance. "There's only one party. Shouldn't a one-party state not have any issues?"

"Well, there's a fight in the Nationalist Party between the Federalists and the States Rights factions." Samuel explained. "The States Rights congressmen believe that if we as Mississippians want to trade with countries outside of Freedonia and Quebec, we should choose to do so. The Federalists, however, believe that we are to follow the wills of the federal government who chooses to not trade outside the eastern bloc."

"Why can't we just trade with other countries?" I questioned aloud.

"Because Freedonia and the Confederacy are partially closed economies, for good reasons. We can't allow harmful ideas to come in and ruin our countries." My father interjected. "I'm with the Federalists."

"I respectfully disagree. I'm a congressman in the state's rights camp. It's time for a new generation of leadership and I believe that every state in the Confederacy should have the rights to trade with whoever they want."

"Well, if we had a two-party system like the Americans before to debate these issues, wouldn't that be better?" I enquired. I was honestly curious. Even though I grew up under one party, I always wondered why we didn't have more. Just like there were issues that Mama and Daddy disagreed upon, I imagined that people in one party would disagree on issues as well.

"You're too young to focus on politics." My father chastised.

"Yes, Daddy." I sighed, understanding that he did not want me to question the system that was in place.

"That's exactly why I didn't want to bring up the subject in the first place." Mama said. "Let's get off that topic. Thomas, what have you been up to lately?"

"I don't wanna bring the mood down." Thomas tried to explain.

"Don't you always do that with your presence?" Jolene sarcastically jested.

"Nah, but you bring the mood down with your face. That lipstick color? Tragic." My brother quipped back before sipping his lemonade.

"Thomas!" My mother exclaimed.

"She started it!" He laughed. "But anyways, I, and other soldiers, are preparing for the fact that we might be going to war."

"With who?" I furrowed my brows.

"Mexico. We've always been a tense neighbor, but now their aggression has heightened. They attempted to fly a drone over our territory, and we shot it down. The tides of war are approaching ever nearer."

"But why?" I asked. "We haven't done anything to them or their people, have we?"

My father shuffled in his seat, like he knew something we didn't. "Because they're hot-headed fools! They've always been suspicious of us and how we run our society. Dixie has a system of apartheid to separate the races and put them in their proper place. And they're happy about it too. Terrell, are you happy?" He asked, motioning our butler to come towards him.

"Yes, sir, I am happy." He faintly smiled before returning back to his position.

"See! The niggers are happy, the spics are happy and us Whites are happy. The Mexicans just want to ruin our way of life. But they wouldn't dare attack us. It'd violate the Treaty of Toronto."

"We'll see..." Thomas retorted.

"Can we please get onto a *lighthearted* topic." My mother seethed through her smile.

"We can talk about my sister's upcoming debutante ball!" Jolene raised her glass. "Do you have a date?"

"Beau will my escort. He's such a gentleman and quite easy on the eyes, I might add." I giggled.

"Leland's little brother?!" Jolene gasped.

"Who's Leland?" Samuel asked Thomas.

"Jolene's first boyfriend. If he's there at the ball, you'll have some tough competition there, buddy." My brother winked back at him.

"Lauralee! My goodness gracious, you have the best guy willing to be your escort to the ball!" Jolene beamed. "Y'all will have the best time! I remember my debut. I felt like the prettiest girl in the whole wide world. The music, the dancing and the lights... it was the most extraordinary night. I can't wait for you to have that experience. Do you know what ball gown you'll be wearing?"

"It's gonna be a surprise! I will have to find a necklace, though."

"Oh, that's no problem! You can find my old jewelry box in the attic. It'll have the necklace I wore to my ball." Mama said.

"Oh, thank you! I'm just so grateful to have y'all as a family." I replied.

We continued to dine and have a thrilling conversation. After supper, my parents sat outside on the porch, laughing, talking, and listening to music from their heyday while Mama drank a glass of wine and Daddy drank some scotch. On the balcony, Jolene and Samuel stood and planned for their wedding, talking about who they were going to invite. Thomas was wandering around the house, looking at old pictures, trying to relive old memories. I went up to the attic by myself. We had a large third floor, where we stored our old collections of clothes, toys, and other materials. I coughed entering in the dusty room, but I attempted to brush that aside. I was on a mission. Determined, I searched through several boxes. Regretfully, I forgot to ask Mama where her old jewelry box was, but I didn't want to disturb Mama and Daddy. I kept pushing through all our junk until I came across a box. It contained a red jacket and college paraphernalia. I recognized it was a box of my father's.

But one important item that I came across was a book, an American history book to be exact. It was something I wasn't expecting to find. I opened it and after hours of reading I was shocked to see that everything I thought I knew was a lie. Remember how I said I knew what I was taught? I was taught that Jim Crow laws changed only in name to apartheid simply because it sounded proper. I was taught that the Civil Rights Movement never happened. You could imagine my shock when I saw there had once been a black president. I gasped. The United States was at one point...equal for everyone. I soon came to some realizations. I was so ignorant.

You can't blame me. In hindsight, our internet was restricted, and we were taught things that didn't exist and wasn't true. Everything was revisionist history. I had never heard of Martin Luther King, Jr. or Rosa Parks or anyone who changed the United States in a way the Confederacy didn't want my generation to know. I had learned that the first civil war was over states' rights and the second civil war was about fighting back against a terrorist organization. The Confederate States of Dixie was founded for the Çaé's most loyal followers as a force against evil. I never considered that we could possibly be the bad guys. So many thoughts swirled in my head that I could not and still cannot comprehend. I was Pandora, gaining forbidden knowledge after opening a box.

From that day forth, I noticed everything that was wrong. After I found my mother's necklace, I hid away the book and went back downstairs. I looked at the maids before they left for the night. I realized that my father was wrong. Black people and Hispanics were not happy with the way things were, when they had once been in tremendous positions of power. Apartheid was not the correct way of living. I hurried to my room to keep my new knowledge secret and the fact that all I knew was wrong. All of the things I've said and done was because I thought that was the way life was. I couldn't make sense of the world anymore. Up was down and left became right. Unable to face these newfound facts, I went to sleep. Little did I know that my world would change even further and the quixotic fantasy that I knew as Dixie would come crashing down.

DANNY

There was a special place within the superblock where Miriam resided that I enjoyed going to whenever I came to the state of Los Angeles. It was a local bookstore with a café. The bookstore was one of a kind, selling vintage books that were managed to be saved from the burnings directed by Çaé Braun before the founding of the Republic. The store retained physical copies of books such as *1984, The Soul of Black Folk, Capital, Les Misérables, Antigone, The Dead Sea Scrolls,* and previous versions of the Bible.

The smell of the old books contained sweet notes of almonds and vanilla flowers, which complimented the rich aroma of coffee and the herbal scent of tea in the café. As a history professor, I cherished the store with all my heart. That day, I asked Chamorra to come with me since she was a frequent visitor. She had a tall cup of black coffee while I had a small cup of chai. After sharing our thoughts on the books we purchased, we conversed about other things.

"Again, I appreciate your hospitality. Thank you for allowing me to stay a few nights with you and Miriam until I go back to Seattle."

"No problem! I'm thrilled to have your company. Miriam and I don't get to see you enough!" She smiled before taking a sip of the strong brew. "However, you didn't stay long for the party. Did you not enjoy it?"

The creamy chai coated my tongue before I could respond. "No, everything was wonderful. I just had a bad talk with Libby."

"What happened?"

"I accused her of forgetting about the people we had to leave behind. When she set me straight, I couldn't stay. I felt ashamed and embarrassed."

"Why would you feel ashamed and embarrassed?"

"Because I realized that I've been resenting her. I felt like it was wrong that she got over what happened to us, but she never got over it. She got through it in order to find some sense of contentment, but she still thinks about those who were left behind daily, like I do. I was just stuck, and I feel stunted. I was jealous that she found happiness by pushing through and I can't."

"You are doing well, though. You're helping to influence and teach a new generation so what happened to you would never happen to anyone else again. And you're still here, making it day by day."

"I know, I just... I just wish I could be the boy I once was before turning into the man I am now. Sorry for being a Debbie Downer."

"You're not a Debbie Downer. You might be a Judy, but you're not a Debbie."

I chuckled. "That was pretty good. But how are you doing?"

"I'm doing good. I just finished a story and my cousin is moving from Guam to Silicon Valley. I think he'll be working on improving green technology to capture carbon and create genetically modified trees in order to plant forests in harsher climates as well as -"

We were both shocked from a simultaneous text message from Miriam telling us to meet her at her place as soon as possible. Chamorra and I both glanced at each other, knowing that it would only be something serious if Miriam would write a cryptic message like that.

***

After receiving the news from Miriam, the next course of action was to tell Libby. Chamorra, Miriam, and I stood outside of their townhouse once their security guard let us through their gate. Andrew opened the door and looked worried.

"Hey, what's going on? Is everything alright?" Andrew voiced out of concern.

"We have some news." Miriam said.

Andrew looked at our expression and knew immediately it was a serious matter. Why else would we travel from Los Angeles to West California? "Libby!" He cried out; the sound rushed from his diaphragm and spread across the house like an echo. Libby came down the stairs after hearing her husband call for her. When she saw us, she was surprised and rightfully so.

"Hey, um... Come in, let's go sit on the couch." She invited us in, and we all went into the living room, which appeared cozy and romantic, perfect for newlyweds. "Danny, I'm glad you came." Libby said to me while Chamorra and Miriam watched alongside Andrew. "I was gonna do a holo-call with you. I'm sorry, for how I reacted the other night. I should have been more sensitive. Yes, we both suffered and lost, but you lost more. You lost your soulmate. And I understand now that to see me in a happy marriage reminds you of everything that was stolen from you."

"Libby... You have nothing to be sorry about, because it's me who should apologize. I was jealous and slightly resentful." I replied. "But that's not why we're here."

"Did something happen?" She asked? Andrew listened intensely while Chamorra held Miriam's hand.

"You should be the one to tell her." Miriam whispered.

"Tell me what?" Libby softly questioned.

"I should explain in the way that Miriam did for me and Chamorra. She was working on a story for *The Standard* and she had a secret contact in one of the last remaining 8Crow groups from Freedonia. She was able to talk to him whenever he called. That person found out that there were rumors that, um, there are slave labor camps in Dixie."

"Oh my God!" Libby was shocked.

"The Confederates are using slaves?!" Andrew was verbally astonished.

"It's been confirmed by the Mexican military. They flew drones across several of the sites and using new technology, they saw through the buildings. The conditions are abhorrent." Miriam quickly added.

"But that's not why I'm here." I continued. "Do you remember Hasan?"

Libby's eyes lit up. "Yes, I do! He...he was there during Operation Eagle. And he was the one who helped us come here."

"Well, apparently, he's undercover as a slave in one of the containment prisons. He was able to get word back to his 8Crow cell and Libby.. Rafael is alive." I broke the news to her as she collapsed into my arms in tears. We both were emotional since this was the first time in years, we could think about Rafael and not fear that he was dead. We hugged tightly, feeling a huge burden of pain and guilt leave our shoulders. She looked up at me and then stopped the hug as she had a horrific realization.

"Does that mean..." She whispered.

"Rafael has been a slave for the past 20 years."

"Oh, dear God." She whimpered, raising her head to the sky above to talk to the Almighty. "Why him, Lord. Will his suffering never end?" She put her head back down to look at me and face the terrible reality. "There has to be something we can do."

"That's why we're here." Chamorra chimed in. "I'm going to go down to the station after I leave here and share Miriam's report to the world."

"And Miriam and I came up with a plan as well." I said. "Because we can't go into the Confederacy without risking becoming slaves ourselves, we'll go meet Miriam's source. We'll take a hypertrain to travel through Mexico and then go through the border back to Freedonia. There, with whoever Miriam's source is, we can work to bring Rafael home. I just want to know if you want to come with us."

Libby pondered and looked to Andrew. "Andrew, I- "

"Go." He said calmly. "Congress is not in session and I know that you've been needing closure. Go and find him. I'll stay here to come up with a bill to work with Mexico on this situation. Danny needs you. Rafael needs you."

Libby looked back at me and squeezed my hand. "Alright then." She gulped. "Back into hell, we go."

Libby

For me, riding in a hypertrain was still somewhat nerve wrecking. It was a relatively new technological feat to be able to travel in a solar powered, high-speed train. Luckily, the interior of the capsules was made to make me as relaxed as possible. The seats were made with comfortable cushions, which were soft enough to make a man fall asleep upright as it was in Danny's case. He was knocked out after the first hour of travel since he was up all night filling out forms in order to have a leave of absence. The capsules were also very posh and sleek. It held eight passengers, each facing each other with fold-away tables in between the seats. In feeling the rushing speed of the vehicle, I sunk into the seat to try to relax.

"Are you okay, Libby?" Miriam asked while assembling some things together on the table.

"Yes, I'm just anxious." I replied.

"You're anxious going back into Freedonia?"

"No. I mean yes, but I'm mainly nervous about this hypertrain."

"Nothing's wrong, this has actually been a great ride." Miriam said.

"I just don't trust something going this fast, it's simply unnatural." I grimaced.

Miriam laughed. "You sound like my grandmother when she flew on her first flight. She claimed that it was unnatural for any man to fly."

"Your grandmother was a wise woman." I responded, remembering the flight I made during the Blitz of St. Louis. The memory still haunted me, watching the city suffer an inhumane fate. To try to get my mind off of the tragedy, I focused on the objects that Miriam fiddled with on the table.

"Hey Miriam. What on earth are you doing with those...thingies?" I said, for lack of a better word.

"They're not just thingies." Miriam chuckled. "Once I put the finishing touches on..." She mumbled. "These will be... new glasses!" She put on what appeared to be sunglasses with a traditional cat-eyed appearance. "These are the new recording glasses that I picked up a couple of days ago. The glasses will record everything I see, through my eyes! Isn't that cool!"

"Actually, I must admit that it is." I admired the new technology that seemed to appear each day. There was so much to reinvent after Braun destroyed so many patents for devices that could threaten her power. The smart glasses were not totally new, but they were finally being reintroduced to our society. "What are you using it for?"

"I'm using it to record a documentary for *The Standard*. I have a feeling our time in Freedonia will be historic."

"Speaking of which, how will we be getting in? The Freedonian border is notoriously hard to get into. I mean, we have our passports, but I doubt that'll cut it."

"I let my source know that we'll be coming in today. He said that he will help us get though the border."

"How do you know your source? You obviously don't even know his name."

"Well, I received his contact information from a colleague of mine who used to work alongside him in 8Crow during the Elysian Revolutionary War, or the Freedonian Civil War, depending how you want to see it. He never gave me his name just so the Fredonian Government Officials would never hunt him down if I mentioned his name in my news stories. It made sense, really. So, I just never pressed him on the issue."

"I hope he comes through to help us if necessary." I said before the capsule rattled ever so slightly. "Do you know how much longer we have to travel on this over-glorified trolley?"

Miriam smiled, amused at my continued displeasure on the hypertrain. "Not long, it's only less than a 2-hour trip from L.A. to the border. I think we may have 45 minutes left."

"Good. Danny had the right idea. I'm taking a nap. Who knows how much sleep we'll catch over the next few days?" I closed my eyes.

I rested so well that it felt like I barely went to sleep. My eyelids seemed to briefly flutter when the train stopped. Danny woke up suddenly, thinking he missed his alarm to catch the hypertrain, briefly not realizing that he was already on it. We got our bags and left the train. We all packed lightly. It brought back some unpleasant memories of old times.

We went out onto the station and was bombarded with the traffic of people walking to their destination. As we walked throughout the place, I took in the sensory delight amidst my apprehension of my situation. The station was full of Mexican flair, with a hint of the old Americana. Old Tejano music played along with old country-pop songs. The fact we were in the state of Missouri still baffled me, knowing that 20 plus years ago, this was part of an American state. It was now a Mexican state. I caught a whiff of churros and pizza and heard both Spanish and English. It was a mix of cultures in this region.

We walked outside to call a car to take us to the furthest end of the city, near to the of the border. Once we made it to the edge of Freedonia, we got out of the car, as we didn't want to get the driver caught up in our plan. We traveled quite a distance and we came across a huge fence with a facility a little further away.

"Of course, Freedonia would still be xenophobic of Mexicans coming across the border." I sighed.

"I think it's more like they don't want anyone to leave." Danny retorted.

"Can you guys climb?" Miriam asked. We looked at her like she was out of her mind. "What? It's like climbing a tree."

"Aren't you from New York? Where did you learn to climb trees in that concrete jungle?" Danny replied.

"There were playgrounds, silly! Climbing is not that hard." Miriam said while looking at me. "Ladies first."

I stared at that behemoth of a fence and sighed even heavily. "There's nothing to it, huh?" I hopped onto a bar and attempted to climb. It was a struggle, grunting all the way to the top while sweat trickled on my forehead. I sat atop the fence and kept my balance. I dropped my bookbag to have some cushion to fall on. I took a deep breath and dove through the air to roll on the ground and land on my knees. I was successful.

"Oh wow! That was impressive!" Danny exclaimed. "Where in the hell did you learn to do that?"

"I used to be a gymnast back in high school. Didn't I ever tell y'all that?" I said.

"That's gonna be a tough act to follow..." Miriam muttered. She did almost the same thing as me, but she just jumped from the top and landed on her feet by bending her knees. "Damn, my body don't work like it used to." She panted, walking up to me. "Danny, it's your turn."

"Yippie..." He was not enthused at all. He struggled climbing up. It took some time for him to make it to the top. But in trying to be balanced, he fell backwards. Luckily, Miriam and I rushed to catch him. He landed on our arms and was rattled.

"Are you okay?" I asked out of concern.

"I'm never doing that again. Next time, y'all ask me to climb anything, you can square up. God, that was so scary." He said, attempting to catch his breath and clenching his chest.

"I guess we should try to get past the border facility." Miriam brushed off any dust that was on her t-shirt. "Can we run from them?"

"Did you not think this far ahead?" I questioned.

"I make it up as I go along." She smiled.

"Uhm, we should start running." Danny pointed out a patrol car coming out ahead.

"Good idea." I said, gathering my bag and running with Danny and Miriam right behind me.

"Hurry up!" I called out to them. But we were no match for the vehicle as it turned and slid in front of us horizontally.

"Hands up!" The man said, getting out of the car. Trying not to ruffle any feathers and further escalate the situation, we listened. We raised our hands in the air. "You were trying to leave the country, weren't you? By the orders of the Çaé, I cannot allow you to do that."

Hearing the phrase 'by the orders of the Çaé' gave me an intense flashback. "Sir, we're entering the country on urgent business." I told the truth. "If you'll just check our passports, you'll see that we're from Elysia."

He seemed to pause, almost giving it some thought. But he had made up his mind that we were criminals. I was attempting to grab my wallet but he got scared and pulled out his gun. "You won't escape! Now get in th-" He was suddenly shot in the head, apparently out of nowhere. It was a Deus Ex Machina, of course. As his body slammed to the ground, we heard the revving of motorcycles. Three of the vehicles were driven by figures dressed in black and covered in shadowy helmets. They came up and parked right next to the patrol car. I must admit; I was frightened. Who were these strange people who came to our rescue? That question was soon answered. The three of them took off their helmets and I wish you could have seen the look of shock and surprise on my face. The woman on the right had ragged, short blond hair and a smile that was utterly familiar. It was Anna. The man on the left stood tall and appeared as kindhearted as ever. It was Josh. The man in the center, had black hair that was shoulder length and it had a sliver streak, just like before almost. He had a goatee and a beard, but he was unmistakable with his sly smile.

"Miss me?" Johannes smirked.

JOHANNES

Twilight began creeping in as Anna, Josh, and I drove back to our place. The pinkish clouds were below a deep purple sky and above a creamy orange-colored sunset. The wind swiftly flew by, a sensation I'm sure was unusual for Libby; she hung on to me for dear life. I revved up the motorcycle to go faster before the authorities could even discover that one of their government officials were dead. However, that man was the last thing on my mind. No one could see it underneath my helmet, but I was grinning from ear to ear. Danny and Libby, my old friends, survived the war. Based on how they looked, they not only survived but thrived as well. I had no idea that Miriam, a new friend, were connected to them whilst I was feeding her information that would force Mexico and Elysia to do what was right.

While Miriam held onto Josh and Danny held onto Anna, we traveled on an empty road and then took a hidden exit towards the forest of southern Illinois. Thank God that we had recently found this cabin, hidden deep into the woods. When we all parked by the trees, and we walked to the front of the tiny home, the happiness overtook all of us. Anna softly hugged Libby, almost in disbelief that she was there in the flesh. Josh lifted Danny up with unimaginable strength and shed tears, which genuinely struck me in the heart since Josh rarely showed emotions like this. I looked at Miriam with a smile, glad to finally be able to see the face behind the voice. She warmly squeezed me and laughed with me like we've known each other for years.

"Do you guys go rescue damsels in distress often?" She said.

"Oh yeah, all the time, that's like totally our norm." I quipped.

"Thank you for saving us." Libby chimed in once she let go from Anna. She walked up to me and stared at me. "You... you look different." She whispered.

"So do you." I replied in awe. "You don't wear an afro anymore. And Danny, you...you have a beard now."

"And Josh has facial hair as well." Danny said. He gazed at me and my new look (in their eyes). "Your hair is longer than it ever was, which is ironic because Anna's is shorter than it ever was."

Josh walked to stand behind Danny, and he signed everything to Anna. Libby had an expression of confusion.

"There's a lot we need to talk about. Let's go on inside." I led them to the front door of the cabin, walking up the tiny stairs and into the entrance where there was a small couch and a huge fireplace. Someone else they weren't expecting was around the corner, holding a bloody knife. He set it on the counter of the mini-kitchen and ran to hug Danny and Libby.

"Lionel!" Danny exclaimed, giving him a bear hug and gaining prints of the deep red liquid onto his clothes. "You're alive!"

"I'm so happy y'all are here!" He uttered in a voice of pure joy. Unhanding him, he realized that he had blood all over his clothes. "Sorry, I just killed a racoon. That's gonna be for supper."

"Oh, okay." Libby seemed surprised, but she went with the flow. I can only imagine the food they got to eat in Elysia, but here, we only ate the food that we had to survive.

"You guys can help us prepare for dinner, if you'd like." Anna said.

"We'd loved to. Just tell us what you would like us to do." Miriam stated, pushing up her cool sunglasses.

After about an hour of chit-chat while shucking corn, we sat in front of the fireplace. I placed the boiler full of corn high above the fire and Lionel placed the raccoon meat wrapped neatly in tinfoil. Not having access to electricity forced us to be creative. The flames, enveloped the room with warmth, danced with fiery colors of bright yellow and auburn. Once dinner was ready, we ate corn on the cob (which was begging for salt and butter, but that was a luxury we didn't have). The raccoon meat had a strong and distinctive flavor with a sort of musky odor, but it was good and tender. Seeing Danny and Libby alive and well gave us the sort of pep that Josh, Anna, Lionel, and I needed to make it through.

"You guys have no idea how happy we are to see you. Ever since St Louis was bombed, we didn't know if you guys made it out of the city." I said, turning our humorous conversation into a serious one. Josh interpreted it into ASL for Anna.

"We didn't know if y'all were even alive!" Danny replied. "When Libby and I were in the air, we... we watched the missiles hit the city and we both assumed the worse."

"It was terrifying." Libby mentioned. "When we hadn't heard from any of you guys afterwards, we just thought the three of you were dead." She was referring to me, Lionel, and Anna. "Josh, how did you get here?"

"Actually, they wouldn't be alive if it wasn't for Brune and me." Josh said as well as signed.

"It's true. After we decided to stay and help 8Crow, someone who was the head of 8Crow in St. Louis got a warning that the city was going to be bombed. We immediately tried to go back to the underground bunkers."

"The warning came from Brune. I had to break my undercover spy role to get the message out. We had to leave Philadelphia immediately before the other government officials knew what we did. Thank God we did before that city tumbled to the ground." Josh added.

"After St. Louis was bombed, we were in a safe area, but we didn't make it to the bunker. We were trapped under some building materials for several days. But we made it out! Some rescuers found us. However, Lionel had a nail stuck in his left eye, which left him partially blind. It's the reason why he's wearing a patch. Also, Anna's cochlear broke and she's not been able to hear anything since then. That's why Josh is her interpreter now, even though she can lip read, she sometime misses part of conversations without him."

"And he's my husband." Anna chimed in after watching Josh. "We've been married for the past 15 years." She looked at him lovingly. "He's been my rock and I don't know what I would have done without him. Especially through these dark times where we always had to move from one place to another, just to avoid getting caught by the F.I.I."

"Wow, uh congratulations!" Libby said to Anna, trying to remember the sign for it. She remembered and Anna smiled.

"Thank you." Anna replied. "I wish you could have been at the reception." She laughed.

"We had exquisite ration packs, the special wedding edition." Josh sarcastically laughed. He took a bite of the meat and kept talking. "Although times were harder right after the war, to spend it with Anna was one of the best times of my life. I remember when they occupied the city of St. Louis. It was right after I escaped back to D.C. from Philadelphia. I knew that the leadership of 8Crow had sent them to St. Louis after Lionel's home was targeted, so I went there to look for them. I was able make it by impersonating my former role, because the military officials that came in weren't updated to the situation of Ryan Oakland." He laughed. "They didn't know that 8Crow held the real Ryan while I acted like him."

"Say, whatever happened to the real Ryan?" Lionel interrupted.

"I don't know." Josh responded. "I think he's dead. I later learned that Ryan was in D.C. when we were college students. He was the one that shot Ace. He was hired by Braun to help her stage a coup."

"What?!" Miriam was shocked.

"Oh yeah. He and several others who became R.O.C.s were directly involved in blowing up sites in D.C. just before that infamous battle. I found out that insidious plot which helped place the Çaé in power when I was in Philadelphia. I still find it quite... what's the word? Appalling, I guess, that a small number of people were able to pull off the greatest coup d'état in history because Braun took advantage of the aftermath of Lumos' death."

"I know, it's odd right?" Anna said. "Freedonia doesn't even seem to stand for much."

"Fascism doesn't have to make sense." Danny stated. "As a history professor, I have spent my time teaching about fascism. All it is a far-right, authoritarian, and ultranationalist form of power that relies on the rule of a dictator. That's it. Freedonia is a fascist oligarchy."

"What is the Confederacy then?" Miriam questioned.

"Ah, that's a tricky statement. It's a puppet state."

"What?" I was confused. I was just trying to munch on some grub.

"Tell us more." Miriam seemed oddly interested until I remembered she was a journalist. Of course, she'd be interested.

"A puppet state is recognized as independent but is completely reliant on a foreign power. A puppet state or government externally appears to be autonomous with a name, flag, anthem, constitution, or whatever. But it's truly controlled by another, more powerful state. Dixie is truly controlled by Freedonia for political and economic reasons. Freedonia is actually in charge." Danny continued and sighed. "At least they're not Quebec, which is just a pussy of a nation, never fully helping out in anything. They claim they're neutral, but they're just a bunch of wimps."

Libby laughed. "Well, that was unexpected and random!"

"You know it's true! I bet you everything I have that Quebec won't get involved in helping stop slavery in the south. Sure, they'll claim neutrality, but they'll have financial reasons as to not get involved since they're the only civilized nation that trades with Freedonia and Dixie." Danny ranted.

"At least when Mexico and Canada witnessed the atrocities that occurred during the war, they helped fortify their democracy so that what happened to us could never happen to them. They recognized the faults that we never did. They saw the cracks in their foundation that we didn't see in our own and fixed them before it crumbled." Miriam said.

"Believe you me, we wanted to leave this treacherous place and go to Canada or Mexico, but..." Lionel began. "We had to be doing something to fix it, not just let this atrocity continue. Who I'm really mad at is Elysia."

"Elysia?" Libby admonished. "What did we do?"

"You all became complicit because you were complacent and content. Because you were happy with your new status quo, you never questioned that the Treaty of Toronto was completely unfair. It stated that Elysia couldn't help the remaining 8Crow members within Freedonia and the Confederacy. We were left here without any support from the main leadership." Lionel argued.

"My mother knew that the Çaé was never going to capitulate and that it would have meant a longer war had she denied those conditions." Libby said. "Was it wrong? Perhaps. But we created a new nation that could fulfill the promises that even the United States of America couldn't reach. But guess what. They're helping now. They, along with Mexico, are going to help free the slaves because now we can see that a dangerous history is being repeated. Besides, we got off topic." She looked back to Anna. "I wanted to know about your honeymoon!"

Anna giggled after Josh signed it, we all laughed, and the mood was light once again. Dinner was over and Danny reached for what looked like a pack of cigarette in his pocket and then looked at me.

"You wanna smoke?" He asked.

"No, I don't smoke tobacco." I replied.

He laughed. "No, you know I would never offer you that! It's marijuana!"

I was surprised. "What?"

"Yeah. In Elysia, weed is fully legalized and decriminalized. It's sold with regulations and it's taxed to make money for the nation. A company called Mary Jane, which is owned by a black woman, was the first one to sell joints in a pack in the country. You want one? I have a hybrid called Earth OG."

I gasped. "That used to be my favorite strain when we were in college."

"Then let's go outside and sit on the steps." Danny said.

This time, he led me through those doors. We sat down and I shivered from anticipation. Realistically, I was probably shivering from the nighttime air. Danny pulled out his phone for light. It was the most technologically advanced cell phone I'd ever seen, especially compared to my burner phone. It was incredibly thin like a credit card. It was also sleek like it came from a sci-fi tv show. It was amazing.

"Do you mind if I play some music?" He propositioned.

Music. I hadn't heard music in forever, other than the occasional humming I did by myself.

"Yeah, I don't mind." I said.

"There's this cool new genre called Minimalé. I think you'll like it." He played a song I had never heard before, the mere fact that it was a novelty for me felt exciting. The pulsating beat and rapid lyrical content were soothing to my ears, reminding me why I loved music in the first place. Music is so healing and makes you feel so many emotions that you'd never think would course through your veins. The instrumentation of music alone was an intense quality to be savored. The delivery of the vocals felt smooth like butter, with voices intertwined to create perfect melody and harmony. The speedy rapping penetrated my gut like bullets, surprising me with every rhyme. There was a certain poetry to music, an art that I so sorely missed.

"Danny...this is fucking awesome! You know I haven't heard any new music in such a long time."

"No?"

"No, we've been busy. Come on, hurry up, I wanna light a joint."

"Okay, okay!" He took out a tiny, yet powerful lighter from inside of his pack. He lit one of the joints and instantly, I was able to sniff an earthy and citrusy scent. He then handed me a reefer. Acknowledging that I wouldn't know how to work the new lighter, he lit the miniscule flame for me. I inhaled the smoke, letting the herb smolder inside and taking in all of the smoke I could. Naturally, because I hadn't smoked in a long time, I coughed loudly, causing my throat to get scratchy and dry.

"You okay?" He laughed.

"Never been better." I joked back. I smoked for a couple minutes and already, the effects of the weed were immediate. I already felt like I had reached a new level of consciousness. I felt relaxed. I didn't realize how much tension I held all the time. It's easy to do that when you live a life like mine, always traveling as to avoid getting killed. The cannabis filled my lungs as if it was filling the deepest part of my soul. I became more sensitive to color, sound, light, touch, and smell.

I became acutely aware just how dark the world was, with the stars providing most of the illumination aside from the bright synthetic light of Danny's phone. I recognized the green color of the trees differed and wasn't all just a homogeneous blend. The smell of the forest along with the smell of the marijuana swirled around my nostrils, creating a woodsy scent that took me back to my camping days when I was younger. The touch of the warm joint and my other hand touching the rough wood of the steps somehow amused me. I giggled, something I hadn't done since I was in my twenties. I then soon reached a state of ecstasy, a difficult yet wonderful sensation to describe. Ecstasy feels like a mind-fuck but like in the best way possible. I was high.

"You good?" Danny checked.

"Yeah, I'm good. I just haven't felt this way in a long time."

"What do you feel?"

"For the first time in forever, free. I feel free."

"What did you mean by 'we've been busy?'" Danny wondered aloud.

"Well, my friends and I have been secretly working with students."

"New 8Crow recruits?"

"No, just students.

There was a gap of quiet, Danny needed time to think. "So, knowledge is your new weapon?"

"Exactly! What we do every now and then, is go to the University of Lynn. It's the premier school in the country. We feed knowledge about democracy and republicanism to a generation that knows nothing about it."

"But how will it work? They're privileged kids that benefit from the institutional power of the state."

"That's right! They're privileged kids. And what do privileged kids want the most?"

"...something they can't have." Danny realized.

"They want democracy because its forbidden. They're learning about choices that don't exist for them and they feel it's unfair to not have those choices because they're used to getting whatever they want. Soon we'll go to the University of Lynn and help them prepare for the protest."

"Protest? How are you gonna just... protest here in Freedonia."

"We'll protest with a massive alliance of people from other universities across the country coming to the capital, in front of the Argenti Palace.

The Çaé won't be able to deny us then. We're going to the university undercover to discuss the final plans with them."

"You know Libby, Miriam, and I will go with you. If we can make this whole eastern bloc crumble for good..." Danny became lost in thought. The lyrics from the new song that just played dealt with issues of a romantic nature. Danny's face became saddened. I knew where his mind was.

"You're thinking about Rafael, aren't you?"

"How can I not... The love of my life is enslaved right now. That sentence alone shows how wrong that is and the Dixies were trying to cover up that they're using slave labor. I can't fathom it."

"We're giving as much information as we can to the Mexican government so that they can use military actions to free them. Don't worry. Come what may, he will be free again. Just like us."

"Gosh, these emotions are just swirling in my head. Should've realized that it would have a bad side effect." Danny sighed. "For the past years, I've been feeling depressed and I don't like it."

"You should allow yourself to feel things. Don't do what I did."

"Which was?"

"Beat myself up for feeling certain things. Remember when I first felt guilty about killing the man who tried to attack me?"

"Yeah, how could I not."

"I've learned to let the guilt of killing go. Sure, I may feel *bad* for the family of those who lost their loved ones that I killed, but I don't experience guilt."

"How did you overcome that?"

"Because I learned to enjoy the killing." I said chillingly. "After killing that officer who treated me like absolute shit, I figured why feel bad for those who try to hurt me. I've learned to not feel badly about protecting myself. Does that sound dark? Maybe so. But these past 20 years have changed me, have changed us, more than you know. I was able to shoot that officer that would probably have killed you guys at the border, and I smiled underneath my helmet. Why? Because I was protecting the ones I love. I feel like I'm sounding cold and brutal, but maybe that's because I am. That's who I had to become to survive in this cruel world. Am I making any sense at all, I feel like I'm not?"

"It's probably the weed talking."

"Yeah, you're probably right. Man, we've changed a lot, haven't we?"

"We have. For better or for worse."

"You know what's never changing? The stars. Look at them, a constant fixture in the sky when you feel like everything you know is turned upside down. The twinkling stars above will guide you home." We both looked at the stars, shining and dimming, and seeing the cloudy gaseous part of space known as the Milky Way. That sight has been seen by humanity before us and will continue to be seen by humanity after us. That was a thought that brought us comfort amidst our toiling emotions and scheming plots to help change the world. The thought that no matter what happened, the stars would always, forevermore, be watching down on mankind.

LAURALEE

F rom my bed, I glanced at the window to admire the wonderment of the stars. The gleaming majesties of the heavens brought a smile on my face. The positions of the starlight signaled the commencement of a special night. It was finally the night of my debutante ball. My hair was already specifically prepared for my coming out into polite society. I had lovely and lengthy thick hair that was styled into volumes of curls from the ear down, with the top of my hairstyle being waved back into a partial half up, half down fashion. My makeup was already done as I wore a natural look with a pink lip tint. The natural look was to showcase a certain type of soft femininity. I saved the most important thing for last: my dress.

"I'm so glad you decided to let me help you with the dress, Lauralee!" Mama said with excitement as she entered my room. "You could've had any of your servants help you with that, but I'm glad you wanted me to share this moment with you." She was already prepared for the ball. My mother had a French Twist hairdo with an outfit that was very becoming of a lady like her. She wore a maroon and dusty rose-colored outfit that was flowing and sweeping out to her calf; she looked quite wonderful. She started to search around the room, seeking to see my secret dress. "Where is it, honey, I've been waiting to see it!"

"It's in the closet, Mama!" I smiled, awaiting her response.

She went into the walk-in closet and exclaimed. "Oh my! It's absolutely beautiful!" She came out and presented my green sprigged muslin ballgown. It had ruffled sleeves that were off-the-shoulder. The skirt was large and full, leading to the expectation that it would be billowing once applied atop of the crinoline petticoat. The outfit was perfect for the ball, as the tight bodice along with the extravagant skirt created an air of elegance and womanliness that was befitting for a belle of the Confederate aristocracy.

She helped me with putting on bodywear that shaped my waist and putting on the petticoat. While doing that, she struck up a conversation with me.

"My, my, times have changed."

"What do you mean, Mama?"

"When I had my debutante ball, we wore white dresses. It was traditional."

"Some traditions must change to make way for new ones." I replied.

"Yes, I suppose so. Besides, the dresses are lively in color now. I do appreciate that. I do remember so desperately wanting to wear a blue ballgown, but it wasn't allowed."

"Thankfully, times have changed. We can wear whatever patterns we want now!"

"As long as it's modest!" My mother added.

"Of course! Do you remember when I was a little girl and I got to witness cousin Charlotte's debutante?"

"Yes! Back at that time, the style was changing to reflect honor on our Confederate heritage. That's why it's important to look like a southern belle, you know. It's time to put your dress on!" She said. I was able to fit the dress without too much difficulty. I spent some time in the mirror admiring how classy I looked. I finally looked like a lady, no longer a little girl. My mother came up behind me to put on the necklace. I touched the jewelry and we both smiled. "This necklace is very special to me. I wore this at my debutante ball. It was a special family heirloom from Georgia. It was one of the only things that survived from antebellum time after Sherman's March. It's been a priceless object to all of your maternal ancestors for centuries. I'm glad to give it to you."

I slowly turned around in shock, not expecting her to say that. "I thought I was only wearing this for tonight?"

"I want you to have it. It's a token of my love and affection for you, my darling daughter. Oh, you're growing up so fast, I can hardly believe it." Tears began to well up in her eyes.

"Don't cry Mama! Your makeup will be ruined!" I comforted her. "Besides, I'll always be your little girl, won't I?"

"Yes, you will." We hugged and tightly embraced each other. I felt treasured and loved. My mother had given me a precious gift, something that has been passed down from mother to daughter since time immemorial. But suddenly, I remembered where I had found it, in the attic, and I remembered all of the things that I learned. I remember reading prohibited knowledge for what seemed like hours. I felt the heavy burden of knowing what I knew. Determined to get some answers, I carefully asked my mother some questions, starting with the necklace.

"Mama, when did your mother give this necklace to you?"

"Why, it was right before my debut, of course." She said.

"What was life like back then? When you were my age?"

"I can never forget. It was during the election season of Ace and Riperton. It was a divisive time for everyone, but everyone in my family were proud members of the Ace base."

"Were you an Ace supporter?"

"To be honest, I was apolitical. Why should I have cared, I was in high school then. I just worried about simple things, such as if a crush liked my picture on social media." She laughed. "My sister was a volunteer for Ace. But then the president died, and the civil war occurred." She looked longingly in the distance. It seemed like there was more of a story there. "But the past is the past."

"Were colored people always in subservient roles?" I quickly questioned before she could move onto another topic.

"Well, that's an odd question to ask." She furrowed her brows.

"It's still pertaining to your youth. What were colored people's life like then?"

"The same as always, I suppose. The people of color occupied the same roles then as they do now. I don't understand what you are talking about, my dear."

"So, they don't deserve to move on to become a part of the aristocracy?"

"Don't be foolish. Their roles have always been to be our cooks, our maids, our servants, and butlers."

"Could one of their roles have been holding the office of the presidency of the United States?" I defiantly asked.

"What has gotten into you?!" My mother reprimanded. "You don't know what you're talking about, Lauralee."

The guilt had taken over me. "Mama, I just don't think that this system of segregation and apartheid is right! We're no better than them, they're human beings too. I've been doing some thinking and I feel that it's wrong that we force a group of people to second-class citizenship." I explained.

Mama grabbed my hands and held them tight. "Facts don't care about our feelings. And the fact remains that the law is the law. White people are to always be segregated from the colored and a colored is never to be of equal status. Lauralee. You can always think about what's right and what's wrong, but never go against the state. It can lead to really serious consequences. Do you understand me? Now I don't ever want to hear you talk about this matter again. We are going to pretend like this conversation never happened. Now look in the mirror." I proceeded to do just that. "My dear daughter, I want you to know that I love you and I hope you have a wonderful night."

Keisha, one of our servants, knocked on the door. I could always tell it was her because she knocked in the beat of Three Men and a Haircut.

"Come in!" Mother said.

"Ma'am, Mister Beau is here for Miss Lauralee." Keisha stated.

"Ahh, perfect timing. Let's go down to greet Beau. I'm sure he's excited to see you." She smiled. Keisha left the room. Mama grabbed my arm in a haste. "Please, don't forget what I said." For the first time, I saw fear in her eyes. I nodded my head ever so slightly. She received the message. She resumed her smile and let me get out of the room first. I made my way down our grand staircase, seeing everyone gathered in the foyer. My father grinned with pride. He wore a tuxedo and kept his hair neat. Thomas maintained a stoic posture with his gray uniform, yet there was a sly smile hidden in his face. Jolene was positively beaming and jumping up and down in her stylish champagne-colored lace column dress. Samuel held her hands, while wearing a tuxedo as well, sharing the same emotions as her. And there was Beau.

Beau was absolutely the most handsome man I had ever laid my eyes upon. He was dressed in a black tuxedo, complete with a light green bowtie to match. His eyes were gray, alluring as the owl of Athena. His hair was short at the sides, but it blended into a longer length at the top, creating a signature curl. He had a pencil mustache that accented his wonderful smile. And oh, how Beau was smiling.

"Lauralee, no one has nor ever will look as gorgeous as you do right now." He reached his hand out for mine once I finished my descent from above. I gently placed my hand in his and he bowed to kiss it, never taking his eyes off me.

"Why, I must declare I've never seen a more handsome man myself!" I said charmingly. "You look wonderful, Beau."

"Alas, my attractive features pales in comparison to your timeless beauty." He flirted.

"Stop it, or you'll make me blush all night." I giggled.

"All right, stop it, you two lovebirds." My father said, attempting to stop the blatant beguilement. "Lauralee, you're the last daughter I have. You're the youngest. I can truthfully say that this moment, seeing you for the first time as a grown-up, may make your father shed a tear."

"Oh, Daddy! I love you too!" I responded. Looking back, I turned to my sister, who left her fiancé's side to talk to me.

"Lauralee! That dress is darling, simply darling!" She squealed.

"I knew you'd love it, Jolene!"

"I have to know, who made this for you?"

"I wouldn't dare tell you!"

"Why not?!" She whined.

"Because if I tell you, she'll start making you dresses. And then when you go back to Jackson, everyone will ask who you're wearing and then my fashion designer will be so busy, she'll never have time for me."

She frowned, but then I laughed.

"What's so funny?"

"I lied! I just got this at the boutique at the town square."

"Oh, you silly little rascal!" She chuckled. "I'll get you back for that."

"Can I talk to you two alone?" Thomas came in, seeming serious.

"Why yes!" I said.

"Let's go into the dining room." Jolene added. We left everyone to talk to each other. We, the Clayton siblings, talked amongst ourselves.

"I already told Mama and Daddy this." Thomas said solemnly. "I wanted to tell you at the last minute."

"Thomas, what's the matter?" Jolene asked.

"I...have been recalled to go back to the base." His voice was shaky. "I have to start preparing for war."

I was stunned. "War? What war? Thomas, what on God's green earth are you talking about?"

"Mexico is planning an invasion into our country and I will be fighting with the army."

"When are you planning to leave?" Jolene voiced out of concern.

"Tonight. I'm actually supposed to be leaving now."

"No!" I cried out. "You can't leave, you just can't! Not tonight of all nights!"

"I'm sorry, Lauralee. I really wanted to see your debut, but I must go."

"I won't let you leave!" I said in fear. "I don't want you to die over some stupid war!"

"I will be safe. I promise. I will do video-chats with y'all all the time, okay?"

"Thomas..." Jolene sadly whispered. "Be careful, brother."

"Be careful, sister." He replied. "If the Mexicans invade Jackson, come right back here. They won't dare mess with civilian homes, understand?"

"Yes." She gulped. Thomas hugged me and Jolene. He looked at me one last time and shed a single tear. It was a tear of fear, fear of the unknown, for no one knew what could possibly happen with the threat of a Mexican-Confederate war. My parents already knew, so when he grabbed his bags, they didn't blink an eye.

"Hey, where's he going?" Samuel questioned, not in the know.

"He's going to serve his country and the state of Mississippi." My father explained. "Farewell, son." My father grabbed Thomas' shoulder and gripped him like a man. Thomas nodded his head. We heard a car pull up from the edge of the property. That was his ride. Thomas looked back, knowing it may very well be the last time he might see his family and his home. He turned around to face forward and went out into the night.

After a moment of silence and realization that we'd be going to war, we all tried, as we southerners tend to do, to continue without mentioning the unfortunate circumstances. It felt like a complete tonal shift, trying to ignore the elephant in the room.

"Let's go to the ball." Mama said once Juan, our valet, brought the limo out front. We made our way and I left the mansion a girl, to come back as a woman.

***

The Daughters of the Confederacy hosted the ball, so naturally near the entrance of the venue there were statues of Robert E. Lee, Ace and the Çaé, along with Zack Claiborne. The outside of the plantation contained a lovely garden with magnolia trees making the area a sight to see. Walking in with Beau alongside me, I saw several of the other girls that were debuting. "My, my, I simply can't take my eyes off your dress." I said to Delilah. She had on a baby blue organdy gown with flowers pinned to the low neckline. Waltzing past her, I saw Courtney. "Wow, what a wonderful gown! Let me know where you got it from after we eat dinner! All right now, don't you forget!" I gracefully complimented. Her dress truly was worthy of a compliment as she wore a pearl pink tulle gown with off-the-shoulder long sleeves that were sheer. We made our way through to the gigantic doors of the towering building. Inside was magnificent. People swirled around this spacious home, which was repurposed to be a huge, almost gilded ballroom. The band played a lively rendition of the national anthem of the Confederacy, which was *Dixie*, of course. On the sides were the stairs which drew your attention to a big floral arrangement that was meant to resemble the Confederate flag, high on the walls of the second floor. The red roses made up the background while the outline of heraldic saltire was made of white roses. The actual saltire was filled with blue roses. There were 10 white bouquets of roses to represent the stars that signified the ten states that were a part of the Confederacy. The setting was phenomenal.

It was time for the debutante ball to officially begin. All of the ladies lined up near the entrance. One by one, we each walked to the center of the ballroom with our escort. Beau winked at me before we walked and made me blush. He brought me to the center in front of the audience where the other girls and I were to be introduced. After the introduction, we were to perform a type of curtsy known as the Texas Dip, which involved us extending our arms outwards and lowering ourselves fully so that one knee can touch the floor while at the same time bowing our head to the side so that our left ear can touch our knee. The audience was silent as we were now becoming women before their very eyes. Once the final person curtsied, there was a joyous applause. The entrances were done, and a formal dinner was held. We were served only the best food by the colored people. When the Black and Hispanic people served us, I felt a tiny sense of shame. My mother looked at me and with a glare, reminded me of what she said earlier. While eating, proper manners were expected to be used at the dinner table, such as laying the napkin on your lap and placing it on the table when you are finished eating. We were taught to take small bites, not talk with a full mouth, and to use the correct silverware for the corresponding course.

After all of the ceremonious traditions were over, it was time for dancing, the part I was most looking forward to. The band played music that was both enjoyable for the young and older people.

"Would you like to dance, m'lady?" Beau offered after we finished eating.

"I would be honored." I cheekily smiled in return. He helped me up and from the corner of my eyes, I saw a strange man. He looked out of place. His hair was short with choppy fringes, which was terribly outdated. It was a style that was closer to my father's era when he was in his twenties. There was more that made him stand out. I had wondered if my eyes were deceiving me. He was wearing a waiter's uniform. Now, that would not have been odd if he was a colored person. But he was white. A white man was always supposed to be above a colored, but here this man was, in equal standing with them. It was quite peculiar.

However, he walked away, and I pushed him out of my thoughts. I focused on dancing with Beau and enjoying the music. The music that was played that night was of the Grasshop sound. The twangy notes of the acoustic stringed instruments along with some rhythmic percussion really was the perfect music for dancing. One song, we did a dance called the Atlanta Stroll, a favorite of mine. Beau and I were having ourselves a mighty fun time. While dancing, I saw the strange man again, looking jittery like he was searching for something. Yet again, I tried to ignore him.

After I had my fill of dancing, I sat back down near my family. While talking to my sister, I noticed the man leave the ballroom and go up the stairs, almost tripping on his way. I politely excused myself because I was curious to see what on earth this person was doing. He snuck up the stairs and I noticed him going to the left. He was going towards the back of the house on the second floor. I went up the stairs gracefully, knowing that anyone could be watching me. I looked down from the second floor underneath the floral Confederate flag arrangement. No one was paying attention, as far as I could tell. I peered around the corner, and saw the man fiddling with a panel down the hallway.

"Explain yourself!" I said in a commanding voice, demanding to know why he was there. The man jumped and tried to place his tools back in his case to hide them from me. "Who are you?"

"Uh, I am a gentleman!" He stammered as I got closer.

"You are no gentleman, I can tell." I scoffed.

"How are you the expert on what a gentleman looks like?" He tried to say without stuttering.

"Because I am a lady!" I admonished.

"A true lady wouldn't followed me upstairs like this. What are you trying to do?"

"What are *you* trying to do? I saw you with those tools!"

"Hey! I'm gonna ask the questions around here." He said. There was a comically long pause where we both stood around, waiting for something.

"Aren't you going to ask a question?!" I exasperatedly replied.

"Well, the first question I have is why all this talk about ladies and gentlemen? What is this, *Gone with the Wind*?!"

"You mentioned it first!" I yelled.

"Hush down!"

"I'll only hush down if you answer my question. If you're a waiter, then why are you white?" The question didn't come out how I meant.

"What an odd question!"

"Well, it applies!"

"I don't understand what you're talking about!" He was adamant in his position.

"Oh, don't you get it, you bumbling fool! You don't belong here! It's too obvious. You have a Freedonian accent, your hair looks ragamuffin, and you are a white man in a servant's clothing! Only colored people here are ever in that role, so it shows me that you're an outsider and you are clearly up to something. So, give it up! Tell me exactly who you are and what you're doing! Quickly!" I demanded.

Realizing that the jig was up, he finally gave in. "My name... is Brune and I'm here for an important reason."

"Which is?" I asked him.

He sighed. "Here in Mississippi, there is someone committing a terrible crime against humanity. I'm here to investigate."

"Well, you sure are a lousy investigator."

"Nevertheless, I'm here to stop a horrific action. Slave labor is being used by the Dixie government and someone here at this very ball owns some of the containment prisons that hold the slaves."

I was confused. "But slavery is illegal! Why would it be here?"

"Because it's hidden under the guise of incarceration and rehabilitation. All of the people of color that are arrested get sent to these slave labor camps. Also, outcasts are sent to death camps as well. It's an atrocity and if you believe in justice, you'll allow me to do my job."

All of the new and recent knowledge I had come to learn swirled in my head once again. I felt compelled to do something right. "I'll do you one better. I'll help you."

Brune scratched his head. "Why?"

"Because I can. I just learned that we are forcing the coloreds to live a life that doesn't guarantee their rights. I have to do something."

"Ah, I suppose you can help me." He said. "You can be on the lookout while I hack this wire through the panel so we can listen into the room on the other side of this wall. There should be men in there right now talking and enjoying their cigars and brandy. Hopefully, there's some damning evidence that one of those men own the Cook Containment Prisons." Brune went back to his toolbox. He went to work and to keep my promise, I stood in front of the hall as a lookout. Several minutes had passed, when I heard footsteps climbing up the stairs. I peeked behind the wall to see who it was. It was Beau. I stepped out of the hallway and stopped him in his tracks.

"There you are! I've been looking all over!" He smiled. "What happened to you?"

"Oh, I'm embarrassed to say!" I lied while leading him back down the stairs as I followed behind him so he wouldn't see Brune. "I've been trying to find the restroom. It isn't fitting of a lady to admit that, I know."

"I would've helped you find it!" He replied. "I know where it is." He held my waist once we were down the stairs. "You might need more help."

"Whatever do you mean?" I questioned.

"How are you going to use the restroom under all those layers of clothes? Perhaps, I can help you undress?"

"Beau, you bad thing!" I giggled. "I would be tempted, but I must maintain my innocence as I do want to be married someday."

"I can always wait for you." He mused.

"I will wait for you too, however, I can't wait to go to the restroom, so lead the way." I said. He led me to the women's room, and I went inside. I didn't really have to use the restroom, but I needed to steer Beau away. After a few minutes of waiting in there, I hurried and snuck back upstairs and ran back towards Brune. He was fiddling with his equipment and breathed a sigh of relief when he saw me.

"Thank you for getting that guy away." He said. "I was able to record them. I have the man responsible."

"Can I hear what they said?" I asked, lowering myself down to the floor.

He prepared his technology for me to hear it. He put a thing on my head he called a headphone, which was big and clunky. It was similar in theory to the earplugs I used, but I struggled to fit it atop my hair. But I got it done. Brune played back what was said within the room.

"Did you hear about the Mexicans?" A gruff voice called out. I recognized it was Mr. Roberts, Beau's uncle.

"Yes. They're most likely going to invade us. They're going to try to destroy our way of life, just like the Yankees did all those years ago." Someone else said. "We must defend ourselves!"

"And we will! We have the help of Freedonia by our side. That has to count for something." Another spoke aloud.

"Maybe so, but we are all to take certain... precautions with our businesses and estates." It was my father's voice. I became even more curious.

"What do you mean, Hunter?" Mr. Roberts said, then coughing, most likely after puffing a cigar.

"I mean, we must have the overseers exterminate the slaves in the prisons. There can be no evidence that there were forced laborers in my containment prisons. I won't go to jail for those lawless niggers and spics. Get that message out to the heads of the Cook Containment Prisons as soon as you can!" My father said. My blood ran cold and I was speechless. I don't remember the rest of the tape, but when it was over, I took the headphones off and gave it back to Brune.

Brune started packing his things. "Thanks again for all your help." I never mentioned that the man he was looking for was my father. "You were on the right side of history. The Mexican government will help bring the criminals to justice, including this Hunter Clayton who owns the properties. Please, don't mention I was ever here."

I nodded my head, and Brune went down the stairs and disappeared into the night. I was left there with bated breath and a pain in my chest. Not only was my country guilty of mass murder and destruction for the colored, but my family was directly responsible and directly benefited from slave laborers. I closed my eyes and tears streamed down my cheek. I had to come to terms with a dark realization. My father was a master of slaves.

RAFAEL

Life as a slave was monotonous. I did the same exact thing almost every morning. I awoke from the same nightmare that I've suffered from for years, only to wake up in an even worse reality. The cell I occupied was always a drab and dreary room, causing me mental torture. In the times I was made to get up, I would always want to drag my feet. I wanted to escape. For years, that was something I did in my mind. I would think about my life before Ace. I was young, growing and learning in a world that seemed brand new to me. I remember being in Sigma Phi Gamma, helping to create some of our steps at our school. I remember being worried about simple things, such as homework and parties. My youth was stolen away every time I looked in the mirror while getting ready. My gray hairs always brought me back to the truth: the world I knew as a young boy existed no longer. There was no escape.

Or was there? For days, I constantly had to remind myself that Hasan was here. Surely, he had a plan. He always did. As a leader in 8Crow, he was a shrewd thinker, planning ahead in everything. Hasan was giving me a renewed sense of hope. Hope was something that I thought had died within me all these years ago, but the feeling of hope arose again. That's why some people fear hope, because among a people that's been oppressed, it can never truly die.

I walked down through the tunnels once more in my uniform. I stood in the booth, calling out names as usual. "Number 83929...Number 18358...Number 78363..." I called out. "Number 172080." Hasan looked at me and I listed he was here. This was his first day out of training and he was finally under me. I nodded my head slightly. We both had each other's back. I continued counting the numbers. Once I finished that unfulfilling work, I moved on to do my job as a foreman. Again, I watched the men toil under the grueling heat, creating steel for the Dixie government. It seemed like there was an increase of production by the way we were forced to work, and we didn't know why at the time. The men literally gave their blood, sweat, and tears to help a nation that didn't give a damn about us.

I did my job, but I also got closer to Hasan's station to talk to him.

"How are you doing?" I asked out of concern.

"As well as I can be." He grunted in pain. "I knew this was going to be a difficult assignment, but I didn't know this was how people were treated. I've had to sleep on the cold floor with other cellmates and I've been beaten by the guards for reasons as simple as waking up a minute after 7."

"I know." I comforted. "Hell is the only place worse than this."

"And the food? How can anybody get by on that? Dirty water and moldy bread should not count as a meal."

"There have been days where I couldn't sleep because of hunger." I whispered. Suddenly, from the corner of my eyes, a guard started carrying other slaves out, dragging them without care. The workplace was filled with screams, panic, and chaos.

"Hasan, what's going on?" I said.

"The people at the top must have gotten wind that the Mexican Army will be coming in to help free everyone across the south." He replied.

"Does that mean?"

"They're gonna be doing an extermination process to cover their tracks." He sighed with a hint of dread. "People are about to start dying by the masses if I don't intervene. It's time for our plan to commence."

"What?"

"I won't get too much into the details, but several of the new guards are undercover and have access to deadly weapons. We, along with other 8Crow and Mexican coverts acting as slaves, have to put our plot into action by giving the prisoners the power to fight back. Rafael, please cover my tracks if you can and continue with your day as if you know nothing." He left and went to God knows where.

"I'll try..." I whispered, still hearing the commotion in the area. Fear struck through me. For 20 years, life had been predictable for the most part. To know that something unexpected would be occurring somehow gave me anxiety. Mister Richards also gave me anxiety.

"Where did Number 172080 go?" Mister Richards questioned, approaching me after Hasan had walked away.

"I sent Number 172080 on an errand." I lied.

"What kind of errand?" He said, getting close to my face. Smelling the sickly scent of tobacco from his clothes, I answered.

"I sent him to fetch one of my workers who left his post early. Number 172080 knew where he went, so I told him to bring him back."

"Why should I believe you?" He sneered. He kneed me in the stomach, making me hunch over panting.

"You don't have to." I groaned, struggling to breathe. "However, I'm still the foreman and I am trying to make sure we make as much steel as we were ordered, sir."

Seemingly satisfied with my answers, he left me trying to pick myself off the floor. I despised that man so much, if I was to be honest. Mister Richards was a hijo de puta, who thought he was better than everyone simply because of the color of his skin. He believed that his cold, pale, and almost scaly *white* skin made him better than me. I had brown skin, leading others in Dixie to believe that I would always be below him, even though I was better than him in every sense of the word. I hated him, but there was nothing I could do about it at that moment.

***

Soon, it was time for lunch, and I sat with Zero. He fiddled with the gag inducing rotten piece of food that was supposed to be considered edible.

"How do we even eat this?" Zero whined. "I don't want to put this in my mouth! Look at it! It's brown and yucky!"

"I wouldn't eat that either. Here." I handed him the extra bread I managed to swipe. "Eat this. It's not much, but it should get rid of the hunger."

He smiled bright, in the way that only a child could. To him, that bread was like dessert. Even though it was partially moldy, it was still the best thing to eat. "Thanks, Thirty-Three!" He tried to wash it down with the water by trying to drink from the top as the dusty material had settled to the bottom of the cup.

"So, how was your day Zero?" I asked, trying to be a good father figure and listen to him.

"It was okay. The overseers made me clean the bathrooms." He murmured.

I was shocked, quite frankly. "Why?" I said, baffled. "You're only five!"

"They said if I can walk, I can clean. Then, when I was tryna bring in a bucket of soap and water, one of the overseers tripped me. I spilled everything and I was wet until one of the other kids loaned me one of their clothes. It wasn't a good day." He sulked.

I felt badly for him. He was starting to realize the troubles of life here. He was quickly losing his childhood innocence and there wasn't much I could do to stop his awareness of the fact that life was not fair.

"Thirty-Three?" He looked up at me with his puppy-dog eyes. "Will I ever see my mother again? They took her to work outside and they won't let me see her."

I was almost speechless for a moment. I didn't know how to respond to his question. I tried to give him an answer in the most dignified way I could. "Zero... If I'm being honest, there's a chance that your mother may not come back. But one thing I do know is that she will always be there in your heart."

"How do you know that?" He pouted.

"Because when I was younger, my mother was taken away from me too. We're a lot alike, you and me. What I know is that my mother is always with me in my heart and soul, just like yours will always be with you."

"Do you miss your mommy?" He said.

Tears began to well in my eyes, but I wiped them before he could see them. "Very much so. But at least we have each other. Zero, you're not alone. You have me to look after you. You also have friends that care deeply about you here. I'm here for you, whatever you need."

Slowly but surely, while he ate, his smile began to come back. I was successful at my mission. He didn't lose all of his innocence and for that, I was thankful. He continued to complain about the food and rant on about his best friend in the children's cell block with him. I was listening to him, but my ears perked up. I started hearing gunfire. It was not only in the distance at the factories, but here in the prison. Everyone in the cafeteria got scared and started to run out.

"Thirty-Three! What's happening?!" He screamed, scared of the unknown.

"Hold onto me, understand?!" I instructed him. He didn't continue questioning. He wrapped his arms around my neck and wrapped his legs around my back as I carried him. He had asked me what was happening. I knew exactly what was going on. The enslaved were leading a revolt. Under normal circumstances, I might have gone ahead and joined in. But my fatherly instinct kicked in and I was going to do everything in my power to protect this little boy. Back in the main area of the prison, it was a full battle for the freedom of the slaves. The prisoners and guards were shooting at each other. Bullets went blazing by and men, women, and children were getting hurt and killed. However, I didn't pay much attention to the fighting. I was really focused on getting Zero to safety. I ran past the scene of the clash and went upstairs to my cell so we could hide in there until it was all over.

Unfortunately, there was a guard in my way. He held a gun in his hands and was prepared to use it. But I could tell he was a green newbie. Not knowing what to do, he tried shooting with the safety on. No bullets came out. I yanked the key to my cell from his necklace and used his panic to my advantage. I kicked him down the balcony when he attempted to get his gun off safety. He crashed down onto the concrete floor, with the impact leading me to hear the sounds of his broken bones. Not paying attention to the body lying in pain below, I tried to get the key into the door that separated me and Zero from safety.

I had almost made it in, but I had heard a shot. I was stunned. I turned to see that it was Mister Richards that tried to shoot at me, but he missed, and he ran out of bullets. My temporary happiness of escaping death once again was gone soon as I realized that the bullet was lodged in Zero's body. The little boy looked at me, gasping for breath. He looked scared. A quiet rage flowed through my body. I tore off my shirt and wrapped it around his wound to try and stop the bleeding, then I carefully set Zero's body on the ground. And stared down the cruel overseer that I had come to know.

Mister Richards had hurt my boy. Somehow, I could manage him bothering me every day, but this time, he had gone too far. He shot his own son. I rushed at him and pushed him against the wall. Punching him and hearing his jaw break and seeing his nose swell up was the only thing giving me satisfaction. I did not hold back. Neither did he. He somehow managed to get the upper hand and then pushed my head to hang over the balcony. Mister Richards started to choke me. He was grunting as his intent was to kill me by any means necessary. Two was willing to play that game.

While I struggled to breathe, I kicked his testicles and quickly got up while he was distracted from howling in pain. I punched him to the floor and sat on him, so he'd have a hard time getting up. I caught my breath. All the years of pent-up anger finally had been released. I put my thumbs over his eyes and just pushed hard while he screamed in agony. I used my nails to tear deep into the flesh of his eye socket, feeling the warm blood gushing all over my hands. Screaming in fury, I found the strength and pulled both his eyes out. I threw the eyes over the balcony, hearing his instrument of sight squish onto the ground. To further hurt him, I choked him. Blind, he gasped for the air I would not let him have. For too long, Mister Richards made me suffer, so I wanted to pay in kindness. He gagged until he couldn't breathe anymore. He was dead. I had killed a man with my bare hands.

With the turmoil still occurring throughout the entire prison, I quickly rushed to Zero's side, who was suffering from a wound that was bleeding. My red-stained hands tried to hold his hands as I knew it would be futile to try to move his body.

"Hey, Thirty-Three?" He weakly called out.

"Yes, Zero." My voice cracked and my tears fell down my cheeks as I watched this sweet boy slip away.

"I finally see Mama…She's beautiful." He exhaled. "She's saying that…it's time for me…to come…home." With that sentence, he took his last breath, finding peace in being welcomed into Heaven by his mother. My tear ducts turned into a faucet. I cried over his body as it wasn't fair. He barely got a chance to live under the mere notion of freedom. The prisoners did gain freedom. They had fought the overseers and the guards, leading to a successful rebellion. Hasan and the others had managed to free the slave labor camp. However, I didn't care to think about the world around me. Distraught, I kneeled over and mourned over the death of the child who never got to have a real name. I was grieving for the boy he was and could have been, if not for the brutal system that was enforced upon him. Zero's innocence and childhood was stolen from him under the oppressive state of Dixie. That was something I vowed I would never forgive, for a pure and young life was taken from the earth.

JOSH

Hearing the fire cackle and feeling a dented absence beside me made me wake up. I stretched and yawned, briefly considering cuddling up in the sleeping bag. However, opening my eyes allowed me to see Anna tending to the fire in the hearth. She smiled and signed "Good morning" to me. I smiled back, getting up to sit right beside her on the brick fireplace. All of our conversation was in sign language, which helped keep things quiet for those still sleeping.

"How did you sleep last night?" I asked her.

"Not well. I had a lot of auditory hallucinations. I couldn't get hardly any rest." She signed.

"I'm sorry, babe. I know how tough it's been for you to lose your cochlear. Are your ears still ringing?" I signed to her.

"Yeah, it's making this weird noise. Like, I'm drowning in outer space." She was clearly frustrated. "I can't really explain it! It's a sound of its own, aquatic, but yet with a spacey reverb? Does that make sense, Josh?"

"It makes perfect sense to me."

"I'm sorry, I must sound crazy."

"No, you don't. It's real and I hate I can't take that pain on for you. You know I would in a heartbeat."

"Thank you. Josh, this sucks. I can handle not having a cochlear. I've been deaf all my life. But it's the constant ringing in my head that's bothering me so much."

"I'll tell you what we can do." I put one hand on her thigh to comfort her and continued signing with one hand. "When we start traveling to Lynn, we can stop by a pharmacy and try to steal some medication to ease your symptoms."

She pondered on that suggestion, but quickly changed her mind. "No, that would be a waste of time and also, we can't risk getting caught by the F.I.I. We're already in dangerous territory."

"You're right. We can't risk having anyone on our trail in Lynn. Ugh. Lynn. Only the Çaé would be egotistical enough to change the name of Springfield, Illinois to her first name."

"Don't work yourself up about that woman." She huffed. "Braun is nothing but a demagogue."

"How can I not work myself up when I think about the past few decades. I just feel like screaming every time I remember what happened to America, the country I so loved. Bigotry and economic anxiety combined to elect Ace. That led our democracy to become fragile as he shook the very foundations of the Constitution. Then Braun saw fit to take control herself by having someone kill Ace and blame it on the liberals. I get so mad when I think about it, it's like a constant loop that plays in my head, that's never-ending and doesn't fully make sense."

"I get exactly what you mean."

"Yeah. It's so frustrating knowing that people essentially handed Braun the keys to the kingdom. They just let our country become a fascist plutocracy. The people thought the far-right wing ideology would make things better, but it only did for the top 1%."

"People would rather keep the elite in power because they think they have a far-fetched chance to be in power as well."

"All Freedonia has ever done for us was create trouble. Everyone but the rich have been starving because of famine and dying because our money and social credit have no real value. We're lucky to even have stolen a good crop of corn and found a fat raccoon. We're the wretched of the world."

"Let's not go down the rabbit hole of thought." Anna assured me. "At least we're going to the University of Lynn to do something that will decide the fate of this country, once and for all."

"What do you think about the new plan that 8Crow will follow?" I questioned.

"I think that the plan for the wealthy's children to come from all across the country and hold a student-led demonstration in front of the palace is a good one. It will create a reckoning that Freedonia will have to face."

"I just pray that nothing bad happens. I don't want students to die. When I remember the Battle of D.C., I remember mourning for our friends in college. I don't want them to go through the same thing. And I pray that it actually produces some results, unlike us taking over D.C. for 8Crow and having to give it back to the Freedonians after the Treaty of Toronto. God, I just pray that everything works out for once."

"I love that you're still a praying man." Anna smiled.

"My faith in God and love for humanity is the only thing that keeps me going. If I didn't have that, I would have given up a long time ago. I know I can't give up. I know that you, Johannes, Lionel, Hasan, and Brune are counting on me."

"How is Brune? We haven't heard from him since he left to provide information for the Mexican army."

"I don't know. But he should be okay. He's a clutz, but he always knows how to land on his feet. Say, do you remember he was my best man at our wedding?"

She chuckled. "Yeah, he almost dropped our rings. But you caught them, and we said our vows in our ratted clothes with the St. Louis 3Crow members to witness. It certainly wasn't the wedding I planned when I was younger."

"That's an understatement. But at least we said, 'I Do' in the most extreme version of the 'for richer or for poorer' passage."

"When was the last time we were rich?" Anna joked.

"Right now, we're rich with each other's love. And that's all the wealth I need in the world. Kiss me, Anna. Let me show you that your love for me is all I desire." We kissed in front of the cackling flame, feeling both the heat of the fire and our passion.

Afterwards, Anna held my hands and we just huddled together by the fireplace in silence. It was rare when we got to experience a moment of peace and quiet. We just enjoyed each other's presence. It wasn't too long when another presence started to wake up.

"You guys ready to hit the road?" Johannes yawned. He was always prepared to get up and go. He was just about prepared for anything, sleeping with a knife underneath his pillow and carrying it in his back pocket in case a fight ever broke out. That morning, Johannes was prepared to leave the cabin behind. It was a nice find, I thought. It certainly beat sleeping on the ground in the middle of the woodlands to hide from the government. But it was time to go.

The three of us awoke everyone. Lionel was the last one to wake up. He was not well. I always heard him sobbing in the middle of the night, crying out for his Ma and Pa. He was depressed, and deeply so. He could never return back home because there was no home to go back to. Also, to put more pressure onto his back, Lionel still suffered from addiction. He was sober before the Blitz of St. Louis, but after hurting from his eye injury afterwards, he was given painkillers. He'd sometime disappear into the night back then and steal drugs from a pharmacy. However, he'd get all of the other necessary medicines like medicine to ease the symptoms for Anna's auditory hallucinations. We started to look the other way.

To be honest, we didn't or rather couldn't blame him. It was a form of escapism, to escape the pains and trouble of living in this world. Luckily, he didn't turn to any harder drugs, but he still struggled with the dependency for over 20 years at that point. It was especially clear, as he was having mild withdrawal symptoms. He couldn't fall asleep and had honestly just begun to rest when it was time for us to go. He was agitated.

But to be fair, so were the others. Miriam, the journalist, had never been on the lam with a group like us beforehand. I could tell. She wasn't as scared when we woke her up. Why would she be? But Danny and Libby knew to be scared if we woke up early. It meant it was time to go. The memory flooded back to them, I could tell, of being on the run. They were slightly grumpy being up so early. We quickly got ready and got on the motorcycles. Libby rode behind on the back of my bike. Danny rode with Johannes and Miriam rode with Anna. Lionel was in my sidecar because he didn't get enough sleep. We left the forest of southern Illinois and traveled to the capital of Freedonia. We went into the belly of the beast.

***

Going into the city of Lynn reminded me of the first capital of Freedonia. Instead of an eastern city, we were deep into the heartland. It was somewhat ironic how certain things never changed. Similar to Philadelphia, on the outskirts of Lynn, there was poverty run amuck. You could see children with bloated bellies and skinny figures that led you to believe the kids had brittle bones. On the outside of the city, there were women who couldn't stop babies from crying because they had no milk, nor the money to buy some. Everything was gritty, dirty, and war-torn. When we entered the central part of the city, we saw people who appeared well-off. The fashion for the affluent Freedonians surprisingly was still similar to what it was when I pretended to be (or was, depending on your point of view) the R.O.C. of Philadelphia. They wore office attire and they were, again, often in the colors of the flag. Some of the women wore black sheath dresses, while others wore white business suits with large shoulder pads and red heels. The men wore white button-up shirts with black ties and red suits. I suspected that the vintage style was just in season that year. The students were a different story, however. The style had changed for them and they had to wear brown uniforms. It was... unstylistic to say the least. But that wasn't important. What was important was getting to the University of Lynn.

We got secret access to the school from the security guard who was an 8Crow spy. He let us in. After parking and getting settled, we went into a hidden lounge on the campus that was only accessed by members of the honors program. We, along with several other 8Crow members that I recognized, stood in the back of the room. The students were at the forefront. It was time to spread the word on how to prepare for the demonstration that was to take place. They decided to get started as more would-be protesters trickled in the salon.

"Thank you all for coming. Quiet down, quiet down! We don't need any of the school administrators to hear our meeting." The red-headed boy said. "As I'm sure most of you know, my name is Nolan Kylesworth. You may know my father as the R.O.C. of Baltimore." Now Kylesworth was a name I hadn't heard in a long time. The father was the one who greeted Brune and I in Baltimore under the guise that we were Wesley and Ryan.

Nolan continued with his speech. "First, let's start by killing the elephant in the room. One may ask, what do we as students from privileged families have to gain in participating in a protest like this? I'll tell you what we'll gain: a future. For years, we have been told that the future belonged to us, that we'd have even more power than our parents did. It's clear that we'll be worse off than the generations before us. Even though we benefit from the corruption of the government, right now at least, people are dying of hunger and we could end up as one of them. The money we have now won't mean much of anything with the rising inflation and an incoming recession. We could leave and go to any other country to live a better life. But we shouldn't have to do that because Freedonia is our home! We have grown up here and will die here. I know I am willing to die for our home. What can we do to make our homeland better, you ask? We will rise up and demand that the Çaé will remove herself from power! We will rise up and push for democracy! Even *we* are not free until all are free! That is why we'll also be calling for freedom of speech, freedom of press, and freedom of association! We're not alone in our thinking. Right now, as we speak, other students and sympathizers all across the country from the far-away states of Maine and even Virginia, are on their way to join us on our mission to occupy Springfield Square outside the gateways of the Argenti Palace. We will disregard our student uniforms and wear the colors of red, white, and blue. It will be symbolic since they are the old American colors. We will represent the ideals of republicanism. The corrupt adults will say that we are spoiled brats. They will we say we're too young. They will say that we don't understand how the world works. Well, I say, they will have to sink or learn to swim because a new tide of change is coming!! I'm not saying that our protest will be easy. But nothing easy is worth dying for. We ARE Freedonians! The term Free is in our name and we ought to act like it. Democracy and the end of tyranny is our goal towards a sustainable future! And us spoiled kids always get our way!!"

His rousing speech was met with an uproarious applause. The clapping in the room was loud as thunder. Miriam pushed her sunglasses up. Libby was nodding in affirmation of what Nolan said. Johannes grinned.

"Nolan's good, isn't he?" Johannes said. "These kids are vivacious and vigorous."

"Just like we once were." Danny added. "They can do it, y'all. I believe in them. They have a fire in them that I haven't seen in a long time."

"I'll introduce you guys to Nolan once the event is over." Johannes responded.

We waited amongst ourselves until the crowd died down. Nolan stepped down from his podium and Johannes motioned him to come over. Nolan caught the flicker of Johannes' hand from the side of his eyes. Parting through the mass, he briefly shook other people's hands and quickly made his way to us. He smiled.

"Johannes! You old son of bitch! You made it!" Nolan laughed, gripping Johannes' arm and patting him on the shoulder.

"I wouldn't have missed it for the world! Everyone, this is Nolan." Johannes introduced us. "Nolan, this is Lionel, Anna, Josh, Libby, Danny, and Miriam. They're my friends."

"Any friend of Johannes is a friend of mine." Nolan smirked.

"How do you two know each other?" Miriam asked.

"Nolan's my protégé." Johannes simply stated. "I've met him twice, but I've had conversations with him on my burner phone. I've been teaching him how much better the world was before the Çaé and how it could change."

"Yes, he's taught me so much and he's been a big help. Without him and the influence of 8Crow, I don't know how we could pull off a protest of this size. It's estimated that at least 500,000 people will be there with us to occupy Springfield Square."

"That's impressive!" Libby said.

"Even though it stands to be a nonviolent protest by the students. I trust that 8Crow will provide some strength in number to fight off the army if necessary." Nolan said, seeking assurance from Johannes.

"You have my word. 8Crow will try to protect the people." Johannes replied.

"How did you become part of a movement that is pushing for democracy?" Miriam instigated. She was a journalist, through and through. "How did you start realizing the injustice of this society?"

"Well," he started to answer. "I have to say it wasn't just one event. I had been recognizing the faults of this country, but I often swept it under the rug. But one moment did change me for good. I remember when I was a teenager back in Baltimore. My father was the R.O.C., so we were a powerful family. One night, we went to the opera. Inside, it was grand and lavish with the Nationalist's Banners on the walls of the theatre. We watched *The Magic Flute* and I enjoyed the Queen of the Night aura. The dramatic vocal gymnastics impressed me as it did many others that evening. We were all dressed in our best clothing, obviously. But when I walked outside, I saw a homeless man and the officers were forcing him to get off the street. I looked and saw it was the former R.O.C. of Annapolis. He used to be a great and accomplished man, but because he wouldn't enforce one harsh rule of the Çaé, he was severely punished. I realized that one day it could be me. I knew the system was wrong, but I didn't understand how. Luckily, I learned about democracy and decided to change the system itself. Being a Freedonian, you're taught self-preservation above all else. This is just me preserving myself."

I was impressed with Nolan. We talked some more, but he got pulled away for business. We snuck out while the students convened and further organized for the protest. We got back on our motorbikes and stayed at the security guard's place since he lived in the city of Lynn. Thankfully, the rest of the day was uneventful. We got to spend time together and enjoy the final moments before the protest at Springfield Square marked a new chapter in our lives.

LAURALEE

The porch was a comfortable place to relax. The fan above kept my sister and me cool, even though it was a warm afternoon. Jolene and I sat next to each other with a small table in between. We were talking, trying to spend more time with each other before she headed back to Jackson. Behind my smile was a whirlwind of thoughts about my father and his egregious business.

"Mmm, this lemonade is so sweet and tart! Uncle Terrell!" Jolene called out while ringing a bell. Our butler came through the front door and stared with a neutral face. "We would like some more lemonade. Oh, and tell Auntie Yolanda we would like some tea cakes. Lauralee, did you want something?"

I had heard her, but I could not pay attention to her. My mind was occupied, and my eyes were blank, gazing at the drifting Spanish moss. All I could think about was hearing my Daddy's voice saying "...*we must have the overseers exterminate the slaves in the prisons. There can be no evidence that there were forced laborers in my containment prisons. I won't go to jail for those lawless niggers and spics.*"

"Lauralee... Lauralee!" Jolene snapped in my face.

"Oh! Sorry, Jolene." I replied.

"Must've been some sort of daydream, huh?" She giggled.

"It wasn't a daydream." I murmured.

"Well, you never answered if you wanted anything, so I asked Uncle Terrell to bring us some tea cakes once Auntie Yolanda finishes making them. Does that sound good?"

"Of course..." I said, in a daze.

Jolene looked at me intensely. "Lauralee, are you okay?"

"No." I considered telling her the truth, but I couldn't let her feel the weight I carried. So instead, I told her another thing I was worried about, a partial truth, if you will. "I'm concerned about Thomas. In fact, I'm concerned about this whole war between us and the Mexicans. It simply isn't right at all!"

"It'll be a short war, I guarantee you. This war will barely register as a blip in the history books once Freedonia comes to our aid! And besides, Thomas will be fine! I made Samuel find out if Thomas was on the frontline. He's not. Father apparently made a huge donation to the base, so long as his son doesn't have to enter battle. We don't have to worry about our brother."

"I guess I'm just sick of men and their silly wars." I tried to act like I was okay. "This Mexican-Confederate war should just end soon. I don't want any of my friends to get drafted. Why if Beau got drafted..."

"You are such a worrier. You definitely gained that trait from Mama!" Jolene laughed.

"Hush, be quiet!" I silenced her. Now she was the one that was worried.

Suddenly, we heard cars and rampant footsteps. Both of us peered beyond our property and saw that it was the Mexican army themselves, speaking of the devil. They stormed onto our land, knocking down the gates and had their guns ready. The Mexican soldiers rushed towards the house.

"Mama!! Daddy!!" Jolene yelled, rushing back into the house. I followed behind her, panicking at the fact that the Mexicans had managed to not only invade the Confederacy, not only invade Mississippi, but breach the privacy of our own home. Mama came running down the stairs, with Samuel and Daddy coming to meet us at the foyer.

"What's happening?!" Mama yelled.

"The Mexicans are here!!" I shouted.

"What?!" Samuel's eyes grew wide in astonishment.

"Didn't you hear her? She just said the Mexicans are here!"

The glass of the windows shattered, and the door was kicked down. My mother shrieked in terror as soldiers had broken their way into our house. A group of people surrounded us, but a number of them tackled my father and placed him in handcuffs.

"What is the meaning of this!" Daddy demanded to know.

"You are under arrest for crimes against humanity." A woman said. "Take him away. Yes, this house will do nicely as a base."

"You can't do this!" My sister cried out. They dragged Daddy, who was kicking and screaming on his way out the door. That day was one of the worse days of my life as I never saw my father until his trial. From then at that moment with the guns still pointed at us, I felt all sorts of emotions. I felt some sense of odd relief as my father would finally have to come to justice. But he was still my father and I didn't want anything to happen to him. I cried a river, my chests bursting with feelings. I felt some sense of guilt that I never told him that I knew and that we could have all left as a family. Because I felt that I was partially responsible for my Daddy going away, I never publicly admitted all that I knew. For years, I kept silent in the role my family played in the history of the South, until now.

RAFAEL

Hasan and I tasked ourselves, along with the others, to finally go outside of the prison. For the first time in a long time, I got to feel a ray of sunshine hit my skin. I basked in the warmth briefly. I closed my eyes and shuddered as tears of both joy and sadness rained down upon my cheeks. Everything was bittersweet. The only reason why I was outside was to bury Zero. He deserved a special spot.

Hasan and I used the tools stolen from the dead guards to dig a grave for him by the tree he saw through the blurred windows. The tree was of a considerable size. After the two of us dug deep enough, we placed the tools down. I took one last look at Zero. He seemed to be at peace finally. I prayed over his body, attempting to say goodbye to the sweetest little boy mankind would ever know. Before Hasan and I could lower him down to his grave, every part of my physical being shook with anger and hurt. Zero should never have had to die. He had so much to offer the world. He was kind, loving, funny, and forgiving. He was more forgiving than those Dixs deserved. Still shaking with conviction, I vowed that the Southerners would face God's wrath.

"In God's Holy name…" I forcefully uttered with a trembling rage. "In God's Holy name, everyone responsible for Zero's death and the suffering of countless others will all pay. May those who ruined my life be disgraced and put to shame! May those who plotted to steal our humanity be brandished as evil for all times, now and forevermore! My Lord, you have seen the injustice placed upon us. Do not answer with silence! Vindicate all of us who suffered under the thumb of slavery and apartheid! No country, no man, and no Çaé will escape Your might! In God's Holy name, let them witness Your vengeance sweep all across the land. Let it be done!"

A strong gust of wind blew, rattling and shaking the leaves of the trees. We buried Zero at his final resting place. After we placed all the dirt back on top, Hasan handed me a pocketknife. I carved his "name" Zero into the tree and what I estimated was his date of birth and his date of death. The tree was Zero's marker. Hasan wrapped his arm around me, and we walked backed towards the prison.

The prison was not as full as it was before the rebellion. Some had left to leave the Confederacy and attempt to cross the border into Mexican territory. But there were those who stayed, like me and Hasan. We stayed behind to bury the dead and take care of the young, old, and the sick.

"I never got to thank you, Hasan." I said. "I can't believe that we're finally free. I never thought I'd ever be able to hear those words escape my mouth."

"You're free. You're all free once again." Hasan assured me.

"We should've never been enslaved in the first place. They used our labor to build up their country and never gave us a dime. They only paid us in disrespect."

Our conversation was interrupted when a teen I knew as Number 46385 came up running with a smile. "Y'all! The Mexicans are here! They're at the gate, ready to liberate us once and for all!" We looked at each other and jogged right behind him.

"I didn't know the army would be here so soon!" Hasan said. "We can finally leave this place behind!

We ran up to the entrance of the prison at the gate to meet the rescuers. We saw the military there prepared to rescue us if the rebellion had failed. They were happy to see that we were successful.

"Please, come in!" Hasan gleefully laughed when he unchained the gate. "The sick, young, and old are in the prison, please take care of them."

One lieutenant smiled at Hasan. "I'm glad that you members of 8Crow were able to lick the dirty Dixs!"

"It wasn't just 8Crow. It was an effort by all of us to get rid of the authority here." Hasan replied.

"Well, we caught the guy who owned the Cook Containment Prison."

"The master I never saw for 20 years." I grumbled.

"I'm sure the general might allow you to see him since we have him in custody." The lieutenant said.

"Where's the general?" Hasan asked.

"I'm right here." I heard in a familiar gruff voice as he parted from behind the sea of rescuers. When I saw the face of the general, I froze and stood still. I was numb.

"Papa?" I whispered.

The general's eyes turned watery and he was shaking his head in disbelief. "Rafael?"

"PAPA!!" I ran up to him and grabbed onto him. He was my father, the man that ICE had arrested to deport all those years ago. My numbness turned into happiness. My father was here, in the flesh. I cried tears of joy onto his shoulders as he did onto mine. We squeezed tightly, as if we couldn't believe that we were seeing each other again.

"My son! Mijo..." Papa cried. We stopped hugging to take a look at each other. "Rafael, you've been a slave here?"

"Yes..." I sobbed, unburdening years of sadness.

"I'm so sorry, mijo." He grabbed my head to place back into his arms. "I'm sorry I wasn't there to help you all these years."

"It wasn't your fault, Papa." I said. "You're here now. How's Mama?"

"She's well. She's in San Antonio, she'll be overjoyed to know that you're alive still! I just wish you didn't have to suffer like this."

"Just take Hasan and me away from here. I want to face the man who enslaved us, the one who's in custody. Please."

He sniffed. "Anything for you." He then proceeded to talk to the soldiers. "You all know your duties. Now I must fulfill mine. Come on, Hasan."

Hasan followed and he looked surprised. I was too. I never thought that Papa would be there right by my side once more.

***

We were in the compound that held all the prisoners of war in the northern part of Mississippi. It was formally another Containment prison until it was liberated by the Mexican military. It looked slightly different than the one I had to live in. It was a lot colder and steelier. Papa took charge of leading us to a room where he was going to introduce to us who helped find the man who owned the Cook Containment prisons.

"This is the man that helped us find Hunter Clayton, the one who owned so many slaves all across the south." My father said with a heavy accent.

"I have a feeling that I know who it might be." Hasan gulped with a hint of excitement.

We walked towards a long hallway. Papa opened the door. There was a man with choppy hair that looked familiar, but I couldn't place a name to his face.

"Brune!" Hasan bear-hugged him.

"I guess this is a day for reunions." My father joked aloud.

"So, this is where Mexico sent you! Brune, I'm glad you made it okay!" Hasan said.

"God, I'm happy to see you too! You got the worse stick of the draw, huh?" Brune noticed Hasan's black and white striped uniform.

"Maybe. But I helped a lot of people. I've done my job." Hasan nodded.

"And you must be Rafael." Brune turned to me. "You may not remember me, but we fought together to free D.C. I was the one who set off the wrong bomb."

"I remember now." I chuckled. "Thank you for bringing justice to all of us who were enslaved. I can never thank you enough for what you've done."

"I'm happy to serve." Brune acknowledged.

"Can we see this Hunter Clayton?" Hasan asked.

"Yes." The general said. "He's in the room next to this. We'll see him through a two-way glass mirror because he's held in an interrogation room." Papa once again took us to a spacious area where security watched the man tied to the table in handcuffs. It was dark with the exception of the interrogation room. That room was bright with florescent lighting. When the door closed, all of us looked upon the man who couldn't see us. His face. I recalled his face first. Memories that stayed deep within my consciousness started to stir. I could never forget his face, even if I had tried. He was older, but I knew exactly who he was.

"Papa...tell your guards to let me in." I said.

"Son..." The general hesitated.

"I'm not asking, I'm demanding!" I lashed back. "Let me in. Now."

He nodded and Hasan and Brune looked at me curiously. The guards opened the door. I knew the others were watching, but it was just me and Hunter. There was a considerable amount of silence.

"Look, when am I getting outta here?" He callously said, breaking the ice.

"The arrogance... the gall... You know, the only thing I always found baffling about some white men is their level of confidence. Where do you get it from? The belief that everything will work out for you?"

"Everything has always worked out for me." He grinned.

"You know, I don't particularly like you." I sneered.

"Why not? I'm a very likeable person."

"That southern charm may work on others, but not on me. You're slacking, you know. You own the Cook Containment prisons and yet, you don't recognize the orange uniform."

His smile changed instantly. "Help! Help!" He cried to the guards.

"Oh, shut up and stop whining!" I punched him with all of my might straight across his face. "Learn to face the consequences of your actions for once." He started to whimper. "You know what, Hunter? You wanna know the man who made you millions of dollars for all these years. You wanna know who allowed you to buy that expensive and tacky suit. It's me, Bucko. I have been a foreman, a damn good one too. But I will never get any credit, not from you. Because of you, I have been wasting my life, enslaved to the Confederacy! Because of you, I have never been able to be with a man since my enslavement. Because of you, my life has been ruined!!" I pounded on the table. I took out an object from my pocket. "This key was used to lock me up in my misery for 20 years!! What do you have to say about that?"

"I don't need to hear this from a faggot." He mocked.

"Well motherfucker, I'm more of a man than you'll ever be." I cackled. "Names and slurs. Oppressing people. That's all you know in this world. What you did was enslave and exploit children born to your labor camps! Zero, my boy, lived and died in the camps because of you! You killed my boy. Give me one good reason why I shouldn't let you die the way you subjected others to. Huh? Can you give you me one?"

He remained silent.

"Really? Not even one? Could my ears be deceiving me? An entitled man actually being quiet for once? What a day! I can, however, give you a reason. Before you die when it's your time, before you vanquish to dust and only have your name spoken aloud to invoke disgust and revulsion from members outside your own family, I want you to remember."

"Remember what?"

"My scar."

His face went from blood red to ice cold.

I circled around him. "I know you remember election night, all those years ago. You and a friend of yours followed me. I remember exactly what the two of you said to me. You yelled out, 'Hey Spic!' Your friend called out, 'Ace is finally gonna build a wall so people like you can't get in no more.'" I stared directly at him as he tried to avoid eye contact. "Aw, poor baby. Is the guilt and shame finally hitting you? Good. Because that's not even the worse of what you did. After you two grabbed me from behind, your friend stomped on my arm. And then you, ever such a gentleman, took out a knife and said, 'Be quiet, you fucking piece of shit, you're gonna get what's coming to you.' You gave me this scar. You wanna know how I remember every word, line, and scene? I see your face repeatedly each and every time I go to sleep. You have been in my nightmares for years! You truly did own me, mind and body. Well, not anymore." I got my key into position. "I believe in justice. The old-fashioned kind. An eye for an eye, a tooth for a tooth..." I used my key to slash him across the face, tearing deep into his skin and causing profound bleeding. "...and a scar for a scar."

I left him there, slamming the door. I soon faced the shocked expressions of Brune, Hasan, and Papa.

"Rafael..." Hasan started to say.

"I don't wanna hear it! I did what I did, and I said what I said." I raised my hand to interrupt him. "Now where do we go from here?"

"Well," Brune said. "I recently talked to Johannes and Danny and Libby are with them in Lynn."

"Take me there!" I yelped upon hearing Danny's name.

"You don't know the danger they're in." Hasan replied

"I don't care! Papa, thank you for all that you have done. I will be home to spend time with you and Mama, but I must go to see the others. I have to."

Papa hugged me and whispered. "Promise me you'll come back."

"I will. I promise." I reassured him. I turned around to my friends. "Hasan, Brune. Take me to see them. Take me to see Danny."

Miriam

Although the others were used to being a part of history, I was quite nervous for the demonstration. In order to comply with the dress code, I wore a plain white t-shirt with my sneakers that were already blue. I looked in the mirror of the security guard's bathroom. Taking a deep breath, I put my sunglasses on. I knew that I'd want footage of the protest. Plus, I looked pretty stellar, if I do say so myself. I walked out of the bathroom and accidently ran into Johannes.

"Hey, I dig the sunglasses, but why do you wear them all the time?" Johannes asked while putting on a clean wifebeater.

"They aren't just sunglasses, it's also a recording device."

"Oh, well, make sure to capture my good side." He grinned and winked.

"I'm ready, how about y'all?" Danny said, appearing from the kitchen. It was a small place and there wasn't much room to change. "The guard is already gone and maybe I'm paranoid, but I don't wanna stay too long and attract attention, especially since we've been his guests for several days."

"I think we're all ready to go." I replied. Suddenly, I had a message on my phone. "Guys! Look! I got this message from Chamorra." Danny, Lionel, Libby, Johannes, Anna, and Josh all huddled in close with me to see the video because they sensed it was important. I made sure to turn on close captioning for Anna.

"Hello, welcome to the Evening News here at *The Standard*. I'm Chamorra Samai and we begin with breaking news from Louisiana and Mississippi regarding the Mexican-Confederate War." She had on a light and slightly pale pink business suit, with golden-rimmed glasses.

"Who's she?" Lionel questioned.

"She's my partner." I smiled.

Chamorra continued with her report. "The Mexican army, with the help of the Freedonian insurgency group known as 8Crow, have freed several of the slave labor camps found in the Southern country as previously reported by Miriam Tabbara. They also have arrested and charged people with crimes against humanity including Hunter Clayton, a prominent man in the Confederacy, for owning the containment prisons and the death centers known as Camps of the Undesirables."

"Hopefully, that means Rafael is safe!" Danny said with an optimism that I hadn't heard in him in a long time.

"The Mexican-Confederate War has a reverberating affect into Elysian politics. Yesterday, the Senator from West California, Congressman Andrew Li had something to say about the war and Freedonia's role in it." Chamorra said before the news showed a clip of Andrew speaking in front of the Senate arguing for the Republic of Elysia to join the Mexican-Confederate War. Andrew was outfitted in a navy-blue suit with a red tie. After the standard introduction to speak to the senate body, he started to talk passionately and fervently. Libby herself began to smile.

"Who's he?" Anna asked, looking at Libby to read her lips.

"He's my husband." Libby said with a loving gaze at the thin screen.

We listened to Andrew's words. "I will speak frankly. I don't have to remind my fellow colleagues of the Elysian Revolutionary War. It was ugly and it was brutal. But out of this darkness came a light, the founding of this great nation. The Republic of Elysia has come to stand for true equality for all. Because we all remember the feeling of oppression under the Çaé in Freedonia, I am ashamed that we became complacent. Our brothers and sisters, who stayed in the South during the Mass Exodus, have had to endure the horrendous rule of apartheid. The sanctioned racial segregation, political discrimination, and violence against nonwhites has been brutally enforced by the Confederate government. And we have done nothing about it! We told ourselves we were too concerned about starting a new country to help. We were too concerned about remaining steadfast to the Treaty of Toronto. We weren't concerned about doing what is morally right. As a member of the Rose Society Party, I am the last person to call for war, but I'll be damned if we do not join the side of the Mexicans to free slaves and death camp detainees. There is a Chinese proverb: fù zhài zǐ huán. The new generation can put right the mistakes of the old. What will your choice be? Remember, the whole world is watching." Andrew finished off his speech, leaving us wowed at his breathtaking words.

The video focused back onto Chamorra. "With the approval of Congress, Elysia, along with Canada, is now at war with the Confederate States of Dixie. We also have word from the House of the President that President Freeman might be taking military action against Freedonia as well, making this a Continental War. Coming up next, a member of the Royal Family from the Commonwealth of Santorini has given birth to a baby girl and will China continue to adopt more of Elysia's climate policies? Stay tuned for more on *The Standard*."

The video ended and we were left with a renewed sense of hope. Anna, Josh, Lionel, and Johannes needed that more than ever.

"All right. It's time to get going." Josh said and signed.

"Don't forget to bring your weapons. I'm bringing mine in my bag. I never know what will happen with those Freedonian bastards." Johannes added. After that statement, we made our way to Springfield Square.

Springfield Square was filled to capacity. The dress code created the illusion of a whitewater rapid rushing in as most people wore white. There were some dressed so loud and outlandish, they were almost caricatures of Yankee Doodle Dandy himself. The Argenti Palace was guarded by officers in black, so that no one could enter the silver-domed Capital. Nolan Kylesworth definitely led the protest. I noticed people carrying signs that were both simple and flamboyant. Some were written plainly on cardboard, saying "Democracy Now!" and "Freedom for Freedonia!" Others were bright and colorful, containing detailed and artistic drawings. It was a pop of life in a bland reality. People from all over the country truly showed up. It wasn't just students, there were parents and normal Freedonians who had struggled under the system they lived under. They all understood the risk of attending this demonstration. And so did we.

It was around 3 or 4 in the afternoon. The temperature was warm enough to make one sweat with all the marching that was taking place. My group walked near the end of the line. The majority of the protestors were in front of us. We were in the back for the same reason other &Crow members were either in the front line or the sideline. We were there to protect the people, just in case things did not go as planned.

"I still can't believe there's this many people." I said, taking in all of the sight.

"I can." Libby responded. "This is what we do when we stand up for our rights. Johannes, do you remember this chant? 'We don't want your tiny hands anywhere near our underpants.'" She giggled.

"Yeah." He laughed. "Wow, you just took me back. There were more people at that march then."

"There're still some people coming in. Look!" Lionel said as we all turned around to look while the rest continued to walk towards Springfield Square. Facing towards the golden sun, which was close to setting, we saw more people coming. It was inspiring, seeing the people taking a stand. In the distance, we noticed three men standing in all-white. The one in the middle, with warm brown skin, walked forward slightly.

"Come on, let's go, we're almost there." Josh stated. We all were ready to move on, but Danny stayed. Danny was frozen as if he was unsure about something. He gasped and his eyes began to water. He saw something, or someone. It was as if his spirit was drawn and compelled to walk towards this person. He began with small footsteps at first, walking into the sunshine. He had a sort of cautious smile.

"Is it? Can it be..." Danny wondered aloud. "Raf..." He whispered. The small footsteps became a jog that turned into a sprint. The whisper turned into a loud voice yelling, "Raf! Raf!" The other man started to run to him, with his arms wide open. They embraced tightly once they ran into each other and kissed with tears rolling down both of their faces. "Rafael! It's you! God, it's really you!" Danny happily sobbed.

"Danny..." Rafael sniffed while cupping Danny's face with his hands. "God knows how much I've missed you! I love you so much!"

"I love you too!" Danny said. The others noticed along with the two other men in white.

"Hasan!" Johannes and Lionel cheerfully yelled, running to hug him.

"Brune!" Josh and Anna joyously voiced aloud.

"Rafael!" Libby jubilantly cried out.

I stayed behind to capture the moment when all of the friends who had all been pulled apart reunited again as a family. It was beautiful. There was affection and warmth between all the friends who had gone through so much together. As the outsider looking in, I saw the love and care that only they had. There was a story that many at that time wished for, but never got to have: reunification. After letting them have their moment, I allowed myself to be introduced. Hasan and Brune were brave men, after describing what they had been through. And I saw why Rafael was Danny's soulmate. I have to say, it felt like they let me into their family too.

Soon, it became after 6. Twilight started to set in. The occupation of Springfield Square became livelier. Once again, we were in the back, basically guarding the people. The protesters were peaceful, singing songs of freedom that dated from years past. The light of the city began to shine. The Argenti Palace sparkled in silver as the light highlighted the metallic color of the dome. Rafael and Danny never stopped holding hands, almost in fear of letting go. Hasan, Lionel, and Johannes talked while also veering off to the sides, making sure that no one would ambush them. Josh, Brune, and Anna signed amongst themselves, happy to be back together as a group.

Suddenly, 5 armed soldiers approached, marching towards the Argenti Palace and marching towards us. Johannes quickly loaded his gun. After one of the soldiers fired a shot towards the crowd, Johannes aimed and shot at the soldiers' heads swiftly and without pause. Their flesh blew apart before they knew it. Johannes was a professional killer. A devilish grin appeared on his face quickly before it dissipated. People started screaming, running in different directions.

"That was a warning. The Freedonian army will be right behind them." Johannes said. Gunshots blared out. The guards at the front of Springfield Square, at the gates of the palace starting to shoot at the crowd in a panic. The loudspeakers across the entire city of Lynn started to blare messages.

"The city is now under martial law. The city is now under martial law." The strangely calming feminine voice on the loudspeakers mixed in the with chaotic and violent noises of the people created an odd and concerning soundtrack of a dystopia. Marching towards us was an army. Behind those men were tanks. We were shocked at the length the Çaé and the government would go to keep their power. Everything happened so fast. The army had not only surrounded the Square but the entirety of Lynn. Quickly, random shots were fired into the civilian population. The troops used expanding bullets, which expanded when entering the body and created larger wounds. They were prohibited by international law. It was deadly.

Some of the 8Crow defense troops gathered to fight the advancing army where we were. The peaceful demonstration became a battlefield.

Hasan yelled at us, while Lionel stood by his side. "You guys go! Run! Lionel and I will take care of them!" Johannes contemplated about joining them, but decided against it, knowing that he'd be of better use at another point. Johannes grabbed Anna's hands, who also held onto Josh, who held onto Brune. They were emulating Danny and Rafael, as if they had some knowledge from previous experience. I was to follow them by holding onto Libby, but before I did, I quickly recorded the experience. Hasan reached into his backpack and pulled out a compact machine gun, which fired off a ton of rounds. Lionel had a handheld gun tucked in the waistband of his pants and he got it out and started shooting as well.

"Take this, you bastards! This is for the Ewings! My parents' death will not be in vain!" Lionel screamed out with a guttural growl. It was a sight to behold, seeing the Freedonian army get smoked by a ragtag group of rebels. But the army was equally as efficient. I saw Lionel get shot right in the heart, causing him to fall down. He died on the spot. Hasan, witnessing the death of his friend, choked up, but continued to shoot down any officer. Suddenly, a bullet entered Hasan's body, instantly striking him dead. Hasan, a believer of the cause, died fighting for freedom.

After witnessing such horrific deaths, I turned around to follow the rest of the gang. We ran headfirst into the jolted crowd. It was pandemonium. From our right, we noticed soldiers had made their way into the crowd and started beating people with batons. The civilians responded by hurling rocks and hitting with sticks. So, we decided to run to the left. Upon running, we noticed that their tanks were encroaching. They ran over some people, letting us hear the crunching sound of people being ran over. The scene was a true horror.

Trying to get through, we, along with dozens of others, narrowly escaped the area where the tanks fired their ammunition, creating a loud explosion and murdering dozens. To our surprise, there were more soldiers behind the tanks. I took out the small gun I was told to carry and starting shooting as fast as I could. The others did too. For them, it was as if muscle memory overtook them. Rafael and Danny had each other's back, protecting themselves from oncoming bullets by quickly grabbing shields from some of the fallen army members. Libby and Anna took their weapons and assembled it to create a bigger weapon. It was damaging to the other side. Josh scavenged the bodies of the dead soldiers and picked up small bombs, which he threw at the other side.

"See, Brune!" Josh yelled. "That's how you throw a bomb!"

Brune chuckled and followed his lead, throwing bombs of tear gases back into the army. In doing so, Brune tripped and fell over another woman. His clumsiness saved her life as a bullet whizzed by her. Johannes was a cold-blooded war assassin. He seemed to have learned to enjoy taking away soldiers' lives, maniacally laughing. His soul seemed dark; he thrived on the battlefield with an odd thirst for blood. One man he killed with a gun, Johannes ran over to use his knife and slit the throat of the officer. But his was a skill that was necessary for a night as dark as that. But it became darker sooner as all the electricity went out across the city and the country. The lights once blazing, were shut off in a flash. The sound of sirens blared. The tanks stopped in their tracks. We were all without sight.

"This must be the military action that Elysia is taking!" I yelled.

"Cyberwarfare! Brilliant!" Both Rafael and Danny said in unison. The cyberwarfare meant that the Continental War had begun.

With the tanks stopped, we were momentarily helpless as none of us could see. It wasn't until a Molotov cocktail was thrown at a tank that we were provided with illumination. The impact of the blast shook the ground, knocking us off our feet. There were screams of people being burnt. People wailed over dead bodies as the army was told to draw back. There were thuds and grunts of people that were resisting arrest from the incoming F.I.I. The whole scene was absolutely tragic. No words can fully describe what occurred that night. The Massacre of Springfield Square, where several thousands died, was truly a terrorizing and frightening time. It was time to put our weapons away and for us to go back to the security guard's place where we knew we'd be safe there. We ran, sneaking past the F.I.I. We made it back only to find out that Johannes and Anna were not with us.

ANNA

The night of the massacre took about as far a left turn as you could imagine. When we were attempting to run away, Johannes grabbed my arms and turned me around. He signed to me in front of a burning tank, the flame providing the only light for me to see him in the dark.

"What are you doing?" I said to my brother. "We need to leave, before anything worse can happen!"

"We can't leave! Not when this is the only opportunity we have!" He frantically emoted with his face and with his hands.

"The only opportunity to do what?"

"Break into the palace! This is our only chance! The power is down, and the guards are out either in the streets or dead. Will you trust me and join me?"

"You know I have always been by your side. Do I think this is a good idea? No. But I will join you. Siblings don't let each other do stupid things alone."

"You're goddamn right." He smiled. "Let's go."

Avoiding people wasn't the hard part. They were too preoccupied with the devastation that was wrecked upon the student demonstration. They were not paying attention. Everyone was in a fight for their life. Johannes and I got to the gate of the Argenti Palace. Usually, there would be guards galore, but like Johannes said, they were all having to take part of the pushback against the protestors. Plus, the gates and fence couldn't shock and electrocute us. It was the perfect scenario for breaking in.

Johannes kicked the gate down to open because it still had a lock. That lock was old and inefficient which was surprising to say the least. When we got onto the premise, Johannes had his gun ready from his bag. To get through the door, I bust through the glass to open the doorknob. We got into the Argenti Palace, which taught me that we relied too much on technology to protect ourselves.

"What's your plan?" I asked Johannes while we crept silently through the building. The adrenaline coursing through my veins made my heart pound so hard, it made me feel like my footsteps were thunderous. I could not describe the interior of the building. It probably was grand and impressive, but I could not focus on that. My mental state was geared towards our task at hand.

"I plan to kill the Çaé. She has had too much control over our lives for far too long. This is the only chance, because I don't know if the Elysian, Mexican, or Canadian military could ever get to her. I can get her myself. Cut off the head of the snake and the Freedonia as we know it will collapse."

"How do you know where we're going?" I asked, signing with one hand to remain quiet and holding a gun with the other.

"Because the propaganda newsreel revealed too much about where Braun might be. I think I know exactly where she is." He led me and I followed. Tiptoeing across the palace was more laborious than I ever could imagine. I was terrified in an unexplainable way. We were in unfamiliar territory. The walk took hours, or rather it felt like it did. My memories of this night are foggy, to say the least. My memories of historic nights always seemed to be foggy. But we made it to a secret room, hidden behind a wall. There was a hidden panel to access the doorknob to turn. We made it through the room, quickly bursting in catching the Çaé off guard. I saw her through the illumination of the pale moonlight. She wasn't as young and spry as I remembered her to be all those years ago. Nay, she aged. She looked old and not up-to-date. We knew that from seeing her in the propaganda, but to see it up close and personal was something else. No longer there stood a powerful Çaé. Lynn Braun was a human who used a dangerous ideology as a weapon to gain power. Just like you can bring down a dangerous ideology such as fascism, we could bring the destroyer to her knees. And that's exactly what we did.

Johannes shot her in the chest. She fell back from the inertia. Johannes smiled like a child. "We did it!" He said. "Braun is finally dead!" He jumped with glee. It was clear he had been dreaming about that moment for years. He got in front of me and hugged me. The woman who had ruined our lives was dead. The woman who was responsible for the death of millions was dead. The Çaé, legendary dictator of Freedonia, was dead. It was over, as quickly as it started. Johannes could finally let his guard down. The cause of his misery was dead.

But Johannes let his guard down too soon. Suddenly, I felt Johannes' gasp, stopping his breath momentarily. He unhanded me and saw that he was stabbed in the back. Bleeding through his wife beater, he stumbled around to see Lynn Braun stubbornly fighting to stay alive. While I was hugging my brother, I couldn't see or hear Braun coming from behind and taking the knife he always kept in his back pocket. Johannes looked to be in obvious pain. I panicked for him. Grunting a sharp breath, he pulled the knife out of his back without a scream. Wobbly-kneed, he faced Braun.

"Come get me, you low-down, dirty dog." I read him huff through his lips.

"A simple 'bitch' would've sufficed." She said, pressing her wound. I shot at her myself, but she still wouldn't die. I had used my last bullet. She was determined to live to fight another day. But Johannes was determined to have her dead. When she had almost no strength left, he stabbed her in the heart with his knife and she fell down. Her mouth gurgled blood. But Johannes made the mistake of not making sure she was dead before. He wouldn't do that again. He continued to slash at her body, piercing her flesh over and over again. The red-stained liquid poured onto the floor and splash across the walls and across Johannes' face. The blood splattered all over him, covering every part of him from his head, arms, and hands down to his feet. He threw the knife across the room and pounded his fist into the older woman's body. He hit the carcass until it was almost unrecognizable. Now she was dead.

I stood back in shock and surprise. Johannes motioned me to come over and press his wound. He shivered across the floor, lying next to the body of the Çaé.

"Anna..." He muttered with every strength he could muster. "Can you read my lips?"

"Yes." I said, while crying.

"I don't think I'm gonna make it." He struggled to breathe. "I need you to tell everyone how I much I love them and how much I valued their friendship."

"Johannes..." I could barely say anything without my eyes watering. My tears fell onto his shirt, mixing with the rust-colored stain.

"And I'm happy that I got be your brother. I only wish we had more time."

"We have enough time. Just hold on!"

"I love you...little sister." He drew me in closer and I pressed my head on his chest.

"I love you too, big brother." I cried. With those final words, my brother passed away. Johannes was dead.

***

I made the trek back to the guard's home by myself. I carried Johannes' bag, feeling numb. Walking through the streets, I remained unfazed by the fogs of war. F.I.I. were arresting people still in the Square and I walked past. I felt the vibration and the boom of the Molotov cocktails hitting buildings, tanks, cars, and soldiers; I walked past. There were thousands upon thousands of cadavers lying on the ground with the stench of death and I walked past. The feeling of sudden emptiness was the only emotion I could muster at that moment of time.

My face was absolutely blank when I walked through the door. I faced Miriam, Brune, Libby, Rafael, Danny, and my husband Josh. They were on the couch, grieving from the events of that night. Miriam and Josh were comforting Brune over Lionel's death. Brune was close to Lionel and he lost one of his best friends. Brune was crying on Josh's shoulder and Miriam was rubbing on his back. She didn't know him that well but was emotionally sensitive to his pain. Libby was taking Miriam's role regarding Rafael who was violently shaking with emotions. Rafael was hugging Danny, sobbing as well. He grew a bond with Hasan who was with him in the slave labor camps.

When I flung the door open, I was standing by myself. They were surprised when I came in. They all stood up, slowly, each one by one.

"What happened to you and Johannes?" Josh asked in sign language. Rafael and Brune both sniffed and wiped away their tears.

"The Çaé is dead..." I gulped. Everyone looked surprised. Brune looked at me with bulging eyes. Libby's mouth was agape. Danny held his hand over his mouth, shocked. I walked to the center of the couch and placed the bloody bag onto the floor. Everyone stood around me, waiting for what I had to say next. My vocal cords quivered, my lips trembled, my brows furrowed, and my eyes became swollen into a well of tears. "And so is my brother." I broke down and wailed. The realization of the fact that Johannes was gone hit them like a ton of bricks. At that moment, I knew that no one could think about the fact that Çaé Braun was deceased. She was not worth any tears. However, Johannes was.

"Johannes told me to tell you that he loved all of you and that he valued each and every one of your friendships." I said.

Danny, Rafael, and Libby were around me, without a dry eye. They wept. They knew Johannes the longest, since they were essentially best friends in college. The man with the bandana was no longer alive on this earth. Josh held my hands while on his knees, letting me cry on his shoulders. I could feel that he was in emotional pain but tried to be strong for me as his wife was having a breakdown. Brune turned around to stare at the wall. He had lost a lot already. Two close friends were already dead, and another was gone. He leaned his forehead against the wall and pounded it with his fist, bawling. Miriam tried to comfort him but to no avail. I couldn't hear Brune, but I emotionally connected with the vibrations of the three thuds he punched at the wall. The first thud was for Hasan, the liberator of D.C. and Mississippi. The second thud was for Lionel, the protector who made sure that we survived when his own family didn't. The third thud was for Johannes, the best friend and brother that anyone could ask for.

We continued to grieve for hours as it sunk in. When the rest of them finally cried themselves to sleep, I stayed in my position, exhausted and numb once again. I looked to the floor and saw the moonbeams upon Johannes' bag. After wiping my snot-filled nose on my arms, I grabbed the bag to look and see what was in it. There were only three things. One of his weapons, a pistol was in there. His favorite pen was in there. And his journal that he's had since his twenties. Feeling the smooth leather, I took a breath and opened it. In his journal were his innermost thoughts. I wanted to read his words so that I could feel closer to him.

"*This is my first entry into this journal and there's something I gotta say. L.A. is the best place in the country, and you can fight me on that. There's nothing better than feeling the warmth of the sun pressed upon your skin like an affectionate hug, especially in May...*"

DANNY

There are moments in life when one experiences a before and after. To make further sense of this peculiar phenomenon, we must look at what happened after the death of the Çaé. Once the country found out she was killed by Johannes, many celebrated as they saw it meant that the authoritarian and brutal regime of Çaé Lynn Braun was finally over. Johannes was lauded as a hero and a martyr. His body was buried in his native home in California, where hundreds of thousands went to pay their respect. The fact that Braun was deceased meant that the Continental War did not have to last long because there was a power vacuum in Freedonia. After several months, the war was quickly won by Elysia, Canada, and Mexico. The losing side included Freedonia and the Confederacy. Quebec remained neutral. One of the aftermaths of the war included freeing all the enslaved and death camp detainees within Dixie. Another result of the Continental War was the beginning of the Great Reconstruction.

The Great Reconstruction has been ongoing for the past 3 years under the administration of President Amaruq Saunik, an Inuit man from Alaska in the Green Party. The former country of Freedonia and the area known as the Demilitarized Zone were divided up into territories under the occupation of Elysia to attempt transformation and reconciliation. Similarly, Mexico oversaw reconstruction with the former Confederate states. The Great Reconstruction has been vital in order to heal the continent for the foreseeable future.

The continent wasn't the only thing that needed healing. All of us needed healing after Johannes' death. The emotional trauma of what we all went through weighed heavy on our hearts. After the war was over, Libby went back to Congress with Andrew to help govern during this new era in our nation's history. Miriam's new passion project at her job with *The Standard* has been to cover everything regarding the Great Reconstruction with Chamorra by her side. Brune went to the territory of Mississippi in Mexico to work with their government to try all of the war criminals and slavers in both former powers of the continent. Josh and Anna lived together in the territory of Illinois to help with the transition to Elysian life for the former Freedonians. I moved to San Antonio, Texas with Rafael, my husband, in Mexico so that he could reconnect with his parents and I taught modern history at a university in the city. But even though we all tried, we were so broken as were all the people involved in those tumultuous times. There was no way to fully heal from the scars of the past.

Anna tried so hard to move on from her brother's death, but she couldn't. She decided she had to move *forward*. The best way in her mind was to write her side of the story to the experiences that Johannes wrote about in his journal. It was therapeutic for her. Sensing that we would need that same relief, she asked us to write our own corresponding stories to weave a narrative with the history of all that transpired and the history of Johannes. She even allowed Brune to find the woman who helped free all those in bondage to include her story. When Brune found Lauralee, it was even more important for her story to be told since he found out that Lauralee made such a huge sacrifice due to the fact her father was tried as a war criminal and her home was under occupation during the Continental

War. We even got a chance to ask Former President April Freeman, Libby's mom, to tell her role and she delivered.

Once a year, we gather together specifically to remember Johannes, Hasan, and Lionel. This year, after asking us to write our chapters, we met at a beach in Santa Barbara. Josh and Anna sat in the cool sand with their toddler, who they named Johannes, to honor his late uncle. Libby, Andrew, Miriam, Chamorra, Brune, Rafael and I all sat next to them. Rafael stared off into the distance, no doubt thinking about Zero, the child he told me was like a son to him. I held his hand to support him. He looked at me and timidly smiled. We all were silent and actively participating in the beauty of nature. We heard the waves crash and felt the water tickle our toes as the tide came in. We smelled the saltiness of the ocean and the squawking of the seagulls somehow beguiled us. The pale pink of the sky with the orange fading sun made us reflective. We became insightful to the tides of change in the world and how the big events affected us personally. We were changed permanently, both internally and for all the people in the land.

Had we stood up and changed our ways earlier, maybe none of the tragedies that befell us would ever have happened. Maybe if we had become kinder to one another and respected each other as human beings, Freedonia and Braun would never have rose to power. But there is no use thinking about the past, unless you use it to teach future generations. As a history professor, I pray that we as a people will never forget all that has happened, lest it repeat itself.

So now you, the reader, have come to end of the book. You, maybe having grown up in a different world, will see the mistakes we've made as a people and the successful growth we've accomplished. I cannot tell you all that we have tried to teach you throughout this book. You will have to draw those conclusions yourself. However, we hope that you take the lessons from our time, to yours.

THE END

ACKNOWLEDGMENTS

I want to express my deepest gratitude to my extraordinary mother, Tralia Rahmaan, for her unwavering support throughout the entire process of writing this book. Her guidance and assistance have been invaluable to me. Additionally, I am immensely thankful to my loving and encouraging grandmother, Gloris Rahmaan, who has gone above and beyond to provide me with the necessary education and resources to embark on this endeavor. I want to give thanks to my marvelous grandfather, Theodis Rahmaan, for his confidence in me. I also want to acknowledge my wonderful Aunt Lanika Rahmaan-Ibeh, affectionately known as Tika, who may no longer be with us physically, but her spirit lives on in my heart. She ignited my passion for reading at a very young age and introduced me to the captivating world of the arts. Their contributions have been instrumental in shaping my journey as an author.

Additionally, I want to show appreciation to the myriad of teachers that helped inspire my writing career, which includes, but is not limited to Caroline Saunders, Elizabeth Shamblin, Heather Lynne Davis, Nicole Scott, Angel Neal, Sandra Longworth, Mark Nabors, Rachel King-Barr, Sharon

Watson, Eric Sullivan, and Paige Franklin.

Next, I want to thank my friend and LOFT twin, Sarah Reinecke, who was the first fan of the book and the most intense shipper of Danny and Rafael! Also, I want to recognize my close friends, Kaylon Neely, Tommy LeRose, and Alli Gregory for letting me skip out on sleepovers so I could write this novel. Next party is at my place!

Furthermore, I am deeply grateful to my extended family and friends for their enduring love and support throughout my journey. Their encouragement has been instrumental in my success.

Lastly, I want to express my heartfelt thanks to all the fans who have supported *Our Time*. Your enthusiasm and support have been truly overwhelming. Thank you sincerely for your dedication!

I0711976

LA GOBERNADORA

Un sexenio de impunidad y saqueos

Editorial
razacero
periodismo ciudadano

razacero | Grupo Editorial
periodismo ciudadano

razacero Periodismo Ciudadano
Cd. Victoria de Durango, Dgo. México.
www.razacero.com

Autor: **Fernando Miranda Servín.**

Investigación: **Erick Marcel Miranda Gamboa.**

Diseño: **Luis Enrique Rodríguez Luna.**

Primera edición, noviembre 2021.
Editado por razacero Grupo Editorial, S.P.G.G, N.L. México.

Edición exclusiva para Amazon.

Índice

Introducción

En la vida política de Durango, José Aispuro es más conocido por sus traiciones que por sus logros, quizá la más conocida sea la que durante las elecciones de 2016 reveló la entonces candidata priísta a la alcaldía de Gómez Palacio, Juana Leticia Herrera. Al respecto, el portal Milenio Digital publicó el día 26 de abril de ese año:

"A mitad de las campañas políticas, circula un víceo en redes sociales que dura 2 minutos con 50 segundos, donde se ve a la candidata a la alcaldía de Gómez Palacio por el PRI, Leticia Herrera, denunciar a José Rosas Aispuro como traidor en 2003, cuando su padre, Don Carlos Herrera, contendió a la gubernatura de Durango. La candidata fue más allá y aseguró que Aispuro traicionó a la familia Herrera a pesar de que se le dieron 5 millones de pesos para que los apoyara. Aquí la transcripción del discurso que realizó Leticia Herrera:

'Porque yo sé que con el apoyo de ustedes nos van a brindar a Esteban y a su amiga Lety... porque es la mancuerna. Porque con el otro... Quiero decirles una cosa y se los digo neto. ¿Quién se acuerda de 2010... no, era 2003, cuando Carlos Herrera quería ser gobernador?. (Enseguida los asistentes levantan la mano gritando yo).

'¿Alguien sabe por qué no fue gobernador? ¿Y quién lo traicionó? Aispuro, sí. A ese viejo le entregó mi papá 5 millones de pesos por sus treinta votos, ya estaban amarrados, por eso le digo traidor en su cara, yo sí tengo huevos para decírselo, yo sí traigo. Es un traidor y en 5 millones vendió sus 30 votos, en un rancho de un exgobernador que tienen pegadito ahí conmigo, se los vendió a Ismael Hernández Deras, por eso Don Carlos no fue gobernador, por culpa de Rosas Aispuro".

Al llegar a la gubernatura en 2016, Aispuro sumaría a su currículum cientos de traiciones más al dar la espalda a muchos protagonistas que colaboraron en su campaña electoral. Pero la traición mayor, sin duda alguna, es la que le asestó al pueblo de Durango, al que engañó de manera infame con los encendidos discursos que pronunciaba en sus mítines para pedir el voto de los electores.

Aquí haremos un recuento de lo que fue el sexenio de Aispuro y el papel preponderante que desempeñó su esposa, Elvira Barrantes, desde su inicio hasta este momento en el que faltan escasos nueve meses para que deje el poder, un poder que él, su cónyuge y los despóticos integrantes de su élite pensaron que era eterno.

Capítulo I
El menos peor

El domingo 3 de abril de 2016, a las 5 de la tarde, en la Plaza del IV Centenario del centro de la ciudad de Durango, ahí frente a la estatua del Benemérito de las Américas, el Lic. Benito Pablo Juárez García, inició su campaña a la gubernatura quien poco más de 5 años después sería considerado el mandatario más corrupto en la historia de esta entidad norteña: José Aispuro.

José Aispuro Torres, en el arranque de su campaña electoral en 2016 junto al ex presidente Felipe Calderón luego de pronunciar un discurso plagado de mentiras.

Desde por lo menos una hora antes comenzaron a llegar las huestes de simpatizantes del PAN, del ya desaparecido PRD y los seguidores del ex senador y candidato de estos partidos, José Aispuro.

A dos calles de la explanada de la Plaza del IV Centenario, sobre la Av. Dolores del Río, también llegaron más de 40 camiones en los que fueron transportados los contingentes aispuristas (acarreados), que sumaban más de 2,500 personas.

En el templete, apoyando a Aispuro, se encontraba la plana mayor del panismo nacional representada por el ex presidente Felipe Calderón Hinojosa, su hermana Luisa María Calderón y el exsenador Ernesto Cordero; alrededor, muchos rostros conocidos del panismo local ese panismo que siempre ha actuado como servidumbre del PRI: Gina Campuzano, Patricia Jiménez, Rodolfo Dorador y el entonces líder estatal, Juan Quiñones; los perredistas Juan Cruz y el exdiputado Israel Soto, y la mayoría de los candidatos a diputados locales, alcaldes y regidores panistas y perredistas, sin faltar José Ramón Enríquez Herrera, quien fue candidato a la alcaldía de Durango por esta coalición PAN-PRD.

En este evento tomó la palabra el ex presidente Felipe Calderón, quien haciendo gala de sus dotes oratorias les recordó a los duranguenses que durante su gobierno entregó suficientes recursos federales al sector Salud del gobierno estatal priísta, para que la ciudadanía no tuviera ninguna carencia de medicinas, acusando al gobierno de Jorge Herrera Caldera de haber hecho uso indebido de esos recursos. Incendiario, Calderón recalcó que el principal problema de Durango era el gobierno estatal priísta. "Hay muchos intereses en juego y, como las puercas, no van a querer soltar la mazorca fácilmente, por eso los invito a votar y a defender el voto para que no se vayan a robar las urnas con sus policías, como sucedió en el 2010", manifestó Calderón, agregando que al ganar José Aispuro la gubernatura se investigarían las enormes fortunas que "misteriosamente ha amasado el grupo en el poder". Por supuesto que esto era una mentira.

José Rosas Aispuro fue el orador principal, señalando: "para que todos ganemos más es necesario que dejen de robar" (refiriéndose a los gobiernos priístas que saquearon esta entidad durante casi 90 años). "Nos prometieron que vendría lo mejor, pero solo vino lo mejor para unos cuantos", abundó.

En su discurso, Aispuro sintetizó su programa de gobierno exponiendo que haría alianza con la ciudadanía de todos los rincones del estado de Durango y con los sectores campesino y empresarial para ofrecer a los duranguenses trabajos bien pagados y no empleos de explotación. Durante su gobierno, dijo, garantizaría la libertad de expresión, la seguridad pública, el combate a la corrupción y la transparencia total. Estas premisas, como sabemos, estuvieron totalmente ausentes en su administración.

Aispuro en su primer mitin de campaña condenó públicamente las fortunas que algunos políticos priístas hicieron de la noche a la mañana y aseguró que devolvería de inmediato la autonomía a la Universidad Juárez del Estado de Durango; así mismo, ofreció su apoyo incondicional al magisterio duranguense. "Seré un gobernante respetuoso de los ciudadanos y de las instituciones y promoveré que todos tengan las mismas oportunidades, sin distinción de partidos". Una mentira más que pudimos atestiguar con el avance de su sexenio.

Alrededor de las 7 de la tarde culminó aquél evento que dejó en claro que en esa contienda electoral solo había dos fuerzas políticas que se disputarían la gubernatura en Durango: la corrupta mafia priísta que ostentaba el poder y José Aispuro, respaldado no tanto por el fragmentado PAN local ni por el casi extinto PRD estatal sino por sectores muy amplios de la ciudadanía que a pesar de los yerros que este político había cometido durante su gestión como senador de la República seguían creyendo en sus propuestas expresando que votarían por él "porque es el menos peor".

Y vaya que sí lo era, pues las demás opciones eran verdaderamente deplorables como Esteban Villegas, candidato del PRI, con un historial de corruptelas interminable, desde haberse dado a sí mismo la categoría de "Médico especialista C" sin jamás haber ejercido su profesión, cuando fue secretario de Salud estatal, y haberle dado una plaza de "aviadora" a su esposa, Marisol Rosso, hasta proteger a sus colaboradores más cercanos que durante su gestión como alcalde de Durango construyeron "casas blancas" con recursos del municipio; Gonzalo Yáñez, el candidato del fantasmal PT, siempre a las órdenes de los gobiernos estatales priístas, y Guillermo Favela, el candidato de Morena rehén de los intereses que el exdelegado estatal de este partido, Rosendo Salgado Vázquez, tenía con el gobierno del priísta Jorge Herrera Caldera, que le impuso a la mayoría de los candidatos a diputados locales, alcaldes y regidores.

Ante ese panorama desolador no dejaba de ser positivo que la ciudadanía tuviera de menos una opción para votar, aunque esa opción fuera la menos peor. Y así fue. Con el voto de la ciudadanía y los acuerdos cupulares entre el PAN de Ricardo Anaya y el priismo peñanietista, José Aispuro ganó la gubernatura de Durango que le fue negada seis años antes.

Capítulo II
Los Beverly de Durango

"Bájale dos rayitas, a mí no me hables en ese tono", fue la frase pronunciada por Elvira Barrantes, esposa del gobernador panista José Aispuro, que con frecuencia escucharon docenas de trabajadores del DIF cuando protestaban ante ella por haber sido despedidos injustificadamente en los primeros días del sexenio, que inició el 15 de septiembre de 2016. En su campaña electoral el mandatario ex priísta, habilitado como panista, había prometido que ningún trabajador del gobierno estatal sería despedido. Mentira.

El DIF estatal fue una de las dependencias en las que más atropellos laborales y violaciones a los derechos humanos se cometieron durante el sexenio de Aispuro Torres.

Así, con actitudes despóticas, altaneras y groseras, los nuevos altos funcionarios del gobierno del estado de Durango, bajo las órdenes de Aispuro Torres y Elvira Barrantes, se dieron a la tarea de despedir de todas las secretarías estatales a cientos de trabajadores institucionales, de todos los niveles y hasta con 25 años de antigüedad, pagándoles miserables liquidaciones. Muchos de estos trabajadores fueron amenazados por el Consejero Jurídico Galdino Torrecillas con ser encarcelados si no delataban a sus ex jefes priístas, revelando las corruptelas que cometían.

Esta "cacería de brujas" se prolongó varios meses, mientras los verdaderos pillos que saquearon el erario estatal durante el sexenio anterior permanecían impunes, unos ocupando cargos en el gobierno blanquiazul y otros negociando su impunidad con personeros de la administración aispurista.

Así, las primeras víctimas de este sexenio fueron los modestos trabajadores del DIF estatal que, argumentaron, fueron maltratados durante todo el sexenio pasado por las anteriores autoridades de esta institución, y luego, sin explicaciones de por medio, fueron despedidos por los directivos entrantes.

Reza el conocido refrán que "el que nunca ha tenido y llega a tener, loco se quiere volver", y así sucedió con esta élite política que por primera vez ostentaba un poder de tal magnitud, pero ya se perfilaba para ser una parodia grotesca de aquellos simpáticos personajes que protagonizaban la famosa serie televisiva estadounidense titulada "Los Beverly Ricos"; si, esos rancheros californianos que de la noche a la mañana se hicieron millonarios al encontrar un yacimiento de petróleo en sus tierras y, con su nueva riqueza, se mudaron al lujoso suburbio de Beverly Hills. Solo que a diferencia de aquellos que eran ingenuos y generosos, estos se mostraron prepotentes, pusilánimes y mezquinos.

Los mismos atropellos que sucedieron en el DIF estatal se dieron en la secretaría de Salud, cuyo titular al inicio del sexenio, el Dr. César Franco Mariscal, eligió a directivos arbitrarios, vengativos e irrespetuosos con los trabajadores, quienes impotentes manifestaron en su momento: "de haber sabido que las cosas se iban a poner así mejor hubiéramos votado por Esteban Villegas". Esto nos da una idea de cómo estuvo la situación en el arranque del gobierno de José Aispuro, un político que sin ningún miramiento arremetió contra los empleados de abajo, muchos de los cuales inclusive votaron por él y por los candidatos de la coalición PAN-PRD, a pesar de las amenazas que les profirieron sus anteriores jefes, representantes del priísmo corrupto.

*Sin duda, este tipo de actitudes chocaron con
la esperanza que el pueblo duranguense había
depositado en el ex senador panista.*

Capítulo III
Aispuro, más de lo mismo

Hacia el 30 de septiembre de 2016, transcurridos 15 días de su gobierno, un amplio sector de la ciudadanía duranguense ya comenzaba a expresar su malestar por los nombramientos de integrantes de su gabinete que el gobernador Aispuro realizaba. En las calles, en las pláticas de café o en las redes sociales se escuchaban y se leían los reclamos de un pueblo que acababa de terminar con 87 años de priísmo corrupto y por ningún motivo estaba dispuesto a soportar un sexenio más de saqueos, corruptelas e inconsistencias.

El pago de cuotas y facturas políticas, el
chambismo, el clientelismo y el amiguismo se
hicieron evidentes.

En La Laguna, por ejemplo, Aispuro Torres recibió fuertes críticas por haber designado al Lic. Manuel Ramos Carrillo como subsecretario de Gobierno en esa región. Ramos Carrillo se desempeñaba como ejecutivo de recursos humanos de la empresa Chilchota, propiedad de la familia de la entonces alcaldesa priísta de Gómez Palacio, Juana Leticia Herrera, por lo que, consideraron los aispuristas laguneros, no tenía el perfil para ocupar este cargo.

José Aispuro utilizó el dinero de los contribuyentes para implementar la política clásica priísta de "comunicación social": Te pago para que te calles.

Otro nombramiento que a simple vista revelaba un inmediato conflicto de intereses fue el de la lectora de noticias, Verónica Terrones, como directora de Comunicación Social. Verónica Terrones dejó su empleo de conductora de noticieros del canal 10 local para inmediatamente tomar posesión de su cargo, aparte de que su esposo, Saúl Maldonado, trabajaba (y trabaja) en el periódico El Siglo de Durango. ¿Cómo ha justificado el gobernador Aispuro los convenios publicitarios que su gobierno ha realizado con este medio de comunicación estrechamente relacionado con su directora de Comunicación Social, Verónica Terrones?

Verónica Terrones, directora de Comunicación Social del gobierno del estado de Durango, opacidad y conflicto de intereses durante todo el sexenio aispurista.

Citando la Ley de Responsabilidades de los Servidores Públicos del Estado de Durango, en su Capítulo II de las Obligaciones de los Servidores Públicos, el Artículo 47 dice:

"Todo servidor público tendrá las siguientes obligaciones para salvaguardar la legalidad, honradez, lealtad, imparcialidad y eficiencia que deben ser observadas en el desempeño de su empleo, cargo o comisión y cuyo incumplimiento dará lugar al procedimiento y las sanciones que correspondan, según la naturaleza de la infracción en que se incurra, y sin perjuicio de sus derechos laborales:

XIV.- Excusarse de intervenir en cualquier forma en la atención, tramitación o resolución de asuntos en los que tenga interés personal, familiar o de negocios, incluyendo aquéllos de los que pueda resultar algún beneficio para él, su cónyuge o parientes consanguíneos hasta el cuarto grado, por afinidad o civiles, o para terceros con los que tenga relaciones profesionales, laborales o de negocios, o para socios o sociedades de las que el servidor público o las personas antes referidas formen o hayan formado parte".

¿Qué tanta legalidad han tenido los convenios publicitarios que el gobierno del estado de Durango realizó con el canal 10 y con el periódico El Siglo de Durango a través de su directora de Comunicación Social?

Con Aispuro, al igual que en los gobiernos priístas, se dió un reparto del erario discrecional a manos llenas a contadísimos medios de comunicación, y se relegó a otros por ser críticos incómodos de este régimen corrupto.

A las anteriores designaciones contradictorias se sumaron las de otros directivos y secretarios que llegaron a sus áreas a despedir personal de manera prepotente y déspota.

Y en este panorama llamó la atención la actitud asumida por algunos integrantes del gabinete aispurista que formaron parte del proceso de entrega recepción de las instituciones que posteriormente pasaron a dirigir, pues jamás se manifestaron sobre el estado físico y financiero en el que encontraron las secretarías e institutos propiedad de los duranguenses; solo uno, el perredista Marcos Carlos Cruz Martínez, quien ocupó la secretaría de Desarrollo Social, hoy SEBISED, manifestó el "total desastre" en que encontró esta secretaría, que durante el anterior sexenio priísta había sido dirigida por Arturo Yáñez Cuéllar. Los demás secretarios del flamante gobierno aispurista brillaron por su sepulcral silencio, sobre todo el de Salud, Dr. César Franco Mariscal, quien nunca informó a la ciudadanía cómo encontró, por ejemplo, el Hospital 450 y lo relativo a los millonarios fraudes que ahí se cometieron durante el sexenio pasado, como el de las camas inservibles que la anterior directora de Administración, C.P. María Eugenia Lourdes Díaz Herrera, compró a 10 mil pesos pero nos las cobró a 100 mil, y mucho tiempo estuvieron arrumbadas en ese piso que sirve como bodega de cachivaches de este hospital.

Lo mismo sucedió con el secretario de Obras Públicas, Ing. Arturo Salazar Moncayo, y el secretario de Finanzas, Arturo Díaz Medina, quienes simplemente no dieron cuentas de uno solo de los monstruosos saqueos que en estas secretarías se llevaron a cabo en la administración priísta. ¿Por qué solamente el secretario de Desarrollo Social, Marcos Cruz, encontró de inmediato "aviadores" y contratos millonarios sin licitación en esta dependencia? ¿Será que las auditorías que supuestamente se realizaron en todas las secretarías e institutos ya tenían sabor a borrón y cuenta nueva? ¿Quién o quiénes negociaron la impunidad de los saqueadores priístas que ocuparon cargos de relevancia?

Otras instituciones a las que el gobernador panista Aispuro no les brindó la atención debida fueron el Tribunal Superior de Justicia y la Fiscalía General del estado, cuyos anteriores titulares, Apolonio Betancourt y Sonia Yadira de la Garza, se caracterizaron no por ser precisamente honestos y transparentes.

Aispuro Torres debió proponer al Congreso estatal la creación de una comisión especial que investigara y resolviera de inmediato todos esos casos de violaciones a los derechos humanos (confesiones obtenidas bajo torturas y sentencias injustas) perpetradas por este par de ex funcionarios y sus secuaces, a través de las cuales encarcelaron a ciudadanos inocentes que en esos momentos se encontraban y aún se encuentran cumpliendo condenas por delitos que no cometieron.

Fueron muchas las expectativas que el pueblo duranguense tuvo con el gobernador José Aispuro, luego de padecer el horror de casi 90 años de gobiernos priístas corruptos, pero el sexenio de este político pusilánime siguió transcurriendo y no corrigió la nota sobre esos nombramientos que la misma vox populi no les daba mucha vigencia por tratarse de personajes notoriamente improvisados y corruptos, que a la postre le harían mucho daño al pueblo de Durango, como por ejemplo los titulares de Finanzas y de la secretaría de Desarrollo Económico, Arturo Díaz Medina y Ramón Dávila Flores, ex ejecutivos de la minera canadiense depredadora First Majestic Silver Corporation, que serían protagonistas de dos de los fraudes más escandalosos que ha habido en la historia de Durango.

Capítulo IV
Comienza la corrupción aispurista

Era tanto el hartazgo que la ciudadanía duranguense tenía del priísmo corrupto que la saqueó durante 87 años, que quizá no recaló en que al tratar de deshacerse de esta onerosa carga estaría llevando al poder a una élite mucho más voraz que la que había rechazado en las urnas el 5 de junio de 2016.

Lamentablemente, como en su momento lo expusimos en medio de aquél proceso electoral, la opción a la gubernatura que propuso la coalición PAN-PRD era la opción menos peor, pues no se podía pasar por alto la larga estancia de José Aispuro en el Partido Revolucionario Institucional, del que fue militante desde 1980 hasta el año 2010 ocupando altos cargos como presidente del Comité Directivo Estatal, diputado federal en tres ocasiones y alcalde de Durango, entre muchos otros; tampoco se podía pasar por alto el deplorable papel que hizo en el Senado de la República, abanderado por el PAN, votando a favor de todas las iniciativas de reformas priístas que hasta la fecha han lesionado gravemente los bolsillos de la mayoría de los mexicanos.

Con un discurso de campaña convincente, pero peligrosamente demagogo, Aispuro logró ganar las elecciones utilizando como punta de lanza su disposición de castigar la corrupción de los todavía en ese momento gobernantes priístas, con la frase: "No me va a temblar la mano para aplicar todo el peso de la ley a quienes le hayan hecho daño al pueblo de Durango". También prometió no realizar despidos de trabajadores de bajo nivel del gobierno estatal. Sin embargo no cumplió ni una ni otra cosa.

Hacia octubre de 2016 causó asombro escuchar a ciertos funcionarios de la secretaria de Salud manifestar que la situación estaba "muy delicada" en esta dependencia pues a más de un mes de haber entrado en funciones el nuevo gobierno de José Aispuro ya se habían detectado casi 200 "aviadores" tan solo en la Jurisdicción Núm. 1, de las 4 jurisdicciones en las que se dividen los Servicios de Salud del estado, por lo que estos servidores públicos calculaban que en total serían por lo menos 400 "aviadores" los que ya cobraban su primer mes de sueldo en esta dependencia de manera ilegal bajo el gobierno de Aispuro Torres. Los directivos, de acuerdo al testimonio de los trabajadores, comentaban descuidados en pláticas de café: "tenemos instrucciones superiores de no tocar a estos 'aviadores'".

Y es en la secretaría de Salud en donde se hizo más notorio el encubrimiento de la corrupción por parte de Aispuro, al grado de que la entonces directora de Administración, C.P. Ruth Elizabeth Reséndiz González, realizaba las mismas prácticas indebidas de su antecesora, la C.P. María Eugenia Lourdes Díaz Herrera, al comprar medicamentos a empresas farmacéuticas cuyas razones sociales no correspondían a las que les fueron otorgadas las licitaciones para abastecer a la secretaría de Salud durante ese año 2016; y lo peor de todo es que los precios de estos medicamentos eran (y siguen siendo) mucho más caros que los que ofrecían otras compañías farmacéuticas. ¿Quién ordenaba hacer esas compras a todas luces fraudulentas?

A medida que pasaban los días y el gobierno de Aispuro no fincaba responsabilidades penales (como la de enriquecimiento ilícito por ejemplo) a los principales protagonistas políticos que ocuparon altos cargos en el sexenio pasado, estaba asumiendo el papel de cómplice de esos saqueadores que dejaron endeudado al pueblo de Durango con más de 15 mil millones de pesos, comprometiendo el presupuesto estatal ¡hasta el año 2038!

Capítulo V
Saqueadores de minas con Aispuro

Con el mandatario panista duranguense llegaron a integrarse a su gabinete personajes verdaderamente peligrosos, entre esos protagonistas destacaron el secretario de Finanzas, Arturo Díaz Medina, y el ex secretario de Desarrollo Económico, Ramón Dávila.

Para comprender mejor el alto grado de capacidad para delinquir que tienen estos individuos es preciso reproducir el reportaje que publicamos el 31 de octubre de 2016 en nuestra página web razacero.com, titulado "Saqueadores de minas con Aispuro":

El ejido Tenochtitlan, ubicado en el municipio de Ocampo, Coahuila, fue creado el 24 de agosto de 1973 por una resolución presidencial que lo dotó de 10 mil 100 hectáreas. En el año 2006, con el apoyo de las autoridades federales (SEDATU) y del gobierno estatal de Coahuila, 2,400 de esas hectáreas fueron invadidas por la Minera La Encantada, propiedad de la compañía canadiense First Majestic Silver Corp; desde ese año, la inexistencia de escrituras por parte de la minera canadiense fue denunciada por los 36 ejidatarios que legalmente son propietarios de estas tierras, y desde entonces libran una batalla legal para recuperar esa extensión que les pertenece.

Este hecho ya ha sido difundido por varias organizaciones internacionales, como el Observatorio de Conflictos Mineros de América Latina (OCMAL).

En el año 2011 las autoridades del ejido Tenochtitlan demandaron ante el Tribunal Agrario del Sexto Distrito, en Torreón, Coahuila, a la Minera La Encantada y a First Majestic Silver Corp, subsidiaria y empresa respectivamente, por usurpar 2 mil 400 hectáreas de su propiedad (expediente 290/2011); coincidentemente, en estas hectáreas despojadas se encuentra la mina de la cual esta empresa extranjera extrae un promedio de 400 mil onzas de plata al mes. Pero el Tribunal Agrario no iniciaba el juicio "porque no encontraba al apoderado legal de la empresa canadiense para notificarlo".

A mediados de 2013, por falta de respuesta de las autoridades, los ejidatarios decidieron bloquear el camino hacia la mina (camino que está

ubicado en terrenos que son de su propiedad), por lo que fueron demanda-
dos por el representante legal de la minera canadiense First Majestic
Silver Corp, C.P. Jesús Arturo Díaz Medina (el mismo que el Tribunal
Agrario no podía localizar para notificarle la demanda de los ejidatarios).
Inmediatamente, los agentes policíacos al servicio del gobernador Rubén
Moreira Valdez, desalojaron a los ejidatarios, en su mayoría mujeres y
ancianos, llevándolos esposados al ministerio público de la comunidad
Laguna del Rey, localizada a ¡700 kilómetros de distancia! Algunos de los
ancianos ultrajados todavía tienen en sus muñecas las cicatrices que les
dejaron las esposas que dolosamente los agentes estatales apretaron a más
no poder.

José Aispuro, el demagogo que integró su gabinete con peligrosos delincuentes de cuello blanco. Durante su gestión fueron más que evidentes los conflictos de intereses que salieron a relucir.

El pasado mes de agosto de este año 2016, debido al alto grado de
corrupción que existe en el Tribunal Agrario del Sexto Distrito, los
ejidatarios coahuilenses recibieron el fallo de su demanda en su contra por
lo que su abogado, Juan Francisco Flores Gándara, anunció de inmediato
que interpondría un recurso de revisión por considerar que la sentencia
no se apegó a derecho pues "no se valoraron documentos para dictar una
sentencia correcta". Flores Gándara dijo también que "las delimitaciones
de los terrenos por parte de los peritos de la empresa, la Secretaría de
Desarrollo Territorial y Urbano (SEDATU) y un tercer perito, fueron
coincidentes y no se apegaron a los planos de dotación inicial (conteni-

dos en el decreto presidencial emitido el 24 de agosto de 1973), donde quedaron pendientes de entregar más de 2 mil 400 hectáreas, las mismas que después ocupó la minera.

Según el abogado, la minera tenía conocimiento de que los terrenos eran parte de la dotación, declaración que venía en un expediente del juicio que tendenciosamente no fue tomado en cuenta por el Tribunal Agrario, por lo que el pleito legal por la posesión de esos terrenos continúa.

Y los ejidatarios, algunos de los cuales ya han fallecido por vejez, no solo reclaman sus tierras e indemnización por las enormes cantidades de plata que esta empresa minera canadiense ha extraído de sus tierras sino también la reparación de los graves daños ambientales que ha ocasionado al haber contaminado los mantos freáticos de la región con las enormes cantidades de cianuro que utiliza para extraer de la tierra el preciado metal, causando enfermedades entre los pobladores y la muerte de animales sin que las autoridades de la secretaría del Medio Ambiente del estado de Coahuila hayan intervenido jamás para evitar este ecocidio.

Arturo Díaz, secretario de Finanzas y Administración en el gobierno aispurista. Negro historial como representante legal de la minera depredadora canadiense First Majestic Silver Corp.

La empresa canadiense First Majestic Silver Corp, tan solo de esta mina coahuilense obtiene un promedio de 1,200 millones de pesos anuales de utilidad bruta pagando solamente 70 mil pesos de impuesto minero; tiene otras 6 minas en igual número de estados como Sonora, Sinaloa, Zacatecas, Jalisco, San Luis Potosí y el Estado de México, y dos en Durango (La Joya y la Parrilla, en los municipios de Poanas y Nombre de Dios); en la mayoría de estas entidades ha tenido conflictos y se ha caracterizado por pagar sueldos miserables a sus empleados y por no cumplir con las promesas que hace a los habitantes de las zonas aledañas a sus miras de reforestar y construir hospitales y escuelas. Son más los daños y depredación que provoca que los beneficios que le deja a nuestra nación; por supuesto, siempre protegida tanto por las autoridades federales como por los gobiernos de las entidades en donde opera.

Con la llegada del gobierno de la "alternancia" y del "cambio", encabezado por el ex priísta y ex senador abanderado por la coalición PAN-PRD, José Rosas Aispuro Torres, muchas sorpresas se han llevado los ciudadanos que votaron por él pensando que las cosas realmente darían un giro de 180 grados respecto a los anteriores gobiernos corruptos priístas que durante 87 años saquearon las arcas públicas. Y los mayores desencantos y decepciones que ha provocado el gobernador José Aispuro han sido las designaciones que ha hecho de personajes que integran buena parte de su gabinete, en el que lo mismo figuran hostigadores sexuales e hijos de ex gobernadores y caciques sindicales priístas, que quienes tienen por ejemplo antecedentes de ser auténticos saqueadores de minas, pues resulta que quien fuera apoderado legal de la minera canadiense First Majestic Silver Corp, el C.P. Jesús Arturo Díaz Medina, hoy es el flamante secretario de Finanzas del gobierno del estado de Durango; sí, el mismo que a mediados de 2013 promovió la agresión a los ancianos ejidatarios coahuilenses que por defender sus derechos fueron detenidos por los policías del sátrapa gobernador Rubén Moreira y llevados a una cárcel que estaba a 700 kilómetros de distancia de sus casas.

También, para completar el cuadro, el pasado 15 de septiembre, el mismo día que José Aispuro tomó posesión de su cargo como gobernador, la empresa First Majestic Silver Corp anunció en su página web la renuncia de su director general, Ing. Ramón Dávila Flores, y el portal de noticias MundoMinero.mx publicó en una nota relacionada al tema: "First Majestic Silver Corp anunció la renuncia de Ramón Dávila de su mesa directiva. Ahora, el Ing. Dávila Flores asumirá el cargo de Secretario de Desarrollo Económico de Durango. Keith Neumeyer, Presidente y CEO de First Majestic, comentó: 'Durante el cargo de Ramón como director de la compañía, First Majestic se convirtió en el segundo mayor productor de plata primaria en México".

Así pues, el gobernador José Rosas Aispuro Torres ha nombrado en su gabinete como secretarios de Finanzas y de Desarrollo Económico a dos de los principales ejecutivos de esta peligrosa empresa minera canadiense. Y la pregunta es obligatoria: ¿Qué clase de compromisos tiene el mandatario estatal Aispuro Torres con esta clase de empresarios?

Ramón Dávila, ex director de la minera canadiense First Majestic Silver Corp., y ex secretario de Desarrollo Económico en el gabinete corrupto del panista Aispuro Torres.

Para cerrar la pinza, Aispuro Torres designó como secretario de Recursos Naturales y Medio Ambiente a su amigo de toda la vida, el dos veces presidente municipal priísta de Tamazula, y ahora panista, Jaime

Rivas Loaiza, ampliamente conocido por el trato despótico y prepotente que le daba a los empleados de este municipio cuando fue alcalde. ¿En verdad este funcionario aplicará la ley a la minera First Majestic Silver Corp por los atropellos ambientales que comete en el estado de Durango, en donde es propietaria de dos minas?

Sin lugar a dudas hay otro tipo de intereses por los que el gobernador Aispuro Torres les cedió dos de las más importantes secretarías de su gabinete a los más altos ejecutivos de la empresa minera First Majestic Silver Corp, que tiene pésimos antecedentes laborales y ecológicos. Y esos intereses, obviamente, no tienen nada que ver con el bienestar y progreso del pueblo de Durango.

Estos nombramientos son preocupantes, como la mayoría de los que ha hecho el gobernador Aispuro Torres, por lo que la ciudadanía deberá estar muy atenta a las actividades que realicen estos funcionarios en especial, ya que por lo aquí expuesto sus antecedentes no son nada recomendables para ocupar los cargos que hoy detentan y por los cuales los contribuyentes les vamos a pagar generosos sueldos".

Hasta aquí el reportaje, y como se sabe, en junio de 2020, en plena pandemia del coronavirus, Ramón Dávila presentó su renuncia como secretario de la SEDECO luego del escandaloso caso llamado SEDECO-GATE, que consistió en la entrega discrecional que Ramón Dávila hizo de fuertes cantidades de dinero a la clase política y empresarial de Durango, relegando a los pequeños y medianos empresarios. El monto de esta operación fraudulenta ascendió a más de 50 millones de pesos. Luego de ser dada a conocer la lista de beneficiados, entre los que destacaban los representantes de las principales cámaras empresariales, funcionarios estatales y del municipio de Durango, así como familiares de connotados políticos, el gobernador de marras instruyó a su incondicional Contralora estatal, Raquel Arreola, para que "investigara" el asunto. Posteriormente, Aispuro ordenó reservar u ocultar estas indagatorias ¡por 5 años!

En lo que se refiere al titular de Finanzas, Arturo Díaz, este personaje se caracterizó por los múltiples atracos que ha cometido en esta dependencia, entre los que sobresalen la deuda de más de 800 millones de pesos por concepto de pagos de quinquenios vencidos que el gobierno de Durango debe a miles de profesores, así como también la ausencia de pagos de pólizas de seguros de vida de los trabajadores estatales. Otro escándalo en el que se vio envuelto este "servidor público" fue el de las listas de "ayudas y subsidios" millonarios, supuestamente entregados a miles de ciudadanos duranguenses por concepto de "tenencia y refrendo" de vehículos. En esta lista aparece una persona física recibiendo un "subsidio" de ¡56 millones de pesos!

¿Cuántos millones de pesos desvió Aispuro durante su sexenio en complicidad con este par de bribones?

Capítulo VI
Las vicisitudes de Galdino
Un Consejero Jurídico inepto o bribón

Luego de la detención de Rafael Herrera, principal asesor político y primo del ex gobernador Jorge Herrera Caldera, que anunció con bombo y platillo el titular de la Consejería General de Asuntos Jurídicos del gobierno del estado de Durango, Lic. Galdino Torrecillas, el miércoles 14 de junio de 2017, fueron más las dudas que certezas las que provocó este hecho en la ciudadanía duranguense, sobre todo en las redes sociales de internet en las que no se dejó de cuestionar el monto por el cual Rafael Herrera fue acusado de supuesto "fraude": 24 millones de pesos. Y esta inquietud se acentuó más cuando el 16 de junio el ex presidente de la Barra de Abogados Benito Juárez, Lic. Mario Pozo Riestra, declaró a varios medios de comunicación locales que Rafael Herrera Piedra "se puede ir a su casa" pues el fraude por el que se le acusa "el Nuevo Sistema de Justicia Penal no lo tipifica como grave".

El imputado, señaló el Lic. Galdino Torrecillas en la espectacular rueda de prensa a la que convocó, "simuló operaciones no documentadas durante el periodo de enero del 2013 hasta septiembre del 2016, pagos que se hicieron a través de la Secretaría de Finanzas y Administración a las empresas Comunicación Trascedente, S.C., e ISO Diseño, S.C., en las cuales aparece como socio el ahora detenido".

Al respecto, llamó la atención que el Lic. Galdino Torrecillas, como Consejero General de Asuntos Jurídicos del gobierno de Durango, se haya preocupado por preparar la detención antes que nada de un proveedor de servicios del anterior gobierno priísta dejando para después la detención de quien o quienes le pagaron esa cantidad de dinero, que en este caso la responsabilidad apuntaba hacia la ex secretaria de Finanzas y Administración, la C.P. María Cristina Díaz Herrera, de quien, según el Lic. Galdino Torrecillas, "solo" encontraron desvíos que ascendían a 72 millones de pesos, de los cuales "gastó un millón de pesos en dulces artesanales".

Como quiera que sea, este pésimo golpe mediático que obviamente tenía las intenciones de legitimar al gobierno "del cambio" ante la ciudadanía en su tardada aplicación de justicia contra quienes lesionaron el erario duranguense, social y políticamente le salió muy contraproducente al mandatario panista corrupto y al Consejero General de Asuntos Jurídicos, Lic. Galdino Torrecillas, pues como dijo el especialista en Derecho, Lic. Mario Pozo Riestra, "Rafael Herrera Piedra en breve podrá irse a su casa", resultado que nos dió el mensaje de que esta mal planeada aplicación de justicia solo fue un mero ajuste de cuentas personal contra el segundo hombre más poderoso del sexenio pasado.

Galdino Torrecillas, el "consejero jurídico" del gobierno del estado de Durango que fue utilizado por el mandatario corrupto José Aispuro para perpetrar su venganza personal en contra del empresario Rafael Herrera Piedra, primo del ex gobernador priísta Jorge Herrera Caldera.

Hoy, estas vicisitudes del Lic. Galdino Torrecillas solo han dejado ver que todos estos años le dio atole con el dedo a la ciudadanía duranguense, pues por inepto o por corrupto no armó bien sus expedientes para fincar responsabilidades penales a los demás ex funcionarios del anterior gobierno priísta que, como todo mundo sabe, junto con sus directores de administración sustrajeron del erario duranguense mucho más que 24 o 72 millones de pesos, como por ejemplo la misma ex secretaria de Finanzas y Administración, C.P. María Cristina Díaz Herrera; el ex secretario de Salud, Dr. Eduardo Díaz Juárez; el ex secretario de Obras Públicas, Arq. César Guillermo Rodríguez Salazar; la ex directora de Comunicación Social, Lic. Arlene Contreras, y la ex Fiscal, Lic. Sonia Yadira de la Garza Fragoso, entre otros tantos ex funcionarios que a discreción le metieron las manos a los bolsillos a los ciudadanos duranguenses.

Capítulo VII
Más familiares de Aispuro y Elvira en la nómina

Hacia el primer año de su gobierno, José Aispuro Torres, su gabinete de impresentables, sus acuerdos inconfesables y su nepotismo representaban el mayor fraude político de los últimos tiempos en esta entidad norteña.

Elvira Barrantes, "La Gobernadora", y José Aispuro, con una corrupción y un nepotismo insultantes representaron el mayor fraude político de los últimos tiempos en Durango.

El 5 de junio de 2016, más del 50% del electorado duranguense votó por el candidato de la coalición PAN-PRD, José Aispuro Torres, llevándolo a la gubernatura y poniendo fin a los regímenes priístas corruptos que gobernaron esta entidad durante 90 años, pero jamás se imaginó que al mismo tiempo se echaría encima una pesadilla de seis años mucho peor. Y es que efectivamente más de la mitad de los sufragantes de esta entidad norteña eligieron a Aispuro Torres para que fuera su gobernador, porque al fin de cuentas fue quien dio la cara en las boletas electorales, pero lo que no sabían los duranguenses, y por supuesto Aispuro Torres no se los dijo, fue que este político aparentemente generoso llegaría al poder acompañado de personajes verdaderamente siniestros y dueños de historiales de corrupción extremadamente preocupantes. También, lo que no dijo en su campaña electoral el ex senador panista fue que al día siguiente de que tomara posesión de su cargo comenzaría a ejercer, junto con su esposa Elvira Barrantes, un detestable nepotismo que ni siquiera los dos últimos gobernadores priístas repudiados por buena parte de la sociedad duranguense practicaron.

Verónica Terrones, directora de Comunicación Social del gobierno del estado de Durango, en la página oficial de Transparencia se ostentó como licenciada, pero no aparecía en el Registro Nacional de Profesionistas de la SEP

A un año de haber iniciado su gestión, Aispuro Torres rendía su primer informe de gobierno en medio de los mismos vicios que en su campaña electoral dijo que eliminaría: el dispendio y derroche del erario proyectando una imagen falsa de su gobierno en los medios de comunicación locales y nacionales; la presentación de datos incorrectos y cifras que no coincidían con las acciones que supuestamente su gobierno había realizado; la organización de eventos mediáticos inútiles, alternos a la presentación oficial de su informe en el Congreso local, en las ciudades de Durango y Gómez Palacio, con el consecuente gasto de enormes cantidades de dinero del erario derrochado en la logística y acarreo de personas; y los ataques a la libertad de expresión perpetrados por personal de la secretaría de Seguridad Pública y empleados del gobierno estatal en contra de ciudadanos que pretendieron manifestar su inconformidad por el mal desempeño que el gobernador Aispuro Torres estaba teniendo.

Dirección Académica
Profr. Jesús Valles Banderas
Directora Academico

618 137.39.04 — Av. Cor. Enrique Carrola Antuna 1814 Fracc. Canelas

Departamento de Planeación Académica
Lic. Edgar Zamarripa Aguirre
jefatura de departamento

618 1373932 — Av. Cor. Enrique Carrola Antuna 1814 Fracc. Canelas

Subdirección Académica
Inq. Karla Cristina Acosta Barrantes
Subdirectora

618 1373950 — Av. Cor. Enrique Carrola Antuna 1814 Fracc. Canelas

Depto. de Proyectos Académicos Especiales
Lic. Tomas Rodríguez Trinidad
Depto. Proyectos Especiales

618 1373918 — Av. Cor. Enrique Carrola Antuna 1814 Fracc. Canelas

Departamento Desarrollo de Infraestructura
C.P. Gudelia Herrera Alvarado
Depto. de Infraestructura

618 1373958 — Carretera al Pueblito 112 El Pueblito

Departamento de Evaluación Institucional
Lic. Marbella Barrantes Blancarte
Depto. de Evaluación Institucional

618 1373936 — Carretera al Pueblito 112 El Pueblito

Depto. de Verificación de Procesos Institucionales
L.I. Claudia Gallegos Rosales

618 1373943 — Carretera al Pueblito 112 El Pueblito

Karla Cristina Acosta Barrantes, sobrina de Elvira Barrantes, sin perfil profesional fue nombrada Subdirectora Académica del COBAED.

Teresa de Jesús Aispuro Torres, fue impuesta por su hermano José Aispuro como Secretaria Ejecutiva de Administración del Poder Judicial del Estado de Durango.

Ese primer año del gobierno "del cambio" dejó un muy mal sabor de boca por todo lo que se observó: la complicidad del gobernador Aispuro Torres con muchos priístas corruptos que permanecieron ocupando importantes cargos en su gobierno; la tibieza de las acusaciones penales en contra de algunos funcionarios saqueadores del sexenio pasado; el encubrimiento de muchos actos de corrupción cometidos por ex servidores públicos del anterior sexenio que fueron detectados desde el proceso de entrega-recepción y de los cuales no se fincaron responsabilidades penales; la corrupción desmedida en las adjudicaciones de contratos favoreciendo a familiares y amigos de buena parte de los integrantes del gabinete aispurista "para pagar compromisos hechos en campaña"; y el nombramiento de perfiles con antecedentes altamente delincuenciales dentro de la iniciativa privada y la administración pública en dependencias sensibles, como por ejemplo la secretaría de Finanzas y de Administración, en manos de auténticos pillos dueños de historiales depredadores en los estados de Coahuila, Sinaloa y Sonora, especialmente, en donde ocuparon altos cargos en los gobiernos panistas de las dos últimas entidades mencionadas.

Así las cosas, el gobernador Aispuro Torres pretendió ocultar bajo la alfombra éste cúmulo de malos resultados patrocinando tras bambalinas una encuesta a modo que lo colocaba como "el segundo mejor gobernador del país". La encuesta fue realizada por la empresa denominada Gabinete de Comunicación Estratégica, propiedad de Liévano Sáenz, aquél ex vocero del candidato presidencial priísta asesinado, Luis Donaldo Colosio, y entre las preguntas que esta encuestadora supuestamente hizo a la ciudadanía se encontraban las siguientes: ¿Considera usted que su gobernador tiene las riendas de su estado o que las cosas se están saliendo de control? Si el gobernador de su estado fuera su vecino y usted tuviera que ausentarse de su casa, ¿le confiaría las llaves de su casa?

Ante estas interrogantes y sabiendo cómo estaban las cosas, surgió la inmediata reflexión de que era obvio que el gobernador duranguense José Aispuro Torres no tenía las riendas de su estado, toda vez que buena parte de su gabinete era ineficaz y cometía actos de corrupción.

En cuanto a la segunda pregunta de la encuesta, por supuesto que en lo personal no le confiaría las llaves de mi casa al gobernador Aispuro Torres considerando que nombró como secretario de Finanzas a un sujeto (C.P.

Arturo Díaz Medina) que apenas hace poco más de un año era representante legal de una empresa minera canadiense (First Majestic Silver Inc.) que despojó a ejidatarios coahuilenses de una mina que produce 1,200 millones de pesos anuales en plata, y también nombró como secretario de Desarrollo Económico al ex director de esta misma minera canadiense, Ing. Ramón Dávila Flores. ¡¡De ninguna manera le hubiera confiado las llaves de mi casa al gobernador Aispuro Torres!!

Londres Botello, cuñado del gobernador de marras José Aispuro, al inicio del sexenio ocupó el cargo de Secretario Técnico de la Comisión Estatal de Suelo y Vivienda en donde se dedicó a violar los derechos laborales y humanos de los trabajadores de esta institución.

Por otro lado, pero sobre lo mismo, un hecho que causó mucha indignación en la ciudadanía duranguense fue la corrupción que el mismo gobernador y su esposa estaban practicando, ejerciendo un nepotismo a ultranza. Aispuro Torres designó a su cuñado, Londres Botello Castro, como Secretario Técnico de la Comisión Estatal de Suelo y Vivienda (COESVI), un puesto estratégico dentro de esta dependencia, además de que este personaje fungió como uno de los principales operadores políticos del gobernador, es decir, una réplica de Rafael Herrera Piedra, el primo del ex gobernador priísta Jorge Herrera Caldera.

DAD

DIRECCIÓN ADMINISTRATIVA

Directora Administrativa

María Julieta
Acosta Barrantes

Direccion:
Blvd. Felipe Pescador 201
Zona Centro
34000

Telefonos:
(618) 137 43 00, 01, 02 y 03,
(618) 137 43 10

María Julieta Acosta Barrantes, sobrina de "La Gobernadora", ocupó un alto cargo dentro de la COESVI.

RECTORIO TELEFÓNICO DE DIF ESTATAL (Anteponer número 13 para convertir en número directo) 13 Sep. 2017

Área	Usuario	Extensión CISCO
Dirección de los Servicios Administrativos		
Blvd. José María Patoni No. 105 "Fracc. Predio Rustico La Tinaja y Los Lugos", Durango, Dgo. C.P. 34217	dif.administrador@durango.gob.mx	
Directora de los Servicios Administrativos araceli.rodriguez@durango.gob.mx	C.P. Araceli Rodríguez Moreno	79166
Secretaria - marthae.hernandezr@durango.gob.mx	Martha Elena Hernández Reza	79153
Subdirección Administrativa dif.subdirector.advo@durango.gob.mx	Acéfalo	
Auxiliar cuotasadvo.dif@durango.gob.mx	L.C. Norma Patricia Ochoa Concha Beatriz Burciaga Hernández	79155
Asesoría Externa	C.P. Mercedes Barrantes V.	79043
Departamento de Servicios Financieros y Contabilidad		
Jefe del Departamento de Servicios Financieros pedro.ramirez@durango.gob.mx	C.P. Pedro Ramírez Jaime	79156
Encargada de Contabilidad alejandra.cardiel@durango.gob.mx	C.P. Alejandra Cardiel Blanco	79123
Auxiliar de Contabilidad comprobaciones.dif@durango.gob.mx	C.P. Ma. Magdalena López Rosales	79123
Auxiliar de Contabilidad	Jesús Antonio Molina Yáñez	79319

Mercedes Barrantes, "La Contadora", hermana de "La Gobernadora" Elvira Barrantes, apareció en el directorio telefónico del DIF estatal como titular de "Asesoría Externa", pero en realidad ejerció funciones fácticas como jefa de Recursos Humanos y de Administración.

La hermana del gobernador, C.P. Teresa de Jesús Aispuro Torres esposa del Lic. Londres Botello Castro, ocupó el cargo de Secretaria Ejecutiva de Administración en el Tribunal Superior de Justicia estatal, que sin duda alguna también es un puesto estratégico. Teresa de Jesús Aispuro, a la par de este cargo, realizaba tareas fácticas en la secretaría de Educación estatal.

Dos sobrinas de Elvira Barrantes, esposa del gobernador, ocuparon altos cargos en el Colegio de Bachilleres del Estado de Durango (COBAED): Marbella Barrantes Blancarte, jefa del Departamento de Evaluación Institucional, y Karla Cristina Acosta Barrantes, titular de la Subdirección Académica. Al respecto, días después de las denuncias publicadas en nuestro medio informativo, razacero, referentes a estos nombramientos nepotistas, la Dirección de Comunicación Social del gobierno de Aispuro Torres emitió un comunicado a los trabajadores del COBAED prohibiéndoles entrevistarse con representantes de los medios de comunicación en sus instalaciones.

Pero los anteriores no fueron los únicos familiares que José Aispuro Torres y su esposa Elvira Barrantes colocaron en la nómina del gobierno estatal inmediatamente de que tomaron posesión de sus cargos, el primero como gobernador y la segunda como presidenta del DIF estatal.

Una sobrina más de Elvira Barrantes, María Julieta Acosta Barrantes, fue nombrada Directora Administrativa de la COESVI, uno de los cargos más altos en esta dependencia.

Perla Aispuro Aispuro, sobrina del goberna-
dor, ocupó una plaza de auxiliar administrativo
en el DIF, pero en los hechos realizaba labores
directivas en la Casa Hogar.

Perla Aispuro tenía a su disposición un vehículo oficial y chofer de tiempo completo que la trasladaba a todas partes, a diferencia de los demás auxiliares administrativos del DIF que son sancionados e inclusive despedidos si se les sorprende utilizando un vehículo oficial de esta dependencia fuera del horario laboral. Pero Perla Aispuro sí podía hacer esto, si no ¿de qué servía ser la sobrina del gobernador?

Otra pariente de Elvira Barrantes que también apareció en la nómina fue su hermana, la C.P. Mercedes Barrantes, conocida en el DIF como "La Contadora". Mercedes Barrantes destacó en el directorio telefónico de trabajadores del DIF como titular de "Asesoría Externa", pero según testimonios de trabajadores de esta institución, Mercedes Barrantes, "La Contadora", es quien decidió todo en las direcciones de Servicios Administrativos y Recursos Humanos del DIF estatal. "En estas áreas no se mueve nada si 'La Contadora' no lo ordena", manifestaron los empleados entrevistados que solicitaron el anonimato por temor a sufrir represalias laborales.

Cabe destacar que la mayoría de estos familiares del matrimonio Aispuro-Barrantes no contaban con el perfil profesional para desempeñar los cargos que les fueron dados.

Este asunto del nepotismo fue solo la punta del iceberg de las corruptelas, privilegios, dispendios y desvíos de recursos que desde el primer minuto de gobierno cometió la dinastía desaseada encabezada por el gobernador José Aispuro Torres.

Capítulo VIII
Más anomalías en el DIF

Luego de la denuncia publicada en nuestro medio de información en cuanto al vergonzoso nepotismo que se practicaba en el DIF estatal, en donde familiares del gobernador José Aispuro Torres y su esposa Elvira Barrantes estaban en la nómina y ocupaban altos cargos de manera táctica, un grupo de trabajadores de esta dependencia acudió a nuestra redacción para ampliar la información sobre más anomalías que se cometían en esta institución, solicitando el anonimato por temor a sufrir represalias laborales.

Elvira Barrantes, "La Gobernadora" y presidenta del DIF. Prepotencia, soberbia, impro- visación y negligencia, algunas de las características de su administración al frente de esta loable institución.

En primer término denunciaron a la sobrina del gobernador, Perla Aispuro Aispuro, quien ejercía funciones fácticas como encargada de la Casa Hogar del DIF. Con plaza de auxiliar administrativo, Perla Aispuro utilizaba un vehículo oficial y chofer de tiempo completo, a diferencia de la mayoría de los trabajadores que eran fuertemente reprendidos, sancionados y hasta despedidos si se les sorprendía utilizando los vehículos de esta institución fuera del horario laboral.

Durango, Dgo., a 16 de Enero del año 2017
Of. D.A./004/2017

ING. HÉCTOR HUGO CRUZ GONZÁLEZ
DIRECTOR DE RECURSOS HUMANOS
DE GOBIERNO DEL ESTADO DE DURANGO
PRESENTE.

Por medio del presente y de la manera más atenta, solicito a Usted realizar el siguiente cambio de percepciones de la **C. MERCEDES BARRANTES VELARDE**, Asesora Administrativa adscrita en Presidencia de este Sistema Estatal D.I.F., el cual seria en:

- Considerar en la Clave P-01 de $10,000.00 al mes por concepto de nivelación al sueldo y en la Clave P-50 la cantidad de $29,160.00 al mes, a partir del 01 de Enero del presente año.

No omito mencionarle que el cambio antes mencionado se genera por la aplicación de la percepción de la Clave P-50 del C. Juan Antonio Álvarez Pérez y cancelación de las percepciones de las Claves P-18 y D-81 del C. Carlos Eduardo Meraz Castro y del ahorro generado con el movimiento de alta de la C. Raquel Leila Arreola Fallad.

Agradezco de antemano sus finas atenciones y esperando verme favorecido con mi petición aprovecho la ocasión para enviarle un cordial saludo.

ATENTAMENTE

C.P. ARACELI RODRÍGUEZ MORENO
DIRECTORA DE LOS SERVICIOS DMINISTRATIVOS
DIF ESTATAL DURANGO

LIC. RICARDO FRANCISCO FAVILA LEÓN
SUBDIRECTOR DE RECURSOS HUMANOS
DIF ESTATAL DURANGO

La fusión de plazas de trabajadores que fueron despedidos injustificadamente fue una práctica aberrante para beneficiar a los familiares de "La Gobernadora", Elvira Barrantes.

Perla Aispuro, manifestaron los trabajadores de la Casa Hogar, "no sabemos qué tipo de preparación tenga, pero se entromete constantemente en el trabajo del equipo multidisciplinario, contradiciendo y manipulando las sugerencias y decisiones de los psicólogos, trabajadores sociales y personal médico con una actitud sumamente intransigente. Con este comportamiento afecta severamente el normal desarrollo del trabajo y, lo peor de todo, afecta la integridad física y emocional de los niños dentro de la Casa Hogar, a quienes con su prepotencia e ignorancia les pone apodos y trata despóticamente".

Los privilegios de Perla Aispuro en la Casa Hogar eran ilimitados, como en su momento lo dieron a conocer los trabajadores del DIF: "Realiza sus tres comidas en el comedor de la Casa Hogar, hecho que no le es permitido a ningún trabajador; ella y su esposo deciden el menú de acuerdo a sus antojos sin importarles las recomendaciones de los médicos o enfermeras", expresaron los trabajadores, puntualizando: "La coordinadora (María Florinda Morán Meraz) es una fina persona que no hace más que obedecer, pero quien decide todo es Perla Aispuro".

Los empleados del DIF estatal también cuestionaron el proceder de la C.P. Mercedes Barrantes, hermana de la esposa del gobernador Aispuro Torres, quien en el organigrama del DIF aparece como "Asesora Externa", pero en los hechos ejerce funciones de mando en las direcciones de Servicios Administrativos y Recursos Humanos: "A un año de haber tomado posesión de su cargo son más los resultados negativos que positivos los que ha dado esta persona, pues ahorra en clips pero en otras cosas despilfarra a manos llenas. Ella y la presidenta del DIF, Elvira Barrantes, negociaron la permanencia en sus plazas de buena parte de funcionarios ineficaces o corruptos de la pasada administración, entre los que destacan la Lic. Claudia Angélica Tynan López, ex titular de la Procuraduría de Protección a Niñas, Niños y Adolescentes en el sexenio pasado; ahora, Claudia Angélica Tynan López ocupa un puesto clave dentro del DIF como titular de Asesoría Jurídica", manifestaron los trabajadores y denunciaron que a más de un año de iniciado el sexenio hubo negligencias y omisiones por parte de las altas autoridades del DIF (léase su presidenta, Elvira Barrantes, la "asesora externa", Mercedes Barrantes, y la directora del DIF, Dra. Rocío Azucena Manzano Chaidez) al ignorar, por indiferencia e incompetencia, un fideicomiso de la Casa Hogar que existe desde hace tres sexenios, "en este fideicomiso hay dinero que debe ser utilizado a favor de la niñez duranguense, pero esta administración, a pesar de que tiene conocimiento de esto, no se ha preocupado por hacerlo funcionar. A tal grado llega la indiferencia de estas autoridades que ni siquiera han hecho los trámites en el banco para cambiar a los titulares de este fideicomiso, que siguen siendo ex funcionarios del sexenio pasado como Jason Eleazar Canales, Lucero González Hermosillo y la C.P. María Cristina Díaz Herrera", expresaron los empleados del DIF a razacero.

Así las cosas, la encargada de solucionar este problema, según los trabajadores del DIF, "era la Lic. Claudia Angélica Tynan López, titular de Asesoría Jurídica de esta institución, pero hizo caso omiso de los correos electrónicos y de las llamadas telefónicas de los ejecutivos de BANORTE, institución bancaria que funge como fiduciaria de este fideicomiso, que en repetidas ocasiones le pidió que se presentara en el banco para hacer los trámites de actualización y presentar a los nuevos titulares", señalaron los trabajadores indignados entregando a nuestra redacción el número de dicho fideicomiso: 204221 en BANORTE.

Rocío Manzano, directora del DIF, complaciente ante los abusos de Perla Aispuro en la Casa Hogar.

Mientras esto sucedía, el DIF (o sea los contribuyentes) seguía pagando al banco los intereses y manejo de cuenta de un fideicomiso que no estaba produciendo ningún beneficio por falta de interés de los principales directivos de esta institución.

Como se ve, lo que menos les interesaba a este tipo de funcionarios del gobierno "del cambio" era el verdadero bienestar de la niñez duranguense. Soberbios, improvisados, prepotentes, despóticos y sin perfil para desempeñar sus cargos, fueron algunas de las características que definieron a esta nueva clase política duranguense que a un año de gobierno ya se había ganado el repudio no solo de buena parte de la planta laboral del gobierno estatal sino de un amplio sector de la ciudadanía que no veía con buenos ojos el nepotismo descarado que practicaba el gobernador Aispuro Torres y su abierta complacencia de actos de corrupción e ineficacia cometidos por casi todos los integrantes de su gabinete.

Capítulo IX
Las placas millonarias

Arturo Díaz, el corrupto secretario de Finanzas del gobierno aispurista, en enero de 2017 anunció el despido del 10 por ciento de trabajadores del gobierno de Durango, como "medida de austeridad", así como reducciones en gastos de combustible, viáticos y telefonía para los empleados gubernamentales, pero ese mismo mes y en diciembre de 2016 su subsecretario de Administración, Ignacio Orrante, firmó contratos con la empresa Talleres Unidos Mexicanos con un sobreprecio de más de 32 millones de pesos.

El estado de Durango es quizá el más pobre del norte de la República mexicana, rezagado en varios rubros importantes como empleo y desarrollo social; en municipios como Mezquital, por ejemplo, la miseria es comparable a la de algunos países africanos y, al igual que allá, ha habido casos en los que por desgracia los niños sufren de desnutrición extrema y llegan a morir de hambre. Pero esto al parecer no les importó mucho al secretario de Administración y Finanzas del gobierno estatal, C.P. Jesús Arturo Díaz Medina, y a su subsecretario de Administración, Luis Ignacio Orrante Ramírez, quienes de la manera más infame dilapidaron el erario de los duranguenses favoreciendo a determinados empresarios, anteponiendo intereses particulares a los intereses públicos.

Así, de acuerdo a una investigación realizada por el equipo de razacero luego de recibir información de fuentes fidedignas de los estados de Sinaloa, Durango y la Ciudad de México, se pudo determinar lo que quizá representaba la punta del iceberg de los saqueos que se realizaron en esta dependencia.

El punto de partida de estos hechos comienza a principios de 2017, cuando el gobierno del estado de Durango, a través de la secretaría de Administración y Finanzas, da a conocer las bases de la licitación pública nacional número EA-910002998-n1-2017, para la "Adquisición de Placas y Calcomanías de Verificación Vehicular", que se declaró desierta a pesar de que cinco empresas se presentaron a concursar, entre ellas la denominada Talleres Unidos Mexicanos S.A. de C.V.

En enero de 2017, inmediatamente después de haber declarado desierta esta licitación, el gobierno del estado de Durango, bajo la figura de Adjudicación directa, otorgó el contrato a la empresa Talleres Unidos Mexicanos S.A. de C.V., propiedad del empresario Manuel Martínez Saldaña, con domicilio en la Ciudad de México.

En este contexto, la empresa Talleres Unidos Mexicanos S.A. de C.V., el 27 de enero de 2017 firma el contrato con el gobierno duranguense para manufacturar las más de 400 mil placas y calcomanías de identificación vehicular que esta administración estatal fue vendiendo a la ciudadanía, específicamente placas y calcomanías de autos, camiones y autobuses, además de otras variantes como placas para motocicletas, remolques, de vehículos para discapacitados, ecológicos y los pertenecientes al gobierno del estado.

Llama la atención que desde diciembre de 2016 el gobierno del estado de Durango ya había signado un contrato con esta misma empresa, también para la adquisición de diversas cantidades de placas y calcomanías.

Según los contratos de adjudicación directa números EA-910002998-n1-2017/01 y GED-SA-005/2016, el precio que el gobierno de Durango, a través de la secretaría de Administración y Finanzas, pagó por cada uno de los más de 400 mil juegos de placas y calcomanías para autos y camiones principalmente, fue de 215.76 pesos (199.52 pesos por juego de placas y 16.24 pesos por calcomanía).

Hasta aquí las cosas aparentemente parecían estar bien, hasta que de acuerdo a información obtenida de otros estados de la República pudimos constatar que esta misma empresa, Talleres Unidos Mexicanos S.A. de C.V., había realizado contratos de esta naturaleza y en ese mismo año, con otros gobiernos estatales, como por ejemplo el de Sinaloa, al que Talleres

Unidos Mexicanos en el Procedimiento de Invitación a cuando Menos Tres Personas Núm. GES IN-31/2017 le ofreció un precio de 135 pesos por cada juego de placas y engomado para autos.

Haciendo cuentas, el secretario de Administración y Finanzas del gobierno del estado de Durango, C.P. Jesús Arturo Díaz Medina, y su subsecretario de Administración, Luis Ignacio Orrante Ramírez, pagaron la friolera de 80.76 pesos más por cada uno de los más de 400 mil juegos de placas y calcomanías de vehículos que adquirió con esta empresa.

Aunque las otras variantes de placas y calcomanías (de remolques, motocicletas y vehículos pertenecientes al gobierno estatal) también presentaron sobreprecios, si tomamos como base el número de 400 mil autos y camiones registrados en el padrón vehicular del estado de Durango, la cifra del sobreprecio asciende a los 32 millones 304 mil pesos que el gobierno del estado de Durango pagó de más a la empresa Talleres Unidos Mexicanos S.A. de C.V., respecto al precio que esta misma empresa ofreció al gobierno del estado de Sinaloa por cada juego de placas y calcomanías de identificación vehicular.

Ignacio Orrante, sus acciones como subsecretario de Administración de la secretaría de Finanzas del gobierno del estado de Durango deben ser investigadas de manera exhaustiva por instancias federales.

Y lo peor de todo esto es que, conforme a fuentes consultadas, "el secretario de Administración y Finanzas, Jesús Arturo Díaz Medina, y el subsecretario de Administración, Luis Ignacio Orrante Ramírez, a sabiendas de esto siguieron dando adjudicaciones directas de contratos a esta misma empresa, a la que le otorgaron otro contrato con el mismo sobreprecio, que jamás apareció en el portal de Transparencia del gobierno del estado de Durango", revelaron las fuentes.

Desde su campaña electoral, el mandatario estatal José Aispuro Torres prometió a la ciudadanía duranguense un gobierno austero y totalmente transparente. El 14 de junio de 2017 el empresario Rafael Herrera Piedra, primo del ex gobernador priísta Jorge Herrera Caldera, fue encarcelado por fraude al patrimonio del gobierno del estado de Durango, que ascendía a 24 millones 372 mil pesos, luego de las pesquisas que realizó el Consejero de Asuntos Jurídicos, Lic. Galdino Torrecillas Herrera, y la pregunta que entonces nos hicimos muchos ciudadanos duranguenses fue la siguiente: ¿Qué harán el Consejero de Asuntos Jurídicos del gobierno del estado de Durango, Lic. Galdino Torrecillas Herrera, la secretaria de la Contraloría, Lic. María del Rosario Castro Lozano, y los diputados del Congreso local? ¿Le fincarán responsabilidades penales al secretario de Administración y Finanzas del gobierno estatal, C.P. Jesús Arturo Díaz Medina, y a su subsecretario de Administración, Luis Ignacio Orrante Ramírez, por este descalabro al erario de los duranguenses que asciende a más de 32 millones de pesos?

Por supuesto que el gobernador de marras, José Aispuro, no hizo absolutamente nada para sancionar a sus dos subordinados ineficaces y corruptos, por lo que poco a poco fue perdiendo su credibilidad y legitimidad.

Capítulo X
Aispuro encubre desvío de recursos millonarios al PD

Luego de la denuncia publicada en el prestigiado periódico The New York Times sobre el desvío de más de 250 millones de pesos que el ex secretario de Hacienda y exsecretario de Relaciones Exteriores, Luis Videgaray Caso, realizó para financiar las campañas del PRI en las elecciones de 2016 a través de los gobiernos estatales de entidades como Veracruz, Chihuahua y Tamaulipas, el escándalo también alcanzó a los estados de Sonora y Durango.

El corrupto gobernador panista José Aispuro, tuvo conocimiento de los desvíos millonarios que el anterior gobierno priísta hizo al Partido Duranguense, pero utilizó esa información para su beneficio político.

Precisamente en esta última entidad, Durango, una fuente fidedigna detalló a nuestro medio informativo, razacero, el entramado que se llevó a cabo durante casi todo el sexenio pasado para financiar no solo las campañas del Partido Revolucionario Institucional, sino las de por lo menos uno de sus partidos satélites: el Partido Duranguense (PD).

Lo peor de todo esto es que, de acuerdo a la fuente, este mecanismo de desvíos millonarios fue encubierto y siguió ocurriendo en el gobierno "del cambio", encabezado por el gobernador panista José Aispuro. El 21 de diciembre de 2017 publicamos en nuestra página web razacero.com:

"En la lista de Proveedores y Contratistas del Gobierno del Estado de Durango, se encuentra Martha Gómez Juárez (prima de Guillermo Juárez Compeán, Coordinador de Audiencias y Atención Ciudadana del Despacho del Ejecutivo en el actual gobierno 'del cambio', y uno de los actores principales en la pérdida de la autonomía de la UJED). Esta persona, Martha Gómez Juárez, recibió 200 mil pesos mensuales depositados a una cuenta del banco HSBC, sin que hubiera de por medio ningún servicio o producto vendido a la administración priísta, estos egresos fueron autorizados por la ex secretaria de Finanzas, C.P. María Cristina Díaz Herrera, por órdenes del ex gobernador Jorge Herrera Caldera. Estas erogaciones ocurrieron entre 2011 y hasta julio de 2016, por lo que en total sumaron un desfalco al erario de más de 7 millones de pesos", denunció la fuente.

¿Cuál fue el destino de este dinero?, la fuente reveló lo siguiente: "Esta partida presupuestal fue destinada a financiar a algunos dirigentes del Partido Duranguense, específicamente a su presidenta actual, Verónica Acosta, ex secretaria de Finanzas del Comité Ejecutivo Estatal, y al entonces Director de Desarrollo Rural estatal, Francisco Acosta Llanes, ex diputado plurinominal del Partido Duranguense en la LXV Legislatura local (2010-2013) y 'consejero vitalicio' de este partido. Este dinero servía para comprar consejeros políticos, hacerse del control del partido y asegurar la participación del mismo en las alianzas con el PRI (derivado de esto el presidente Raúl Irigoyen intentó renunciar y presentó un documento con este propósito, donde detalló todas estas anomalías, pero fue obligado a permanecer en el cargo con amenazas a través de la entonces Fiscal, Sonia Yadira de la Garza Fragoso, y de la policía a su cargo)".

De acuerdo a las investigaciones realizadas por la fuente, Martha Gómez Juárez solo era una secretaria en el Partido Duranguense y su estilo de vida no correspondía al de una empresaria que durante 5 años ganó 200 mil pesos al mes, libres de impuestos.

La fuente abundó: "Adicionalmente, ninguno
de los bienes y servicios que se describían en sus
facturaciones entraron como parte del inventa-
rio al gobierno estatal".

Para finalizar, la fuente precisaba que "hay algunas fotografías de Martha Gómez recogiendo algunas entregas de dinero, que el gobierno actual (de Aispuro) las guarda como evidencia para en caso necesario, a conveniencia, detenerla y usarlas en su contra, así como también este gobierno tiene pruebas de estos desvíos millonarios en contra de la presidenta del Partido Duranguense, Verónica Acosta, y de la ex secretaria de Finanzas, C.P. María Cristina Díaz Herrera, ya prófuga".

Así las cosas, todo parece indicar que el gobernador duranguense, José Aispuro, tenía conocimiento de estos hechos delictivos, pero por intereses políticos particulares y de grupo no los dio a conocer al pueblo de Durango.

Verónica Acosta, como dirigente del Partido Duranguense fue utilizada por el gobierno aispurista para atacar al ex alcalde de Durango José Ramón Enríquez Herrera.

A finales de 2017, la presidenta del Partido Duranguense, Verónica Acosta, de manera poco usual presentó media docena de denuncias en contra del entonces alcalde de Durango, José Ramón Enríquez Herrera, de su esposa, la Dra. Ana Beatriz González Carranza, y de la directora de Comunicación Social de este municipio, Lic. Patricia Salas Name, por supuestos desvíos de recursos públicos "para la promoción de la imagen personal del alcalde capitalino en pleno proceso electoral", ante el Tribunal Electoral del Poder Judicial de la Federación, entidad que al no tener facultades para resolver este caso dio vista al Congreso local de

Durango para que procediera a determinar lo correspondiente.

En la misma situación de sometimiento forzoso al gobierno "del cambio" pudieron encontrarse algunos dirigentes y ex dirigentes locales del Partido Verde Ecologista, el PRD, PT y Nueva Alianza, que recibieron fuertes cantidades de dinero del anterior gobierno priísta.

Capítulo XI
Los guadalupanos perversos

El 8 de diciembre de 2017, los perversos guadalupanos encabezaron la peregrinación en las calles de Durango para rendirle tributo a la Virgen del Tepeyac.
¿Qué pensará La Virgen Morena sobre el comportamiento de estos fieles devotos?

El hartazgo estalló la noche del viernes 15 de diciembre de 2017, las llamadas comenzaron a llegar a nuestra redacción, eran decenas de empleados del DIF estatal de Durango: "¡Son las 9 de la noche y no nos han depositado la quincena ni el aguinaldo!", exclamó un empleado sumamente enojado.

"Solo dependo de mi salario, tengo una hija pequeña y no tengo para comprarle sus pañales", informaba desesperado otro de los trabajadores afectados.

"Ya estamos hartos de esta gente, nos hacen trabajar horas

extras y se niegan a pagárnoslas", denunciaron.

"Podrán decir lo que sea del ex gobernador Ismael Hernández Deras, pero su esposa doña Gabriela, cuando fue presidenta del DIF, fue una finísima persona... nada que ver con lo que está pasando ahora. Los directivos nos dijeron que la falta de pago era por culpa del banco, pero fuimos al banco y los ejecutivos nos confirmaron que las autoridades del gobierno estatal no habían hecho el depósito correspondiente", manifestó vía telefónica una trabajadora de esta institución.

Elvira Barrantes, "La Gobernadora", y Rocío Manzano, como presidenta y directora del DIF, respectivamente, implantaron un régimen de terror laboral en esta institución provocando el hartazgo y el repudio de los trabajadores.

Por nuestra parte, hicimos la denuncia inmediata vía twitter, y otros medios de comunicación locales de esta entidad, muy pocos, hicieron eco de los reclamos de los trabajadores. Así, tuvo que haber presión para que los funcionarios del gobierno estatal de Durango, encabezados por el ya controvertido ex senador panista, José Aispuro Torres, solucionaran este problema hasta el sábado 16, pasado el medio día. Y es que en este gobierno, parece ser que las finanzas estuvieron totalmente en manos de verdaderos pillos, el principal de ellos fue el titular de la secretaría de Administración y Finanzas, Arturo Díaz, quien contaba con antecedentes realmente peligrosos dentro de la iniciativa privada como ex apoderado legal de la empresa minera canadiense First Majestic Silver Corporation, que en el año 2011 fue demandada por los campesinos del ejido Tenochtitlán, del estado de Coahuila, por usurpar 2,400 hectáreas de su propiedad, extensión en la cual se encuentra una mina de plata que produce utilidades de 1,200 millones de pesos anuales. Hasta la fecha, este proceso legal continúa vigente.

A 15 meses de iniciado este gobierno "del cambio", de corte panista-perredista, el repudio de la planta laboral ya era generalizado, tanto en las secretarías como en las direcciones, sobre todo en el DIF, institución en la que ya era inaguantable la actitud prepotente y déspota de la presidenta y esposa del gobernador, Elvira Barrantes, quien junto con su hermana, Mercedes Barrantes, "asesora de administración", y la directora, Azucena Manzano, implantaron un verdadero régimen de terror laboral en esta dependencia, auxiliados por un pequeño grupo de directivos de marras que conspiraban en sus oficinas para seleccionar a las empleadas que iban a hostigar sexualmente y a los trabajadores a los que les iban a hacer la vida imposible hasta despedirlos injustificadamente.

Con sueldos miserables de 2,200 pesos a la quincena, la mayoría de los empleados del DIF estatal de Durango tuvieron que soportar los abusos de poder de esta élite aborrecible que podía tener todo, menos cultura y sensibilidad social.

Así las cosas, "a nombre del gobernador Aispuro", como solían decir con frecuencia estos detestables "servidores públicos", esta estirpe ruin que "dirigió" al DIF cometió todo tipo de tropelías en agravio de los trabajadores, que conocían perfectamente las corruptelas que cometían, desde sus negocios sucios con proveedores favoritos hasta la disposición desmedida de vales de gasolina para sus vehículos particulares.

Otra parcela de poder en manos de un patán
fue la secretaría de Salud, con su entonces
titular, el Dr. César Franco.

"En la secretaría de Salud también nos han quitado varias prestaciones que nos daban en el sexenio pasado, el desabasto es peor que cuando estaba el ex gobernador Jorge Herrera Caldera y ni siquiera hay vendas para enyesar a los lesionados", denunció en nuestra redacción un doctor que labora en esta dependencia al enterarse de la falta de pago a los empleados del DIF.

También, algunos policías de la secretaría de Seguridad Pública llamaron a la redacción de razacero preocupados porque no les habían pagado su bono sexenal, que ascendía a 18 mil 500 pesos anuales y les era entregado cada fin de año.

Así gobernó Aispuro Torres, este profesional de la demagogia y del engaño que llegó al poder prometiendo un cambio, pero no les dijo a los electores que ese cambio sería para mal, pues traería consigo a una cauda de colaboradores prepotentes, mezquinos y extremadamente corruptos.

Así gobernó Aispuro Torres, este pequeño aprendiz de dictadorzuelo que, al igual que los sátrapas priistas que gobernaron el sexenio pasado, también aplicó la regla del "te pago para que te calles" auxiliado por una ex conductora de noticieros que tristemente devino en censuradora de medios de comunicación. Y los comunicadores que no se adherían a esta regla inmediatamente pasaron a ser candidatos para sufrir alguna represalia.

Lo extraordinario de esto es que a muchos de estos personajes nefastos, encabezados por el gobernador Aispuro Torres y su esposa Elvira Barrantes, se les vio desfilar por las calles de Durango el 8 de diciembre de 2017, en peregrinación para rendirle tributo al máximo ícono religioso de los mexicanos: la Virgen de Guadalupe.

¿Qué pensará La Virgen del Tepeyac sobre el comportamiento miserable de estos detestables personajes?

CAPÍTULO XII
Contralora de Durango, 15 meses simulando

Hacia diciembre de 2017, el gobernador Aispuro y su entonces Contralora estatal, Rosario Castro, seguían encubriendo la corrupción del anterior gobierno priísta y el periodista lagunense Juan Monrreal López escribía en su portal de noticias Demócrata Norte de México:

Quince meses después de que el llamado "gobierno de la alternancia" se instalara con la figura de José Rosas Aispuro Torres como gobernador, los fincamientos de responsabilidades a ex funcionarios del gobierno del estado que dirigió Jorge Herrera Caldera por daños patrimoniales a Durango poco a poco se van diluyendo envueltos en un mar de palabrería que semana tras semana ha vertido la Contralora panista María del Rosario Castro Lozano, quien hace exactamente un año declaró en entrevista con la periodista Shaila Rosagel, acerca de los daños presupuestales ocasionados por el ex gobernador Herrera Caldera por al menos 4 mil 500 millones de pesos de acuerdo con las irregularidades señaladas por la Auditoría Superior de la Federación (ASF); "pero sólo son la punta del iceberg porque los daños son mayores e incuantificables", dijo la Contralora a la reportera. 430 días después, los castigos legales a "quien la hizo la paga" (Aispuro dixit) siguen disolviéndose en el mar de las negociaciones políticas, y hasta ahora sólo se mantiene en la cárcel a Rafael Herrera Piedra, primo del ex gobernador, pero a ningún ex funcionario público se ha tocado e incluso ya se exoneró de toda responsabilidad administrativa a Jorge Herrera Caldera.

Y es que la Contralora del estado, María del Rosario Castro Lozano, tiene fama y antecedentes de ser perfecta simuladora y de pactar con quien le reditúe mayores dividendos políticos y económicos, de manera que rendir buenas cuentas a la ciudadanía poco importa.

De hecho, Rosario Castro ha trabajado con mayores compromisos con fuerzas y grupos priístas que con los propios militantes del PAN, partido al que pertenece formalmente. Un ejemplo: las pasadas elecciones locales de 2016.

La hoy Contralora realizó campaña diferenciada con los candidatos a los puestos de gubernatura, presidencia municipal y diputaciones locales.

Así, mientras por un lado empujaba la candidatura del ahora gobernador José Rosas Aispuro, al mismo tiempo promocionaba a la aspirante priista a la presidencia municipal de Lerdo, María Luisa González Achem, así como a la diputada local Jaqueline del Río López, por compromisos adquiridos con el entonces alcalde priista Roberto Carmona -beneficiario actual de la obra pública lerdense-, boicoteando abiertamente las campañas de Salomé Elyd de Katsicas y Raúl Villegas Morales, candidatos de la coalición formada por los partidos PAN-PRD, Unidos por Ti.

De hecho, el sexenio de Jorge Herrera Caldera
fue un periodo de ensueño para María del
Rosario Castro Lozano.

Amarrada la alianza con el ex gobernador, se dedicó a cultivar colaboraciones con los jefes de los poderes, entre éstos con el ex presidente del Tribunal Superior de Justicia, Apolonio Betancourt, y otros funcionarios señalados como saqueadores de los bienes del estado de Durango, de manera que difícilmente se llevará ante la ley a quienes como pandilla asaltaron las arcas públicas.

"Daños incuantificables al erario": Rosario Castro Lozano

"Hasta el momento la cifra es incuantificable, se irá precisando conforme se vayan desahogando las audiencias y conforme se den los resultados de las auditorías estatales. Las federales ya se tienen, hay que esperar las estatales", dijo Castro Lozano hace un año.

Sin embargo, han pasado 430 días y nada se ha hecho público de los avances de las auditorías estatales, aun cuando la Contralora declaró que la Federación detectó cuando menos "234 soluciones de responsabilidad administrativa de parte de la ASF y la Secretaría de la Función Pública", pero nada se ha hecho por llevar ante los tribunales a los 14 ex funcionarios que mencionó Rosario Castro Lozano, o a los 27 burócratas que según el secretario General de Gobierno, Adrián Alanís Quiñones, participaron en el saqueo estatal.

Todavía el 25 de noviembre de 2016, la Contralora presumió que "nos están exigiendo (de la Federación) requerir a los ex funcionarios. Nosotros somos coadyuvantes, la Federación se reserva las facultades de recuperar el dinero federal y la facultad para hacerlo punitivo. Nosotros tenemos que demostrar que sí se requirió y se llevó el procedimiento. Si cumplieron se les notifica, y si no se pasa el expediente para el debido proceso", explicó en ese entonces, pero a la fecha los duranguenses siguen esperando que el llamado "gobierno del cambio" presente ante las autoridades judiciales a quienes causaron "daños (patrimoniales) incuantificables" a las arcas del estado.

Jorge Herrera Caldera incrementó la deuda 405 por ciento, está exonerado

El gobierno de Jorge Herrera Caldera fue de saqueo. De 3 mil 697 millones de deuda oficial heredada del gobierno de Ismael Alfredo Hernández Deras -"El campesino nylon encargado de la CNC"-, la elevó hasta 15 mil millones de pesos, sin obra pública que la justifique.

Aun así, el ex gobernador fue exonerado
públicamente por el actual mandatario estatal
José Rosas Aispuro Torres.

Es tal la carga de esta herencia deudora que los habitantes de Durango adeudan 13 mil 780 pesos per cápita, una cantidad más elevada que Chihuahua y Veracruz cuyos habitantes deben 11 mil 308 pesos y 5 mil 621 pesos respectivamente, cuando existen cuando menos 234 observaciones de responsabilidad administrativa, según aseveró la Contralora, señalamientos que no han servido para fincar responsabilidades a ninguno de los jefes políticos frente a un juez.

Ahora, los duranguenses verán, como en Coahuila, la impunidad en todo su esplendor, mientras las finanzas públicas pujan hasta para cubrir las necesidades más ingentes; en tanto, María del Rosario Castro Lozano seguirá hablando a los medios acerca de la diferencia del previo "proceso de entrega-recepción, (que) anteriormente se llevaban entregas formales, pero no legales; hoy, con la alternancia, se están llevando entregas formales y legales", pero los resultados son peores pues la ciudadanía es engañada.

Rosario Castro Lozano; alianzas 2018, otra vez con el PRI

Con la enjundia de haber derrotado en las urnas al PRI el 5 de junio de 2016, los nuevos funcionarios no escatimaron en seguir prometiendo y prometiendo; uno de estos burócratas fue la Contralora del gobierno del estado de Durango.

Luego, exaltada en rueda de prensa, María del Rosario Castro Lozano reveló el nombre de 3 ex secretarios a los que se les imputaron responsabilidades administrativas, sin que hasta la fecha el proceso prosiga. Unos porque están amparados, como Eduardo Díaz Juárez, ex secretario de Salud, con el expediente 1206/2016, así como César Guillermo Rodríguez, titular de Comunicaciones y Obras Públicas, con el expediente 1164/2016, y otros porque se dieron a la fuga, como la ex jefa de Finanzas María Cristina Díaz Herrera.

Rosario Castro, ex titular de la Contraloría del gobierno panista sucio encabezado por José Aispuro, quince meses engañó al pueblo de Durango sancionando a empleados de bajo rango mientras los autores de grandes saqueos al erario durante el sexenio pasado permanecieron impunes o prófugos.

El asunto es que ningún funcionario público de la era de Jorge Herrera Caldera –el exonerado-, se encuentra frente a tribunales, y mucho menos en prisión.

En este contexto, Rosario Castro Lozano ha declarado tener a 14 ex funcionarios en investigación; en tanto, el secretario General de Gobierno, Adrián Alanís Quiñones, hizo público que 27 ex burócratas de Jorge Herrera se encuentran amparados para no ser reclusos.

Han pasado 15 meses desde que el gobierno de la alternancia encargó a Rosario Castro Lozano llevar a cabo los procesos jurídicos para fincar responsabilidades a quienes saquearon el patrimonio de los duranguenses, en este tiempo a nadie ha encarcelado, salvo a Rafael Herrera Piedra, primo del ex gobernador que nunca fungió como empleado público.

Eso sí, María del Rosario Castro llenó la nómina con fieles seguidores que ya se encuentran haciendo amarres políticos para el próximo proceso electoral 2018, y no precisamente con el PAN, como siempre ha sido la escuela mafio partidista de la Contralora que le ha fallado a Durango desde su nombramiento mismo.

Hasta aquí la nota de Juan Monrreal López. Como se sabe, Rosario Castro posteriormente, luego de haber realizado un "excelente" papel como Contralora estatal, es decir, encubriendo la corrupción de los ex funcionarios del sexenio anterior priísta y del gobierno aispurista, fue nombrada "coordinadora de gabinete", un cargo inexistente en el organigrama oficial del gobierno del estado de Durango, inventado por el gobernador de marras José Aispuro para integrar a las actividades de gobierno a su fiel asistente, Carlos Maturino, actual diputado federal panista.

Capítulo XIII
Aispuro, el gobernador
de la impunidad

El gobernador de Durango, José Aispuro, al momento de emitir su amenaza al gobierno municipal de Durango. "*Mi respaldo a los empresarios, no están solos, vamos a buscar por todos los medios legales y con la fuerza que tiene el Estado para que se respeten sus derechos*".

El 20 de febrero de 2018 el gobernador de Durango, José Aispuro Torres, apareció en los canales de televisión local haciendo declaraciones inusuales, se le notaba nervioso, tenso, sin control de sus emociones. Amenazante, advirtió al gobierno municipal de Durango, específicamente al alcalde, Dr. José Ramón Enríquez Herrera, diciendo:

"Mi respaldo a los empresarios, no están solos, vamos a buscar por todos los medios legales y con la fuerza que tiene el Estado para que se respeten sus derechos", refiriéndose al sector empresarial de esta entidad que, según este mandatario, se sentía agredido por la clausura de la construcción de la plaza comercial Distrito Hampton, por no tener su licencia de construcción en regla y de la que es socio el conocido empresario Jaime Mijares Salum, beneficiado sobremanera durante el anterior sexenio priísta, en el que adquirió a un precio irrisorio (40 millones de pesos) los valiosos terrenos en donde se encontraban las instalaciones del DIF estatal y el Centro de Salud Núm. 1, mismos en los que se edificó la polémica plaza comercial Distrito Hampton y el fastuoso Hotel Hampton.

También, en sus declaraciones viscerales, Aispuro Torres sentenció: "Hago un llamado al ayuntamiento capitalino para que se conduzca con respeto a la ley y que cese el hostigamiento a los empresarios. Aquí yo estoy defendiendo a un sector que coadyuva al desarrollo económico y que genera empleo".

Minutos antes de emitir estas fuertes declaraciones, el gobernador duranguense había tenido una reunión con los representantes de los principales sectores empresariales de Durango: Elier Flores, de la Confederación Patronal de la República Mexicana (Coparmex); Guillermo Falomir, del Sector Privado Empresarial, y Miguel Castro, de la Cámara Nacional de Comercio (Canaco) y representante del Consejo Coordinador Empresarial (CCE) quienes acusaron a las autoridades municipales de Durango "de realizar actos sistemáticos de bloqueo en contra de los empresarios".

Jaime Mijares, el conocido empresario duranguense favorecido por el gobierno corrupto priista del sexenio pasado. Compró los terrenos donde se encontraban las instalaciones del DIF estatal y del Centro de Salud Núm. 1 al precio irrisorio de 40 millones de pesos, cuando el valor de estas propiedades era muy superior.

Un día antes de este entramado mediático, las autoridades del municipio de Durango habían retirado los sellos de clausura de la construcción de la plaza comercial Distrito Hampton, pues los encargados de la obra habían cumplido ya con los requerimientos legales que el municipio le exige a cualquier ciudadano para realizar construcción alguna.

Es evidente que la reacción sobrada del gobernador Aispuro Torres no se debió tanto al supuesto hostigamiento que las autoridades municipales de Durango ejercieron sobre el sector empresarial en lo general, sino a la afectación de los intereses de un empresario en particular: Jaime Mijares Salum, muy cercano a su círculo político y también muy cercano a quienes durante el sexenio pasado se dedicaron a saquear el erario de los duranguenses.

En este contexto, resultó contradictorio que el gobernador Aispuro Torres exigiera al Ayuntamiento de Durango que se condujera con respeto a la ley cuando precisamente por cumplir con la ley fue que suspendió la ostentosa construcción del empresario Mijares Salum.

Si todos los ciudadanos, en materia de construcción, debemos cumplir con los requisitos que marca la ley inclusive para comenzar a levantar una pequeña barda en nuestras casas, ¿por qué al empresario Mijares Salum debía exentársele de tal obligación? ¿O es que de acuerdo a Aispuro Torres en Durango debía haber ciudadanos de primera y de segunda?

Independientemente del trasfondo político que pudo haber tenido este asunto porque se dio en pleno proceso electoral y en medio de las disputas internas por las candidaturas en los partidos, en este caso en el PAN, donde el empresario Jaime Mijares podía obtener una candidatura para contender por una diputación local, lo que proyectó este incidente fue el autoritarismo de un gobernador que a toda costa pretendió seguir salvaguardando los privilegios de algunos empresarios por encima de la ley, la igualdad y el piso parejo que la mayoría de los empresarios y ciudadanos exigieron que se respetaran en este gobierno del cambio.

Por otro lado, con este hecho quedó manifestada públicamente la adversidad política, y quizá hasta personal, que el gobernador duranguense siempre mantuvo hacia el entonces alcalde de Durango, José Ramón Enríquez Herrera, quien designado ya oficialmente como candidato a senador por Durango representando al partido Movimiento Ciudadano, dentro de la coalición "Por México Al Frente", se convertía de ribete en fuerte candidato natural a la gubernatura de esta entidad norteña para las elecciones del año 2022.

Como quiera que sea, fue patético ver y oír a un gobernante defender furiosamente no tanto a esos sectores empresariales y a sus cúpulas sino a un individuo que se ha enriquecido a la sombra del poder. De esta misma manera, a los ciudadanos y a muchos comunicadores nos hubiera gustado ver al gobernador Aispuro defender con idéntica enjundia al periodista lagunense Juan Monrreal López, cuando en mayo de 2017 fue amenazado con ser encarcelado por el cabildo del municipio de Gómez Palacio, en un acto maquinado por la alcaldesa gomezpalatina Juana Leticia Herrera Ale, por no querer revelar sus fuentes de información y por publicar denuncias de corrupción en contra de autoridades de este municipio. Además de esto, Juan Monrreal López fue amenazado anónimamente en su integridad física y patrimonial si persistía en seguir publicando sus denuncias en su medio de comunicación digital, Demócrata Norte de México.

En este tema, al gobernador Aispuro Torres jamás se le escuchó en los medios de comunicación exigir de manera enérgica a la alcaldesa de Gómez Palacio, Juana Leticia Herrera Ale, y a su cabildo que dejaran de hostigar al periodista Juan Monrreal, y a pesar de la solicitud que le hizo la Comisión Nacional de los Derechos Humanos, Aispuro Torres no fue capaz ni siquiera de otorgarle la más mínima protección a Juan Monrreal, pues la Fiscalía General de Durango puso a disposición del periodista dos agentes ministeriales a los que el mismo Juan Monrreal debía de pagar alimentos y alojamiento. Vaya ayuda. Pero si se trata de defender a un empresario bribón y ventajoso, el gobernador Aispuro Torres, ni tardo ni perezoso, pone a su disposición "la fuerza que tiene el Estado para que se respeten sus derechos".

Por lo demás, a 17 meses de gobierno, la aceptación social del otrora popular gobernador José Aispuro Torres seguía en picada, pues a diferencia de los gobernadores de Chihuahua y Veracruz, Javier Corral y José Ángel Yúnez, que llegaron al poder apoyados por la alianza PAN-PRD (la misma que cobijó a Aispuro), este gobernante duranguense por razones inconfesables no cumplió su promesa de aplicar la ley "a todos aquellos que le hicieron daño al pueblo de Durango", y más aún, no recuperó un solo centavo de los miles de millones de pesos que se robó la mafia priísta que gobernó esta entidad el sexenio pasado. Por el contrario, Aispuro Torres se definió como un mandatario nepotista, complaciente, tolerante y protector de los oprobiosos actos de corrupción que cometieron la mayoría de los integrantes de su gabinete, actos que contemplan desde el saqueo del erario hasta hostigamientos sexuales y violaciones a los derechos laborales de cientos de empleados que fueron despedidos injustificadamente de todas las dependencias estatales, especialmente del DIF, donde su esposa, Elvira Barrantes, y la directora de esta institución, Rocío Manzano, practicaron un terrorismo laboral humillante, sin precedente en la historia de Durango.

A 17 meses de comenzado su sexenio, acompañado de un gabinete de pillos y aventureros improvisados, José Aispuro Torres, de gobernador "del cambio", pasó a ser El Gobernador de la Impunidad.

Capítulo XIV
Secretaría de Salud, más de un año sin pagar a proveedores

A 18 meses de haber llegado al poder, el gobierno "del cambio", encabezado por el panista José Aispuro Torres, ya había recibido dos presupuestos "históricos" de la federación: el de 2017, de 27 mil millones de pesos, y el de 2018, de 28 mil millones. De estos, anualmente, más de 2 mil millones eran destinados al sector Salud; sin embargo, esta considerable suma de dinero no se veía reflejada en la satisfacción de las necesidades primordiales que cotidianamente tienen tanto los centros de salud como los hospitales que esta secretaría administra en el estado.

Así, y para desgracia de la ciudadanía que tiene que hacer uso de los pésimos servicios que otorga esta institución, el desabasto de medicamentos y equipo médico se convirtió en un hecho cotidiano, como cotidianos fueron y son los maltratos de los directivos hacia los empleados de esta secretaría y sus derechohabientes. Pero el titular de esta dependencia en ese momento, Dr. César Franco Mariscal, con un desparpajo que rayaba en el cinismo e indignaba al pueblo de Durango, seguía culpando a la pasada administración priísta por la supuesta mala situación financiera de la secretaría a su cargo.

¿Por qué no había dinero para solucionar estos problemas si en menos de dos años esta secretaría había tenido un presupuesto superior a los 4 mil millones de pesos?

Proveedores locales y foráneos denunciaron ante la redacción de razacero que desde hacía más de un año el gobierno "del cambio" se negaba a pagarles los servicios que le habían prestado. "Algunos proveedores ya estamos a punto de quebrar pues desde hace más de un año el gobierno del estado de Durango no nos paga los suministros y equipos médicos que le hemos vendido, son deudas que ascienden a un millón, dos millones, tres millones o más, y las autoridades de este gobierno solo pagan abonos de 20 mil o 30 mil pesos, y encima de eso nos siguen pidiendo productos a pesar de que no tienen solvencia económica", denunció un proveedor desesperado que por razones obvias solicitó el anonimato.

"Ya no sabemos qué hacer, les pedimos que nos paguen y no hacen caso, y si exigimos nuestros pagos por la vía legal sabemos que nos vamos a ir a juicios interminables y menos nos van a pagar", concluyeron.

Estos proveedores se suman a los empleados estatales de casi todas las dependencias que quincena tras quincena filtran a los medios de comunicación locales y en las redes sociales quejas por la falta de pago puntual de sus salarios y descuentos leoninos que ni siquiera en el anterior gobierno priísta corrupto les hacían.

Este desaseo en el manejo de las finanzas del gobierno del estado de Durango comenzó a darse en esta entidad con el secretario de este rubro, Arturo Díaz Medina, personaje muy cercano al gobernador José Aispuro Torres.

Este funcionario desde el inicio del sexenio se caracterizó por otorgar adjudicaciones directas de contratos con sobreprecios a empresarios amigos de este gobierno de corte panista-perredista, a quienes dio un trato preferencial para pagarles puntualmente.

Arturo Díaz Medina, apenas un día antes de integrarse al gabinete del gobernador duranguense Aispuro Torres, el 15 de septiembre de 2016, era apoderado legal de la empresa minera canadiense depredadora First Majestic Silver Corporation, misma que bajo este gobierno comenzó a extraer oro y plata de las minas de Tayoltita, en el municipio de San Dimas. La minera First Majestic Silver Corporation es conocida a nivel nacional por los atropellos que ha cometido en estados como Coahuila y Zacatecas, en los que ha violado derechos humanos y legales dañando el medio ambiente y despojando a ciudadanos y ejidatarios de grandes extensiones de terrenos en los que se encuentran minas de metales preciosos.

La alta corrupción e ineptitud de este personaje, protegido por el gobernador pusilánime Aispuro Torres, ha sido la razón por la que las finanzas del estado de Durango fueron empeorando durante todo este sexenio, pues al dejar de pagar hasta por más de un año a cientos de proveedores y prestadores de servicios duranguenses muchos de ellos han quebrado, agudizándose el desempleo y disminuyendo el circulante de dinero entre la ciudadanía.

Por el contrario, trascendería que muchas empresas selectas, sobre todo del estado de Sinaloa, siempre han recibido sus pagos puntuales por parte del gobierno panista de Aispuro, empresas relacionadas de alguna u otra manera con su dinastía familiar liderada por su esposa, Elvira Barrantes, quien desde el inicio del sexenio decidió tras bambalinas qué empresas debían ser contratadas por el gobierno estatal y cuáles no.

Capítulo XV
Salud, el desastre

Bajo la administración de César Franco Mariscal la secretaría de Salud del estado de Durango pasó por la peor crisis de su historia.

18 meses bastaron para que la secretaría de Salud del estado de Durango, bajo el gobierno "del cambio", se resquebrajara y presentara resultados mucho peores que los que dejó el gobierno priísta corrupto que gobernó esta entidad el sexenio pasado.

Al despotismo, prepotencia y vulgaridad que el titular de esta dependencia, el Dr. César Franco Mariscal, ejerció desde el primer día de su gestión afectando a la planta laboral, le siguieron la corrupción e ineficacia pues con este funcionario siguieron practicándose los mismos vicios de la administración anterior.

Con Franco Mariscal el desastre fue tal que los empleados del "mejor hospital de Durango", el 450, se quejaron en el anonimato: "El desabasto de medicamentos y equipo médico es grave, estamos usando las jeringas con el mismo paciente todo el día porque no hay. Tampoco hay sondas para aspirar a los pacientes, no hay catéteres centrales ni guantes, ni tubos para entubar a los enfermos; en urgencias no hay reactivos para sodio, para potasio, para magnesio; no hay Alkacide, tampoco hay ventiladores, y en el colmo algunos directivos nos piden que esterilicemos las sondas desechables. Los carros de paro están casi vacíos, el autoclave está descompuesto".

En esta secretaría, las adjudicaciones directas de contratos estuvieron a la orden del día pues por lo general no se realizaron licitaciones públicas para la adquisición de medicamentos, equipos médicos y servicios, y solamente los empresarios de Sinaloa fueron los que siempre recibieron sus pagos puntualmente.

"Franco Mariscal debe más de 300 millones de pesos a proveedores que han prestado sus servicios y entregado mercancías a esta secretaría desde hace más de un año, lo que está ocasionando que algunos de ellos ya estén a punto de quebrar financieramente", denunciaron los trabajadores de Salud entrevistados.

En cuanto al Seguro Popular las cosas no pintaron tan bien para este funcionario nocivo, pues de acuerdo a los testimonios de trabajadores de este sector: "El Seguro Popular es un ente financiador que paga a la secretaría de Salud por la atención que le brinde a cada uno de sus afiliados; la última campaña de afiliación fue hace tres años. Durante este gobierno no ha habido ningún avance en ese aspecto. Por ineficacia e inoperancia la secretaría de Salud no atiende al número de derechohabientes del Seguro Popular que debería atender y, por lo tanto, el Seguro Popular no paga a la secretaría de Salud lo que le debería pagar, dejando de percibir esta institución más de 50 millones de pesos en lo que va de este gobierno 'del cambio'. Lo mismo sucede en Cancerología, específicamente en la atención a los niños con cáncer, en donde la secretaría de Salud ha dejado de percibir más de 20 millones de pesos", detallaron los trabajadores denunciantes.

En los primeros meses de 2018, el Seguro Popular donó a la secretaría de Salud 20 ambulancias para trasladar a los derechohabientes que lo requirieran, "pero todas están estacionadas en el patio del Hospital 450, empolvadas, sin usarse", relataron los empleados de esta institución.

Para entonces, más de 2,500 empleados ya habían sido despedidos injustificadamente por la administración del Dr. César Franco Mariscal: "Despidieron a más de 2,500 compañeros y contrataron a 1,500 a los que les pagan sueldos muy superiores a los que ganaban los despedidos; también, muchos de los contratados son personas sin perfil para ocupar sus cargos, pero son allegados de Franco Mariscal, de Elvira Barrantes y de los principales directivos", expusieron los trabajadores de Salud que solicitaron el anonimato por temor a sufrir represalias y ser despedidos.

Además de esto, el gobierno del estado tuvo que pagar conforme a la ley las liquidaciones de centenares de trabajadores que optaron por interponer demandas en los tribunales correspondientes por despido injustificado.

El acoso laboral, otro lastre que llegó a esta dependencia con el gobierno "del cambio", no cesó durante todo el sexenio, haciendo menos productivo y más estresante el rendimiento de los trabajadores.

Ante todos estos abusos laborales, los distintos secretarios de la sección 88 del Sindicato Nacional de Trabajadores de la Secretaría de Salud, fueron comparsas del gobierno sátrapa aispurista.

Capítulo XVI
Secretaría de Salud de Durango: La licitación fétida

El 25 de abril de 2018, luego de un proceso totalmente amañado, la Secretaría de Salud del estado de Durango le otorgó a la "empresa" Servicios de Alimentación Vizcaya S.A. de C.V., el contrato de Adquisición del Servicio de Suministro de Alimentos Preparados para el Hospital General 450 y el Hospital de Salud Mental Dr. Miguel Vallebueno, que ascendió a más de 15 millones de pesos, para prestar este servicio a partir del mes de mayo hasta diciembre de 2018, que consistió en servir entre 18 y 20 mil dietas al mes a razón de 70 pesos por dieta. Sin embargo, los directivos de estos centros hospitalarios no sabían el viacrucis que les esperaba con los representantes de esta empresa supuestamente profesional. Y los conflictos que comenzaron de cero, llegaron a su punto más áspero en mayo de 2019, como lo revelaron a razacero trabajadores del Hospital 450 que solicitaron el anonimato por temor a sufrir represalias laborales: "La situación en el Hospital 450 ya es insostenible, pues desde que la empresa Servicios de Alimentación Vizcaya ganó de manera ilegal la licitación para otorgar el suministro de alimentos ha cometido una serie de irregularidades graves que ponen en peligro la salud y la vida de los pacientes y del personal", reveló la fuente.

El Dr. Sergio González Romero, titular de la secretaría de Salud, y el Dr. Martín Ernesto Delgado Gómez, director del Hospital 450, sabían perfectamente las violaciones graves a las leyes sanitarias que cometía la "empresa" Servicios de Alimentación Vizcaya S.A. de C.V., pero no hicieron absolutamente nada para sancionarla.

"Se sabe que inclusive algunos trabajadores de esta empresa laboran padeciendo enfermedades contagiosas, como parasitosis, pues la empresa Servicios de Alimentación Vizcaya S.A. de C.V., no los somete al control epidemiológico exigido por las autoridades sanitarias", denunciaron los trabajadores.

Así las cosas, en el Hospital 450, por esta situación, todos los días se respiraba un ambiente laboral tenso ya que el dueño de esta empresa, José Luna Herrera, y su representante, la Licenciada en Nutrición Mayra Alejandra Pérez Rincón, confundieron su papel de prestadores de servicios y actuaban como directivos.

"Se supo en todo el Hospital 450 que el dueño de la empresa Servicios de Alimentación Vizcaya S.A. de C.V., José Luna Herrera, amenazó a la Jefa del Departamento de Nutrición, L.N. Karen Alejandra Ballesteros, diciéndole de manera violenta que utilizaría sus influencias para despedirla por las constantes quejas que ésta ha presentado ante el secretario de Salud, Dr. Sergio González Romero, por el pésimo servicio que presta este empresario, quien fanfarronea de ser amigo cercano del gobernador Aispuro Torres", informaron los empleados entrevistados.

Pelos en los alimentos, gusanos en verduras mal lavadas, moscas cocidas en medio de las dietas y piezas de pollo crudas eran servidos con frecuencia en las dietas a pacientes y personal del Hospital 450 por esta empresa de marras, a la que de manera increíble le fueron otorgadas por la secretaría de Turismo las licencias 14449 y 14491 conocidas como "Distintivo H", por supuestamente cumplir con los estándares de higiene que marca la Norma Mexicana NMX-F605 NORMEX 2004, y en hospitales la Norma 251.

A todo esto se sumó el manejo fraudulento de los registros de controles de dietas: "Ya no es un secreto en el Hospital 450 que esta empresa abulta en sus registros el número de dietas que sirve a pacientes y personal. Las nutriólogas se niegan a firmar esos registros y han implementado un sistema de vales para evitar el saqueo que realiza esta empresa, ya que cobra un promedio de 4 mil a 5 mil dietas ficticias al mes, pero este esquema de vales ha sido boicoteado por la empresa, que prepara menos dietas dejando sin comer a pacientes y personal culpando de esto a la jefa de Nutrición, Karen Alejandra Ballesteros", especificaron las fuentes.

Con esta actitud extremadamente voraz operó la "empresa" Servicios de Alimentación Vizcaya S.A. de C.V., propiedad de José Luna Herrera, sin que ninguna autoridad en el gobierno estatal la metiera en cintura, y lo más grave de esto es que este agresivo empresario fue por todo pues también "ganó" los contratos para ofrecer este mismo "servicio" en el Hospital 450, en el Centro Estatal de Transfusión Sanguínea, Hospital General Durango, Centro Estatal de Cancerología, Hospital de Salud Mental Dr. Miguel Vallebueno, Hospital General de Gómez Palacio y en el Hospital General de Lerdo, de acuerdo a la licitación número LP/E/SSA/012/2019, emitida el 3 de mayo de 2019 por el secretario de Salud Dr. Sergio González Romero, para la Adquisición del Servicio de Suministro de Alimentos Preparados por un periodo de 6 meses, del 1 de junio al 31 de diciembre de 2019, contrato que, como en el año 2018, se extendió por 5 o 6 meses más.

"Servicios de Alimentación Vizcaya S.A. de C.V., no cumple con uno de los requisitos principales para obtener este contrato, que es el de contar con instalaciones especiales en caso de alguna contingencia. El domicilio que proporcionan en la ciudad de Durango es el de una bodega de abarrotes llamada "Dorado del Pacífico", ubicada en el Mercado de Abastos de la colonia El Refugio", expresaron los trabajadores de la secretaría de Salud.

Por esta razón, en el margen superior derecho de la licitación pública se estableció premeditadamente que "No habrá visita a instalaciones".

SERVICIOS DE SALUD DE DURANGO
SUBDIRECCION DE RECURSOS MATERIALES

Convocatoria: 012

De conformidad con lo que establece el Artículo 134 de la Constitución Política de los Estados Unidos Mexicanos, 160 de la Constitución Política del Estado Libre y Soberano de Durango, y el Artículo 17 fracción I inciso a) de la Ley de Adquisiciones, Arrendamientos y Servicios del Estado de Durango, y su reglamento, se convoca a los interesados en participar en la licitación para la Adquisición del Servicio de Alimentos Preparados para diversas Unidades Hospitalarias de Servicios de Salud de Durango, de conformidad con lo siguiente:

Licitación Pública Nacional

No. de licitación	Costo de las bases	Fecha límite para adquirir bases	Junta de aclaraciones	Visita a instalaciones	Presentación y apertura de proposiciones
LP/E/SSA/012/2019	$5,000.00	10 de mayo de 2019	13 de mayo de 2019 12:00 horas	No habrá visita a instalaciones	20 de mayo de 2019 12:00 horas

PARTIDA	UNIDAD	UNIDAD DE MEDIDA	CANTIDAD MINIMA	CANTIDAD MAXIMA
1	HOSPITAL GENERAL 450	DIETA	114,611	142,947
	CENTRO ESTATAL DE TRANSFUSIÓN SANGUINEA	DIETA	7,616	9,940
	HOSPITAL GENERAL DURANGO	DIETA	35,231	93,520
2	CENTRO ESTATAL DE CANCEROLOGIA	DIETA	7,112	17,780
	HOSPITAL DE SALUD MENTAL DR. MIGUEL VALLEBUENO	DIETA	48,419	121,037
	HOSPITAL GENERAL DE GÓMEZ PALACIO	DIETA	23,667	56,000
	HOSPITAL GENERAL DE LERDO.	DIETA	23,940	59,850

- Las bases de la licitación se encuentran disponibles para consulta en: La página del Sistema de Compras Gubernamentales comprasestatal.durango.gob.mx y para consulta y venta en el domicilio de la Convocante, sito en Cuauhtémoc Número 225 norte, colonia Centro, C.P. 34000, Durango, Durango, teléfono: 01 (618) 1 37 70 20 / 1 37 74 82, correo electrónico licitaciones.ssd@durango.gob.mx, los días del 07 al 10 de mayo de 2019, con el siguiente horario: 8:30 a 15:00 horas. La forma de pago es: mediante deposito en Banco Santander (México) S.A. a la cuenta No. 65-50261256-4 clabe 014190655026125647, plaza 3762 sucursal principal Durango a favor de los Servicios de Salud de Durango.
- La junta de aclaraciones se llevará a cabo el día 13 de mayo de 2019 a las 12:00 horas en: Sala de Juntas anexa a la Subdirección de Recursos Materiales, de los Servicios de Salud de Durango, ubicado en Cuauhtémoc Número 225 norte, colonia Centro, C.P. 34000, Durango, Durango.
- El acto de presentación y apertura de proposiciones se efectuará el día 20 de mayo de 2019 a las 12:00 horas, en Sala de Juntas anexa a la Subdirección de Recursos Materiales de los Servicios de Salud de Durango, Cuauhtémoc, Número 225 norte, colonia Centro, C.P. 34000, Durango, Durango.
- El idioma en que deberán presentarse las proposiciones será: Español.
- La moneda en que deberán cotizarse las proposiciones será: Peso mexicano.
- No se otorgará anticipo.
- Lugar de entrega: Unidades Hospitalarias de los Servicios de Salud de Durango, establecidas en las bases, los días lunes a domingo las 24 horas.
- Plazo de entrega/Inicio de Servicio: 01 de junio de 2019.
- El pago se realizará: dentro de los 20 días naturales posteriores a la fecha de prestación mensual del servicio, de conformidad en tiempo y forma y presentada la factura original.
- Ninguna de las condiciones establecidas en las bases de licitación, así como las proposiciones presentadas por los licitantes, podrán ser negociadas.
- Los criterios de adjudicación serán en base a lo establecido por el Artículo 35 de la Ley de Adquisiciones, Arrendamientos y Servicios del Estado de Durango.
- No podrán participar las personas que se encuentren en los supuestos del Artículo 37 de la Ley de Adquisiciones, Arrendamientos y Servicios del Estado de Durango.

DURANGO, DURANGO, A 03 DE MAYO DE 2019

DR. SERGIO GONZALEZ ROMERO
SECRETARIO DE SALUD Y DIRECTOR GENERAL DE SERVICIOS DE SALUD DE DURANGO
RÚBRICA

La convocatoria de la licitación pública LP/E/SSA/012/2019, para concursar por el contrato de Adquisición del Servicio de Alimentos Preparados en los principales centros hospitalarios de Durango. "El Contralor Interno de la secretaría de Salud, Ing. Miguel Vázquez Cabrera, preparó todo para que ganara la 'empresa' Alimentación Vizcaya S.A. de C.V., propiedad de José Luna Herrera", denunciaron trabajadores de esta dependencia.

OSIEL FRANCISCO LUNA CONTRERAS
LUCO950916VE0
Domicilio Fiscal
BLOCK B, BODEGA 17-A
Col. EL REFUGIO 34170
MERCADO DE ABASTOS EL REFUGIO DURANGO
DURANGO México
Tel. 618-8-27-32-73

Factura No: 10096

FOLIO FISCAL (UUID):
07217227-4A04-4745-A434-4A5421D0101...
NO. DE SERIE DEL CERTIFICADO DEL SAT:
00001000000403498740
NO. DE SERIE DEL CERTIFICADO DEL EMISOR:
00001000000306591228
FECHA Y HORA DE CERTIFICACIÓN:
2017-11-09T21:18:38
FECHA Y HORA DE EMISIÓN DE CFDI:
2017-11-09T21:11:38

CLIENTE: SERVICIOS DE SALUD DE DURANGO
RFC: SSD950927CR4
DIRECCIÓN: CUAUHTEMOC 225 NTE.
C.P. 34000
DURANGO Durango
MEXICO

Régimen Fiscal: Régimen de las Personas Físicas con Actividades Empresariales y Profesionales
Lugar de Expedición: DURANGO, DURANGO
Forma de Pago: Pago en una sola exhibición
Método de Pago: 03-Transferencia electrónica de fondos
Fecha de Expedición: 09 noviembre 2017
Clave de Moneda: MXN

CANTIDAD	UNIDAD DE MEDIDA	NO. IDENTIFICACIÓN	DESCRIPCIÓN	PRECIO UNITARIO	IMPORTE
[illegible].00	PAQUETE	HOSPANTI	PAN TOSTADO INTEGRAL	$ 30.00	$ 180.00
[illegible].00	BARRA	HOSPANI	PAN BIMBO INTEGRAL	$ 35.00	$ 7[illegible]0.00
32.00	BARRA	HOSPANB	PAN BIMBO BLANCO	$ 35.00	$ 1,1[illegible]0.00
6.00	PAQUETE	HOSPANTB	PAN TOSTADO BLANCO BIMBO	$ 30.00	$ 1[illegible]0.00
80.00	KILO	HOSTORH	TORTILLA DE HARINA	$ 30.00	$ 2,4[illegible]0.00
10.00	CAJA	HOSHCT	HARINA HOT-CAKES	$ 25.00	$ 2[illegible]0.00
15.00	CAJA	HOSLECHEE	LECHE ENTERA C/12LTS	$ 215.00	$ 3,2[illegible]5.00
5.00	CAJA	HOSLECHEL	LECHE LIGHT C/12LTS	$ 215.00	$ 1,0[illegible]8.00
4.00	FRASCO	HOSMAYOL	MAYONESA LIGHT .800GRS	$ 75.00	$ 3[illegible]0.00
4.00	FRASCO	HOSMAYON	MAYONESA 1.9KGS	$ 170.00	$ 6[illegible]0.00
3.00	BOTELLA	HOSCAT	SALSA CATSUP .330GRS	$ 30.00	$ 9[illegible].00
80.00	LATA	HOSCHICHARZ	CHICHARO C/ZANAHORIA	$ 8.50	$ 6[illegible]8.00
120.00	LATA	HOSATUN	ATUN	$ 18.00	$ 2,16[illegible].00
1.00	FRASCO	HOSACEI	ACEITUNA	$ 90.00	$ 9[illegible].00
100.00	PAQUETE	HOSCUERN	CUERNITOS BIMBO	$ 21.00	$ 2.10[illegible].00
40.00	LATA	HOSELOT	ELOTE .220GRS	$ 8.50	$ 51[illegible].00
[illegible].00	PIEZA	HOSFLAN	FLAN	$ 12.50	$ 30[illegible].00
1.00	KILO	HOSPIM	PIMIENTA	$ 280.00	$ 28[illegible].00
2.00	KILO	HOSGRENE.	GRENETINA	$ 65.00	$ 13[illegible].00
2.00	LITRO	HOSACEID	ACEITE DE OLIVA	$ 140.00	$ 28[illegible].00
60.00	LATA	HOSCHAM	CHAMPIÑON .380GRS	$ 25.00	$ 1,50[illegible].00
5.00	CAJA	HOSTEMANZA	TE DE MANZANILLA C/100 SOBRES	$ 50.00	$ 25[illegible].00
25.00	LATA	HOSCHICHI	CHILE CHIPOTLE	$ 25.00	$ 62[illegible].00
10.00	BOTE	HOSAVE	AVENA .375GRS	$ 22.00	$ 22[illegible]00
10.00	BOLSA	HOSPANHOT	PAN P/HOT DOGS	$ 30.00	$ 30[illegible]00
1.00	KILO	HOSPASAS	PASAS	$ 80.00	$ 8[illegible]00
2.00	KILO	HOSSAL	SAL	$ 10.00	$ 20[illegible]00
48.00	PIEZA	HOSSOP	SOPA YEMINA	$ 8.00	$ 384[illegible]00
48.00	PIEZA	HOSSOP	SOPA YEMINA ESPAGUETI	$ 8.00	$ 384[illegible]00

La bodega de abarrotes Dorado del Pacífico, la principal proveedora de la secretaría de Salud, su domicilio fue la "instalación especial para uso en caso de contingencia" de la "empresa" Alimentación Vizcaya S.A. de C.V.

"Ya está todo arreglado para que Servicios de Alimentación Vizcaya S.A. de C.V., gane esta licitación, pues inclusive ya hicieron las contrataciones de personal. La otra empresa concursante, MARVINO S.A. de C.V., es la misma que participó y perdió el año pasado; este año volverá a perder", finalizaron las fuentes.

Posteriormente a estos hechos, los propietarios de esta empresa, familiares de una conocida conductora de un programa televisivo de noticias locales y muy cercanos a Elvira Barrantes, esposa del gobernador de marras Aispuro Torres, asumieron realmente un papel fáctico de directivos al interior de la secretaría de Salud del estado de Durango, llegando al grado de ordenar represalias en contra del personal de nutrición del Hospital 450 que se atrevió a manifestar sus inconformidades por la forma de "trabajar" de esta empresa. Así, varios trabajadores fueron cambiados de su centro de trabajo y enviados a laborar a lugares lejanos de la capital de Durango.

Capítulo XVII
Gobierno "del cambio" hostigó a sindicato independiente de la COESVI

La historia del Sindicato Independiente de Trabajadores de la COESVI es una historia de lucha que se remonta a las postrimerías del sexenio del ex gobernador duranguense Ismael Hernández Deras, cuando a principios del año 2010 un grupo de empleados de esta dependencia descentralizada encabezado por Raúl Quezada Pacheco, Juan Carlos Galarza, Mario Alberto Gámiz y Arturo Barrios solicitan su registro como sindicato ante la Junta Federal de Conciliación y Arbitraje y éste les es negado.

El hampón Londres Botello Castro, cuñado del gobernador de marras José Aispuro, hostigó laboralmente a los trabajadores de la COESVI. Posteriormente, como regidor del municipio de Durango sería señalado tácitamente por el alcalde panista Jorge Salum por sus nexos con grupos delincuenciales en el rubro de licencias para venta de bebidas alcohólicas.

"En ese tiempo era el Instituto de Vivienda del Estado de Durango (IVED) y, luego de solicitar nuestro registro, varios de nuestros compañeros, bajo presiones y amenazas, son despedidos injustificadamente y obligados a recibir liquidaciones que no cumplían con lo que establecen las leyes laborales, por lo que al inicio del sexenio de Jorge Herrera Caldera nuestros compañeros Raúl Quezada, Mario Alberto Gámiz y Eduardo

Arellano Villa exigen su reinstalación y reposición de sueldos caídos, juicios que hasta la fecha siguen vigentes", expresó en mayo de 2018 en entrevista exclusiva para razacero el Ing. Juan Carlos Galarza Martínez, secretario general de este pequeño pero valeroso gremio integrado por 22 trabajadores.

En julio de 2011 las convicciones y firmeza de estos trabajadores rinden frutos y la Junta Federal de Conciliación y Arbitraje les otorga el registro oficial como Sindicato Independiente de Trabajadores del IVED (hoy Comisión Estatal de Suelo y Vivienda, COESVI).

"El gobierno priísta de Jorge Herrera Caldera designa como director del IVED al Lic. Javier Hernández Flores (el tristemente célebre ex delegado de la SEDESOL denunciado en julio de 2016 por los saqueos millonarios que perpetró en esta institución federal en Durango). Javier Hernández Flores, con todo el apoyo del gobierno estatal, forma otro sindicato para quitarnos el Contrato Colectivo. A este sindicato oficialista la JFCA le otorgó el registro en menos de 15 días", recordó Raúl Quezada, uno de los fundadores del Sindicato Independiente de la COESVI.

En la entrevista concedida a este medio a principios de mayo de 2018, Juan Carlos Galarza y Raúl Quezada rememoraron:

"En 2010, fastidiados por el hostigamiento del gobierno priísta de Ismael Hernández Deras, nos acercamos al entonces candidato opositor José Rosas Aispuro Torres para informarle nuestra problemática, prometiéndonos que si ganaba la gubernatura nos ayudaría para reinstalar a nuestros compañeros despedidos, pero Aispuro no ganó las elecciones y durante todo el sexenio de Jorge Herrera Caldera estuvimos batallando para que se respetaran nuestros derechos laborales".

En 2016, cuando finalmente José Aispuro Torres llegó a la gubernatura de Durango, los integrantes del Sindicato Independiente de Trabajadores de la COESVI se acercaron al recién nombrado Secretario Técnico de esta institución, Lic. Londres Botello Castro.

"Pensamos que por fin se nos haría justicia ya que el Dr. José Rosas Aispuro en el año 2010 prometió ayudarnos, pero con sorpresa vimos que el Lic. Londres Botello en lugar de apoyarnos comenzó una campaña agresiva para amedrentar a nuestros compañeros con el objetivo de obligarlos a abandonar nuestro sindicato y afiliarse al Sindicato de Trabajadores al Servicio de los Tres Poderes, cuya lideresa es María del Carmen Villalobos Valenzuela", denunciaron los fundadores del Sindicato Independiente de la COESVI.

Así las cosas, y luego de un largo juicio de más de siete años ante la JFCA, Raúl Quezada y Mario Alberto Gámiz Medina son reinstalados en sus trabajos, pero la COESVI se niega a pagarles sus sueldos caídos. El otro empleado despedido injustificadamente en el sexenio de Ismael Hernández Deras, Eduardo Arellano Villa, falleció en el año 2013.

"Hasta la fecha, tanto la COESVI como la Dirección General de Pensiones del estado de Durango se echan la pelota una a otra y se niegan a pagarle la pensión a la viuda de nuestro compañero Eduardo Arellano Villa", manifestó el secretario general del Sindicato Independiente de la COESVI, Juan Carlos Galarza.

En el gobierno "del cambio" panista-perredista, las cosas lejos de mejorar para los integrantes de este sindicato independiente empeoraron:

"El director de la COESVI, Ing. Raúl Flores Hernández, y el Secretario Técnico, Lic. Londres Botello Castro, comenzaron a orquestar el desmantelamiento de los dos sindicatos, el oficialista creado por Javier Hernández Flores y el nuestro, para afiliar a los trabajadores de estos sindicatos al Sindicato de los Tres Poderes, ofreciéndoles, a unos con engaños y a otros con amenazas, prestaciones que supuestamente son mejores, pero en los hechos son las mismas que ahora tienen. De esta manera once de nuestros compañeros fueron coaccionados para afiliarse al Sindicato de los Tres Poderes, por lo que ahora quedamos veintidós", denunciaron Juan Carlos Galarza y Raúl Quezada.

Estos directivos de la COESVI arriba mencionados solicitaron ante la JFCA la cancelación del registro del Sindicato Independiente de Trabajadores de la COESVI, "pero lo hicieron bajo la vía administrativa y no bajo la vía legal", expuso el secretario general de este sindicato, Juan Carlos Galarza, y abundó: "Según la Suprema Corte de Justicia de la Nación, no es legal que el Sindicato de los Tres Poderes represente a trabajadores de dependencias descentralizadas ya que estas no pertenecen a ningún poder".

Ante la resistencia de los 22 trabajadores de este sindicato independiente que advirtió ampararse ante la justicia federal, los directivos de la COESVI, encabezados por el Secretario Técnico, Lic. Londres Botello Castro, que en los hechos era el auténtico director de esta dependencia, intensificaron el hostigamiento laboral en contra de estos empleados en particular.

El gobernador de Durango, José Aispuro Torres, en un acto de traición acordó con su cuñado Londres Botello aplastar laboralmente a los trabajadores del Sindicato Independiente de la COESVI.

"Nos están negando prestaciones de ley aún con el convenio, no hacen los descuentos de cuotas sindicales vía nómina, no recibimos ayuda de transporte y renta, que es de 750 pesos al mes, e inclusive niegan apoyo para gastos funerarios. Tenemos que reclamar todas estas prestaciones por medio de oficios mientras los empleados que ilegalmente han sido afiliados al Sindicato de los Tres Poderes reciben todas sus prestaciones sin ningún problema", denunció el dirigente Juan Carlos Galarza.

El 25 de abril de 2018, el trabajador Javier Garza Siller, integrante del Sindicato Independiente, fue despedido injustificadamente. Javier Garza se atrevió a solicitar el pago del porcentaje que le correspondía por la recuperación de las carteras vencidas de varios créditos hipotecarios.

"En el contrato laboral se establece que la COESVI pagará al trabajador el 1% de comisión por cada cartera vencida recuperada", explicaron los líderes del Sindicato Independiente. "Los directivos de COESVI se negaron a pagarle a Javier Garza el porcentaje de las carteras vencidas que había recuperado argumentando que no tenían ninguna obligación legal de hacerlo, por lo que Javier Garza Siller pidió que le entregaran su contrato laboral, en el que se especifica esa obligación por parte de la COESVI. Al verse acorralados, los directivos encabezados por el Lic. Londres Botello inmediatamente decidieron despedir de manera injustificada a Javier Garza", relataron los dirigentes sindicales.

Todos estos abusos laborales fueron protegi-
dos por la presidenta de la Junta Federal de
Conciliación y Arbitraje, Lic. Marcela Quiñones.

Otro detalle que raya en lo absurdo e inverosímil es que los trabajadores de la COESVI no tienen derecho a la vivienda a través del FOVISSSTE.
Por lo anterior, los integrantes del Sindicato Independiente de Trabajadores de la COESVI solicitaron la intervención inmediata del gobernador José Aispuro Torres, pero este los ignoró por completo.

"Queremos creer que el gobernador Aispuro Torres no está enterado de lo que realmente sucede en la COESVI y de las ilegalidades en las que están incurriendo el director general, Ing. José Flores Hernández y el Secretario Técnico, Lic. Londres Botello Castro", finalizaron los trabajadores.

Lo cierto es que Aispuro siempre estuvo al tanto de este conflicto y, en los hechos, estaba de acuerdo con los directivos de la COESVI para aplastar al Sindicato Independiente de Trabajadores de la COESVI.

Este fue el panorama al que se enfrentaron los integrantes de este sindicato, que en los sexenios de los priístas Ismael Hernández Deras y Jorge Herrera Caldera fueron hostigados y reprimidos; y, bajo el gobierno "del cambio", de tendencia panista-perredista, lejos de recibir el apoyo esperado simplemente quisieron desaparecerlos.

*Así se las gastó Aispuro y los funcionarios
de esta dependencia que durante todo el sexenio
no han construido una sola vivienda para la
ciudadanía duranguense.*

Cuatro meses después, en septiembre de 2018, los trabajadores de la COESVI harían un paro de labores para destituir a Julieta Acosta Barrantes, sobrina de Elvira Barrantes, esposa del gobernador Aispuro Torres, por el trato despótico y abusivo que daba a los servidores públicos de esta institución.

Capítulo XVIII
Festival Revueltas, los contratos millonarios

Durango es uno de los estados más pobres de la República mexicana, sin embargo, en el año 2018 realizó la edición del Festival Revueltas más cara de su historia. Creado por decreto desde el año 2009 como un organismo público desconcentrado, los directivos de la institución encargada de realizarlo, el Instituto de Cultura del Estado de Durango (ICED), jamás han podido darle el sentido y la proyección que establece la ley que le dio origen, que es primordialmente fortalecer el sentido de identidad de los duranguenses y difundir, promocionar y divulgar la obra de los hermanos Revueltas (Silvestre, Fermín, José y Rosaura).

Por el contrario, el Festival Revueltas ha devenido año con año en un evento más de entretenimiento comercial que de interés cultural y, lo peor, ha servido para enriquecer a unos cuantos vivales.

Si ya de por sí la programación de este festival siempre ha sido polémica por no adaptarse a la ley que lo rige, en 2018 el Festival Revueltas rompió todos los esquemas en lo que respecta al monto de los contratos que el ICED signa con algunas empresas para que reconocidos artistas participen en el.

El primero y más notorio, sin duda alguna, fue el contrato del tenor español Plácido Domingo, que le costó a los ciudadanos duranguenses 16 millones de pesos, de acuerdo a lo informado por el propio ICED, y a partir de este dato, las conjeturas e información de primera mano no dejaron de fluir en las redes sociales en cuanto al costo desproporcionado de las contrataciones de éste y otros artistas que estuvieron presentes, a tal grado que el tema llegó al mismo Congreso local, en cuya tribuna el diputado morenista Iván Gurrola Vega exigió a los directivos del ICED que dieran a conocer los contratos que realizaron con las empresas que trajeron a determinados artistas. Y las sospechas de este diputado no fueron infundadas.

Diversas fuentes del ambiente cultural, especializadas en este tipo de eventos, revelaron a razacero en noviembre de 2018 que efectivamente los costos que el ICED dio a conocer por las contrataciones de algunos artistas que actuaron en el Festival Revueltas 2018 fueron excesivamente elevados: "Las cifras que proporciona la Dirección de Finanzas y Administración del ICED (a cargo del C.P. José Luis Chávez Samaniego), son realmente ofensivas; por ejemplo, informa que el concierto de Tania Libertad, celebrado el 7 de octubre en la Plaza de Armas de la ciudad de Lerdo, tuvo un costo de 980 mil pesos, más 136,800 pesos del IVA, y que dicho concierto fue contratado con la empresa llamada Enlace Cultural Managment. Pero resulta que la empresa Producciones Aztecas ofrece el mismo concierto de Tania Libertad en 350 mil pesos más IVA y viáticos, dando una cifra total que no llega a los 500 mil pesos", informó la fuente que prefirió omitir su nombre.

La otrora "revolucionaria de la cultura", Socorro Soto Alanís, directora del ICED, terminó como cómplice de improvisados y pillos que dañaron severamente al erario duranguense.

Y lo mismo sucedió con el concierto titulado "Juntas Juntísimas", que brindaron las cantantes Regina Orozco y Susana Zabaleta el 12 de octubre en la explanada del museo El Acertijo, en la ciudad de Gómez Palacio, cuyo monto del contrato manifestado por el ICED fue de un millón 850 mil pesos más 296 mil pesos del IVA; la fuente comentó: "A través de la empresa Producciones Aztecas, Regina Orozco cobra 200 mil pesos más IVA y viáticos que no exceden más de 50 mil pesos, y Susana Zabaleta, a través de la empresa Escénica Producciones cobra 600 mil pesos más IVA. Entre las dos cantantes cobrarían aproximadamente 800 mil pesos más

IVA; es decir, menos de un millón de pesos, pero el ICED pagó por ellas 2 millones 146 mil pesos a través de la misma empresa llamada Enlace Cultural Managment".

Aunado a lo anterior, la selección del artista en cuestión se considera que cumple con la esencia de la LEY del FESTIVAL CULTURAL REVUELTAS, ya que procura en el fortalecimiento de su programación el sentido de identidad de los duranguenses, además de generar difusión y promoción turística de la entidad.

DATOS DEL PRESTADOR

NOMBRE: "ENLACE CULTURAL MANAGMENT"
NACIONALIDAD: MEXICANA
MONTO ESTIMADO DE LA CONTRATACIÓN: El monto total de la adjudicación asciende a la cantidad de $1'136,800.00 (UN MILLÓN CIENTO TREINTA Y SEIS MIL OCHOCIENTOS PESOS 00/100 M. N.) que incluye el impuesto al valor agregado I.V.A.

C R I T E R I O S
DE ANALISIS Y EVALUACIÓN

Se requiere la colaboración la sociedad anónima de capital variable "ENLACE CULTURAL MANAGMENT" para el desarrollo de la presentación artística del concierto "TANIA LIBERTAD" mismo que se llevara a cabo el día domingo 7 de octubre a las 20:00 horas, en la Plaza de Armas en la ciudad de Lerdo, en este estado, lo que representa una gran oportunidad de presentar un evento de talla internacional, generando gran impacto entre la comunidad que gusta de la música de la cantante TANIA LIBERTAD misma que cuenta con una gran trayectoria y reconocimiento, además de que aportan todo el equipo técnico necesario para llevar a cabo la presentación del evento.

En mérito de lo antes expuesto, conforme a lo dispuesto por los artículos 17 fracción II, 57 y 58 fracción XI de la Ley de Adquisiciones Arrendamientos y Servicios del estado de Durango, así como el artículo 28 inciso d) de su reglamento, se propone contratar los servicios especificados en el párrafo que antecede. Esta acción que se ejerce tiene fundamento en los criterios siguientes:

Fragmento del contrato del concierto de Tania Libertad signado por el director ejecutivo del Festival Revueltas, Daniel Hernández Vela, con la empresa Enlace Cultural Managment, cuyo monto fue de un millón 136 mil 800 pesos.

Para el concierto del grupo Los Ángeles Azules, titulado "Los Ángeles Azules Sinfónico", llevado a cabo el 19 de octubre en la Plaza IV Centenario de la ciudad de Durango, el ICED realizó un contrato con la multicitada empresa Enlace Cultural Managment que ascendió a los 3 millones de pesos, más 480 mil pesos del IVA. Al respecto, la fuente precisó: "La empresa Escénica Producciones ofrece el mismo concierto 'Los Ángeles Azules Sinfónico' en un millón 350 mil pesos, más 216 mil pesos de IVA, cuando este grupo se presenta con la orquesta sinfónica de la ciudad donde se realiza el evento, como fue el caso del Festival Revueltas de Durango, más gastos de transportación, hospedaje y viáticos de los artistas y su equipo de logística, que no exceden más de 250 mil pesos".

Todas las contrataciones de los artistas foráneos que participaron en el Festival Revueltas 2018 fueron signadas por el controvertido exdirector ejecutivo de este festival y también exdirector de Promoción y Difusión del ICED, Daniel Hernández Vela, ampliamente conocido por el trato despótico que le daba tanto a los empleados de este instituto como a los creadores duranguenses.

Regina Orozco

Costo:

$200,000.00 más IVA.

Requerimientos:

Transporte aéreo

    02 boletos de avión en primera clase

    14 en clase turista

    (La Sra. Orozco y 05 personas más viajarán un día antes, considerar su viático)

Hotel 5 estrellas

    01 junior suite

    05 habitaciones sencillas

    04 dobles

    (La Sra. Orozco y 03 personas más viajarán un día antes, considerar su viático)

Viáticos

    6,850.00 para el grupo por día (considerar tiempos de viaje)

Transporte local

    03 camionetas tipo van express grande

Equipos de audio e iluminación según rider (inclusive backline)

Tania Libertad

Costo:

$350,000.00 más IVA.

Requerimientos:

Transporte aéreo:

    02 boletos de avión en primera clase

    10 en clase turista

Hotel 5 estrellas:

    01 suite

    05 habitaciones sencillas

    03 dobles

Viáticos:

    Artista y manager 1,000.00

    resto del grupo 500.00

Transporte local

La empresa Producciones Aztecas ofrecía el concierto de Tania Libertad en 350 mil pesos más IVA.

LOS ANGELES AZULES

Los Ángeles Azules es un grupo musical mexicano de cumbia sonidera proveniente de la colonia Los Ángeles, Iztapalapa, Ciudad de México, conformada en 1976 pero activa oficialmente desde 1983, popular en varios países de América Latina y parte de Estados Unidos. Actualmente, la alineación principal la forman los fundadores Hermanos Mejía Avante: Elías, Alfredo, José Hilario, Jorge, Cristina y Guadalupe. Recientemente en el año 2015 el grupo inaugura el nuevo edificio de vinculación de la UPAEP con motivo a su 42 aniversario. Por otro lado, interpretan el tema principal de la Telenovela La vecina producida por Televisa. Posteriormente, estrenaron el álbum "De plaza en plaza", donde se destacan la participación de Rodrigo & Gabriela, Natalia Lafourcade, Ha*Ash, Gloria Trevi y Pepe Aguilar entre otros.

Video Angeles Azules

Honorarios: $1, 350,000 MN más IVA

Costo del grupo con producción puesta

ESCÈNICA PRODUCCIONES
escenicamty@gmail.com **Facebook y Twitter @EscenicaOficial**
Alicia Vázquez **81-12275664**   Bruno Sangar **81-18808794**

La empresa Escénica Producciones ofrecía el concierto "Los Ángeles Azules Sinfón co" en un millón 350 mil pesos, más 216 mil pesos de IVA.

Daniel Hernández Vela, ex director ejecutivo del Festival Revueltas y ex director de Promoción y Difusión del ICED, sus rapacerías fueron abiertamente protegidas por el gobernador José Aispuro.

La ley que crea el Festival Cultural Revueltas establece en su artículo 12: "Para la vigilancia y el control del Organismo, éste contará con un Comisario Público, que será designado por la Secretaría de Contraloría del Gobierno del Estado. Le corresponde al Comisario el control y fiscalización de los recursos del Organismo".

¿Quién es ese Comisario que no cumplió eficazmente con su trabajo? En este evidente descalabro al erario duranguense es indudable que hubo responsables directos que deben responder no solo ante el Congreso del estado de Durango, sino ante las autoridades administrativas y hasta judiciales ya que inclusive pudieron haber incurrido en graves actos ilícitos, pues es inadmisible que servidores públicos de este nivel, por acción u omisión, por dolo o ignorancia, provoquen este tipo de daños tan severos al erario.

¿Quiénes se beneficiaron en esta danza de contratos millonarios desaseados mientras buena parte de la ciudadanía duranguense padece hambre y desempleo?

Este fue uno de los atracos al erario duranguense más descarados y protegidos por Aispuro.

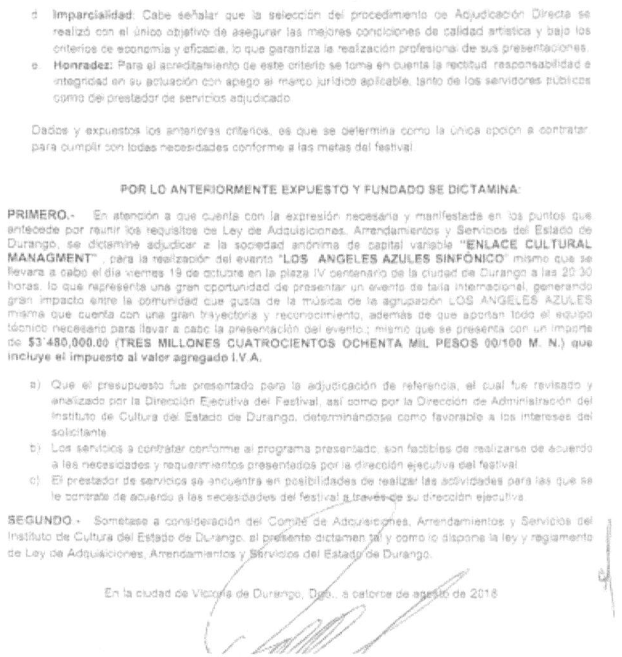

d. **Imparcialidad:** Cabe señalar que la selección del procedimiento de Adjudicación Directa se realizó con el único objetivo de asegurar las mejores condiciones de calidad artística y bajo los criterios de economía y eficacia, lo que garantiza la realización profesional de sus presentaciones.

e. **Honradez:** Para el acreditamiento de este criterio se toma en cuenta la rectitud, responsabilidad e integridad en su actuación con apego al marco jurídico aplicable, tanto de los servidores públicos como del prestador de servicios adjudicado.

Dados y expuestos los anteriores criterios, es que se determina como la única opción a contratar para cumplir con todas necesidades conforme a las metas del festival.

POR LO ANTERIORMENTE EXPUESTO Y FUNDADO SE DICTAMINA:

PRIMERO.- En atención a que cuenta con la expresión necesaria y manifestada en los puntos que antecede por reunir los requisitos de Ley de Adquisiciones, Arrendamientos y Servicios del Estado de Durango, se dictamine adjudicar a la sociedad anónima de capital variable **"ENLACE CULTURAL MANAGMENT"**, para la realización del evento **"LOS ANGELES AZULES SINFÓNICO"** mismo que se llevara a cabo el día viernes 19 de octubre en la plaza IV centenario de la ciudad de Durango a las 20:30 horas, lo que representa una gran oportunidad de presentar un evento de talla internacional, generando gran impacto entre la comunidad que gusta de la música de la agrupación LOS ANGELES AZULES misma que cuenta con una gran trayectoria y reconocimiento, además de que aportan todo el equipo técnico necesario para llevar a cabo la presentación del evento.; mismo que se presenta con un importe de **$3'480,000.00 (TRES MILLONES CUATROCIENTOS OCHENTA MIL PESOS 00/100 M. N.)** que incluye el impuesto al valor agregado I.V.A.

a) Que el presupuesto fue presentado para la adjudicación de referencia, el cual fue revisado y analizado por la Dirección Ejecutiva del Festival, así como por la Dirección de Administración del Instituto de Cultura del Estado de Durango, determinándose como favorable a los intereses del solicitante.

b) Los servicios a contratar conforme al programa presentado, son factibles de realizarse de acuerdo a las necesidades y requerimientos presentados por la dirección ejecutiva del festival.

c) El prestador de servicios se encuentra en posibilidades de realizar las actividades para las que se le contrate de acuerdo a las necesidades del festival a través de su dirección ejecutiva.

SEGUNDO.- Sométase a consideración del Comité de Adquisiciones, Arrendamientos y Servicios del Instituto de Cultura del Estado de Durango, el presente dictamen tal y como lo dispone la ley y reglamento de Ley de Adquisiciones, Arrendamientos y Servicios del Estado de Durango.

En la ciudad de Victoria de Durango, Dgo., a catorce de agosto de 2018

Fragmento del contrato del concierto "Los Ángeles Azules Sinfónico", que el ex director ejecutivo del Festival Revueltas, Daniel Hernández Vela, firmó con la empresa Enlace Cultural Managment por 3 millones 480 mil pesos.

Posteriormente a esta publicación, el ex diputado morenista Iván Gurrola Vega presentó las pruebas de estos desvíos ante la Contraloría estatal, a cargo de Raquel Leila Arreola, y ante la Fiscalía Especializada en Combate a la Corrupción, a cargo de Héctor García Rodríguez, pero hasta la fecha ambas instituciones mantienen esta investigación archivada.

Capítulo XIX
Miseria humana en la Secretaría de Salud

Si el sexenio pasado la secretaría de Salud del estado de Durango pasó por lo que se pensaba que era el peor ciclo de su historia, la ciudadanía no se imaginó que al deshacerse del PRI en las urnas vendría a gobernar una mafia burocrática mucho peor.

Dr. Sergio González Romero, secretario de Salud en el gobierno aispurista, su prestigio quedó por los suelos como titular de esta dependencia.

Y es que el gobierno "del cambio", panista-perredista, llevó la corrupción e ineficacia en esta dependencia a grados de miseria humana inaceptables.

Trabajadores de esta institución denunciaron en nuestra redacción, nuevamente, a la directora administrativa y supuesta contadora pública, Ruth Vázquez, por establecer medidas de "austeridad" que rayaban en la ignominia, como restringir a los directivos de los principales hospitales de la entidad que hicieran gastos supériores a los dos mil pesos. Al respecto, los empleados manifestaron: "Si se presenta una emergencia, los directivos de hospitales no tienen facultades para realizar gastos superiores a los dos mil pesos, tienen que hacer la solicitud correspondiente para que la administradora Ruth Vázquez autorice el gasto, que tiene que ser debidamente justificado, tardando este trámite varios días. Ya ha habido ocasiones en que por este tipo de limitaciones no se puede disponer de algún medicamento o equipo de inmediato, poniendo en riesgo la vida de los pacientes".

El último piso del Hospital Materno Infantil sin energía eléctrica y los techos cayéndose a pedazos, denunciaron los trabajadores.

La situación que vivió la secretaría de Salud debido a la pésima administración de sus recursos y al saqueo desmedido que se llevó a cabo de medicamentos y de su presupuesto provocó que, por ejemplo, las instalaciones del Hospital Materno Infantil colapsaran por falta de mantenimiento. "En algunas áreas del último piso no hay energía eléctrica y las fugas de agua en los baños son constantes sin que ninguna autoridad se preocupe por resolver estos problemas. Los techos se están cayendo a pedazos", denunció uno de los trabajadores de este hospital.

Y ya en el colmo de la vileza que esta funcionaria de marras practicó, los trabajadores describieron indignados: "Recientemente se le solicitaron guantes quirúrgicos para que los médicos ginecólogos realizaran las revisiones de rutina a las pacientes del hospital, este tipo de guantes, como se sabe, son especiales, pero la administradora Ruth Vázquez nos envió guantes de plástico desechables de ínfima calidad, de esos que las tiendas Walmart y Soriana obsequian a sus clientes para que escojan el pescado. ¡¡Es increíble!!", finalizaron los entrevistados.

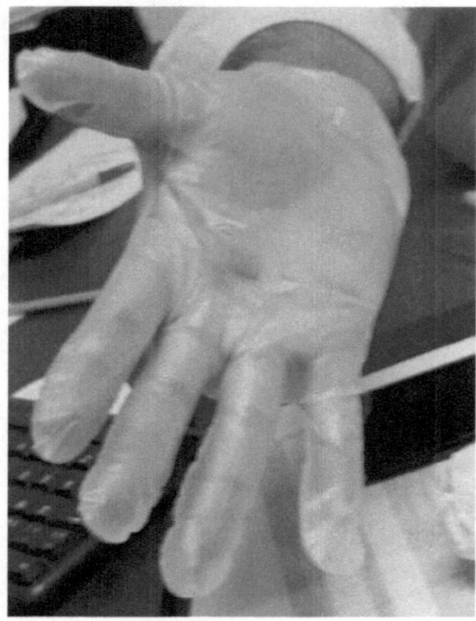

*En lugar de guantes quirúrgicos especiales,
la directora de administración, Ruth María
Vázquez Barraza, le envió a los ginecólogos del
Hospital Materno Infantil guantes de plástico
desechables, "de los que las tiendas Walmart
y Soriana les regalan a sus clientes para que
escojan el pescado", denunciaron trabajadores
de este nosocomio.*

Y más increíble fue, por supuesto, que esta "servidora pública" permaneciera en su cargo luego de la infinidad de denuncias de corrupción y negligencia que hubo en su contra. Este nivel de corrupción, ineptitud e impunidad solo pudo haberse dado por la cercanía que esta funcionaria nefasta tuvo con el gobernador de marras José Aispuro y su esposa Elvira Barrantes.

Capítulo XX
El secretario feliz

El 15 de septiembre de 2016, unas horas antes de integrarse al gobierno estatal de Durango como secretario de Desarrollo Económico, el Ing. Ramón Dávila Flores todavía ostentaba el cargo de director ejecutivo en México de la conocida minera depredadora canadiense Firts Majestic Silver Corporation. Sin ninguna experiencia en el servicio público, y mucho menos en el ramo de desarrollo económico, Ramón Tomás Dávila Flores llegó a ese importante cargo más por pago de cuotas electoreras que por capacidades profesionales reales.

De inmediato, Dávila Flores organizó una burda red de corrupción alrededor de la promoción económica del estado y, aprovechando el acceso a información privilegiada, se hace socio principal de compañías inmobiliarias para construir plazas comerciales en el sur de la ciudad de Durango, como Central Plaza, un consorcio que de antemano resultó "casualmente" beneficiado en su plusvalía por la remodelación escogida del Boulevard Domingo Arrieta.

Pero este funcionario de marras no solo realizó este tipo de negocios al amparo del gobernador Aispuro Torres, sino también fue el promotor número uno del peligroso proyecto de la planta química estadounidense Chemours, que violando un amparo federal continuó construyendo dicha planta en Gómez Palacio con la intención de producir 65 mil toneladas de cianuro de sodio al año, componente que es fundamental para la extracción de oro y plata. Como se sabe, la minera canadiense Firts Majestic Silver Corporation, de la que Ramón Tomás Dávila Flores fue director ejecutivo, durante este sexenio fue beneficiada con varias concesiones para explotar minas en Durango.

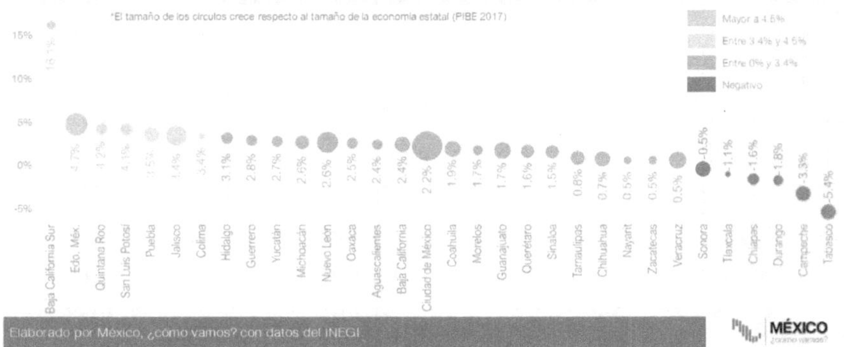

De acuerdo al INEGI, entre 2017 y 2018 Durango ocupó uno de los últimos lugares a nivel nacional en cuanto a crecimiento económico.

Así, ante las demandas legales que interpusieron los pobladores gomezpalatinos para impedir la instalación de la planta Chemours, Dávila Flores y los representantes de esta empresa pusieron a trabajar a un equipo de "especialistas" para convencer a los afectados de que retiraran sus demandas, ofreciéndoles fuertes dádivas.

Una de las anomalías más escandalosas en esta secretaría de Desarrollo Económico bajo la administración de Dávila Flores fue el desfalco de 7.9 millones de pesos destinados a la creación de nuevas tecnologías a través de la modalidad de startup (proyectos de empresas emergentes), en alianza con la compañía privada iLab. En tres meses, iLab y la SEDECO desarrollaron un producto "milagro" prácticamente inservible: una banda "para ayudar a dormir", cuando lo que les quita el sueño a los duranguenses es la falta de trabajo.

Uno de los proyectos que sí tenía potencial para ser patrocinado por esta secretaría y la empresa mencionada, de acuerdo a fuentes internas de esta dependencia, fue el Medidor de azúcares reductores totales para el agave mezcalero, realizado por jóvenes investigadores de la compañía Agavart. Se trataba de una tecnología pionera en la producción sustentable de agave en Durango, "pero el proyecto fue robado con el consentimiento del secretario Ramón Dávila, pues la documentación y planos del proyecto fueron entregados a un particular ajeno a la compañía iLab que tramitó la patente, misma que le fue otorgada, por lo que los jóvenes que desarrollaron esta tecnología quedaron legalmente imposibilitados para comercializarla", denunciaron las fuentes a razacero en marzo de 2019.

Éste exsecretario de Desarrollo Económico del gobierno estatal de Durango solo se dedicó a pasear por toda Europa, Asia y Canadá (su país favorito), con un nutrido séquito de aduladores que muy caro le costaron al pueblo de Durango. El argumento clásico para justificar estos viajes fue el de "promocionar a la entidad para atraer inversiones extranjeras", un machote ya sumamente trillado y utilizado por quienes han ostentado el mismo cargo en anteriores sexenios y han obtenido los mismos pésimos resultados.

En 2019 las estadísticas de la Secretaría de Economía del gobierno federal fueron duras e indicaron que durante los dos años anteriores, 2017 y 2018, el flujo de Inversión Extranjera Directa cayó un 73% en Durango, y a nivel nacional el Crecimiento Económico de esta entidad norteña decreció a -1.8%, ocupando los últimos lugares de desarrollo económico en el país.

En el colmo de la ineptitud y corrupción de este exfuncionario del gobierno "del cambio" muy cercano al gobernador Aispuro Torres, todos los eventos de gala que esta dependencia organizaba para "empresarios" y amigos del exsecretario Ramón Dávila Flores, fueron atendidos por la empresa Dávila Gourmet que, por supuesto, entregaba facturas infladas y totalmente desproporcionadas. ¿Y de quién creén, apreciados lectores, que era propiedad esta empresa de banquetes palaciegos? Pues sí, del mismo Ramón Dávila Flores.

Ya en la víspera de los últimos cambios que el gobernador José Aispuro Torres realizó en su gabinete en diciembre de 2018, se mencionó en los corrillos políticos la posible salida de este secretario por los nulos resultados positivos que había obtenido, pero fue tolerado por el mandatario estatal corrupto. Poco más de un año después, Ramón Dávila Flores protagonizaría uno de los casos de corrupción más sonados en la historia de Durango: El SEDECOGATE.

Capítulo XXI
Contralora incontrolable

A finales de 2019, el INEGI ubicaba a Durango como el sexto estado más corrupto del país, pero en esta entidad hubo "servidores públicos" que se esmeraron para que en 2021 ocupara el primer sitio. Y a pesar de que el gobernador Aispuro Torres dictó supuestas medidas de "austeridad", no todos los integrantes de su gabinete estuvieron dispuestos a obedecerlo. Una de estas funcionarias fue la titular de la Contraloría del gobierno del estado de Durango, Lic. Raquel Arreola, quien se suponía debía poner el ejemplo de cordura, honestidad y pulcritud por la labor que le tocó desempeñar, que es precisamente la de vigilar que haya transparencia y rendición de cuentas claras por parte de todos aquellos que ocupan cargos públicos, así como de aplicar sanciones a quienes incurran en actos de corrupción u omisión. Pero esta contralora resultó incontrolable.

Fuentes internas fidedignas de esta dependencia dieron cuenta en nuestra redacción de anomalías relacionadas con despilfarros y desvíos de recursos cometidos por esta funcionaria: "La Contralora Raquel Leila Arreola ha contratado a su conveniencia a varios despachos particulares favoritos a los que les ha asignado honorarios estratosféricos que oscilan entre los 150 mil y 350 mil pesos por cada una de las 60 auditorías externas que han realizado durante este año 2019 a algunas dependencias del gobierno estatal, cuando es obligación de esta dependencia realizar esos procedimientos con el personal que tiene a su disposición", revela la fuente.

Raquel Leila Arreola Fallad, titular de la secretaría de Contraloría del gobierno del estado de Durango, encargada de aplicar sanciones a funcionarios corruptos, pero utilizó recursos públicos para adquirir joyería de uso personal.

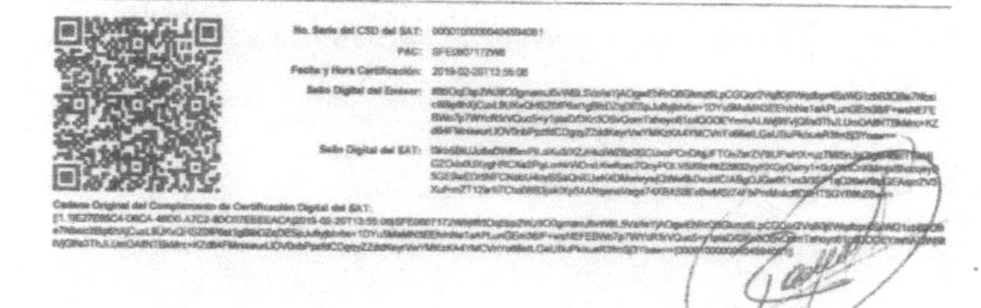

ULTRA BOUTIQUES SA DE CV

UBO171231225
LOS OLIVOS, MANZANA 66 LOTE 66, BODEGA 6C, SMZA 310, 77560,
BENITO JUAREZ, CANCUN, QUINTANA ROO, México
General de Ley Personas Morales (601)

Folio Fiscal	E27655C4-D6CA-48D0-A7C 3-9DC07E6666ACA
No. CSD	00001000000412935686
Serie/Folio	AEG - 36
Tipo comprobante	Ingreso
Fecha expedición:	2019-02-20T13:55:03
Expedido en:	Benito Juárez, Ciudad de México, 03920

RFC: GED620101652
Nombre: GOBIERNO DEL ESTADO DE DURANGO
Dirección: BOULEVARD FELIPE PESCADOR, 900, DURANGO CENTRO,
DURANGO, DURANGO, MEX, 34000
Uso CFDI: Gastos en general (G03)

Forma pago: 28 - Tarjeta de Débito
Método pago: Pago en una sola exhibición (PUE)
Condiciones pago:
Tipo cambio:

ClaveProd	No id	Cantidad	Unidad	Descripción	Valor Unitario	Descuento	Impuestos	Importe
61101804	080184843	1	(H87) PIEZA	EARRING STUDS FOREVER PANDORA WITH CZ CL	$1,166.10		IVA 16 % $186.90	$1,166.10
54101503	000227800	1	(H87) PIEZA	FW17 PAND LOGO RING STERLING CZ SILVER W	$1,379.31		IVA 16 % $220.69	$1,379.31
54101502	000227854	1	(H87) PIEZA	FW17 PANDORA NECKL STERLING CZ SILVER W	$1,913.79		IVA 16 % $306.21	$1,913.79

CANTIDAD EN LETRAS:

CINCO MIL CIENTO SETENTA Y CINCO PESOS 00/100 MXN

Subtotal:	$ 4,461.20
IVA 16%	$ 713.80
Total:	$ 5,175.00

No. Serie del CSD del SAT: 00001000000404094081
PAC: SFE080717ZW6
Fecha y Hora Certificación: 2019-02-20T13:55:06
Sello Digital del Emisor: [illegible]
Sello Digital del SAT: [illegible]

Cadena Original del Complemento de Certificación Digital del SAT:
[illegible]

Factura expedida por la tienda ULTRA BOUTIQUES S.A. DE C.V., el 20 de febrero de 2019, con cargo al gobierno del estado de Durango, por un monto de 5 mil 175 pesos, firmada por la Contralora Raquel Leila Arreola.

Y si lo anterior era preocupante, el siguiente testimonio simplemente rayó en lo inaudito: "Todos hemos visto que la Contralora Raquel Leila Arreola anda siempre muy enjoyada, pero lo que no sabe la ciudadanía es que las joyas que porta las adquiere con recursos públicos". Y como prueba, la fuente proporcionó un par de documentos: Una factura de una boutique ubicada en la ciudad de México (ULTRA BOUTIQUES S.A. DE C.V.), por un monto de 5 mil 175 pesos, y una "Tarjeta Informativa" con la que la Contralora y su secretaria particular, Lic. Hilda Payán Díaz, solicitaron al gobierno estatal el reembolso de dicha adquisición por concepto de "Gastos de Orden Social y Cultural" (sic).

TARJETA INFORMATIVA

Se solicita de la manera más atenta su apoyo con la finalidad de realizar el pago correspondiente efectuado por concepto de Gastos de Orden Social y Cultural por la cantidad de $5,175.00 (Cinco mil ciento setenta y cinco pesos 00/100 M.N.)

Le agradezco la atención que se sirva prestar a la presente.

A T E N T A M E N T E
Durango, Dgo., a 20 de febrero de 2019

LIC. HILDA PAYÁN DÍAZ
SECRETARIA PARTICULAR

Vo.Bo.

M.D. RAQUEL LEILA ARREOLA FALLAD
SECRETARIA DE CONTRALORÍA

"Tarjeta Informativa" con la que la Contralora Raquel Leila Arreola y su secretaria particular Hilda Payán solicitaron al gobierno estatal el reembolso de la misma cantidad facturada por la tienda ULTRA BOUTIQUES S.A. DE C.V., pero bajo el concepto de "Gastos de Orden Social y Cultural".

Por menos de esto, en otros países (obviamente con una cultura cívica y política mucho más desarrollada que la nuestra) este tipo de comportamiento amerita la destitución inmediata del servidor público en cuestión y la exigencia de la reposición del recurso público dispuesto indebidamente, pero bajo el gobierno de Aispuro Torres, a pesar de haberse hecho esta denuncia de manera pública, no sucedió absolutamente nada.

Capítulo XXII
Aispuro, el encubridor

"¡¡Les puedo hablar de frente porque no le debo nada a nadie, porque no me he robado ni un centavo y puedo ver a todo mundo de frente!'", gritó furioso en el presídium el gobernador de Durango, José Aispuro Torres, cuando increpó a una multitud de ciudadanos que lo abuchearon y lo llamaron corrupto durante la visita del presidente de la República, Andrés Manuel López Obrador, a Gómez Palacio, el 15 de junio de 2019.

Y aunque pudiera ser cierta la aseveración de este mandatario estatal, lo que no deja lugar a dudas, porque hay firmes evidencias de ello, es el encubrimiento que practicó para proteger a la mayoría de los integrantes de su gabinete que cometieron abiertos actos de pillería, lesionando gravemente el erario.

Estos hechos, desde los primeros días de su gobierno ya se veían venir por la inclusión en su gabinete de personajes con perfiles altamente peligrosos, como los empresarios mineros Jesús Arturo Díaz Medina, ex representante legal de la nociva minera canadiense First Majestic Silver Corporation, a quien Aispuro Torres nombró titular de la joya de la corona: la secretaría de Finanzas del gobierno del estado, y el ex director de esta misma empresa minera depredadora, Ramón Dávila Flores, a quien designó como secretario de Desarrollo Económico.

Así, a más de tres años de iniciado el gobierno del panista Aispuro Torres, estos dos protagonistas ya tenían al estado de Durango hundido en una de sus peores crisis financieras y sociales, pues el primero, Jesús Arturo Díaz Medina, titular de la secretaría de Finanzas, fue el responsable de que por primera vez en la historia de Durango no se pagaran a los empleados del gobierno estatal en tiempo y forma sus sueldos correspondientes a la última quincena del año 2019, ni sus aguinaldos.

Jesús Arturo Díaz Medina, secretario de Finanzas del gobierno de Durango, y Ramón Dávila Flores, ex titular de la Secretaría de Desarrollo Económico, como ejecutivos de la minera canadiense depredadora First Majestic Silver Corp., saquearon minas de oro y plata en Coahuila; pero en el gobierno "del cambio", encabezado por el gobernador bribón José Aispuro Torres, les fue mucho mejor.

Algo o mucho tuvo que ver la millonaria "asesoría profesional financiera" que esta secretaría recibió durante todo el sexenio del conocido consultor sonorense Pedro López Elías, que en los hechos no sirvió absolutamente para nada, mas que para pagar facturas políticas y para sangrar los bolsillos de los contribuyentes.

Adjudicaciones directas de contratos y licitaciones amañadas con escandalosos sobreprecios (robos) que favorecieron a exclusivos proveedores y prestadores de servicios muy cercanos al círculo del gobernador duranguense y su esposa, Elvira Barrantes, fueron dadas a conocer en razacero sin que el gobernador Aispuro Torres realizara diligencias para sancionar a los responsables, como Las placas millonarias y La licitación fétida. Este par de ejemplos fueron solo la punta del iceberg, y por esta vía de las adjudicaciones directas y licitaciones plagadas de ilegalidades varios miles de millones de pesos del erario duranguense fueron a parar a los bolsillos de unos cuantos vivales bien identificados, que despacharon en la secretaría de Finanzas del estado de Durango y cotidianamente realizaron negocios con conocidos empresarios.

La ineptitud para manejar recursos públicos y el saqueo sistemático que llevó a cabo el titular de la secretaría de Finanzas, Arturo Díaz Medina que tuvieron en jaque financiero al gobierno del panista José Aispuro Torres, fueron de la mano con la nula experiencia (y también corrupción) del exsecretario de Desarrollo Económico, Ramón Tomás Dávila Flores quien a pesar de sus incontables viajes al extranjero (la mayoría de ellos improductivos), no logró atraer las inversiones que Durango necesitaba para alcanzar un verdadero desarrollo económico pleno. Por el contrario esta entidad norteña ha ocupado invariablemente los últimos lugares a nivel nacional en las gráficas de estadísticas que diversas organizaciones expertas en la materia publican periódicamente. Sin embargo, la economía personal y familiar de este "servidor público" (El secretario feliz) tuvo mucho auge por los jugosos negocios que hizo aprovechándose de su cargo y cercanía con el gobernador que no se ha robado ni un centavo y puede ver a todo mundo de frente, José Aispuro Torres.

En el aspecto cultural, el gobernador duranguense no mostró mas que desinterés total, dejando al Instituto de Cultura del Estado de Durango a la deriva, en manos de directivos improvisados y corruptos. La mejor (o peor) muestra de esto fue el grotesco fraude millonario perpetrado en el Festival Revueltas del año 2018, en el que el ex director de este evento Daniel Hernández Vela, realizó contrataciones de conocidos artistas con descarados sobreprecios millonarios (Festival Revueltas: Los contratos millonarios). Este caso, como los anteriores y muchos otros, fueron olímpicamente ignorados por el gobernador que no se ha robado ni un centavo y puede ver a todo mundo de frente.

Y ya en el colmo, en el gobierno del panista Aispuro Torres la titular de la secretaría de Contraloría, Lic. Raquel Leila Arreola, encargada de sancionar a los servidores públicos del gobierno estatal que cometieran actos de corrupción, es una de las integrantes del gabinete aispurista que más actos indebidos e ilegales cometió en el cumplimiento de sus funciones, al grado de disponer de recursos públicos para satisfacer sus gustos personales (Contralora incontrolable).

Estos son solo algunos de los personajes cuyos actos de pillería fueron exhibidos públicamente con pruebas documentadas, actos que vergonzosamente permanecieron impunes, ignorados y encubiertos por el gobernador José Aispuro Torres, sí, el mismo que el 15 de junio de 2019 vociferó frente al presidente de la República, Andrés Manuel López Obrador, que no se ha robado ni un centavo y puede ver a todo mundo de frente.

Capítulo XXIII
SEDECOGATE, la ignominia panista

No cabe duda que la pandemia del coronavirus sacó lo mejor y lo peor de las sociedades a nivel mundial, nacional y local. Así, en estos duros meses la ciudadanía atestiguó desde muestras desinteresadas de solidaridad hasta detestables acciones de proselitismo emprendidas por políticos corruptos. Pero lo que sucedió a mediados de 2020 en Durango con la entrega de créditos financieros a empresarios, por parte del gobierno estatal panista, para que soportaran el impacto económico del COVID19, simplemente no tuvo nombre.

Ramón Dávila Flores, ex director de la depredadora empresa minera canadiense First Majestic Silver Corporation y ex secretario de Desarrollo Económico del gobierno de Durango, autor del desastre conocido como SEDECOGATE. Hasta la fecha, "El Secretario Feliz" continúa impune, protegido por el gobernador de marras José Aispuro.

Fue la Secretaría de Desarrollo Económico a través de su peculiar titular, Ramón Dávila Flores, la que se encargó de repartir fuertes cantidades de dinero a por lo menos tres centenares de empresarios duranguenses, dirigiendo los préstamos de mayor cantidad a connotados empresarios amigos y hasta funcionarios del gobierno municipal de Durango.

Sin especificar los criterios para entregar dichas cantidades, en la lista de beneficiados aparecieron inclusive empresas que al buscarlas en el directorio telefónico y en las redes sociales simplemente no aparecían, y las que aparecieron no contaban con domicilio establecido, como Baluarte del Patrimonio de México S.A. D.I. de C.V., y Aguas y Drenaje de Durango S.A. de C.V.

No.	NOMBRE	MUNICIPIO	TIPO DE GARANTIA	ACTIVIDAD	INGRESOS	EMPLEOS CONSERVADOS	SOLICITADO	SUGERIDO
12	Jose Miguel Castro Carrillo	Durango	prendaria	Notaria Publica	170,000.00	22	50,000.00	500,000.00
13	Servando De Jesus Quiñones Mares	Durango	obligado solidario	Venta de diversos articulos	35,000.00	3	120,000.00	100,000.00
14	MOVIMIENTOS INDUSTRIALES DURANGO SA DE CV	Durango	prendaria	Fletes foraneos	102,000.00	6	500,000.00	450,000.00
15	MAELSA SA DE CV	Durango	obligado solidario	Instalaciones elecetricas y	500,000.00	33	500,000.00	450,000.00

"El Notario Pobre", José Miguel Castro Carrillo, padre del presidente del Consejo Coordinador Empresarial, José Miguel Castro Mayagoitia, recibió un crédito de 500 mil pesos.

En lo que se refiere a los empresarios pudientes que sin ningún empacho ni pudor solicitaron y recibieron importantes créditos sin tener necesidad apremiante, los más señalados fueron el presidente de la CANACO, Mauricio Holguín, ortodoncista, quien recibió la exorbitante cantidad de 500 mil pesos; Miguel Ángel Reveles Pérez, presidente de la Cámara Mexicana de la Industria de la Construcción (CMIC), recibió 500 mil pesos, y su hijo Miguel Ángel Reveles Valdez también recibió 500 mil pesos; María Teresa Vivó Prieto, presidenta del Consejo para el Desarrollo de Durango y dueña de una cremería, recibió 300 mil pesos, y su esposo, Alejandro Wallander Hernández, 500 mil pesos; Otilia Wallander Hernández, cuñada de María Teresa Vivó, recibió 80 mil pesos. José Miguel Castro Carrillo, notario público y padre del presidente del Consejo Coordinador Empresarial, José Miguel Castro Mayagoitia, recibió 500 mil pesos. La vicepresidenta de la Asociación Mexicana de Mujeres Jefas de Empresas (AMMJE), Adriana Miranda Nájera, empresaria carnicera, recibió 400 mil pesos, y su hermana, Nancy Sarahí Miranda Nájera, con el mismo giro, recibió 450 mil pesos. La ex diputada panista y empresaria mueblera, Patricia Jiménez, recibió 400 mil pesos.

Josué Segovia Mijares, propietario de una carnicería y hermano del acaudalado ex alcalde interino de Durango, Carlos Segovia Mijares, recibió

500 mil pesos.

El director del CONALEP, Alfredo Parra Aguilar, propietario de la empresa Maquinados Industriales Durango S.A. de C.V., recibió 300 mil pesos. Bernardo Loera Carrillo, dueño de un gimnasio y director de Servicios Regionales de la Secretaría de Educación del Estado de Durango, recibió 200 mil pesos.

Funcionarios del municipio de Durango y familiares de estos también solicitaron y recibieron apoyo financiero de la secretaría de Desarrollo Económico, siendo los más beneficiados María José Santiesteban Soto, dueña de una tienda de souvenirs y directora de Fomento Económico, quien solicitó y le fue entregada la cantidad de 400 mil pesos; Carmen Soler Bourillón, madre del director de Medio Ambiente Municipal, Francisco Franco Soler, y propietaria de un restaurante bar, recibió 150 mil pesos.

Alejandro González Martínez, dueño de un "taller de motos" y hermano del regidor panista Francisco González, recibió 50 mil pesos.

Y para cerrar con broche de oro, Liliana Guadalupe Salum del Palacio, propietaria de un restaurante (no especificó cuál) y hermana del presidente municipal de Durango, Jorge Salum, solicitó y recibió la nada despreciable suma de 500 mil pesos, mientras su esposo, Roberto Esteban Álvarez, dueño de una cafetería (tampoco especificó cuál), recibió 100 mil pesos.

Luego de que los nombres de algunos de los favorecidos y fragmentos de esta lista comenzaran a ser difundidos en las redes sociales, la bomba mediática estalló y la indignación de la ciudadanía duranguense provocó que algunos empresarios beneficiados declararan en los medios de comunicación locales que no harían uso de los créditos que ya les habían entregado. En un comunicado emitido por la secretaría de Desarrollo Económico, luego que los diputados Iván Gurrola Vega y David Ramos Zepeda, de los partidos Morena y PRD, respectivamente, exigieran la renuncia inmediata de su titular, Ing. Ramón Dávila Flores, la dependencia anunció que habían decidido "revisar y fortalecer los lineamientos de asignación del Programa de Créditos a Micro, Pequeñas y Medianas Empresas con el fin de mantener y ampliar el apoyo a aquellos empleadores que atraviesan dificultades en la crisis económica derivada de la emergencia sanitaria". Sin embargo, esta dependencia, su titular, los empresarios más favorecidos, familiares y funcionarios estatales y del municipio de Durango ya habían quedado exhibidos ante la ciudadanía duranguense por el alevoso y ventajoso oportunismo que demostraron para desplazar a cientos de empresarios que realmente merecían recibir un crédito para salvar a sus empresas y a sus trabajadores.

Este vergonzoso escándalo representó un duro golpe para el panismo duranguense en la antesala del proceso electoral de 2021, un golpe perpetrado desde las entrañas del mismo gobierno estatal por ese secretario de Desarrollo Económico, Ramón Dávila Flores, que se caracterizó más por sus incontables viajes improductivos al extranjero y por los negocios personales que hizo al amparo del poder que por impulsar la economía de esta entidad norteña.

Días después de este atropello a la ciudadanía duranguense, Ramón Dávila Flores presentó su renuncia y el gobernador Aispuro Torres "ordenó" a la titular de la Contraloría estatal, Raquel Leila Arreola, que iniciara una "investigación" de los hechos, para más tarde anunciar que reservaría u ocultaría los resultados de estas indagatorias durante ¡5 años!, al más puro estilo de los gobiernos priístas y lopezobradorista.

Capítulo XXIV
Villa Ocampo, Durango.
La justicia al mejor postor

El secuestro y despojo de sus tierras que sufrió la familia Soto Carrillo, en Villa Ocampo, Durango, es una de las atrocidades más graves de las que tuvo conocimiento el gobernador de marras, José Aispuro, y no hizo absolutamente nada para impedirla.

La pesadilla de Doña Elpidia Carrillo Portillo, de 67 años de edad, comenzó en el año 2013, cuando falleció su esposo, Carlos Soto Cañas, poseedor del predio conocido como "Agua Puerca", de 119 hectáreas de extensión, localizado en la comunidad llamada Providencia, en el municipio de Villa Ocampo, ubicado al norte del estado de Durango, colindante con Chihuahua.

La Fiscal de Durango, Ruth Medina Alemán, un caso más de despojo de tierras en el que lejos de defender los intereses de las víctimas se puso al servicio de los agresores.

Al poco tiempo de la muerte de Don Carlos Soto Cañas, en 2014, Armando Soto Cañas, su hermano, reclamó la posesión del predio "Agua Puerca" con una escritura apócrifa. En 2015, luego de un Juicio Sucesorio llevado a cabo en el Tribunal Unitario Agrario del estado de Durango, Doña Elpidia Carrillo Portillo obtiene la posesión legal del predio "Agua Puerca".

Pero la justicia en Durango, en el sexenio panista "del cambio", siempre estuvo al alcance del mejor postor, y a la pesadilla de Doña Elpidia Carrillo le siguió un auténtico calvario, pues el 20 de abril de 2017 su hijo Mario

Arnoldo Soto Carrillo, de 47 años de edad, fue secuestrado por elementos de la Policía Investigadora de Delitos bajo las órdenes del agente del ministerio público Emmanuel Cardiel Hernández, patrocinados por Armando Soto Cañas.

De acuerdo a las declaraciones de testigos y de la víctima, contenidas en la Carpeta de Investigación Núm. 3MRV7/2018, los elementos de la PID y el agente del ministerio público, Emmanuel Cardiel Hernández, primero privaron de su libertad al señor Martín Antonio Herrera Cano, de 37 años de edad, empleado de la familia Soto Carrillo, quien, esposado, fue llevado a la casa de Armando Soto Cañas, en la comunidad Providencia, y obligado a estar bajo el sol durante cinco horas mientras el anfitrión y sus captores comían y bebían bebidas alcohólicas.

El gobernador de Durango, José Aispuro Torres, ignoró a la familia Soto Carrillo cuando en un evento le pidió ayuda y prefirió encubrir los atropellos de la Fiscal Ruth Medina y de sus agentes secuestradores de la PID.

Ahí, desde la casa de Armando Soto Cañas, un elemento de la PID le llamó por teléfono a Mario Arnoldo Soto Carrillo diciéndole que habían detenido a su empleado y que querían hablar con él en el predio "Agua Puerca". Alrededor de las 8 de la noche, Mario Arnoldo Soto Carrillo llegó al predio "Agua Puerca", propiedad de su madre Doña Elpidia Carrillo, e inmediatamente fue secuestrado por el grupo de elementos de la PID y el ministerio público Emmanuel Cardiel Hernández, quienes fuera de su jurisdicción y sin orden de aprehensión alguna trasladaron a Mario Arnoldo Soto Carrillo a la ciudad de Bermejillo, en el municipio de Mapimí.

Al día siguiente, 21 de abril de 2017, Sandra Soto Carrillo, hermana de Mario Arnoldo Soto, recibió una llamada de un agente de la PID no identificado, quien le dijo que su hermano estaba "bajo su resguardo", exigiéndole la entrega de 15 mil pesos para dejarlo en libertad, de lo contrario lo pondría a disposición del juez penal que "lo estaba requiriendo".

A la ciudad de Bermejillo se presentó Doña Elpidia Carrillo, quien fue citada por un elemento de la PID que se identificó como "comandante de la PID adscrito en la ciudad de Bermejillo"; ahí, en los separos de la PID ubicados a un costado de la policía municipal, Doña Elpidia Carrillo fue presionada por el comandante de la PID y el ministerio público Emmanuel Cardiel Hernández: "Me dijeron que para liberar a mi hijo era necesario que les firmara un documento cediéndole todos los derechos del predio 'Agua Puerca' al señor Armando Soto Cañas y a su esposa, Ivonel Olivas Muñoz. Minutos antes ya les había entregado los 15 mil pesos que nos exigieron para liberar a mi hijo, y como me negué a firmarles el documento no me devolvieron el dinero y enviaron a mi hijo ante el juez penal de Gómez Palacio, acusado de despojo", declaró Doña Elpidia Carrillo en octubre de 2018 en la Fiscalía General del estado de Durango.

El 23 de abril de 2017, con el apoyo de elementos de la PID y del ministerio público Emmanuel Cardiel Hernández, Armando Soto Cañas invadió el predio "Agua Puerca" y metió a su ganado en esta propiedad.

Doña Elpidia Carrillo y sus hijos, Mario Arnoldo, Sandra y Araceli fueron acusados de despojo y absueltos en junio de 2018, fecha en que acudieron a la Fiscalía General del estado de Durango para poner su denuncia en contra de Armando Soto Cañas por el delito de despojo y lo que resulte (Causa Penal 814/2018). En diciembre de 2018 Armando Soto Cañas fue detenido y liberado de inmediato y, hasta el momento continúa ocupando ilegalmente el predio "Agua Puerca".

"En marzo de este año 2020, el juez Carlos Reséndiz se negó a dictar las medidas cautelares para que pudiéramos recuperar el predio 'Agua Puerca', y el 2 de octubre pasado, de manera inverosímil, la Fiscal Ruth Medina Alemán solicitó al Juez de Control el sobreseimiento de la causa" manifestó a razacero Sandra Soto Carrillo en noviembre de 2020.

El sobreseimiento, como se sabe, es una resolución judicial que dicta un juez para suspender un proceso por falta de causas que justifiquen la acción de la justicia.

Así, de manera olímpica, la Fiscal Ruth Medina Alemán, sin dar a conocer las razones específicas para solicitar el sobreseimiento de esta causa penal, perjudicó a las víctimas y benefició al despojador Armando Soto Cañas, cómplice de los elementos de la PID y del agente del ministerio público Emmanuel Cardiel Hernández que privaron de la libertad y secuestraron a los señores Martín Antonio Herrera Cano y Mario Arnoldo Soto Carrillo.

En octubre de 2020, las hermanas Sandra y Araceli Soto Carrillo durante un evento en la Fiscalía General de Durango abordaron al gobernador José Aispuro Torres para exponerle el grave atropello del que estaban siendo objeto, pero éste las ignoró.

El gobernador Aispuro Torres, en éste como en muchos otros casos similares, hizo oídos sordos a la petición de estas ciudadanas y un mes después la Fiscal corrupta Ruth Medina Alemán protagonizaría uno de los más grandes escándalos en la historia de Durango con el secuestro y tortura de la Dra. Azucena Calvillo.

Capítulo XXV
¡¡Fuera la Fiscal!!

El domingo 13 de diciembre de 2020 se llevó a cabo la manifestación más grande que ha habido en la historia de Durango. Médicos, enfermeras, personal administrativo de salud y ciudadanos se dieron cita a las 5 de la tarde en el Hospital 450 para marchar en caravana vehicular y a pie a la Plaza IV Centenario de la capital duranguense. El grito era unánime: "¡¡FUERA LA FISCAL!!". El motivo ya era más que conocido a nivel nacional y hasta internacional: por el secuestro, desaparición forzada, amenazas y tortura que perpetraron el lunes 7 de diciembre agentes de la Fiscalía de Durango bajo las órdenes de la fiscal Ruth Medina Alemán en contra de la Dra. Azucena Calvillo Carrillo, jefa del área de COVID19 del hospital del IMSS en Durango, a quien los sátrapas agentes de la Fiscalía obligaron a firmar una confesión en la que se inculpaba "por haber intentado asesinar" al magistrado Héctor Emmanuel Silva Delfín, internado de manera irregular en el hospital del IMSS Durango y hermano de la delegada federal del IMSS en Tamaulipas, Dra. Velia Patricia Silva Delfín.

El martes 8 de diciembre, la Dra. Calvillo fue encarcelada en el CERESO de Durango y vinculada a proceso, así, sin haber mediado denuncia oficial, proceso ni orden de aprehensión.

Gracias a la presión del gremio médico a nivel nacional y a la ciudadanía que protestó enérgicamente en las redes sociales, la Dra. Calvillo fue liberada la madrugada del miércoles 9 de diciembre y comenzó a destaparse la cloaca.

Se supo de la amistad que la delegada federal del IMSS en Tamaulipas, Velia Patricia Silva Delfín, tenía con la fiscal Ruth Medina Alemán por haber sido compañeras de trabajo en el IMSS hace varios años, y se supo de un encuentro ríspido que la Dra. Calvillo tuvo con la delegada del IMSS en Tamaulipas, Velia Patricia Silva Delfín, quien utilizando sus influencias con el delegado del IMSS en Durango, Julio Gutiérrez Méndez, ingresó varias veces a la zona restringida de enfermos de COVID19 y dispuso de una enfermera particular para cuidar a su hermano, el magistrado Héctor Emmanuel Silva Delfín, interfiriendo en las labores de la Dra. Calvillo.

Este tráfico de influencias y el supuesto (novelesco) intento de homicidio del magistrado Silva Delfín, hicieron blanco de una vendetta a la Dra. Calvillo, quien en menos de 24 horas de "investigación" fue secuestrada y llevada a una casa de seguridad ubicada en el fraccionamiento Acereros, en donde fue torturada por agentes de la Fiscalía, obedeciendo las órdenes de la fiscal Ruth Medina Alemán, para obligarla a firmar una declaración aceptando haber intentado asesinar al magistrado de marras, quien, por lo demás, se encontraba vivo en un hospital militar de Mazatlán, a donde fue trasladado, también de manera anómala, en un helicóptero propiedad del gobierno del estado de Durango.

En las calles de la capital de Durango miles de ciudadanos le exigieron al gobernador José Aispuro la destitución inmediata de la Fiscal Ruth Medina, pero el mandatario panista le dio la espalda al pueblo y decidió mantener en su cargo a la funcionaria corrupta.

Hoy, hasta el momento de cerrar la edición de este libro, la fiscal corrupta Ruth Medina Alemán continúa en su cargo, protegida por el gobernador panista Aispuro Torres, quien con esta decisión no solo le dio la espalda al pueblo de Durango, sino también le mandó el mensaje claro de que en esta entidad, bajo su administración, no hubo Estado de derecho y, de facto, hubo patente de corso para que esta fiscal deliquiera hasta el final de su sexenio con sus agentes secuestradores y torturadores, violando las leyes y los derechos humanos universales, sin consecuencias.

No era la primera vez que Ruth Medina y sus agentes esbirros cometían este tipo de delitos. El caso de Villa Ocampo, en el que el señor Mario Arnoldo Soto Carrillo fue secuestrado por agentes de la Fiscalía para obligar a su mamá, Doña Elpidia Carrillo Portillo, a ceder la propiedad de su rancho de 119 hectáreas a un tercero, es uno de los muchos ejemplos de las atrocidades que cotidianamente se cometieron en la Fiscalía de Durango, con la abierta complicidad de la fiscal Ruth Medina Alemán y la complacencia del gobernador omiso José Aispuro.

"¡¡FUERA RUTH MEDINA!!", fue el grito generalizado que se escuchó en las calles de Durango el domingo 13 de diciembre de 2020.

Son muchas las atrocidades que durante el sexenio de Aispuro Torres cometió la Fiscal corrupta Ruth Medina Alemán y sus agentes secuestradores, por lo que debe ser investigada en instancias nacionales e internacionales.

¿Cuántos ciudadanos inocentes estarán en el CERESO de Durango pagando delitos que no cometieron?

Capítulo XXVI
Aispuro, el más corrupto de México

El ex priísta José Aispuro Torres es un político muy especial, desde su primer intento para llegar a la gubernatura de Durango como flamante panista, en 2010, explotó el discurso de la honestidad señalando a gritos en sus mítines las corruptelas cometidas por el gobierno priísta en turno, logrando convencer a buena parte del electorado duranguense con sus histriónicas actuaciones.

José Aispuro, un demagogo profesional que estafó al pueblo de Durango con sus discursos incendiarios de hombre íntegro y transparente.

Como se sabe, en 2010 fue derrotado por el ex gobernador Jorge Herrera Caldera y al poco tiempo obtuvo la senaduría por Durango. Ahí, en el Senado de la República, fue beneficiado en esos oscuros tratos que la dirigencia nacional del PAN hizo con el ex presidente Enrique Peña Nieto para obtener algunas gubernaturas a cambio de que sus legisladores votaran a favor de la reforma energética. Aispuro, por supuesto, fue uno de los senadores que votó a favor de esta reforma para posteriormente ser ungido sin problema alguno como gobernador de Durango en septiembre de 2016.

Desde la conformación de su gabinete, Aispuro Torres dio muestras de que su gobierno sería tremendamente depredador designando en la secretaría de Finanzas al representante legal de la empresa minera contaminante First Majestic Silver Corporation, Jesús Arturo Díaz Medina, con pésimos antecedentes en el despojo de minas a ejidatarios de Coahuila.

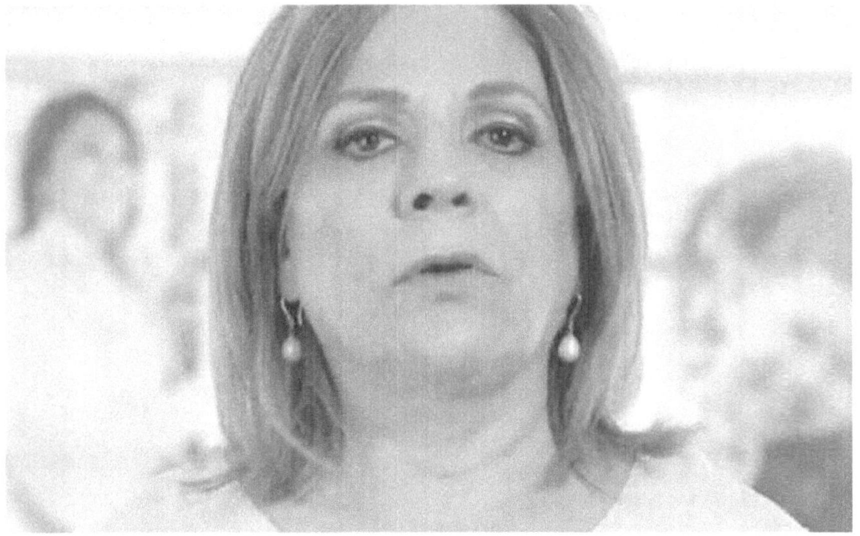

Elvira Barrantes, pieza clave de los saqueos que se dieron en el gobierno estatal de Durango, obligatoriamente debe ser investigada por la Unidad de Inteligencia Financiera del gobierno lopezobradorista. La esposa del mandatario duranguense podría superar en tropelías a la ex primera dama veracruzana, Karime Macías.

En la secretaría de Desarrollo Económico Aispuro nombró como titular a Ramón Dávila Flores, ex director de la misma empresa minera canadiense. Ramón Dávila Flores renunció a mediados de 2020 por el escándalo del SEDECOGATE, en el que otorgó créditos millonarios en plena pandemia a conocidos personajes pudientes pertenecientes a las principales cámaras empresariales de Durango, así como a familiares de políticos, servidores públicos estatales y funcionarios del municipio capitalino.

El gobierno de Aispuro, a su manera, inició una "investigación" para sancionar a este funcionario opaco y a otros dos directivos de la SEDECO, indagatoria que simplemente fue archivada en la secretaría de la Contraloría, a cargo de Raquel Arreola, esa corrupta "servidora pública" que utilizó el erario de esta dependencia para comprarse alhajas en la Ciudad de México.

Pero un personaje clave en la corrupción rampante que agobió a

Durango durante todo este sexenio es la esposa del gobernador, Elvira Barrantes, quien dejó sentir su peso mediante el tráfico de influencias que practicó para colocar en la nómina gubernamental a una veintena de sus parientes, mientras a otros más les otorgó jugosos contratos por adjudicación directa en las secretarías estatales.

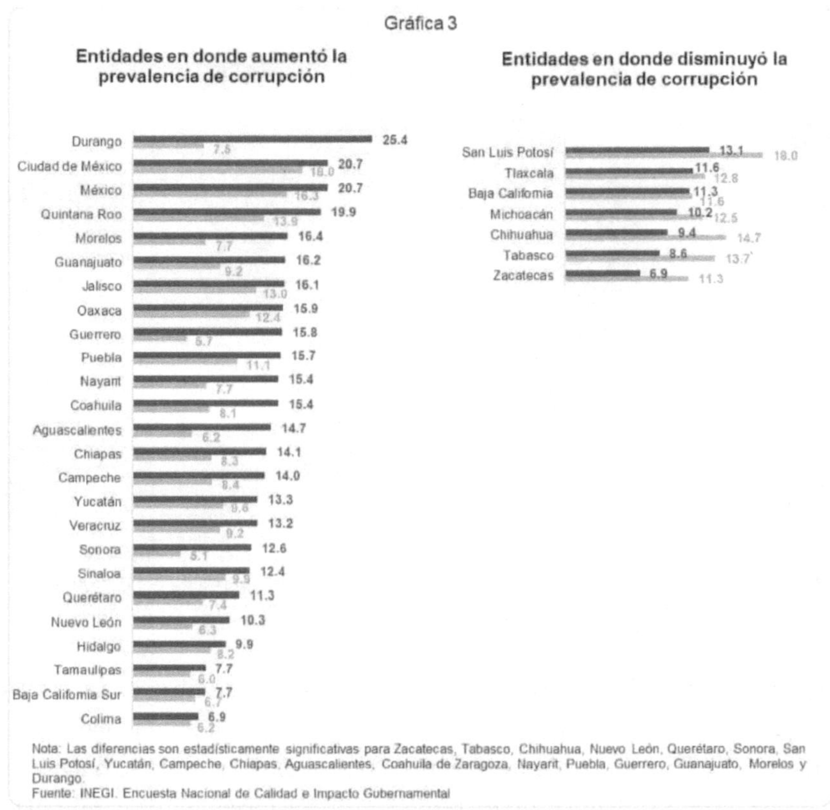

De acuerdo a la última Encuesta Nacional de Calidad e Impacto Gubernamental, realizada por el INEGI en 2019, Durango ocupa el primer lugar a nivel nacional en Tasa de Prevalencia de Corrupción y Tasa de Incidencia de Corrupción, superando a la Ciudad de México.

Elvira Barrantes, desde que comenzó el sexenio, impuso a todas las directoras de administración de las secretarías del gobierno del estado de Durango, creando una red de corrupción ahí precisamente donde están los recursos financieros, decidiendo sobre los titulares de las secretarías a qué proveedores y prestadores de servicios se les debía otorgar contratos, la mayoría de las veces con sobreprecios y por la vía de la adjudicación directa. Al respecto, un alto funcionario de la secretaría de Salud, que pidió omitir su nombre por razones obvias, detalló a razacero: "El ex secretario de Salud, César Franco Mariscal, tuvo varios desacuerdos con Elvira Barrantes, quien le exigía que otorgara contratos por adjudicación directa a determinadas empresas que vendían medicinas, productos y equipos médicos con excesivos sobreprecios. Al final de cuentas, ante este tipo de presiones César Franco Mariscal prefirió renunciar, no sin antes reclamarle al gobernador el turbio proceder de su esposa", reveló la fuente.

La Fiscal General de Durango, Ruth Medina Alemán, famosa por haber mandado secuestrar y torturar a la Dra. Azucena Calvillo, es uno de los ejemplos más claros de corrupción e ingobernabilidad en el sexenio de Aispuro Torres.

El saqueo que perpetró durante todo este sexenio Elvira Barrantes, su parentela y su séquito de directoras de administración de las secretarías estatales, principalmente en Obras Públicas, Salud y en el DIF, es inimaginable. Por ejemplo, revelaron fuentes fidedignas del mismo gobierno estatal: "su hermana, Mercedes Barrantes, 'Asesora Externa' del DIF, actuó como directora de facto de los Servicios de Administración y Recursos Humanos de esta dependencia. En lo que va del sexenio ha comprado tres casas en el fraccionamiento Privanzas, el más exclusivo de Durango luego del Campestre, y un terreno en las cercanías de la principal zona turística de la ciudad de Durango conocida como El Pueblito. Las casas en el fraccionamiento Privanzas oscilan entre los 7 y 8 millones de pesos cada una, mientras el terreno en El Pueblito cuesta la friolera de más de 3 millones de pesos".

Así, en las secretarías estatales, de acuerdo al testimonio otorgado a razacero por trabajadores gubernamentales, "no se mueve nada ni se toman decisiones sin el consentimiento de Elvira Barrantes", quien a estas alturas del sexenio ya se perfila para superar en fechorías a Karime Macías, la celebérrima esposa del ex gobernador de Veracruz, Javier Duarte de Ochoa.

El puente del Blvd. Francisco Villa, monumento a la corrupción con el que José Aispuro Torres se despide como el gobernador más corrupto del país.

El papel desempeñado por el gobernador duranguense que no se ha robado ni un centavo, pero ha sido altamente permisivo y omiso para sancionar a sus colaboradores cercanos que han cometido saqueos e infinidad de actos de corrupción e ineptitud es muy discutible, pues las últimas estadísticas del INEGI de 2019 colocaron al estado de Durango en el primer lugar a nivel nacional en cuanto a Tasa de Prevalencia de Corrupción y Tasa de Incidencia de Corrupción, por encima de la Ciudad de México que tiene una densidad poblacional de más de 9 millones de habitantes, mientras Durango tiene un millón 800 mil habitantes.

En el sexenio de José Aispuro la corrupción se disparó a niveles nunca antes vistos en la historia de esta entidad norteña, con él, por supuesto, a la cabeza como principal garante de la impunidad y encubridor de altos funcionarios de su gabinete transgresores de la ley. El mejor ejemplo de esto, además de la primera dama duranguense, lo representó la Fiscal General, Ruth Medina Alemán, quien saltó a la fama nacional e internacional no precisamente por su buen desempeño profesional sino por haber mandado secuestrar y torturar a la Dra. Azucena Calvillo Carrillo, el 7 de diciembre de 2020, para obligarla a declararse culpable de intentar asesinar al ex magistrado Héctor Emmanuel Silva Delfín. A pesar de la clara desaparición forzada y amenazas sufridas por la Dra. Azucena Calvillo por parte de elementos de la Fiscalía bajo las órdenes de Ruth Medina Alemán y de la mayor marcha que ha habido en los últimos tiempos en Durango, de ciudadanos que exigieron la destitución inmediata de la Fiscal de marras, el gobernador Aispuro, de manera más que vergonzosa, la mantuvo en su cargo a pesar de ser señalada en otros casos similares como cómplice de tortura, secuestro y despojo de enormes extensiones de tierras.

Pablo Gómez Álvarez, titular de la Unidad de Inteligencia Financiera de la secretaría de Hacienda del gobierno lopezobradorista, por obligación debe investigar al gobernador de Durango, José Aispuro Torres, y a su esposa, Elvira Barrantes.

Ya en las postrimerías de su sexenio, Aispuro Torres continuó entregando malas cuentas a la ciudadanía con tasas negativas, inferiores a la media nacional, en Crecimiento Económico, Empleos Formales, Productividad y Deuda Pública, de acuerdo a la prestigiada organización denominada "México, Cómo Vamos" (https://mexicocomovamos.mx).

En lo que se refiere a la Deuda Pública, el periodista Rodrigo Rosales, del periódico El Economista, el 2 de junio de 2021 reveló: "Al cierre del primer trimestre de 2021 Durango fue la única entidad que registró cambios en el Sistema de Alertas respecto al mismo período del año pasado, al pasar de endeudamiento sostenible (semáforo verde) a endeudamiento en observación (amarillo), es decir, empeoró en este indicador".

En cuanto a la pandemia de COVID19, aunque la responsabilidad fue compartida con el gobierno federal, el grave deterioro del sistema de salud estatal, producto de la enorme corrupción que se dio en este sector, y las pésimas estrategias de prevención de contagios implementadas por Aispuro Torres contribuyeron para que más de 2 mil quinientos duranguenses perdieran la vida, conforme a los últimos registros.

A menos de un año de dejar el poder, Aispuro se retira con más pena que gloria, rubricando su administración con el puente del Boulevard Francisco Villa, una obra plagada de actos de corrupción cometidos desde antes de que iniciara su construcción, como la emisión de licencias violatorias de los reglamentos municipales y la carencia de un estudio serio de impacto ambiental que provocó la tala irracional de cientos de árboles y la muerte de infinidad de tordos de pecho amarillo que perdieron su hábitat.

Con el priísmo duranguense como gran ganador en el último proceso electoral, dentro de su alianza con el PAN y el PRD, y el partido Morena acechando el poder, Aispuro Torres llegó al final de su sexenio debilitado por sus mismos actos de corrupción y sin margen para elegir a un sucesor de su confianza, fuerte, que le cubra la espalda de manera efectiva por la infinidad de tropelías y atrocidades que cometió junto con su esposa, su parentela y su séquito de incondicionales saqueadores.

Aispuro Torres y su cónyuge, Elvira Barrantes, sin lugar a dudas, son candidatos a ser investigados por esa temible Unidad de Inteligencia Financiera de la secretaría de Hacienda, la que no tendrá ningún problema para seguirle la huella a cada centavo mal habido que hayan obtenido durante estos últimos seis años.

Tomando en cuenta las estadísticas del INEGI y lo que los ciudadanos hemos observado, Aispuro termina su administración como el gobernador más corrupto de México.

Capítulo XXVII
La Gobernadora

Finalmente, el político demagogo que en campaña electoral dijo que no le iba a temblar la mano para castigar a todos los que le hubieran hecho daño al pueblo de Durango, terminó no solo exonerando a los saqueadores del sexenio pasado sino protegiendo a ultranza a los integrantes de su gabinete que durante su administración asaltaron el erario de manera descarada para enriquecerse ilícitamente.

A la ciudadanía no se le engaña y en las redes sociales el comentario más frecuente es que José Aispuro Torres y su élite de bandidos llegaron al poder "con hambre vieja de robar".

El gobernador de Durango, José Aispuro Torres, un mandatario farsante, encubridor de corruptos y facilitador de enriquecimientos ilícitos de familiares y colaboradores cercanos.

Aispuro Torres fue alcalde priísta de Durango de 2001 a 2004, y no vuelve a gozar de privilegios hasta el año 2012 en que fue ungido como senador de la República representando al PAN, conformando la LXII

Legislatura del Senado, una de las legislaturas más corruptas que ha habido en la historia de México pues en ella se dio la famosa entrega de gubernaturas al partido blanquiazul a cambio de que sus legisladores votaran a favor de la reforma energética de Enrique Peña Nieto. Aispuro, por supuesto, fue uno de los beneficiados con este trato sucio.

En 2016, Aispuro ocupa de nuevo un cargo como mandatario, pero esta vez como gobernador de Durango, y aquí es donde "el hambre vieja de robar" comienza a manifestarse pues a su lado trae a su esposa, Elvira Barrantes, quien desde los primeros minutos del sexenio aispurista, especialmente en el DIF, se manifiesta implacable despidiendo injustificadamente a cientos de empleados pagándoles paupérrimas liquidaciones.

Uno de los primeros personajes que se quejó amargamente de la voracidad del gobernador panista Aispuro Torres y de su esposa fue el ex alcalde del municipio de Durango, José Ramón Enríquez Herrera, quien en pláticas con políticos y periodistas manifestaba haber sido despojado de los presupuestos del DIF municipal y de Comunicación Social por el gobernador Aispuro, y señalaba la intervención de Elvira Barrantes en este y otros asuntos de gobierno.

Elvira Barrantes, "La Gobernadora", ya está por terminar el mandato de su esposo, José Aispuro Torres, durante el cual cometió todo tipo de atropellos en agravio del pueblo de Durango.

Al más puro estilo de los políticos hampones, Aispuro Torres manifestó a voz en cuello que no se ha robado ni un centavo; sin embargo, su esposa

Elvira Barrantes tejió una red de corrupción bien estructurada para saquear recursos millonarios de todas las secretarías estatales a través de las directoras de administración que impuso desde el inicio del sexenio. Una de las más notorias fue la de la secretaría de Salud, Ruth Vázquez Barraza, quien fue señalada infinidad de veces por el personal de esta dependencia debido a los actos de corrupción en los que incurrió. Los testimonios de los trabajadores fueron incontables y demoledores: "Ruth Vázquez Barraza subrogó el servicio de lavandería de los hospitales 450 y Materno Infantil a la empresa Lavartex y ahora la secretaría de Salud paga mucho más que cuando operaban las lavanderías de los hospitales".

En noviembre de 2018, el gobierno federal realizó una auditoría en la que se detectaron transacciones millonarias ilícitas como la compra de camas de hospital con sobreprecios 10 veces superiores a su valor real, lo mismo en la adquisición de incubadoras, un tomógrafo y equipo médico, "hasta la fecha nunca se supieron los resultados de esas auditorías", revelaron a razacero trabajadores de Salud.

Mercedes Barrantes, "asesora externa" y administradora de facto de los recursos financieros del DIF estatal de Durango, y Ruth Vázquez Barraza, directora de Administración de la secretaría de Salud, deben ser investigadas por el gobierno lopezobradorista.

La subdirección de Recursos Materiales y la Coordinación de Abastos son piezas clave en los saqueos que se llevaron a cabo en esta dependencia pues en ellas se controlaron las compras de materiales de curación, licitaciones, inventarios y compras de medicamentos especializados. "El ex subdirector de Recursos Materiales, Manuel Peleato, de la noche a la mañana enriqueció. Llegaba en camión a su oficina y de pronto se compró un vehículo Land Rover último modelo", denunciaron empleados de este sector.

Pero sin duda alguna, entre las pocas empresas favorecidas en el sexenio aispurista la favorita de Elvira Barrantes fue Servicios de Alimentación Vizcaya, propiedad de José Luna Herrera. Esta empresa desde abril de 2018 obtuvo de manera ilegal el contrato de Adquisición del Servicio de Suministro de Alimentos Preparados para el Hospital General 450 y el Hospital de Salud Mental Dr. Miguel Vallebueno. "Ahora Servicios de Alimentación Vizcaya tiene el monopolio del suministro de alimentos preparados en todos los centros de salud estatales y en casi todas las secretarías del gobierno de Durango. En el Hospital 450 tenían un contrato por un máximo de 5 mil dietas diarias, pero facturan hasta 8 mil dietas y no suministran ni 2 mil. Esta empresa también tiene monopolizados los servicios de limpieza", señalaron a razacero trabajadores del gobierno estatal.

La secretaría de Salud, una de las dependencias en las que más saqueos cometió la élite cercana a Elvira Barrantes.

Algunos empleados del Hospital 450 que tuvieron problemas con la empresa Servicios de Alimentación Vizcaya, pues se atrevieron a reclamar su falta de profesionalismo al servir a los pacientes y personal médico alimentos en mal estado, fueron objeto de actos de represión al ser cambiados a centros de salud lejanos por órdenes de los propietarios de esta empresa de marras que ejercieron un poder fáctico al interior de la secretaría de Salud, con la anuencia del titular de esta dependencia, Dr. Sergio González y, por supuesto, con el visto bueno del gobernador panista Aispuro Torres y de su esposa Elvira Barrantes.

Una empresa más que fue utilizada para realizar grandes saqueos en la secretaría de Salud es la denominada Comercializadora ARMOM, que vendió desde camas de hospital y aparatos médicos hasta papel higiénico, todo con sobreprecios exagerados.

"Bajo la administración del Dr. César Franco Mariscal, Elvira Barrantes le exigía que depositara en su cuenta personal cantidades millonarias. En una ocasión llegaron participaciones federales que ascendían a 7 millones de pesos y a pesar de que estos recursos estaban destinados para la compra de insumos médicos, Elvira Barrantes, a gritos, le exigió al Dr. Mariscal que los depositara de inmediato en una de sus cuentas personales", denunció a razacero una fuente interna de la secretaría de Salud.

En la secretaría de Obras Públicas no fue un secreto que la mayoría de los contratos fueron otorgados a empresarios de la construcción sinaloenses, cercanos a Elvira Barrantes.

La empresa Publimark, propiedad de Roberto Jiménez, fue la que tuvo el monopolio de los servicios de impresión en todas las secretarías estatales. "Son insultantes los sobreprecios que esta empresa le da al gobierno estatal de Durango", se quejaron impresores duranguenses que simplemente no fueron contratados por el gobierno aispurista como lo eran durante las administraciones priístas.

En el DIF, Mercedes Barrantes, hermana de Elvira, aunque en el organigrama apareció como "asesora externa" fue la que manejó las finanzas de esta institución. La familia Barrantes durante el sexenio aispurista adquirió tres lujosas residencias en el fraccionamiento Privanzas, uno de los más exclusivos de Durango, cuyos costos oscilan entre los 6 y 7 millones de pesos cada una.

En la secretaría de Finanzas, de acuerdo a testimonios de trabajadores estatales, quien decidió el manejo del erario fue el conocido asesor financiero Pedro López Elías, el mismo que prestó servicios similares al ex gobernador saqueador de Sonora, Guillermo Padrés Elías, quien gobernó esta entidad de 2009 a 2015 y fue encarcelado en 2016 acusado de defraudación fiscal equiparable. La Contraloría General de Sonora detectó daños al erario estatal por el orden de los 30 mil millones de pesos. El Partido Acción Nacional suspendió los derechos de Guillermo Padrés y se desligó de las acusaciones, por lo que no es nada lejano ni descabellado que algo parecido suceda con el mandatario duranguense, José Aispuro Torres.

A menos de un año de terminar el sexenio del político más demagogo y traidor que ha tenido Durango, muchos ex trabajadores institucionales del gobierno estatal despedidos injustificadamente recuerdan que una de las promesas de campaña de José Aispuro Torres fue precisamente la de no despedir a ningún trabajador. Y uno de los principales personajes que fungió como verdugo fue Elvira Barrantes.

"Ella decidió a quién despedir y a quién no, más de un millar de duranguenses se quedaron sin empleo, algunos acusados falsamente de dar información a la prensa sobre las corruptelas que se cometían en el DIF. Lo mismo sucedió en las compras y licitaciones, Elvira Barrantes durante todo el sexenio decidió a qué empresas les otorgarían contratos y a cuáles no. Desde que Aispuro tomó posesión de su cargo los trabajadores en las secretarías estatales comenzaron a llamarle 'La Gobernadora'", expresaron las fuentes a razacero.

Con un Congreso local dócil, una Contralora incondicional, una Fiscal deshonesta y un Fiscal Anticorrupción de ornato, el gobernador de Durango ha pretendido obtener impunidad para él y los suyos, pero por obligación el gobierno del presidente Andrés Manuel López Obrador debe llamarlo a cuentas para que responda por los delitos que perpetró en su administración.

Ya sin el mismo poder político que tuvo al inicio de su sexenio, desprestigiado y repudiado por muy buena parte de la ciudadanía duranguense, Aispuro Torres entró en una pugna interna con la dirigencia nacional del PAN para imponer a su candidato a la gubernatura, ese que pudiera encubrir las tropelías que él y su esposa cometieron. Por otro lado, José Aispuro no es bien visto por el gobierno federal, por haber integrado esa "Alianza Federalista" opositora al gobierno de López Obrador.

La pelea por la gubernatura de Durango comenzó desde octubre de 2021 y después del mes de septiembre de 2022, sea quien sea el próximo gobernador de Durango, lo más probable es que José Aispuro Torres y "La Gobernadora" tengan que rendir cuentas por las atrocidades que cometieron durante su sexenio.

Capítulo XXVIII
Aispuro, ¿puros logros o puros robos?

José Aispuro Torres llegó a su quinto año de gobierno con una larga cauda de promesas incumplidas y traiciones al pueblo de Durango. Finalmente, no solo le tembló la mano para castigar a sus antecesores que le hicieron daño al pueblo de Durango, sino también las rodillas y la voz, para terminar siendo lo que tanto criticó: un político corrupto y dirigente de una administración saqueadora.

Más de 2 mil millones de pesos anuales sustrajo el gobierno que encabezó José Aispuro Torres para pagar "ayudas y subsidios" a familiares, amigos y empresarios

Desde el inicio de su sexenio él, su esposa Elvira Barrantes y su séquito de bandidos se dedicaron a sustraer el erario conformando una estructura férrea para controlar todas las direcciones de administración de las secretarías e institutos estatales, para desde ahí contratar a empresas de familiares y amigos creadas al vapor y otorgar a discreción adjudicaciones directas para obras y servicios a un grupo muy selecto de empresarios, generalmente foráneos.

Así, con un gabinete de vivales encabezado por un par de peligrosos delincuentes de cuello blanco (Jesús Arturo Díaz Medina, secretario de Finanzas, y Ramón Dávila Flores, ex secretario de Desarrollo Económico) el progreso de Durango se estancó todo un sexenio, agravándose la pobreza y el desempleo por el manejo corrupto que el gobernador Aispuro y estos personajes hicieron de los recursos públicos, especialmente durante la pandemia, como el famoso SEDECOGATE, a través del cual desviaron el erario para beneficiar a la clase política y empresarial de Durango con créditos millonarios a fondo perdido, que en este caso ascendieron a poco más de 50 millones de pesos.

GOBIERNO DEL ESTADO DE DURANGO
MONTOS PAGADOS POR AYUDAS Y SUBSIDIOS
PERIODO: PRIMER TRIMESTRE 2019

CONCEPTO	AYUDA	SUBSIDIO	SECTOR	BENEFICIARIO	RFC	CURP	MONTO
OTROS SUBSIDIOS		X	ECONOMICO	GM FINANCIAL DE MEXICO SA DE CV SOFOM ER	X	X	$ 5,137,698.56
OTROS SUBSIDIOS		X	ECONOMICO	COMERCIALIZADORA DE LACTEOS Y DERIVADOS SA DE CV	X	X	$ 2,600,284.48
OTROS SUBSIDIOS		X	ECONOMICO	FISCALIA ESPECIALIZADA EN COMBATE A LA CORRUPCION DEL ESTADO DE DURA	X	X	$ 1,139,492.89
OTROS SUBSIDIOS		X	ECONOMICO	GOBIERNO DEL ESTADO DE DURANGO	X	X	$ 1,117,513.66
OTROS SUBSIDIOS		X	ECONOMICO	CHILCHOTA ALIMENTOS SA DE CV	X	X	$ 485,299.83
OTROS SUBSIDIOS		X	ECONOMICO	ARRENDADORA Y FACTOR BNTE SA DE CV SOFOM ER GFB	X	X	$ 463,438.75
OTROS SUBSIDIOS		X	ECONOMICO	MARGARITA SAMANIEGO LARA	X	X	$ 123,103.33
OTROS SUBSIDIOS		X	ECONOMICO	GRUPO MINERO BACIS SA DE CV	X	X	$ 93,135.34
OTROS SUBSIDIOS		X	ECONOMICO	SECRETARIADO EJECUTIVO DEL CONSEJO ESTATAL DE SEGURIDAD PUBLICA DEL	X	X	$ 45,589.83
OTROS SUBSIDIOS		X	ECONOMICO	INMOBILIARIA DEL PILON SA DE CV	X	X	$ 42,901.37
OTROS SUBSIDIOS		X	ECONOMICO	SERVICIO GAMO DE DURANGO SA DE CV	X	X	$ 35,558.55
OTROS SUBSIDIOS		X	ECONOMICO	BEBIDAS MUNDIALES S DE RL DE C V	X	X	$ 34,227.03
OTROS SUBSIDIOS		X	ECONOMICO	AEREO SERVICIOS EMPRESARIALES SA DE CV	X	X	$ 98,989.64
OTROS SUBSIDIOS		X	ECONOMICO	ROBERTO ARTURO ENRIQUEZ MARTINEZ	X	X	$ 78,769.93
OTROS SUBSIDIOS		X	ECONOMICO	LUZ ELENA RONQUILLO BARRAZA	X	X	$ 39,929.86
OTROS SUBSIDIOS		X	ECONOMICO	PABLO CHAVEZ ROSSIQUE	X	X	$ 36,969.41
OTROS SUBSIDIOS		X	ECONOMICO	COMBUSTIBLES Y GASES DE TORREON S A DE C V	X	X	$ 08,527.64
OTROS SUBSIDIOS		X	ECONOMICO	NR FINANCE MEXICO SA DE CV SOFOM ENR	X	X	$ 05,886.9C
OTROS SUBSIDIOS		X	ECONOMICO	ELEMENT FLEET MANAGEMENT CORPORATION MEXICO SA DE CV	X	X	$ 74,783.83
OTROS SUBSIDIOS		X	ECONOMICO	JIBE CONSTRUCCIONES Y PAVIMENTOS SA DE CV	X	X	$ 68,360.86
OTROS SUBSIDIOS		X	ECONOMICO	START BANREGIO SA DE CV SOFOM ER BANREGIO GRUPO FINANCIERO	X	X	$ 68,038.33
OTROS SUBSIDIOS		X	ECONOMICO	MAXICAR AUTOMOTRIZ SA DE CV	X	X	$ 51,970.16
OTROS SUBSIDIOS		X	ECONOMICO	SERVICIOS DE SALUD DEL ESTADO DE DURANGO	X	X	$ 13,157.78
OTROS SUBSIDIOS		X	ECONOMICO	HERMANOS BATTA SA CV	X	X	$ 11,322.03
OTROS SUBSIDIOS		X	ECONOMICO	MIGUEL ANGEL MIRELES MORENO	X	X	$ 89,946.04
OTROS SUBSIDIOS		X	ECONOMICO	CESAR ARMANDO CORRAL CAMPOS	X	X	$ 87,728.84
OTROS SUBSIDIOS		X	ECONOMICO	OSCAR GARCIA DE LEON	X	X	$ 76,791.39
OTROS SUBSIDIOS		X	ECONOMICO	BBVA LEASING MEXICO SA DE CV	X	X	$ 55,272.29
OTROS SUBSIDIOS		X	ECONOMICO	RIGOBERTO ROSALES SERNA	X	X	$ 54,824.44
OTROS SUBSIDIOS		X	ECONOMICO	HUMBERTO SANCHEZ MARTINEZ	X	X	$ 49,820.87
OTROS SUBSIDIOS		X	ECONOMICO	SOFOM INBURSA S.A. DE C.V. SOFOM, E.R., GRUPO FINANCIERO INBURSA	X	X	$ 77,229.98
OTROS SUBSIDIOS		X	ECONOMICO	SAN JUANA FABELA GONZALEZ	X	X	$ 77,061.73
OTROS SUBSIDIOS		X	ECONOMICO	VICTOR MANUEL BOJORQUEZ OSUNA	X	X	$ 77,040.54
OTROS SUBSIDIOS		X	ECONOMICO	GABRIELA SILVEYRA FAYA	X	X	$ 77,025.70
OTROS SUBSIDIOS		X	ECONOMICO	JOSE EDUARDO AISPURO BARRANTES	X	X	$ 76,928.50
OTROS SUBSIDIOS		X	ECONOMICO	OMEGA PROVEEDORA DE ALIMENTOS SA DE CV	X	X	$ 76,908.29
OTROS SUBSIDIOS		X	ECONOMICO	TRANSPORTADORA ALEJANDRA SA DE CV	X	X	$ 76,907.22
OTROS SUBSIDIOS		X	ECONOMICO	MARICELA CAÑEDO SANCHEZ	X	X	$ 76,668.61
OTROS SUBSIDIOS		X	ECONOMICO	DELI DIETA SA DE CV	X	X	$ 76,510.26
OTROS SUBSIDIOS		X	ECONOMICO	MANUEL GUILLERMO HERRERA SILVEYRA	X	X	$ 76,493.62
OTROS SUBSIDIOS		X	ECONOMICO	MA DE JESUS BARRON GARCIA	X	X	$ 76,296.19
OTROS SUBSIDIOS		X	ECONOMICO	SAGAR CONSTRUCCIONES SA DE CV	X	X	$ 75,981.84
OTROS SUBSIDIOS		X	ECONOMICO	SERVICIOS INDUSTRIALES Y EMPRESARIALES DE LA LAGUNA SA DE CV	X	X	$ 75,923.66

Empresas de políticos, familiares del gobernador Aispuro Torres y entregas ficticias de dinero en las listas de "ayudas y subsidios" del gobierno del estado de Durango.

Posteriormente nos enteraríamos que durante el gobierno aispurista cada tres meses se perpetraron atracos diez veces mayores al del SEDECOGATE con las entregas de "ayudas y subsidios" a conocidos políticos duranguenses, así como a familiares y empresas de estos.

Bajo el rubro de "Montos Pagados por Ayudas y Subsidios. Período Primer Trimestre 2019", contenido en un link del gobierno del estado de Durango que circula en internet, destacan los nombres de las empresas GM Financial de México S.A. de C.V. Sofomer, recibiendo 5 millones 337 mil 698 pesos; Comercializadora de Lácteos y Derivados S.A. de C.V., con 2 millones 600 mil 284 pesos; Chilchota Alimentos S.A. de C.V., propiedad de la ex alcaldesa saqueadora de Gómez Palacio, Juana Herrera, recibiendo 885 mil 299 pesos, y la Inmobiliaria Del Pilón S.A. de C.V., sin página web ni antecedentes de su existencia, recibiendo 742 mil 901 pesos.

En el enorme listado de más de 11 mil nombres de empresas y personas físicas se encuentran conocidos personajes de la política local como el hijo del gobernador, José Eduardo Aispuro Barrantes, recibiendo 76 mil 928 pesos; el diputado federal Juan Carlos Maturino Manzanera, con 74 mil 298 pesos; Jesús Óscar Reyes Escalera, ex director de la facultad de Odontología de la UJED, recibiendo 73 mil 725 pesos; y hasta la Contralora estatal, Raquel Leyla Arreola Fallad, con 4 mil 266 pesos. Llaman especialmente la atención los nombres de Roberto Arturo Enríquez Martínez, regidor del Partido Verde en San Juan de Guadalupe, recibiendo la cantidad de 678 mil 769 pesos, y Luz Elena Ronquillo Barraza, empleada de la Coordinación de Personal Académico de la UJED, recibiendo 639 mil 929 pesos.

Y lo peor: una vez dado a conocer este link en la red social de Twitter, fui alertado por un usuario de que mi nombre también aparecía en esta lista, supuestamente recibiendo la cantidad de 3 mil 551 pesos, cuando jamás he solicitado "ayuda ni subsidio" al gobierno del estado de Durango.

Lo anterior, lejos de ser anecdótico es grave pues esto también se trata de entregas ficticias de "ayudas y subsidios" a miles de ciudadanos que ni siquiera estábamos enterados de que aparecíamos en esa lista. En lo personal, acudí a las instancias correspondientes para interponer la denuncia de hechos en contra de quien resulte responsable.

El monto total de las entregas de "ayudas y subsidios", tan solo del primer trimestre de 2019, asciende a 539 millones 669 mil 376 pesos.

En el rubro de "Montos Pagados por Ayudas y Subsidios. Período Primer Trimestre 2018", se observa otro modus operandi pues en la lista de más de 49 mil empresas y ciudadanos beneficiados se registran entregas que van desde los 300 mil pesos hasta los ¡21 pesos! que supuestamente recibió el ciudadano Roberto Covarrubias Contreras.

La suma total de los montos aparentemente pagados por el gobierno estatal de Durango por "ayudas y subsidios" del primer trimestre de 2018 asciende a los 466 millones 344 mil pesos, desconociéndose bajo qué criterios el gobierno estatal de Durango otorgó estas "ayudas y subsidios" a determinadas empresas y ciudadanos.

En promedio, el gobierno que encabezó el panista José Aispuro Torres pagó por "ayudas y subsidios" a sus familiares y amigos, y también de manera ficticia a una cantidad incierta de ciudadanos, la friolera de 2 mil millones de pesos anuales durante casi todo su sexenio, lo que podría considerarse como el fraude más escandaloso en la historia de Durango.

Desafortunadamente los diputados de oposición de Morena y PT de la flamante LXIX Legislatura del Congreso duranguense que entró en funciones en septiembre de este año 2021 no han tenido el más mínimo interés en iniciar una exhaustiva investigación sobre estos hechos y sancionar a los responsables de este gigantesco saqueo.

Mientras el desempleo y la pobreza han azotado a la ciudadanía duranguense, las empresas de la familia Aispuro Barrantes fueron viento en popa con jugosos contratos por adjudicación directa otorgados por las secretarías del gobierno estatal.

Mientras esto sucedía, en la víspera de su quinto informe de gobierno el mandatario José Aispuro Torres solicitó al Congreso de Durango autorización para endeudar las finanzas estatales con un préstamo de más de 7 mil millones de pesos. La aprobación de este endeudamiento le fue otorgada al mandatario de marras gracias a la complicidad de los diputados de la fracción del partido Morena que votaron a favor de este atropello a la ciudadanía duranguense.

Ante estas evidencias de graves actos delictivos, es obligatorio que el gobierno federal, a través de la Unidad de Inteligencia Financiera de la SHCP, investigue a fondo los manejos turbios del erario que el gobernador Aispuro Torres y su círculo cercano de colaboradores hicieron en agravio del pueblo de Durango.

Un par de semanas después de realizada esta denuncia, el secretario de Finanzas del gobierno del estado de Durango, Arturo Díaz, declaró ante un medio de comunicación local que dichas "ayudas y subsidios" se otorgaron a miles de ciudadanos en sus pagos de tenencias y refrendos acumulados durante los últimos 10 años, creando aún más suspicacias y dudas pues muchas personas que jamás han tenido vehículos aparecieron en esas listas y otros destacaron en las mismas recibiendo "ayudas y subsidios" de hasta ¡56 millones de pesos! Por lo demás, los rubros de "ayudas y subsidios" se encuentran etiquetados anualmente en los Presupuestos de Egresos de la Federación.

Capítulo XXIX
El edificio de doña Elvira

Mientras la pobreza aumentó en Durango, el auge económico de la familia Aispuro-Barrantes fue inusitado.

Durante el sexenio del gobernador panista José Aispuro Torres, la pobreza en el estado de Durango aumentó de manera alarmante. De acuerdo al Observatorio de Finanzas Públicas y Desarrollo Regional, basado en datos del Consejo Nacional de Evaluación de la Política de Desarrollo Social (CONEVAL), en 2020 esta entidad norteña con una población de un millón 833 mil habitantes registró 716 mil ciudadanos en situación de pobreza; es decir, casi 40% o más de un tercio de los duranguenses viven en la pobreza. Esto, sin tomar en cuenta que durante 2021 la pandemia y el desempleo se agudizaron por la pésima administración gubernamental aispurista y su total ausencia de políticas publicas en cuanto a desarrollo social y económico, por lo que la cifra de 716 mil habitantes en situación de pobreza podría ser mucho mayor.

Sin embargo, estos datos parece que nunca le preocuparon al mandatario blanquiazul, el mismo que a gritos vociferó frente al presidente de la República, Andrés Manuel López Obrador, que no se ha robado ni un centavo del erario, pero sí fue altamente permisivo para que sus familiares e integrantes de su gabinete se enriquecieran ilícitamente de manera escandalosa. Así, mientras más de un tercio de los duranguenses sufre pobreza el séquito que rodeó a José Aispuro Torres vive en la abundancia, con la confianza plena de que al final de este sexenio habrá impunidad.

Una de las principales protagonistas de la corrupción en Durango fue la esposa del mandatario estatal, Elvira Barrantes, quien desde el primer minuto de este sexenio incrustó en la nómina gubernamental a una veintena de parientes en puestos clave e implementó una red en todas las direcciones de administración de las secretarías para desde ahí saquear el erario a través de empresas familiares y de amigos creadas al vapor. Y el auge económico de este personaje no podía pasar desapercibido.

SEXTO.- Mediante oficio número DMDU/0702/17, el Ing. Tomas Héctor Mitre Camargo, Director Municipal de Desarrollo Urbano, envía a la Secretaria Municipal y del Ayuntamiento documento para que a su vez sea turnado a esta H. Comisión, donde manifiesta que la C. María Elvira Barrantes Velarde, solicita cambio de uso de suelo del terreno ubicado en Calle Rubí #108 del Fraccionamiento Esmeralda, para la construcción de un edificio habitacional; y explica que se trata de un terreno con una superficie total de 1,044 M2, contemplado en el Programa de Desarrollo Urbano de la Ciudad Victoria de Durango 2025 para comercio y servicios; actualmente es un terreno baldío bardeado que colinda al norte con locales comerciales, al este con centro de acopio de materiales reciclables; se pretende la construcción de un edificio habitacional con 2 departamentos y área de estacionamiento en planta baja; en planta alta primer y segundo nivel 2 departamentos por piso.

En base a lo anteriormente expuesto, éste H. Ayuntamiento emite el siguiente:

RESOLUTIVO No. 921

EL HONORABLE AYUNTAMIENTO DEL MUNICIPIO DE DURANGO 2016-2019, DE CONFORMIDAD CON LAS FACULTADES QUE LE OTORGA EL ARTÍCULO 65 DEL BANDO DE POLICIA Y GOBIERNO DE DURANGO, RESUELVE:

PRIMERO.- Se Autoriza el cambio de uso de suelo a la C. María Elvira Barrantes Velarde, del terreno ubicado en Calle Rubí #108 del Fraccionamiento Esmeralda, con una superficie de 1,044 M2, para la construcción de un edificio habitacional.

SEGUNDO.- La presente autorización queda sujeta al cumplimiento de las siguientes restricciones: deberá considerar cajones de estacionamiento para visitas a parte de los reglamentados para los departamentos, respetar los coeficientes de utilización, ocupación y absorción de suelo C.U.S de 6, C.O.S del 80% y C.A.S del 20% respectivamente; además de cumplir con todos y cada uno de los requisitos necesarios para el trámite; así como lo indicado en la Ley General de Desarrollo Urbano para el Estado de Durango, el Reglamento de Construcciones para el Municipio de Durango y demás normatividad vigente, en cuyo caso contrario se nulificará al presente resolutivo.

Fragmento del Resolutivo 921 del Ayuntamiento del municipio de Durango, publicado en la Gaceta Municipal del día 9 de junio de 2017.

A menos de un año de haber llegado José Aispuro a la gubernatura, en la Gaceta Municipal del Ayuntamiento de Durango, del 9 de junio de 2017, se publicó el Resolutivo Núm. 921 que autorizaba a María Elvira Barrantes Velarde el cambio de Uso de suelo del terreno ubicado en la calle Rubí Núm. 108 del fraccionamiento Esmeralda, con una superficie de 1,044 metros cuadrados, para la construcción de un edificio habitacional.

El edificio de Doña Elvira, construido durante este sexenio, tiene un costo superior a los 30 millones de pesos.

El proyecto inicial manifestado ante el municipio de Durango era la edificación de un conjunto habitacional con planta baja y dos pisos, con dos departamentos por piso, pero ahora consta de planta baja y cuatro pisos, con dos departamentos por piso.

El inmueble, ubicado en una de las zonas de mayor plusvalía de la ciudad de Durango, rebasa los tres mil metros cuadrados de construcción y, de acuerdo a los peritos consultados, su valor supera los 30 millones de pesos.

Construida totalmente durante este sexenio, esta propiedad nos da una idea del auge financiero que tuvo la familia Aispuro-Barrantes, considerando que la primera dama de Durango, o "La Gobernadora", como le dicen, no percibió sueldo alguno en su cargo honorífico de presidenta del DIF.

Mientras tanto, en redes sociales continuó la polémica que se desató por la revelación de las listas de "ayudas y subsidios" del gobierno estatal de Durango, en las que aparecieron desde familiares del gobernador Aispuro Torres hasta empresas de conocidos políticos y ciudadanos que recibieron cantidades millonarias de dinero, hecho que tendrá que aclarar el secretario de Finanzas, Arturo Díaz. Y también tendrá que aclarar la razón por la que ordenó eliminar temporalmente de la página oficial del gobierno del estado de Durango el archivo pdf que contenía la información de los "Montos Pagados Por Ayudas y Subsidios. Período: Primer Trimestre 2021", en el que aparecen ciudadanos recibiendo "ayudas y subsidios" de manera individual por hasta 56 millones de pesos.

GOBIERNO DEL ESTADO DE DURANGO
MONTOS PAGADOS POR AYUDAS Y SUBSIDIOS
PERIODO: PRIMER TRIMESTRE 2021

CONCEPTO	AYUDA	SUBSIDIO	SECTOR	BENEFICIARIO	RFC	CURP	MONTO
OTROS SUBSIDIOS		X	ECONOMICO	MARIA NIEVES MARQUEZ VIDAÑA	X	X	$ 56,986,045.47
OTROS SUBSIDIOS		X	ECONOMICO	KARLA VANESA HERNANDEZ ARGUIJO	X	X	$ 25,647,763.71
OTROS SUBSIDIOS		X	ECONOMICO	GM FINANCIAL DE MEXICO SA DE CV SOFOM ER	X	X	$ 7,225,561.67
OTROS SUBSIDIOS		X	ECONOMICO	MIRIAM LORENA MARCOS WONG	X	X	$ 3,989,104.16
OTROS SUBSIDIOS		X	ECONOMICO	LUIS ANTONIO CHAVEZ AGUIRRE	X	X	$ 3,304,929.52
OTROS SUBSIDIOS		X	ECONOMICO	GOBIERNO DEL ESTADO DE DURANGO	X	X	$ 2,474,191.96
OTROS SUBSIDIOS		X	ECONOMICO	VANESSA YEN PIÑA	X	X	$ 2,220,055.74
OTROS SUBSIDIOS		X	ECONOMICO	ELEMENT FLEET MANAGEMENT CORPORATION MEXICO SA DE CV	X	X	$ 1,721,514.87
OTROS SUBSIDIOS		X	ECONOMICO	JUAN ANTONIO CHAVARIN CHAVARIN	X	X	$ 1,716,792.46
OTROS SUBSIDIOS		X	ECONOMICO	MA DE LOS ANGELES VILLEGAS GUTIERREZ	X	X	$ 1,662,005.08
OTROS SUBSIDIOS		X	ECONOMICO	HEBER GARCIA CUELLAR	X	X	$ 1,546,945.15
OTROS SUBSIDIOS		X	ECONOMICO	MARGARITA GAMBOA TORRES	X	X	$ 1,510,161.51
OTROS SUBSIDIOS		X	ECONOMICO	GARCIA VILLARREAL CONSULTORES SC	X	X	$ 1,415,011.42
OTROS SUBSIDIOS		X	ECONOMICO	KARINA RUBI AGUILAR ALONSO	X	X	$ 1,269,934.40
OTROS SUBSIDIOS		X	ECONOMICO	MARGARITA SAMANIEGO LARA	X	X	$ 1,268,951.52
OTROS SUBSIDIOS		X	ECONOMICO	MARIA DE JESUS CHAVEZ GARCIA	X	X	$ 1,247,295.52
OTROS SUBSIDIOS		X	ECONOMICO	KARLA CECILIA GAMEZ MORELL	X	X	$ 1,246,053.20
OTROS SUBSIDIOS		X	ECONOMICO	DIANA JANETTE ZUÑIGA SANTANA	X	X	$ 1,228,170.44
OTROS SUBSIDIOS		X	ECONOMICO	NR FINANCE MEXICO SA DE CV	X	X	$ 1,200,264.99
OTROS SUBSIDIOS		X	ECONOMICO	MARIA BERTHA REYES NAJERA	X	X	$ 1,106,323.70
OTROS SUBSIDIOS		X	ECONOMICO	CHILCHOTA ALIMENTOS SA DE CV	X	X	$ 1,089,570.87
OTROS SUBSIDIOS		X	ECONOMICO	MARIA FERNANDA GURROLA ALCARAZ	X	X	$ 1,059,828.52
OTROS SUBSIDIOS		X	ECONOMICO	CRAIG PHILLIP OSSO	X	X	$ 1,044,912.70
OTROS SUBSIDIOS		X	ECONOMICO	HERMANOS BATTA SA CV	X	X	$ 1,031,017.11
OTROS SUBSIDIOS		X	ECONOMICO	FERNANDO RIOS ANDRADE	X	X	$ 1,003,873.70
OTROS SUBSIDIOS		X	ECONOMICO	JESUS EMMANUEL FLORES DURAN	X	X	$ 970,664.99
OTROS SUBSIDIOS		X	ECONOMICO	GILBERTO VALENCIA ROSALES	X	X	$ 959,512.80
OTROS SUBSIDIOS		X	ECONOMICO	JOSE GUADALUPE RODRIGUEZ CISNEROS	X	X	$ 955,871.39
OTROS SUBSIDIOS		X	ECONOMICO	ROBERTO ARTURO ENRIQUEZ MARTINEZ	X	X	$ 928,776.73
OTROS SUBSIDIOS		X	ECONOMICO	GABRIELA SILVEYRA FAYA	X	X	$ 914,225.50
OTROS SUBSIDIOS		X	ECONOMICO	JOPER SA DE CV	X	X	$ 850,225.51
OTROS SUBSIDIOS		X	ECONOMICO	SERVICIO GEOLOGICO MEXICANO	X	X	$ 816,101.06
OTROS SUBSIDIOS		X	ECONOMICO	CAROLINA MARTIN ZAZUETA	X	X	$ 796,158.94
OTROS SUBSIDIOS		X	ECONOMICO	ROGELIO ALMERAZ DIAZ	X	X	$ 779,457.98
OTROS SUBSIDIOS		X	ECONOMICO	TRANSPORTES GARZA LEAL SA DE CV	X	X	$ 769,884.63
OTROS SUBSIDIOS		X	ECONOMICO	KENIA MARBELLA MEDRANO ACOSTA	X	X	$ 766,464.01
OTROS SUBSIDIOS		X	ECONOMICO	ARRENDADORA Y FACTOR BANORTE SA DE CV SOFOM ER GRUPO FINANCIERO B	X	X	$ 694,865.01
OTROS SUBSIDIOS		X	ECONOMICO	SERGIO BAYONA SERRANO	X	X	$ 673,394.67
OTROS SUBSIDIOS		X	ECONOMICO	SECRETARIADO EJECUTIVO DEL CONSEJO ESTATAL DE SEGURIDAD PUBLICA DEL	X	X	$ 663,030.26
OTROS SUBSIDIOS		X	ECONOMICO	A2DAHT HEALTH MEXICO SA DE CV	X	X	$ 651,812.24
OTROS SUBSIDIOS		X	ECONOMICO	CESAR ARMANDO CORRAL CAMPOS	X	X	$ 647,806.34
OTROS SUBSIDIOS		X	ECONOMICO	GRUPO ACERERO CAHVEZ SA DE CV	X	X	$ 641,703.00
OTROS SUBSIDIOS		X	ECONOMICO	ROMAN OROZCO DE LOS SANTOS	X	X	$ 641,383.93
OTROS SUBSIDIOS		X	ECONOMICO	MIGUEL ANGEL MIRELES MORENO	X	X	$ 637,335.16
OTROS SUBSIDIOS		X	ECONOMICO	CARLOS MANUEL HERRERA ALE	X	X	$ 628,640.51
OTROS SUBSIDIOS		X	ECONOMICO	JUAN ANTONIO ANDRADE LOSORIA	X	X	$ 611,993.54
OTROS SUBSIDIOS		X	ECONOMICO	CSI LEASING MEXICO S DE RL DE CV	X	X	$ 556,152.59
OTROS SUBSIDIOS		X	ECONOMICO	RASHITH ASKAR TORRES	X	X	$ 554,873.31

El archivo pdf que contenía los "Montos Pagados por Ayudas y Subsidios. Período: Primer Trimestre 2021" fue eliminado temporalmente de la página oficial del gobierno estatal de Durango por órdenes del secretario de Finanzas, Arturo Díaz Medina.

Así las cosas, Aispuro Torres se encamina a la recta final de su sexenio con el sambenito de gobernar el estado que ocupa el primer lugar a nivel nacional en cuanto a incidencia y percepción de la corrupción, de acuerdo a las estadísticas del INEGI, y extrañamente también, Aispuro Torres termina su sexenio sin estar siendo investigado por el gobierno federal lopezobradorista, lo que confirmaría el rumor de que este mandatario rapaz habría pactado la entrega de la gubernatura de Durango al partido oficial, Morena, a cambio de impunidad.

El gobernador de Durango, José Aispuro Torres, ya habría pactado su impunidad con el gobierno lopezobradorista a cambio de entregar la gubernatura al partido Morena en las próximas elecciones de 2022.

Capítulo XXX
SEBISED, los contratos millonarios de Jaime Rivas

De acuerdo a las últimas estadísticas del Consejo Nacional de Evaluación de la Política de Desarrollo Social (CONEVAL), durante el sexenio del gobernador panista José Aispuro Torres la pobreza aumentó de manera dramática en Durango. Con un millón 833 mil habitantes, en el año 2018 esta entidad registraba 694 mil 500 personas en situación de pobreza; para el año 2020 esta cifra había aumentado a 715 mil 500 personas.

En 2018, el CONEVAL registró en Durango a 38 mil 500 personas en situación de pobreza extrema (2.2% de la población); para el 2020 esta cifra aumentó a más del doble, llegando a las 79 mil 600 personas (4.3%).

En el rubro de Población con al menos tres carencias sociales, en 2018 Durango manifestaba 169 mil personas; para 2020 este número ascendió a 250 mil 300 personas.

Y así en todas las clasificaciones relativas a la pobreza, Durango presentó resultados negativos, tanto en las estadísticas del CONEVAL como en las del INEGI.

Estas son solo algunas de las consecuencias nefastas que trajo el sexenio del panista José Aispuro Torres, un sexenio perdido para el pueblo duranguense, en el que solo los familiares de este mandatario y su séquito de allegados progresaron.

Jaime Rivas Loaiza, hermano putativo del gobernador Aispuro Torres y titular de la secretaría de Bienestar (SEBISED), fue uno de los principales responsables de las cifras deplorables que publicó el CONEVAL en su página oficial (coneval.org.mx).

Designar a personas incompetentes en cargos de enorme responsabilidad es corrupción, y eso es lo que el gobernador Aispuro Torres hizo desde el comienzo de su sexenio, colocando como titulares de despacho y en puestos relevantes a sus parientes y amigos sin importarle si tenían o no capacidad para desempeñar dichos cargos.

Lo que sucedió en la SEBISED con Jaime Rivas Loaiza fue la misma historia que aconteció en todas las secretarías estatales, en las que el uso de recursos públicos para hacer negocios personales fue la constante. Así, revisando las actividades financieras de este funcionario, el equipo de razacero pudo detectar de inmediato una serie de contratos millonarios insultantes que contrastaban con los pobres resultados que este "servidor público" obtuvo en el combate a la pobreza y en el impulso de un verdadero desarrollo social en Durango.

Medición multidimensional de la pobreza,* Durango
Porcentaje, número de personas y carencias promedio por indicador de pobreza, 2018 - 2020

	Porcentaje		Miles de personas		Carencias promedio	
	2018	2020	2018	2020	2018	2020
Pobreza						
Población en situación de pobreza	38.8	38.7	694.5	715.5	1.7	1.9
Población en situación de pobreza moderada	36.6	34.4	656.0	635.9	1.6	1.8
Población en situación de pobreza extrema	2.2	4.3	38.5	79.6	3.3	3.4
Población vulnerable por carencias sociales	23.2	23.3	415.0	430.8	1.6	1.8
Población vulnerable por ingresos	12.3	12.4	220.2	228.9	0.0	0.0
Población no pobre y no vulnerable	25.7	25.6	460.9	474.1	0.0	0.0
Privación social						
Población con al menos una carencia social	62.0	62.0	1,109.5	1,146.3	1.7	1.9
Población con al menos tres carencias sociales	9.4	13.5	169.0	250.3	3.3	3.3
Indicadores de carencia social						
Rezago educativo	16.3	16.9	292.6	313.0	2.2	2.3
Carencia por acceso a los servicios de salud	13.1	22.9	233.9	423.5	2.5	2.5
Carencia por acceso a la seguridad social	44.5	45.7	796.5	845.6	1.9	2.1
Carencia por calidad y espacios de la vivienda	4.8	5.8	85.6	107.6	2.5	2.7
Carencia por acceso a los servicios básicos en la vivienda	5.7	5.9	101.3	109.4	2.6	2.9
Carencia por acceso a la alimentación nutritiva y de calidad	19.0	18.9	339.9	349.6	2.1	2.2
Bienestar económico						
Población con ingreso inferior a la línea de pobreza extrema por ingresos	13.1	14.0	235.1	259.5	1.5	1.9
Población con ingreso inferior a la línea de pobreza por ingresos	51.1	51.1	914.7	944.4	1.3	1.5

*De acuerdo con los *Lineamientos y criterios generales para la definición, identificación y medición de la pobreza* (2018) que se pueden consultar en el Diario Oficial de la Federación (https://www.dof.gob.mx/nota_detalle.php?codigo=5542421&fecha=30/10/2018) y la *Metodología para la medición multidimensional de la pobreza en México*, tercera edición (https://www.coneval.org.mx/InformesPublicaciones/InformesPublicaciones/Documents/Metodologia-medicion-multidimensional-3er-edicion.pdf).
Fuente: estimaciones del CONEVAL con base en la ENIGH 2018 y 2020.

Las cifras de medición de la pobreza en Durango proporcionadas por el CONEVAL son lapidarias y revelan la ineptitud del titular de la SEBISED, Jaime Rivas Loaiza, y del gabinete económico del gobierno del estado de Durango.

En la página oficial de Transparencia del gobierno de Durango aparece manifestado un contrato absurdo por "Prestación de servicios de consultoría para conocer la opinión ciudadana sobre los programas sociales", que asciende a 3 millones 190 mil pesos, adjudicado de manera directa a la empresa Consulta S.A. de C.V., representada por Alejandro Mejía Manjarrez (Contrato de Adquisición No. SBS/CONSULTORÍA/001/2020). Sin embargo, al querer acceder al link para ver los pormenores del contrato este no aparece en la página de Transparencia.

Jaime Rivas Loaiza fue secretario de Recursos Naturales y Medio Ambiente, en donde también realizó un papel mediocre. Su único mérito en este sexenio fue ser hermano putativo del gobernador panista saqueador José Aispuro Torres.

Otro contrato desconcertante es el que tuvo por objeto la "Adquisición de despensas en apoyo a las familias duranguenses para mitigar los efectos de la contingencia ocasionada por el virus SARS-COV2", que asciende a 11 millones 253 mil 200 pesos. El contrato de adquisición No. SBS/DFD/01/2020, que supuestamente respalda esta operación, tampoco está disponible en la página oficial de Transparencia del estado de Durango; en el rubro donde debe aparecer el nombre de la empresa, se señala que "carece de razón social" y fue adjudicado de manera directa al ciudadano Rodrigo Valenzuela Núñez.

Un contrato más por "Servicios Profesionales para el Proyecto denominado Capacitación Durango 2020", con un monto de 15 millones 550 mil pesos, también fue adjudicado de manera directa a la empresa Sinaloa Conection S.A. de C.V., representada por Elsa Mariel Mendivil Sánchez. El contrato No. CAP/SBS/02/2020 que respalda esta millonaria entrega sí aparece en la página de Transparencia del gobierno de Durango, plagada de contratos por adjudicación directa con empresas sinaloenses, que son las preferidas de la esposa del gobernador, Elvira Barrantes, por lo que muy buena parte del presupuesto ejercido por el gobierno de Aispuro Torres durante estos últimos 5 años fue a parar a las cuentas bancarias de empresas y personas físicas de esta entidad vecina.

Con Jaime Rivas como secretario de la SEBISED las adjudicaciones directas de contratos millonarios a empresas sinaloenses fueron cotidianas.

La lista de contratos millonarios otorgados por la vía de adjudicación directa y firmados por el titular de SEBISED, Jaime Rivas Loaiza, es copiosa y difícilmente soportaría una auditoría profesional autónoma.

Es por demás decir que si el presupuesto de esta dependencia se hubiera ejercido durante este sexenio de manera responsable y con verdadera transparencia por lo menos la pobreza extrema en Durango ya habría sido eliminada, pero desgraciadamente en 2016 el panista José Aispuro Torres llegó a gobernar esta entidad acompañado de una auténtica banda de saqueadores.

Capítulo XXXI
SEBISED, más de 100 millones para una sola empresa

Según el ranking del World Justice Project, presentado recientemente, México es el quinto país más corrupto del mundo, ocupando el lugar 135 de 139 entre las naciones más corruptas del planeta, sólo por debajo de Uganda, Camerún, Camboya y el Congo. En este contexto, y de acuerdo a las estadísticas del INEGI, el estado de Durango ocupa el primer lugar en Prevalencia y Percepción de la corrupción en México, sitio ganado a pulso durante el sexenio del panista José Aispuro Torres.

Considerando la anterior información de estas fuentes especializadas, Durango puede considerarse como una de las entidades más corruptas del mundo.

Con el control absoluto de las principales instituciones impartidoras de justicia como la Contraloría estatal, la Fiscalía General, la Fiscalía Especializada en Combate a la Corrupción, el Tribunal Superior de Justicia y el Congreso local, al mandatario de marras panista José Aispuro no le fue difícil cometer todo tipo de tropelías y encubrir los saqueos y enriquecimientos ilícitos de sus familiares y de los integrantes de su gabinete, entre los que se encuentra el titular de la secretaría de Bienestar, Jaime Rivas Loaiza, su hermano putativo cuya familia le dio refugio en su casa desde la infancia.

Este personaje opaco hizo y deshizo en la SEBISED, y más en los últimos meses del sexenio en los que reparte el erario de esta dependencia a diestra y siniestra entre diversos actores de todas las fuerzas políticas con el fin de ganar adeptos e intentar comprar, sí, comprar la candidatura del PAN a la gubernatura de Durango.

Así, utilizando bastos recursos públicos de manera descarada, Jaime Rivas realiza un proselitismo insultante, aparte de promocionar su imagen (con cargo al erario) en los principales medios de comunicación masiva duranguenses. En pocas palabras, nosotros los contribuyentes pagamos la precampaña de este político ex priista ambicioso que a toda costa busca ser candidato del PAN a la gubernatura de Durango. De esta manera vimos el manejo de una institución pública como una parcela de uso particular.

Jaime Rivas Loaiza, titular de la SEBISED, en plena pandemia se dedicó a pintar escuelas y viviendas beneficiando a una sola empresa con contratos de adjudicación directa por más de 100 millones de pesos.

Los resultados de esta "política" solapada por el gobernador panista Aispuro Torres están a los ojos de todo el mundo con los resultados negativos en el combate a la pobreza que obtuvo Jaime Rivas Loaiza como titular de la SEBISED, manteniendo a un tercio de la población duranguense (más de 700 mil ciudadanos) en la pobreza y duplicando el número de habitantes en situación de pobreza extrema (de 38 mil 500 duranguenses en 2018 a 79 mil 600 en 2020).

Pero hay un grupo de empresarios a los que les fue demasiado bien en este sexenio con este "servidor público", entre los que destacan en especial los propietarios de la empresa Proyección Integral Total S.A. de C.V., que entre los años 2020 y 2021, en plena pandemia, fueron beneficiados con un par de contratos que ascendieron a más de 100 millones de pesos.

CONTRATACIÓN DE SERVICIOS PROFESIONALES PARA EL PROYECTO DENOMINADO "REHABILITACIÓN DE EDIFICIOS Y EXTERIORES/REHABILITACIÓN DE ESPACIOS EDUCATIVOS 2020", QUE CELEBRAN POR UNA PARTE LA SECRETARÍA DE BIENESTAR SOCIAL DEL ESTADO DE DURANGO, REPRESENTADA POR EL **LIC. JAIME RIVAS LOAIZA**, EN SU CARÁCTER DE TITULAR DE LA DEPENDENCIA, FACULTADO LEGALMENTE, ASISTIDO POR LA **LIC. BLANCA LILIANA CORTÉZ MONTOYA**, EN SU CARÁCTER DE DIRECTORA DE ADMINISTRACIÓN, A QUIENES PARA LOS EFECTOS DEL PRESENTE SE LES DENOMINARÁ COMO **"LA CONTRATANTE"**; Y POR LA OTRA PARTE LA EMPRESA **PROYECCIÓN INTEGRAL TOTAL S.A. DE C.V.**, POR CONDUCTO DE SU REPRESENTANTE LEGAL, EL **C. LUIS FERNANDO POMPA LIZÁRRRAGA**, A QUIEN EN LO SUCESIVO SE LE DENOMINARÁ **"EL PROVEEDOR"**; ASÍ MISMO, SE HACE CONSTAR QUE CUANDO AMBAS PARTES ACTÚEN DE FORMA CONJUNTA, SE DENOMINARÁN **"LAS PARTES"** DE ACUERDO CON EL SIGUIENTE GLOSARIO, DECLARACIONES Y CLÁUSULAS:

GLOSARIO:

ÚNICO.- **"LAS PARTES"** acuerdan que para los efectos del presente contrato, se entenderá por:

NOMBRE ABREVIADO	NOMBRE COMPLETO
Administrador del Contrato	Dirección de Bienestar Social
Código Civil	Código Civil del Estado de Durango.
Contrato	EE/SBS/03/2020.
Constitución	Constitución Política del Estado Libre y Soberano de Durango.

SEGUNDA. MONTO DEL CONTRATO.- El monto del presente contrato es por la cantidad de $ 42'241,168.33 (Cuarenta y dos millones doscientos cuarenta y un mil ciento sesenta y ocho pesos 33/100 M.N.) antes de I.V.A., debiendo agregarse la cantidad de $6'758,586.94 (Seis millones setecientos cincuenta y ocho mil quinientos ochenta y seis pesos 94/100 M.N.), por concepto de I.V.A. es decir, que la cantidad total es por $48'999,755.27 (Cuarenta y ocho millones novecientos noventa y nueve mil setecientos cincuenta y cinco pesos 27/100 M.N.) siendo a precio fijo.

TERCERA. VIGENCIA DEL CONTRATO.- El contrato tendrá vigencia desde la fecha de firma del presente y hasta el 15 de diciembre de 2020, plazo en el cual se deberá dar cumplimiento a los servicios objeto del presente instrumento legal y su **ANEXO 1**. Una vez que se reciba el anticipo, contará **"EL PROVEEDOR"** con un plazo de ciento ochenta días naturales para ejecutar las acciones.

CUARTA. TERMINACIÓN ANTICIPADA.- **"LA CONTRATANTE"** podrá dar por terminado anticipadamente el presente contrato y sin responsabilidad para ésta, mediante aviso por escrito que le dé **"LA CONTRATANTE"** a **"EL PROVEEDOR"**, con 15 días naturales de anticipación, por los siguientes motivos:

a) Cuando concurran razones de interés general.
b) Por extinguirse la necesidad de requerir los servicios contratados.
c) Cuando por la continuidad del presente contrato, se genere un daño o perjuicio al Estado de Durango.
d) Cuando se determine la nulidad total o parcial de los actos que dieron origen al presente instrumento.
e) Por resolución de la autoridad competente.
f) Por cualquier deterioro o menoscabo que reporte el servicio prestado por **"EL PROVEEDOR"** ya sea que no reúna las características estipuladas en el presente contrato y su **ANEXO 1** o que sea deficiente, a juicio de la **"LA CONTRATANTE"**.

QUINTA. LUGAR Y PROCESO DE RECEPCIÓN DE LOS SERVICIOS.- La prestación de los servicios será en los Municipios de: Durango, Gómez Palacio, Lerdo, Santiago Papasquiaro, Guadalupe Victoria, Rodeo y Mezquital, todos del Estado de Durango, como se precisa en el **ANEXO 1** y en cualquier otro lugar indicado por **"LA CONTRATANTE"** que se requiera para el cumplimiento del objeto del presente contrato; la recepción de los entregables e informes objeto del presente contrato, será en el edificio de la Secretaría, ubicada en Boulevard Domingo Arrieta número 200, esquina con Gral. Ismael Lares, Fraccionamiento Domingo Arrieta, C.P. 34180, en la Ciudad de Victoria de Durango, Dgo. ante el Administrador del Contrato.

El contrato otorgado por Jaime Rivas a la empresa Proyección Integral Total S.A. de C.V., por casi 49 millones. En la Cámara Mexicana de la Industria de la Construcción esta empresa aparece registrada con un rango de 10 empleados.

El 30 de abril del año 2020, el "Comité de Adquisiciones, Arrendamientos y Servicios de la Secretaría de Bienestar del estado de Durango" otorgó a la empresa Proyección Integral Total S.A. de C.V., el contrato por adjudicación directa número EE/SBS/03/2020 por un monto de 48 millones 999 mil 755 pesos con 27 centavos, por concepto de "Rehabilitación de Edificios y Exteriores/Espacios Educativos en el Estado de Durango, del proyecto denominado: 'Espacios Educativos Durango 2020'", firmado el 11 de mayo de 2020, que consistió supuestamente en pintar escuelas de mayo a diciembre de 2020, cuando todos los planteles educativos de Durango se encontraban cerrados por la pandemia y los recursos del erario debieron haberse utilizado para ser repartidos entre la ciudadanía para combatir los efectos del COVID19.

Fragmento de uno de los contratos otorgados por el titular de la SEBISED, Jaime Rivas, a la empresa Proyección Integral Total S.A. DE C.V., por un monto de 68 millones 500 mil pesos, por concepto de "aplicación de pintura en fachadas", firmado el 29 de marzo de 2021, cuando la ciudadanía necesitaba otro tipo de apoyos para paliar los graves efectos de la pandemia del COVID19.

El 26 de marzo de 2021, ese mismo "Comité de Adquisiciones, Arrendamientos y Servicios de la Secretaría de Bienestar del estado de Durango" asignó a la misma empresa Proyección Integral Total S.A. de C.V., otro contrato por adjudicación directa, esta vez por un monto de 68 millones 500 mil pesos, por concepto de "Servicios de Aplicación de Pintura en Fachadas e Impermeabilización de Techos de Viviendas en el Estado de Durango 2021", firmado el 29 de marzo de 2021. En el contrato de marras se menciona un número indeterminado de colonias y fraccionamientos de los municipios de Durango, Pánuco de Coronado, Guadalupe Victoria, Santiago Papasquiaro y Gómez Palacio en donde supuestamente se proporcionaron estos beneficios.

Así las cosas, el titular de la SEBISED, Jaime Rivas Loaiza, destinó durante los peores años de la pandemia, 2020 y 2021, más de 100 millones de pesos para pintar escuelas y fachadas de casas a lo largo y ancho del estado de Durango, beneficiando a una sola empresa, Proyección Integral Total S.A. de C.V.

Con esa cantidad de dinero, ¿cuántos pequeños y medianos empresarios hubieran salvado sus negocios y conservado las fuentes de ingresos de sus trabajadores?

Cabe resaltar que en el contrato que la empresa Proyección Integral Total S.A. de C.V., celebró con la SEBISED el 11 de mayo del año 2020, esta se manifestó como una empresa constituida conforme a las leyes mexicanas "lo cual se hace constar con Escritura Pública Num.26193 volumen número 1140, de fecha 5 de octubre de 2016", representada por el C. Luis Fernando Pompa Lizárraga, mientras en el contrato celebrado el 29 de marzo de 2021 la misma empresa manifiesta haber sido constituida mediante la Escritura Pública Núm. 2319, volumen 246, de fecha 11 de enero de 2006, y fue representada por el C. Saúl Machado León.

Este tipo de contratos fueron recurrentes en la SEBISED desde que su titular, Jaime Rivas, tomó posesión de su cargo el 11 de julio de 2018.

Epílogo

Esta retrospectiva del sexenio del gobernador panista José Aispuro Torres recapitula los actos de corrupción más notorios que se cometieron durante su administración, actos de corrupción que indudablemente impactaron en la vida social de los duranguenses que en 2016 llevaron al poder a este político ex priista que llegó acompañado de una verdadera mafia de colaboradores saqueadores e inescrupulosos. El papel más relevante dentro de este grupo depredador lo protagonizó Elvira Barrantes, esposa del gobernador de marras Aispuro Torres, quien, como se expone en esta recopilación, desde el inicio del sexenio tejió una red bien organizada para controlar las direcciones de administración de todas las dependencias estatales para desde ahí ordenar la entrega de contratos por la vía de adjudicación directa para beneficiar a empresas de familiares y a empresarios foráneos y locales selectos, afines a sus intereses.

Este menosprecio hacia la mayoría de prestadores de servicios y proveedores duranguenses, agudizó en los últimos años del sexenio la crisis económica de esta entidad, agregando a esto el pésimo desempeño del gabinete económico-social aispurista, cuyos saqueos en las secretarías de Finanzas, Desarrollo Económico y Bienestar Social fueron más que evidentes. Con Aispuro, el crecimiento económico y el combate a la pobreza fueron prácticamente nulos y, entre los años 2018 y 2020, la pobreza extrema se duplicó pasando de 38 mil 500 a 79 mil 600 ciudadanos duranguenses que sobreviven en esta situación.

Hacia la primera mitad del sexenio, ya era más que notoria la ingobernabilidad en la administración del mandatario bribón, José Aispuro, sobre todo en el rubro de impartición de justicia, superando el 90% de impunidad en casos de violencia de género, despojos de tierras y actos delictivos cometidos por "servidores públicos". Los casos de secuestro y tortura de la Dra. Azucena Calvillo, de la familia Soto Carrillo, en Villa Ocampo, y el de Las Niñas Peyro, arrancadas de manera infame de su seno materno por "autoridades" del DIF estatal, encabezadas por Elvira Barrantes y la directora de esta institución, Rocío Manzano, en contubernio con personajes siniestros de la Fiscalía General de Durango, son solo tres ejemplos de los muchos que sucedieron durante el sexenio de terror del panista José Aispuro, quien a pesar de haber tenido conocimiento pleno de estos crímenes de lesa humanidad optó por proteger a los agresores dándole la espalda a las víctimas.

En esta administración vergonzante, miles de millones de pesos fueron desviados del erario, lo mismo a través de contratos ventajosos con empresarios inescrupulosos que en entregas ficticias de "ayudas y subsidios" supuestamente entregados a miles de ciudadanos.

Es innegable que el gobierno del panista Aispuro Torres superó en corrupción a las administraciones de sus antecesores priistas y produjo muchos nuevos ricos, especialmente en su círculo familiar, cuyos enriquecimientos ilícitos fueron más que notorios.

Todos estos hechos de marcada corrupción e ineptitud que convirtieron al gobierno panista duranguense en un gobierno totalmente impopular, llevaron al dirigente nacional del Partido Acción Nacional, Marko Cortés, a declarar el 25 de septiembre de este año 2021 ante líderes locales de Aguascalientes: "Se los digo en casa, la única gubernatura que tenemos posibilidades de ganar, reales, auténticas y bien ganada es esta (la de Aguascalientes). No hay más. Está muy complicado Durango, Tamaulipas, Quintana Roo, Hidalgo y Oaxaca, ¿qué les cuento?".

Es obvio que si el mandatario demagogo duranguense hubiera gobernado de manera impecable no estaría en esta situación, al frente de una entidad señalada por el mismo INEGI como la más corrupta de México.

Por estas razones y conociendo los pactos de impunidad que sexenio tras sexenio suceden, en los que los titulares de los gobiernos entrantes protegen las pillerías de los que se van, es determinante que como sociedad exijamos a quienes lleguen, y sobre todo al gobierno federal encabezado por el presidente Andrés Manuel López Obrador, que realicen las investigaciones correspondientes para que el grupo delincuencial que gobernó Durango de 2016 a 2022, dirigido por José Aispuro Torres, sea sometido al imperio de la ley por los hurtos y atrocidades que cometió.

Organigrama de la corrupción

El sentido de las flechas indica la cadena de obediencia

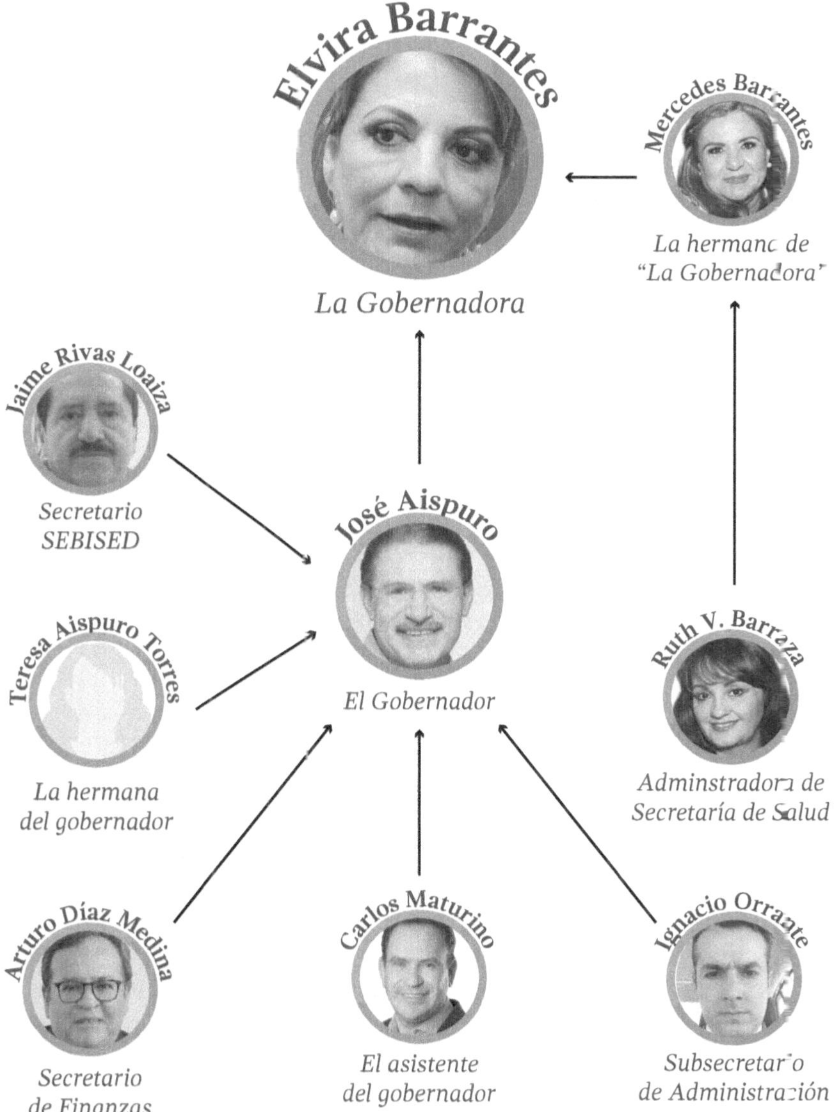